HERAKLES

Vijay Hare

BY THE SAME AUTHOR

THE SAGA OF MAJESTY
Herakles

THE IRONBREAKERS SERIES
Legion That Was (novel)
Aquilifer (short story)

OTHER SHORT STORIES
Ode to an Odyssey
The Carrion Rain

FROM WHOM THE GODS GRANT POWER, THEY FIRST DEMAND PAIN…

Greece, in the Age of Legends.

Heroes quest across a land haunted by gods and spirits. Prophecies and pride drive them to complete mighty deeds. All except one of them. The greatest of them all.

Wearied from his many Labours, broken by the lives lost along the way, the fabled Herakles has rejected the hero's path forevermore. Never again will he perform deeds of legend. Never again will he be a weapon of Fate.

Until word reaches him of a Thessalian upstart named Jason, and a gathering of foolhardy lords and champions. Their aim, to sail to the distant land of Colchis, and steal the legendary Golden Fleece.

But as Jason's reckless quest throws the power of the gods themselves into jeopardy, Herakles must rejoin the world he left behind… and change the Fate of gods and men forever.

A NOTE ON TRANSLITERATION

In the text that follows, I have tried to walk the tightrope between transliterating names as faithfully to the original Greek as I can, while also trying to keep the more iconic names close to how we would recognise them in English.

In most cases this is fairly superficial, with words ending in the more Latinised -*us* (instead of the more strictly accurate -*os*), and the odd flipflopping between *c*, *k* and *ch*. Examples include *Iolchus* instead of *Iolkos*, *Chiron* instead of *Kheiron*, and *Athena* instead of *Athene*.

The one very obvious exception, as you have probably gleaned from the front cover, is the titular Big Man himself, whom I have very deliberately transliterated with a *k* instead of the *c* you commonly find in English. There is no deep-seated intellectual reason for this change; I simply like how the more archaic spelling looks on the page, and felt it was only right that the Gods' Last Son stands apart from his friends and enemies, as he does in so many other ways.

I imagine every Classicist or reader of myth retellings has a different take on this. I simply wanted to reassure you that this glaring inconsistency was, in fact, an indulgence rather than an oversight.

For Arjan, Anjali, Ishaan, Yash and Ayla.

Your move, Nisha Bhua.

PROLOGUE
COMPOSED IN THE SHADOW OF SEVEN GATES

The oracle asked me what I dream about.

Can you believe that, Iolaus? Who else would seek to pry into my thoughts like that? Who else would dare intrude upon my nightmares?

Who else would even guess I had them?

Of all the men I left behind in Thebes, he is the one who unnerves me most. He is also one of the few I truly miss.

That false smile of his, that spreads like a noose pulled tight. Those rheumy, red-veined eyes, blind and yet seeing so much. They are the oldest thing about him, older than that squalid cave on Cithaeron he makes a home of. Older than the plains and prairies that surround it.

I have known a fair few seers and prophets in my time, scryers of birds and rattlers of bone. But there is only one Tiresias. It is as well that he is Fated to live so long. When he perishes, the House of Cadmus will be much bereft. There will never be another like him.

I came to him, on that distant evening. I came alone, unarmed, bare in all the ways that matter. Without my club, without the Nemean Lion's pelt around me. Without even Hylas. My prophetic host seemed to find his absence particularly amusing, but there are some secrets that even my boy cannot know about.

So come I did, on this long and lonely pilgrimage, back to the city and kingdom that first gave me shelter.

This was the first time I'd been back in Thebes since... well. Since I left, all those years ago. I hardly need to tell you that, Iolaus. It was for your sake I stayed away. Yours, and your father's.

I close my eyes and I can still see it all. Those seven immense gates, looming over the sands. The towering, sculpted boars with their tusks of dark quartz. And the pale autumnal sky that frames them.

But not this time. I gave my former home a wide berth, crossing the Cithaeron Plateau with only the distant howls of wolves and prairie dogs for company.

He knew I was coming, of course. The seer's lot. There is no surprise or wonder to his life. He has to live out all his days in waiting.

And he was waiting for me. He and I were never close, even before the exile, before the Labours. But he'd heard the stories, of course. Those accursed tales of mine, that have spread far too widely and too thinly. He related them back to me as we sat, the wispy candlelight doing nothing to banish the cold, and he seemed to relish every moment of it.

Slaying the lion born among the stars. Robbing the Glade of Hesperide, and looting the apple that a Titan held dear. Crossing down into the World Beneath, and bringing the Hound of Hell to heel.

By the time he'd got to Atlas, he could scarcely contain his laughter. All spittle, no mirth, baring his yellowed teeth to the world. All lies, he judged. All fictions. After all, what man born of woman could take up the sky-bearer's burden? What man could bear the stars upon his back?

I chose not to answer that last question.

But then his amusement passed. He knew why I'd come. Either his capricious gods had whispered the truth into his ears, or he simply had enough nous to see this moment for what it was.

Only one thing could have brought me crawling back to Thebes, back to him, *after all these years. These years of my self-imposed exile, when* my former friends and erstwhile foes believe me dead, or lost to time. As the memories of my deeds grow dimmer, decaying into song and legend.

Tiresias met my gaze, with eyes that no longer work. And he asked me what I dream about.

Forgive me my slowness, Iolaus. These are memories I have little wish to unpack. Even picking up my stylus is more burdensome than I'd hoped.

Here I am, the Gods' Last Son, a Child of Thunder, a slayer of beasts who has fought with deities. Digging deep into my courage to put ink on parchment.

Oh, how the mighty fall.

But Tiresias was right. I have rarely ever dreamed in my life, even as a child. Growing to manhood did little to change that, and after that. . . you can imagine. My eyes have seen a great deal, more than most mortals. Plenty of fertile ground for nightmares, I would guess.

But I only ever dreamed rarely, happily or otherwise, and when I did, they rarely lingered.

Until now.

This dream is more than just a dream. I think this, more than anything, was what led me to seek the prophet out. This is no mere nightmare, but a memory. A memory that never happened to me.

I see a ram soaring through the sky, as swift as it is silent. Above it, the sunlit sky gives way to rich, airless blue, and then the inky black of starless space. Below it, verdant grassland glides on with a stately lack of haste.

Clouds of dewy vapour and billowing air caress it, washing it clean. A storm, yet to fully brew, from a god's eye view.

The ram is not a natural beast by anyone's reckoning. A natural ram could not grow to such a size, not least sail through the heavens, without wings, without aid, without any real effort. And a natural ram would have a thatch of dirty white wool, not gleaming naked sunlight. Its curled horns would look like ivory, not burnished glass. Even the flesh beneath its skin simmers like molten ichor. But even that, dear nephew, is not the most wondrous thing.

Upon its back, nestled within the shimmering fur-fire fronds, I see two wide-eyed children holding on for dear life. I know, somehow, that they are brother and sister. I know that the boy is Phrixus, and that the girl is called Helle.

I know those names because they reverberate through legend. These twins died years before I was even born. But something is wrong, even here, even now. Phrixus' features narrow and blur, his long unkept hair now reminding me of a wild shepherd from Thessaly. And Helle shines, not like a beauty but a star, her skin the caramel gold of those living in eternal sunlight without ever feeling its burn. Artful henna and foreign cuneiform curl and spiral across her skin, a language I do not recognise and hope I never will.

As if in sympathy with my unease, the ram plunges higher into the air. Even without foreknowledge, I know what is coming.

Helle's hand slips loose, too weak and moist to hold the sunlit fleece any longer.

Only for Phrixus to grab that empty hand, and grab it firm.

And for a moment, just one single shining moment, they hold together, palm in sweaty palm, as the entire axis of creation spins around them.

And then Helle is gone, cartwheeling away into nothingness.

You never put any stock in dreams, Iolaus. Even as a boy. Or if you did, you never admitted it.

I sometimes wish I had your clarity.

Tiresias had little clarity for me, at any rate. Nothing, at least, that didn't simply raise more doubts. Always the way with seers, I find. You ask one straight question, and they give you three answers, which are all unhelpful and terrifying to know.

This was more than just a nightmare, that much he could guess. This was an augury, plain and simple. A shard of the past, carrying tidings of the future. That was the sum of his wisdom, his precious divination. That was all he had to say about it.

I can never abide uncertainty, but Tiresias thrives on it.

I had half a mind to leave, then, without the answers I'd come for, when the oracle halted me with a hollow smile. He wasn't quite finished with me yet. He had a revelation of his own for me. One he'd clearly been waiting to impart.

We are both used to living in exile, keeping the world around us at arm's length. But he still has a home, a kingdom, an allegiance. He is still privy to the ebb and flow of life outside, and it was news of the outside world he gave me.

A summons had arrived from Thessaly. From the great city of Iolchus, to be precise. A summons that I should give some thought to heeding.

For a moment, Phrixus' face drifted across my gaze, blurring into the features of a Thessalian youth. But I resolved not to think about it.

I told the prophet the truth. That those days were over. I was done doing the dirty work of kingdoms. King Pelias — if he even still ruled in that ancient land — could find some other fool to slay his monsters.

Again, that foetid smile from Tiresias. It showed not only how little my answer had impressed him, but that I'd stumbled into the exact trap he'd hoped I would. Oh, how he loves to do this. To kick out the crutches from beneath you.

He drily berated me, for my vanity in assuming this summons had come for me alone. And he reminded me, gently but firmly, that not a single soul who mattered had seen me alive in years. My voluntary exile since completing the Last Labour and leaving Eurystheus' court had seen to that. The memory of Herakles still endured, but few across the kingdoms believed I did.

All Thebes had been awash with the contents of this message, as had the entire Achaean headland. Every city and kingdom from here to Parnassus had received the same summons. A call to all heroes, or any man who fancied himself one. No number of valiant souls was too high. All were welcome, for all would be needed.

Tiresias had little respect for such lofty posturing, that much I could see. But just this once, he wasn't quite able to hide his surprise. His memory is long, perhaps the longest of us all, yet he had never even heard of such a summoning before.

This would be no mere monster hunt, no wanton day of bloodletting. This was... something more.

His unease was as unnerving as his earlier glibness. Truth be told, I wasn't sure which was worse.

So here I find myself, Iolaus. Here, as I finish scrawling out my thoughts on parchment, ready to brave the open road once more. The first of the Seven Gates stands behind me, its outline picked out by winter sunset. I cannot dally within Thebes' borders much longer. Not if there is a chance I will be recognised.

He knew, of course. Tiresias knew. Be it prophetic gift or simple intuition, he knew the choice I'd make.

Because he knew just how to pull my strings.

Whatever was transpiring on Thessaly's shores... what would be the point of it, beyond the brief amusement of my Olympian forebears? So what if the Fates had more troubles in store for me. So what if it transpired I needed more tempering on their anvil, if twelve debilitating Labours somehow weren't enough for one lifetime. I could stay, or I could go. The gods would have their sport, either way.

I said as much to Tiresias as I prepared to take my leave. I had intended it to be my parting gift before I left him for this final time. The nomad's path was calling to me once more, and I doubted anything would ever bring me back to Thebes again.

And then he called out, from the mouth of his hovel, as I was leaving. One last twist of the blade.

The Allslayer could well ignore the gods, he observed. But could he ignore his friends?

I stopped, midstride, already turning back against my will. Damn him, and his tongue of dripping silver. I could feel my resolve dry and crumble, even as I mustered reasons not to listen.

Because he was right, as he always damn well is. How many of my old friends and comrades would answer this fool's clarion call? How many of them could resist such a gathering of might, a legend that would doubtless echo down through the ages?

Whatever storm the Fates were brewing for them… was I truly going to let them weather it without me?

I tried to argue the point, as if anyone can win an argument with Tiresias. What good would my presence bring, beyond the bad? There is a reason I wander this world alone. How many souls have I called friend, have I made family of, over the years? And how many of them burned in divine rage, taken from me by godly whims, whenever the Olympians decided I needed scourging?

Gods above… you know that, nephew, better than anyone. You and the others. You lived that truth.

I told the oracle I wouldn't go to Iolchus. If I wasn't with them, I could not doom them.

But if I wasn't with them, he retorted, I could not protect them.

Do you see, Iolaus? I am damned if I do, and damned if I don't.

I told Tiresias that, and turned once more to be finally on my way. I remember how heavy my feet felt as I left his mountain hovel, this time resolutely for good.

Only for the seer to call out, one final time. He asked me when my life had ever been any different.

And then he told me to watch my back. And to keep Hylas close, in the days to come. For Thessaly, he'd heard, was an unkind place to travellers.

ACT I

THE MOUNTAIN BOY

'When we tire, we are attacked by ideas we conquered long ago.'

– attributed to the Titan Prometheus

I

ONCE, UPON PELION

The only light in the dungeon is the moon's.

Gilded robes have no place in so foetid a crypt, but the new arrival has no patience to dress for the occasion. A threat to his supremacy walked into his *megaron*, and he did what any man would do in his place. He charmed it, outwitted it and entrapped it. Now, he weighs up the risk of its survival against the sin of its murder.

But then, he is hardly a stranger to such things. His name is Pelias, lord of all Thessaly. Once nothing more than a noble spare to a nobler heir, he won his way to a kingdom through guile and skill instead of birth.

And what did it cost him? Nothing. Nothing but a dead brother, and a sullied soul.

Until tonight. Tonight, almost twenty years since that fateful moment, when the past walked back into Iolchus without fear or shame.

Even now, the prisoner knows nothing but defiance. Whether feigned or genuine, it is seemingly undimmed by an evening's hanging in chains from the rafters. There is no mistaking his common status, but this is no mere herder of swine. Here, tonight, he is so much more than that.

And his face. At first, Pelias could scarcely stand to look at it. His own haughtiness shines out from the prisoner's features. He knows that face all too well, for it was once his own, and was once his brother's, too.

'My, my, Uncle!' the hanging man taunts him. 'The years have not been kind to you!'

The prisoner is in high spirits for one in his predicament. His few threadbare garments were torn off him upon incarceration, and his other personal effects – a shepherd's crook hewn from old teak, and a week's supply of water and stoned bread – have likely already found new homes.

All except one thing. Pelias has it in his hands even now. It is nothing, just a common pastoral trinket. And yet it has thrown the king's carefully guarded future into disarray.

He tosses it across the cell, where it lands in the grime beneath the hanging prisoner. A sandal, poorly crafted and falling apart, shaped to clasp a man's left foot.

'I have never put much stock in prophecy. And I never believed I'd see you again.' He sighs. 'That is twice I have been wrong today, Jason of Pelion.'

The prisoner raises his hanging head, a face full of defiance glaring through strands of filthy hair.

'Jason of Iolchus,' he balefully corrects him. 'I have a better claim on that name than you, *Uncle*. Murderer. Usurper.'

'Perhaps.' Pelias' head shifts, as if ceding the point. The King of Thessaly begins to slowly pace the cell's circumference, hawklike eyes never leaving Jason's hanging form all the while.

The boy has grown. Changed. A fully-grown youth, on the edge of manhood, is suspended before Pelias' eyes where once a babe in arms lay ready for the slaughter. Sentiment stayed Pelias' hand then, and twenty years later he is paying for that flaw.

'Two decades,' the king recalls. 'Two decades I had my spies and riders hunt for you. For even the *rumour* of you. A fortune, there for the taking, for any man who could bring me Aeson's missing son.'

Jason manages another half-smile through his pain. For a man who has spent the evening hanging in irons, it is no small feat.

'And here I was the whole time, Uncle. Tending flocks in your very own backwater.' His smile becomes a sneer. 'Fitting, no? The great usurper Pelias, murderer of kin, thief of thrones. Undone not by valour, nor piety, but simple snobbishness. You couldn't hold your nose long enough to grace the slopes of Mount Pelion, and that failing of yours shielded me from you.'

Pelias finally slows to a halt, directly before the suspended prisoner once again.

'Until now, Jason. Until now.'

Uncle and nephew regard each other in the moonlight. Pelias, at last, breaks the silent stalemate.

'What changed?' he asks. 'You had a life beyond my reach. In that respect, you had beaten me. So what made you come back after all this time? There is nothing heroic in marching toward death.'

The king forces himself not to look away as he speaks those words. There can be no secure future for him now, or his line. Not while Jason draws breath. But whatever he says... can he truly bring himself to go through with it?

'Everything has changed, murderer. I had a visitation from the gods themselves.' Jason's moonlit leer conveys both malice and heroism. 'The Fate you claim has no power caught up with me at last. The goddess Hera, Uncle! Can you imagine? The Queen of Olympus showed me the truth of who I was. And the truth of who I'll be when I'm done righting your wrongs.'

Pelias digests this in silence. He is not surprised that Jason lived out his youth and childhood in ignorance of his familial truth. No better way for his father's loyalists to hide him.

The King of Thessaly forces himself to smile without warmth. Power. Control. Even the illusion of those things matters.

'Is that truly what you believe?' he asks, walking over to the stony slit that serves as a window. 'That you have the protection of the immortals on your side?'

But in truth, Pelias fears it may be so. There is something in the way his errant nephew holds himself. A confidence, silent but not hidden, something beyond a shepherd's cocksure cheek. And a vitality, too, about his build and sinew. This boy may well have the protection of Hera, but that could mean anything at all. When the gods grant mortals favour, it does not always end well. Whether Jason is cherished, amusing, or languishes under the direst of obligations, it can be a double-edged sword.

Pelias turns to face his nephew once more, abandoning that umbral line of thought.

'I hazard you may be wrong, nephew. The messages of gods have brought you doom, instead of deliverance. It is quite the irony, no?'

Jason's face contorts from its rictus of grim resolve. Defiance is not entirely able to hide confusion.

'What are you talking about, murderer?'

'Why this, of course.' Pelias draws closer, picking up the discarded sandal for Jason to inspect. 'Perhaps there is more to Fate after all, boy. A seer once told me, a clutch of years after you left… dear gods, how I remember his fevered auguries even now! He told me that my doom would come one day, *wearing one sandal*. And sure enough, after twenty years apart, here you are in Thessaly once more, seeking what you think is yours.'

Jason swallows. He is able to hide his doubts, but not skilfully. Not skilfully enough for the likes of Pelias. The shackles around his arms and shoulders feel a little heavier.

'I lost the other one. On my trek down the Mountain into Iolchus, crossing the river.'

'Oh, that is a pity.' The king's voice is dripping in irony, seemingly oblivious to how naturally he plays the role of villain. 'Do you comprehend what that means, Jason? If it weren't for your beloved Hera, if not for her revelation of truth, you would still be out there, free of me. Roaming Pelion's summits, supping milk from the lambs and flowers, having your way with mountain daughters. Free. Contented.'

'Ignorant,' Jason stubbornly retorts. 'Unfulfilled. It is not about what I want.'

'Isn't it?'

'It is about destiny, Uncle. The obligation of Fate. Not that *obligation* means a thing to a man like you. Destiny called to me, and I will not begrudge it. I will see this to the end.'

'My, oh my.' Pelias claps his hands together theatrically, mocking the younger man's conviction. 'You have your father's taste for dramatics, Jason. Do you truly believe, after twenty years of my unfailing stewardship, that it is somehow still your destiny to rule Thessaly?'

'I do,' Jason ripostes. 'By all rights I should never have survived you. I was only a babe, after all. What defence could I have had against a man prepared to kill his own kin?'

For whatever it is worth, Pelias has the dignity not to argue that charge.

'And yet here I am,' Jason continues. 'Dead I should be, but clearly it was my destiny to live.'

'So far,' the king cautions him. 'Every breath you take, from now on, comes at my mercy.'

And for a moment, Pelias isn't seeing his long-lost nephew. Nor the oubliette around them. The usurper-king's thoughts flicker back to that bloody night, when his defectors broke him into the *megaron* that was still Aeson's, and brought Pelias face to face with his naïvely honourable brother.

He makes no attempt to hide his derision.

'What would you know of kingship, shepherd boy? What skills and talents have twenty years on Pelion furnished you with, beyond a head full of dusty ideals? You would take this throne from me, take this *kingdom* from me, for no better reason than vengeance. And then what? You will rule justly? Fairly? Is that it?'

This time, Jason has no answer. His streak of stubborn righteousness seems temporarily halted, wary of the sting that lurks behind Pelias' words.

The king takes another step closer, drawing level with Jason's waist. At this range, the youth could kick him savagely. If he had any strength left.

'Idiot boy. Do you think *fairness* is in a king's remit? A king's duty is to protect his kingdom, Jason, and all who dwell within it. As savagely, as dishonourably, and with as black a heart as needed. All other concerns — honour, even-handedness — are merely gilding!'

Jason's broken conviction is evident in his slouch. He makes less effort to hold himself firm, but it will take more than pretty words to cloud his purpose.

'You have had many years to repeat these lies to yourself, Uncle. Anything to avoid meeting your own gaze in the mirror. To avoid facing up to the Fate that comes for you.'

'Oh, please.' The king cracks his knuckles, as if this is the most commonplace conversation a man could have. 'You call it Fate, nephew. I call it hindsight. Aeson was f—'

'*Don't you speak his name!*' Jason takes this moment to curse him. 'He was my *father!*'

'He was my brother,' Pelias drily retorts, 'long before he was your father.'

And with that, the king continues with his diatribe as if uninterrupted.

'Aeson was foolish enough to miss the signs. Too naïve to see me coming. And too weak to protect his kingdom from me. His inability to hold his rule merely proved how unsuited he was to ever have it. Now his palace and halls are mine. All Iolchus is mine, and I have ruled over Thessaly ever since. No usurpers have prised it from my grasp, and believe me, many have tried.'

The king risks holding Jason's gaze with his own. He does not seek to rile the boy, though his words undoubtedly do so. It dawns on Jason, with slow and unwelcome clarity, that his uncle believes every word of what he says.

'But they don't succeed,' Pelias says. 'Because I am strong, where Aeson was weak. Cunning, where he was naïve. And the means my brother was too honourable or squeamish to employ?' He smiles, piteously and contemptibly in the moonlight. 'Well, I do not shirk from such methods. Reflect on this, Jason, while I decide how long you have left to live. There are no rightful heirs and usurpers. There are only strong kings, and weak kings. I know which one I am, boy. Which do you think you would be?'

Jason's head hangs low as he digests these truths in silence. Pelias does not wait for an answer, reading the youth's silence as submission.

The king turns on his heels, leaving his nephew to rot in the dark.

The royal cabal is in fine voice that night, each of the king's counsellors wishing to say their piece on Jason. A great many of them — Pelias' son and heir, Acastus, foremost among them — would slice their errant kinsman's throat this very night, leaving his corpse for the vultures or dumping it on the next boat out of Thessaly. Several others urge a more cautious and meandering approach, fearing the backlash from gods and onlookers at committing so impious a sin so brazenly. There is talk of sending Jason on his way back to the mountain, laden with gold and food and kingly favour.

Or subsuming him into palace life, perhaps. Where he can be watched, and contained, and guarded against. A meaningless royal appointment or two, physically and politically beneath Acastus' heels. Something to slake the people's thirst for fairness, giving them a powerless idol while keeping the king's daggers clean of scandal.

As is so often the case in Pelias' life, two wolves inside his soul jockey for favour. The reason, that shows him the winding path through the fog, and the paranoia, that closes the chinks in his armour. Either one of them can ride high in his heart, depending on time and mood and circumstance.

But more often than not, it comes down to which of the two Pelias feeds.

A part of him wonders what Alcestis would say if she were here. She was always the most perceptive and level-headed of his children, even before following Admetus to Pherae. But then again, she was always a woman who loved honour. Who favoured the high road.

Enough of this.

The king dismisses his sect of advisors with a handwave, too wrapped up in his ruminations to even bid them a pleasant night. The throne room is empty but for him, even his precious guards permitted only to surround the hallowed hall, not enter it.

He stays in his throne for some time. Night deepens. The oil in the braziers around him slowly depletes, and light fades.

Pelias' contemplation is deep indeed, as he weighs up the danger that lies before him with the desires that haunt his dreams.

And then he is gone, leaving an empty regnal hall behind him.

Jason doesn't look up as the door grinds open a second time. Perhaps this is to feign nonchalance. Or maybe he is simply too weak to even move.

He opens rheumy eyes with more effort than is seemly, trying not to show how much pain the binding chains are giving him. He is not surprised, or pleased, at who he sees.

'Perfect,' he croaks through a parched throat. 'I was really hoping, just now, for yet another family talk.'

'Still defiant,' Pelias wryly observes. 'I'm glad to see it.'

Thessaly's king takes a step, two steps, three steps forward. He is practically standing right under Jason where he hangs, head craned up with no loss of superiority.

'I have a mind to set you free, boy. This very moment. What say you?'

Jason does not respond, struggling to wrap his thoughts around this fresh battle of wills.

'And more,' Pelias continues. 'To have you fed and tended, in the halls of this palace, as an honoured guest.'

'I seek no *xenia* from you, murderer. To Hades with your poisoned goodwill.'

Jason tries to spit defiance down into his uncle's face, but such a gesture takes strength and control. A tendril of drool, viscous and pitiful, simply trails down his chin to land on the rank floor.

But Pelias ploughs onward, seemingly unable to hear his nephew's words.

'And what is more, I will swear by any oath you like that I will give you what you seek. I will step aside from your path, disavow Acastus as my heir, and invest you with the kingship of all Thessaly. What say you, boy?'

Silence greets this maddening vow. Whether shocked, bemused or enthralled by Pelias' words, Jason has no answer to any of this.

'I mean it,' the king insists. 'Your father's throne. Your supposed birthright. Say the word, and it will be yours… upon completion of a task.'

Jason is not a royal scion, whatever his heritage. He was not raised to walk in courts and royal concourses. He is a shepherd of Pelion, a child of the mountain, eking out a hard, pastoral life.

He understands the basics of trade, of barter, of bared teeth and negotiations, better than any king or prince.

'Go on,' he hisses. 'What do you want from me, assuming I can even trust you?'

'Why, I want to prove you wrong.' Pelias cannot help but crack a little smirk. 'The thing you call Fate, that I call hindsight… I want to prove that it is made by men, not gods. You can have your precious dreams of kingship, if that is what you truly want. Far be it from me to defy the will of Hera. But in return… I want something greater still. What is a throne, boy, when compared to the power of gods?'

Again, Jason's silence answers. And again, Pelias cannot give a single damn from where it comes.

'What do you know of Colchis, nephew? What do you know of the Golden Fleece?'

II

THE MOUNTAIN WAY

No kingdom is ever truly rid of banditry, but the arid wildlands of Thessaly are a poor example of stewardship. King Pelias measures his power from the centre of his world, and rarely is that stately attention lavished beyond the walls of Iolchus.

Out here, where rugged mountains dot the landscape, and twisting lowland valleys run between their feet, justice is less sacrosanct and more provincial. For the rural communities who nestle in the peaks' shadows, might has an uncomfortable way of making right.

This is particularly apt in the case of Xanthias the brigand, an outcast outlaw from the lower country, who has eked out a living these long years by crushing farmers, shepherds and his own compassion beneath his sandalled feet. His men have felled a great tree, blocking the road as it winds upcountry, and his scouts tell him there are two unwary travellers afoot.

It is a game the brigands have played a thousand times before, more than once on this very spot. Blocking the easiest path, to herd unsuspecting passers-by into an ambush. Caught unawares on the open road, even a seasoned warrior becomes easy prey. And the harder they fall, the greater the pickings.

But not today. By the time Xanthias and his honourless wretches have ridden their 'prey' to ground, there is nothing to prey upon. No hoary old warrior of yore. No stuttering squire, bringing up the rear.

And the tree… That is, perhaps, the most unnerving thing of all. The sundered oak, uprooted from the ground days before, has been lifted clean off the stony road. Xanthias knows this, for he can see where it has landed, thrown a good way down the steep mountain drop by the crumbling roadside.

Thrown.

'What manner of…' a henchman begins. 'It took ten of us to even lift that blasted thing. Let alone move it!'

A desolate chill is climbing Xanthias' backbone. He gives his horse's reins another tug, betraying his mounting nerves.

'The travellers you were following, Alexius. Could they have done this?'

The scout looks uncertain. 'Just the two of them? Hardly. The big one, the war dog? Looked like a has-been, all worn around the edges. And that mewling little servant with him couldn't have managed it. He could barely carry their bags!'

Xanthias breathes out, looking about their hilly, defenceless, surroundings. The hunters, he realises with sick revelation, might just have become the hunted.

'Easy meat, but little sport. Still,' he calls to his idling men, trying to rekindle their cruel confidence, 'what do we say to easy pickings, boys?'

A few of them jeer, but their leader does not join them. The hackles on his neck are stood on end, that same feeling of walking through the wilderness and hearing wolves howl in the distance.

The metaphor, he realises, is horrifically apt.

'Maybe we should go,' Alexius mutters. His heart is beating hard, and not with anticipation. 'Maybe thi—'

A missile of polished pine shatters his skull, thrown end over end. Any man would struggle to lift it, let alone wield it with such force.

Any mortal man.

Xanthias and the other brigands recognise the club that hurls Alexius' body to the ground. None of them have ever seen this weapon with their eyes before. But they all know it. They know its fell legacy.

Ten armed men against one unarmed newcomer. The outcome is like Fate itself. Fixed in stone, unbreakable by mortals.

'A terrifying prospect, no?' growls Herakles, drawing nearer. His fists are balled, but strangely, there is no real anger in his gaze. 'To be ambushed on the road. What a terrible way to die, gentlemen.'

What follows is brief, brutal, and scarcely worthy of written recollection.

Hylas helps him strip the camp when it is done. The two of them are no strangers to living off the land, and over the years have become shamefully good at it.

Fresh food and water are a welcome boon, to fill their bellies on the last road to Iolchus. Sheets of satin and cured leather, too, if they need to sleep beneath the sky again. A little extra gold, scavenged from dead men's pockets, never goes amiss either.

The warrior and the squire enjoy a bowl of pilfered stew, cooked on the open fire as they consign the rest of Xanthias' empty camp to the flames.

In time, they are graced with company. Not many, merely ones and twos, but a steady stream of it as the sun begins to fall. Villagers from the next valley, and herders of sheep and swine from the mountain slopes. Every one of them grateful for the slaying of Xanthias' piratical band. And all keen to pay homage to their itinerant saviour, whoever he is.

'Herakles,' he tells them, putting down his bowl of stew. 'Son of Amphitryon and Alcmena. Born of Tiryns. Former ward of Thebes.'

If the rural folk of Thessaly know the import of such names, they do not let on. All their concern is for what offerings and sacrifices would appropriately honour their deliverer and hero.

'Sacrifice,' Herakles tells them, 'cannot be made to a living man.' He rises from his seat, taking in the dusk-lit valley one last time. 'And I am no hero. Look to your own defence, if you truly wish to honour me. And never let another take your Fate into his hands.'

They are on the road again by first light, leaving scarcely a trace of their passing.

'Has Thessaly changed much?' Hylas asks him, following a little way behind. In a rare moment of confidence, his master actually replies.

'I cannot say,' Herakles admits, without turning or stopping on his path. 'I was never here when Aeson was king. And only a handful of times since then.' They crest the top of another highland peak, giving them their most spectacular view yet of the plateauing plain that stretches before Iolchus.

'But still,' Herakles continues, beginning to make his way down. 'We can at least count upon a royal welcome when we arrive. We've lived like jackals long enough, boy.'

Scrambling over the crest to catch up, Hylas doesn't feel so inclined to agree with that.

'Are you sure?' he risks asking. 'What of your... *our* reputation? What if it has proceeded us to this kingdom already?'

Herakles' sandaled foot crunches stone, scraping as he fights not to slip. For a moment, just a moment, another landscape lies before his eyes... a sunlit plain near Thebes, three small bloody bodies slumped in the grass at his feet. A bow of sturdy maple hangs in one loose hand. A bow that is not there.

He shakes his head, dispelling Theban grasslands and the mosaic floor of Eurystheus' throne room from his mind's eye. When he finally speaks, he snarls with empty venom.

'I am not speaking of ancestry, boy. I am speaking of deeds. Do you forget how I rescued the princess Alcestis? How I delivered Admetus' bride back into his loving arms? I fancy Pelias will welcome the man who saved his daughter's life.'

Hylas pulls himself over another small ridge, his shorter legs straining to keep up.

'Of course. I meant no slight.'

His master does not reply, or stop. The squire is not surprised by this.

'Well,' he continues, trying to raise their spirits. 'Whatever awaits you in Iolchus... what threat could it possibly pose to the Gods' Last Son? The man who has vanquished Death itself?'

That finally halts his master, though he does not turn around. Herakles' gaze remains fixed on the distant city, his face untainted by his follower's confidence.

Far above them, over the ridge the two travellers have put behind them, something watches their unsteady progress. Something that has no eyes with which to see. No tongue to call out a greeting or warning. And no breath with which to speak.

They make their way onwards, down-country and onto evermore agreeable ground. The stone outline of Iolchus becomes a little less distant with every hour, though trying to measure progress by that gauge can be disheartening.

But Herakles has deeper concerns right now. There is still so little about this he knows, and he is not a man who relishes a mystery. They haven't passed a single soul since returning to the road, and have little means of picking up news or rumours. Speed may be of the essence, but walking into this summons blind doesn't appeal to his few vestiges of caution.

His gaze snaps up, head cocked. What is that he can hear? Are those…

'Hooves,' Hylas confirms. 'Hooves on stone. Must've taken our path up the mountain.'

Herakles' hand drifts to his lower back, where the handle of his club hangs ready to be grasped. Were they really as careful as they'd hoped? Has someone followed them all this way?

The first charger makes her way over the rocky summit, a piebald grey whose mane is dusted with silt. The mare is ridden well, cautious yet swift over the treasonous terrain.

Another pair of darker steeds follow in quick succession, and another two after that in various mottled shades. The riders are lightly armoured, but their rich patronage is evident in their clothes and equipment. Royal guards, escorting a royal guest. Herakles recognises the colours of Athens. But the heraldry trailing from the chargers is not that of King Aegeus.

'Hail!' Herakles calls with a spreading grin, releasing his club handle. He motions for Hylas to loosen up. 'Who is your master, men?'

As if he needs to hear the answer. The lead rider gallops all the way up to him – on the finest-looking horse Herakles has ever seen, gilded with royal teal and saffron – and swoops down to the ground, throwing his exquisitely woven cloak over one shoulder.

'Old man!' he bellows. 'Are you truly still alive?'

The Allslayer pulls the new arrival into a crushing hug. The Athenian is almost as broad, but a good head closer to the ground.

'By the gods, Theseus! I had hoped you would answer the call, boy. But I never thought you'd make the whole journey by land.'

Herakles lets the Athenian go at last, and he motions for his riders to dismount.

'It is *King* Theseus now,' he pretends to chide him. But the smile is apparent in his twinkling eyes. To Herakles, he has always been *boy*, and likely always will be.

'So I'd heard.' Herakles claps Theseus' shoulder once again, more affectionately this time. For the first time in far too many years, he almost starts to feel like himself again. 'I was sorry to hear about Aegeus. The news only reached me recently.'

Theseus smiles, a little too easily, though his gaze briefly flickers with something umbral. His attention drifts to the diminutive presence at their side.

'Hylas, old thing. Good to see he hasn't gotten you killed yet.'

Hylas simply cringes for want of a reply, as Theseus ruffles the squire's hair without affection. This gentle mockery won't dampen his mood, however. Herakles hasn't smiled this earnestly in years, and that is more than enough for him.

A clattering of wood and stone heralds the first of Theseus' carriages arriving, making its cumbersome way along the mountain path behind the riders. Athens' new king is far too impatient to forsake his own steed, but this wagon must be carrying the rest of the royal party.

'Quite the entourage you have with you,' Herakles notes. 'Do you know any more about this summons than I do?'

Theseus' eyes twinkle, clearly relishing knowing something his old mentor does not.

'Come, both of you. Ride into Iolchus with my retinue, and I can share with you what news has reached us.'

'Are you sure, Theseus?' Herakles shares a glance with Hylas. 'I would hate to impose.'

The King of Athens waves his objection aside, already walking toward the waiting wagon.

'Nonsense,' he assures them. 'Phaedra will be happy to walk, I'm sure.'

III
A FATE AWAITED

'The old Thessalian rumours are true,' Theseus confesses, skinning a piece of fruit with his knife and handing his passengers a little flesh. 'Prince Jason is alive. The lost heir of King Aeson has been found!'

If he is hoping to strike Herakles with revelation, then he is off the mark. The Allslayer's misgivings are already riding high, having surfaced the moment he and Hylas climbed aboard. Seeing his old friend and protégé after all these many years is a brief but sincere cause for joy. Hearing of his many exploits – ridding Athens of the treacherous sons of Pallas, slaying the foul Minotaur of Crete – is sincerer still.

And yet, after riding in the new king's personal carriage, while Queen Phaedra and her handmaidens dutifully trail the slow-moving train on foot, Herakles cannot quite shake the feeling that something is awry. That this isn't quite the same Theseus he remembers.

Phaedra's sudden absence is the starkest reminder. Neither master nor squire risks asking after her sister, the Princess Ariadne of Crete, the woman rumours once abounded Theseus yearned to marry. But from the look that passes between them all when Phaedra dismounts, the King of Athens clearly isn't blind to their reticence.

The carriage joggles and bumps on the uneven ground as they converse.

'And from where has this Jason sprung?' Hylas asks.

'Mount Pelion, of all places!' Theseus rakes his fingers through the air theatrically. 'They say the babe was spirited from the Iolchan *megaron* the very night Pelias usurped his brother's crown. And Jason has supposedly been tending flocks on the Mountain ever since!' He chuckles, one king deriding the folly of another. 'That was two decades ago, would you believe it. A rather damning oversight for Pelias, no?'

Herakles is nonplussed, neither the situation nor the humour Theseus sees in it particularly moving him. Stranger things have happened, after all. And taking either side feels petty without knowing all the facts. He never once met Aeson, and has only crossed paths with Pelias a handful of times.

'Would it even matter?' he finally retorts. 'If this shepherd really is King Aeson's little foundling? It is deeds that make the measure of a man, Theseus. Not birth. I taught you that, long ago.'

A dry and brittle laugh answers that before Theseus can, from the fourth occupant of the carriage.

'That is a strange sentiment coming from a prince of Tiryns,' the laughing man tells him. 'Or a son of Zeus.'

Herakles feels his teeth grind together, relaxing himself with an unwilling breath. Here, sat across from him, is the most telling source of his unease. This is the first time he has ever met Pirithous, the much-maligned king of the Lapiths. He knows him by reputation, if not by character, and what he has heard does not please him.

Finding him here, in such close confidence of King Theseus, is a cold and unwelcome surprise. Herakles cannot help wondering what history runs between them. And then, belatedly, if he truly wishes to know the answer.

Pirithous' knowing smirk is so brief, the others could well have imagined it.

'Your reputation proceeds you, Allslayer. And there is far more interesting gossip ahead of us, that I promise. They say that heralds took word to every kingdom and royal house. Kings, princes, the best and brightest stars of every tribe and sept. The call went out to all of them.'

'And what is more,' Theseus interjects, 'none of those summonses came from King Pelias. It is *Jason* who has been rallying the greatest heroes of the land to sail to Thessaly. On his own behalf!'

'Then Jason is still alive?' Hylas asks, perplexed. 'And walking free?'

'So it would seem.'

'And openly makes moves against Pelias?'

Herakles' brow furrows. Now, maybe now, he starts to realise that this is no ordinary undertaking he is walking into. Not another Bull, or Boar, or Lion in need of putting down. This sorry endeavour, whatever it turns out to be, has the unwelcome stench of a quest.

Tiresias' knowing face rises from his memories. He forces the image away.

'Well then,' Hylas' optimism cuts through his maudlin thoughts. 'We are not without friends among the lines of kings and heroes. Phthia, Thrace, Ithaca… the name of Herakles is not nothing, your majesty. Even after all these years.'

Herakles half-smiles, for that is a fair appraisal indeed. It would be good to cross paths with his dauntless friends once more, wherever in life they now find themselves. But all the same… how will they react? To see the man they once knew, reduced to… to whatever in Hades he is now?

'And what of Sparta?' Pirithous asks, his bright eyes drifting to Theseus even as he addresses the Allslayer. 'Would you receive fair welcome among Tyndareus' sons, do you think?'

Whatever that is supposed to mean, Herakles is none the wiser. But from the way Theseus' gaze darkens, shifting away from the others, this is clearly something he would rather not talk about.

A kingdom is nothing without the man who rules it.

As Pelias stands in the tower of his palace's central keep, casting his gaze out over the numberless masses of central Iolchus, he wonders if his long-dead brother ever fully grasped that truth.

From his distant vantage point, he has a decent view over the bottommost lip of the harbour. Making out faces or figures among the crowd is a fool's hope, but from the odd royal banner fluttering in the breeze, he has some idea of the newcomers gracing Thessaly with their presence today.

Heroes. The word alone almost makes him sneer. Such eager little children, crying out with a thirst that no roll of deeds will ever quench. These proud and valiant men doubtless have little idea of what this summons will truly entail.

But then, neither does Pelias' erstwhile nephew. Jason may believe, for now, that his destiny to rule is written in the very stars themselves, but stars are not always the faithful guides people hold them to be. Stars can fall from heaven. They can be shrouded, their movements misread.

For any other lord, or even king, such a gathering of royalty and valour beneath one sky could be construed as a threat to one's power. But Pelias' mettle is sterner than that.

His ambition burns as bright as a forge in flow, as bright as it did the day he seized Iolchus. That forge is fed, even now, by his cunning and his daring.

So, no. The many heroes gathering in his shadow do not worry him. Naïve little Jason believes they are congregating for *him*, and not their own precious legacies, and that worries him even less. These men – proud, headstrong, leaders one and all – are not soldiers, not men trained to move and act with one will. Each of these new arrivals to Iolchus will be as stubborn, independent and glory hungry as the last. What challenge can they pose to Pelias' true designs, when they are too busy posing challenges to each other?

Still, there is little point in judging them personally. Pelias can hardly scorn the ambition of others, after all. The heroes' paths – self-centred and spiritually empty as they are – are their own to walk.

His goals are simply loftier still.

If poor little Jason truly desires the throne of Thessaly, to salvage his family's soiled honour, then he is welcome to it. If he truly believes such ascension will recompense the mewling dog's death his father suffered, the years spent living like a stray on Mount Pelion, he can seize the crown with hands outstretched. In time, it will hardly matter.

Pelias will have little need of a throne once the Golden Fleece is his. Or a kingdom. Or the acclaim of mortal men.

'Your majesty…' a palace guard breaks his mythic reverie. He must carry lofty news to warrant disturbing Pelias' solitude. 'The man from Tiryns, who you beseeched us to watch for. The one with the lion pelt.'

'Herakles?'

'Indeed, my lord. He was sighted entering the southern gates, alongside a delegation from Athens.'

Pelias does not dignify this with a reply. Now *there*, at last, is a hero he can respect. It would not matter that Herakles was the one to wrest his beloved daughter, Alcestis, from the darkest of fates so long ago. There stands a man with more deeds to his name than any other prince or hero could ever emulate; and yet, a man who has never once in life sought to channel that acclaim into gain. Simply wandering between kingdoms as a hermit and hero, believed dead after so many years without word.

Now here, resurfaced at last, in answer to the call.

Pelias allows himself the honesty of a smile. Convincing this coterie of self-important monster slayers to follow a beardless shepherd from Pelion might not be the easiest of tasks, even with the Fleece as a prize to dangle before them. But the Allslayer's presence is enough to change the landscape. If the Gods' Last Son throws in his lot with Jason's folly… then the others will surely follow.

Win Herakles over and this will work.

IV

CONCLAVE

'I know those colours.' Herakles scours the crowd around
the harbour with his gaze. 'And I know that damned voice.'

Behind him, Hylas tightens his grip on their travelling
rack. Since parting ways with Theseus and his entourage,
the two of them have made their way into the inner citadel.
Here, the pulse of urban life beats all the faster in the
megaron's great shadow. The coming of so many outlanders
to Thessaly's shores have made the inner city, and the
harbour district, busier still.

But even over the din, Herakles is right. He recognises
that rough-edged, gravelly voice all too well. And the man it
belongs to.

Hylas finds him first, moving more nimbly through the
crowd. Only for a colossal hand to clamp down on his
shoulder, pulling him to one side. Herakles doesn't even
need to see the newcomers' faces. He would recognise them
anywhere; recognise the way they blundered through life.
No matter how many years pass, he will never stop valuing
that trait.

'I told you he'd be here! It's our gods-damned brother
in arms!'

Their bodies crash together in fraternal joy, three
pinnacles of human strength and endeavour who fit together

like chainmail links. The reek of sea salt and honestly earnt sweat fills Herakles' nostrils before the bear hug finally breaks, and he can admire his comrades of old once more.

'Peleus! Telamon! Blood of Olympus, it is good to see you both again.'

He feels a twitch of that feeling from before, the way his load had seemed to lighten when he greeted Theseus on the road. He came here expecting heroes, and heroes he has found.

But more than that. These men are his friends.

Peleus' laughter only kindles Telamon's own. 'My, oh my. Has it really been that long, kinsman?'

There is a sheepishness to their humour, however. As sheepish as two heroic battle kings in their golden years can look. Time and war have changed them both since their last meeting, and Herakles can see that all too clearly.

'Oh, and here he is!' Telamon gives Hylas a playful slap, and somehow the squire remains standing. 'Growing up fast, boy! Good to see you're still picking up Herakles' mess.'

That has them all laughing this time, though Herakles' is a little more forced. They have history, these four men, going back far too many years. As princes, the two Phthians once sailed with him to capture Troy and put the honourless King Laomedon down. And long before that, both brothers had accompanied the Allslayer's quest to Themiscyra, fighting in the bloody debacle with the Amazons that had followed.

So many scars from that pointless war alone. So many regrets.

'Who else is coming, then?' Telamon asks. 'I don't remember ever hearing of a summons like this. I fancy we'll see some familiar faces.'

'We arrived here with King Theseus,' Hylas admits. 'And King Pirithous was travelling with him. Nothing else for sure we can tell you, though King Pirithous had heard rumours of a Spartan delegation.'

The mention of the Lapith King kindles no favour. But nevertheless, Peleus' laughter begins anew, this time snide and without mirth. It no longer galls the Allslayer to feel so adrift from his fellow men – his years of isolation, after all, have been entirely of his own volition – but he cannot help wondering what nerve he has just touched.

'Something to say, friend?'

'Nothing, kinsman. It's just quaint to see you still standing by your pet Athenian. I don't know what Theseus has told you, but I can't imagine he'll be keen to cross paths with any Spartans this day.'

Herakles' eyes narrow. He thinks back to Theseus' reticence in the carriage. The way he'd reacted to Pirithous' goading.

'Enough gossip, brother.' Telamon claps the Allslayer's shoulder once again, and this bleeds all tension from the moment. 'Wine beckons as the sun falls! I've heard fine tales of Iolchan hospitality. And in the court of King Pelias, no less. I wonder what golden haired delights will be warming our beds tonight?'

Even Hylas is chuckling now, despite himself.

Crowds reluctantly part at their passing as they make their way toward the *megaron* at last. Apropos of nothing, Telamon clasps the Allslayer's forearm with his hand.

'I knew you weren't dead, my friend. No matter what anyone else said. Not even the Hellhound, or his kingly master, could ever lay you low.'

Herakles smiles, without comfort, at that quaint little sentiment. He returns the fraternal gesture, but is thankful when Telamon lets him go.

A part of him, small and distant but a part of him nonetheless, wonders if he ever truly left those shadowed shores after all.

Further down the harbour crescent, another ship has dropped its anchor stones. A small army of helots and indentured serfs carry its passengers' many belongings and provisions off deck.

A pair of muscular princes are the last to descend the gangplank. Their ornate bronze armour, edged with cold iron and earthen pewter, turns reflected sunlight into argent blindness. Beneath this they wear robes dyed in the royal colours of King Tyndareus, beautiful but stark. Like everything else that comes out of Sparta's kingdom.

The two princes are cast in the very image of one another, twins in the truest, purest sense of the word. Nurture, however, has set them apart in ways nature cannot. The first twin sports a mane of dark, shaggy hair that could put Herakles to shame, hanging loose and freely about his shoulders in the general way of his countrymen. The second, though no-one sees it under his princely helm, has shorn his hair and face down to the roots, features framed by stubble instead of locks. His face is a touch craggier and more scarred than his brother's, though what that means is anyone's guess.

The two of them share the same pale eyes, though the longer-haired brother's are less narrow. Not quite hopeful, not quite simple, but willing to see the world as it appears to be, perhaps. The other prince's gaze is darker, contemplative, and a cynic might have plenty to say about it.

The first twin's sandals touch the ground. The gentle sound of music meets his ears, carried on the air above the vibrant chaos of twenty disembarking ships on either side of him.

'I have never heard the panpipes played so beautifully.'

'Focus yourself!' his short-haired brother counsels him. 'We are here for a reason, and it isn't to admire the fauna.'

'Really, Castor? Spartan dignity to the fore, same as ever.'

'Just keep your eyes open, Polydeuces, and your wits about you. However long we spend on these shores, I foresee us making more enemies than friends here.'

The panpipes have ceased their gentle melody, as if in agreement with Castor's maudlin thoughts. Around them, their helots and handmaidens go about their work, unnoticed and unthanked.

'Always so fatal!' Polydeuces chides him. 'It is a just thing we seek to do here, brother. And we stand among heroes, paragons of virtue and nobility. People may be kinder than you think.'

Castor gives his brother a tiresome look as he disembarks, removing his helmet and baring his crudely shorn features to the world. Justice can look savage to other pairs of eyes, and heroism is no guarantee of virtue. This, he knows.

'I wish I could see the world as you do, brother.'

Polydeuces smiles at that, taking the words quite erroneously as a compliment. Only for another voice to answer over the bustling throng.

'Your brother is probably right, you know. Though he is not as subtle as he thinks he is.'

The princes turn, one hostile, the other faintly amused. The voice's source can hardly be mistaken, even across Iolchus' chaotic port. A man, dark skinned and lightly clothed, spread languidly across a marble wall. His rather dreamy expression, until now gazing wistfully across the harbour bay, nonchalantly meets Castor's gaze.

'Excuse me?' The prince steps forward, royal primness masking a dangerous temper. 'What is it to you, my Thessalian friend?'

The supine man doesn't rise, doesn't move. 'What would I know?' he ponders. His softly spoken words carry over the harbour noise without difficulty. 'I'm just a pipe player.'

Polydeuces steps closer, following his brother. 'Oh, I don't think that is quite the whole truth. Even in Sparta, we've heard word of the Pierian Bard.' His smile is far more genuine than Castor's. 'Orpheus, is it not? We are honoured to stand before a Muse's son.'

The pipe player gently laughs, and even that sound is honey to the ears.

'Enough pleasantries,' Castor growls. 'What did you mean just now, Pierian?'

'I mean that rumours in this land are fleet of foot.' Sandalled feet alight as Orpheus slides off his stony perch. 'And doubtless I am not the only one who will divine the real reason you are here.'

'Why, to answer the summons from Jason of Pelion,' Polydeuces answers. 'Whoever that is.'

Orpheus raises a delicate eyebrow. 'Really? Not to settle your blood-debt with King Theseus?'

Castor is about to say something most unprincely, but thankfully his brother gets there first.

'Whatever rumours you have heard, singer, are rumours and nothing more. We had no idea any Athenians had even answered the call.'

'Well, that is fortuitous indeed.' Orpheus finally pockets his pipes, gracing the twins with another smile. 'For

I have come to Thessaly in answer to that very same summons.'

Castor scowls. Polydeuces does not.

'Care to join me, princes? We can make our way to the palace of Iolchus together.'

Castor grits his teeth, replacing his helm as he gives his ship one last look.

'Of… of course, Bard. We would be honoured.'

V
HUNTRESS

Little notice is paid as the three men depart the harbour. Life continues much the same without them. Hawkers and traders go on loudly flogging their wares. Heralds and messengers scamper up and down the docks, proclaiming the arrival of yet more visitors to Thessaly.

Except for one. One striking, unassuming woman, dressed like a supplicant but with a bearing far less malleable. Her hair is cropped and bound a little above shoulder height, in the manner of Arcadian farming folk. She is dressed in a loose, unhitched chiton, with a simple flaxen girdle for easy movement over uneven ground.

Only the hunting knife sheathed at her thigh sets her apart from a common peasant. That, and the shortbow slung across her back.

Now Orpheus and the twins have left, she stops feigning interest in a nearby market stall, revealing herself at long last. Even then, she is scarcely noted by a single soul. This is the truest of her patroness's many gifts. To pass unseen, unnoticed, through the world around her. Not like a ghost, but an afterthought.

Sure enough, she slopes off at a cautious, measured pace, tailing the Spartan twins at some distance.

VI
THE GLADE OF IO

'I meant to ask about your wedding,' Herakles confesses.

At his side, Peleus pulls a face that could be boyish embarrassment, or carefully masked trauma. He doesn't stop, or make them break their stride. He doesn't even turn.

'Aye,' he finally agrees. 'That was a night to remember, Allslayer. A night when we'd have been greatly honoured to have you with us.'

Momentarily shamed, Herakles at least has the decency to look away.

'She is a fine woman,' Telamon chips in.

Even as they descend the woody mountain path, the marble roofs of inner Iolchus framing the sky around them, that makes them all smile. All three know the legends of Thetis the water-nymph — indeed, every scion of noble birth this side of Parnassus does — but none of them ever suspected, in their wildest fancies, that she would deign to take a mortal hand. Not least the hand of a man they call friend.

Whether driven by divine whim, or all too mortal longing, Peleus of Phthia's marriage has elevated him to a level of power and influence few kings and lords will ever dream of. But from the distant look in the prince's eyes, there is clearly more to being a goddess' consort than basking in her aura.

'Telamon mentioned your son,' Herakles prompts him. That rekindles his bonhomie once more.

'He grows,' Peleus confirms. 'He prospers. Thetis and I were… unlucky. More than once. But little Achilles is blessed with good health, and a great spirit.' His smile creases into a grin at the thought. 'He's a little rascal, to tell you the truth. These days I can scarcely even—'

A hoarse and ugly shout breaks the spell, and their gazes all snap forward. Three men up ahead, two of whom are known to Herakles, and one of whom is particularly beloved of him. Only right now, the Allslayer's joy at seeing him feels strangely empty.

Telamon calls out to the man with familiarity, if not friendliness.

'King Theseus!' he shouts. 'A long time since we've crossed paths! Herakles told us you'd be here.'

Theseus steps forward, head bowed with little eye contact, Pirithous predictably in his shadow. The Athenian's bearing seems nonchalant, but Herakles is not a fool. Theseus is trying to mask his surprise. Or is that shame at being caught red handed?

'Phthians,' he finally replies. 'I am honoured to meet you both again.'

Behind Theseus, an old and feeble-looking man lies sprawled in the dirty verge bordering the road. He looks run down even for a traveller. In fact, from his shaken mien and posture, it is shamefully apparent what was happening before they were discovered. Even without the torn rag and stolen satchel still hanging in Pirithous' hand.

'This man's name is Idmon,' Theseus begins to explain. 'We were simply having a little misunderstanding. He sought to impugn Pirithous' honour, and—'

'Hardly a difficult feat, I'd imagine,' Telamon chides him. Peleus has already stepped forward, shooting the Lapith a venomous glance as he helps Idmon back to his feet.

'Not good form, Pirithous,' Telamon continues. 'Not good form at all, to trouble a seer. Not on the eve of so auspicious a day.'

Herakles says nothing. His gaze remains locked on Theseus' as his friends say their pieces. Whatever the Gods' Last Son feels about what he has just witnessed, the King of Athens has no difficulty inferring.

Theseus belatedly takes the satchel from Pirithous' grasp, handing it back to its rightful owner. 'My apologies, seer. Forgive us our testiness. We were simply... tired. It has been a long day of travel.'

'Thank you, my lords. Think no more of it.' Idmon isn't quite able to hide his grumble. He slowly retrieves his wooden staff from where it lies in the muck, a little too far off to have fallen there by accident.

Herakles has little love for most prophets. But their craft, being the mouthpiece of gods, that at least he respects. Whatever the gods themselves might say. Toying with an ailing seer is the sort of low he would expect Pirithous to sink to... but Theseus?

'Well then, no point in standing around all evening.' Telamon seems to sense the atmosphere building between the others. 'The hour is nigh, and our summoner must be waiting for us at last.'

And with that, the six of them – kings, princes, heroes and a ragged old prophet – resume the winding mountain trek to their destination.

Jason does not lie at their journey's end, but other souls have waited for their arrival.

The Glade of Io is not an easy place to find. An ancient stone circle overrun by grass and climbing weeds, it predates the kingdom it lies within, predates even the gods its people pray to. Even the name itself is a misnomer, an attempt from Thessaly's earliest settlers at bringing their own light to this place of darkness. Perhaps it was once a temple. Or arena. Or burial site.

Few set foot here now. Rumours abound of the circle's *miasma*, the pollution of the profane and unsanctified, that taints the soul as much as the body. Idmon, trailing behind the other five with his shorter strides, makes several gestures of warding as he draws close.

And yet, as every missive and messenger in the *megaron* has maintained in Pelias' absence, this place is where Jason will meet those he has called to him.

How curious.

Herakles takes the scene in with one glance as he arrives, as well as those who have already arrived. The glade is easily the size of a racing stadium, but instead of tiers of seating there are only shattered altars and plinths, some taken by the greenery, others simply weathered by time.

Two very different men await the Allslayer and his ragged entourage, and neither notices the new arrivals. They are locked in a bout of wrestling, apparently heedless of the glade's dubious sanctity, too engrossed to even realise they are observed. The younger of the pair is quicker on his feet, while his opponent has more power in his throws and takedowns. In terms of skill, neither yet displays an edge.

'Anyone you know?' Telamon asks. His brother merely shakes his head.

Herakles waits a moment, stealing the odd glimpse of each man's face and reaching back into his memory. He has seen the younger one before, long ago. An infant in the royal house of Calydon, running about King Oeneus' robed feet and causing havoc.

Meleager.

A crash of bone on marble jolts him back to the present. The Calydonian prince is down, sprawling, clutching his right temple. The fight, for now at least, has gone out of him.

'Easy now,' his older opponent cautions. He offers the boy a hand to help him rise, magnanimous in victory. 'Best to sit it out for a little while, lad. Head wounds can catch up to you when you least expect it. Take it from me.'

Herakles recognises the accent, if not the voice. The victor is from Pylos, a coastal kingdom with only one prince to accept summons to faraway quests. Which gives the Allslayer a good idea of whom he is talking to.

He steps forward, ignoring Meleager for the time being. 'Nestor, I presume? Nestor of Pylos?'

'You do indeed presume.' The victorious wrestler wipes dust from his hands onto his thighs, before clasping Herakles' wrist in greeting. 'But yes. I am Nestor. And you would be?'

Nestor's eyes rake the Allslayer's figure, taking in the deep-set brow and jawline, the dark silvering curls of hair, and the lion's maw that frames his head.

'Herakles?' he gasps. His awe is measured, but genuine. 'The rumours were wrong, then. I am honoured to finally make your acquaintance. And heartily glad you still draw breath. People said you had—'

'Died,' Herakles fills in. 'During the Last Labour. Merely rumour, as you can see.'

The young man from Calydon is now rising to his feet, not quite able to believe what he has heard. His glee is too pronounced to be considered princely.

'*You* are Herakles? Is it truly you?'

Puppyish charm is more than the Allslayer is used to. He tries to his best to deflect it.

'Hail, Meleager,' he greets him. 'You have grown since last I saw you, boy.'

The young Calydonian turns to the others. 'Theseus,' he begins. 'It is good to see you once again. Though I can't say I recognise your friends.'

The King of Athens looks Meleager up and down, not especially pleased with what he sees.

'Is that how you address a king, boy? Oeneus clearly hasn't taught you any manners since our last meeting.'

The Calydonian's expression shifts, and a hand drifts uncomfortably near the blade hanging at his belt. His honour is an incendiary thing, worn tightly about him, and all too easily set alight. A malady that often afflicts princes fresh out of the cradle.

'Enough with it,' Nestor growls as he takes a step between them. His hand both rests on Meleager's shoulder and pushes him a pace or two back. 'We'll all have time to test each other's mettle later, I'm sure.'

The Pylian gestures to the men standing either side of Herakles. 'These fine men are from Phthia.'

'Hail,' Telamon smiles.

'It is good to know you,' Peleus greets him.

Nestor spares the others a look, not knowing one face, and recognising the other with a flicker of unease. Prophets often have that effect on people, but he tries at least to mask it.

'And Idmon, you old snake! Good to see you're still alive.' He then extends a rough hand in Pirithous' direction. 'And I cannot say I know you, friend. From where have you come?'

The Lapith draws breath to answer, but never gets the words out. What happens next catches every last one of them off guard.

Precisely as their attackers planned.

Herakles lunges.

He falls.

He crashes down, his bulk splintering the stone floor beneath the cloying moss and grass. Theseus has fallen beside him, which was deliberate. It was Theseus he sought to throw aside, for it was Theseus in the line of fire.

The discus shatters the ground, thrown like a thunderbolt, barely a handspan from where the Athenian lies. It strikes like an almighty gong, ringing in the ears of every man present.

Herakles rolls over, head snapping up. Just in time to see them.

Two blurs of bronze armour and flowing cloaks, moving faster than any metal-clad man has any right doing. Shock has paralysed Meleager, while Idmon and Pirithous are little better off. Nestor scrabbles for his nearby blade, while Telamon and Peleus have at least drawn iron.

Pointless, all of it.

'*Wretch!*' the first one howls as he barrels into Theseus, sending them both cartwheeling down a grassy slope. '*Honourless! Wretch!*'

Herakles is already moving. One lunge, one crash, and he bears the second assailant end over end into earthen marble. He takes a punch, a knee. This bastard is fast. And well trained. He strikes hard, even while thrown down, without surrendering any speed or defence.

He has a glimpse of battered armour, and crudely cropped hair.

'Enough!'

One blow against his metal breastplate is enough to throw the attacker clear. He risks a leftward glance. Theseus and the other assailant, down in the ashen dirt, are pummelling each other into oblivion. Another flurry of flesh hides the combatants from view.

And then it is over, as Peleus and Meleager haul Theseus' swearing, flailing attacker clear. The King of Athens is left to lie in the dust, blood leaking from a host of ignoble wounds.

The Allslayer turns, muscles unclenching after being caught so unawares. With an unsurprised sneer, he spots Pirithous standing a little way off away from them, having moved to the circle's far side the moment the fight began.

Not that he need worry. The other aggressor is already down, one of Telamon's oaken arms locked around his neck and torso.

'Don't try anything.' Telamon warns him. His catch – a young, haughty-looking man with shoulder length hair and a freshly blackened eye – spits a gobbet of bloody phlegm from the corner of his mouth.

'As you wish. This was my brother's idea, anyway.'

A defeated yet defiant roar steals their attention, as that very man throws the lanky Meleager clear. Peleus tries his best to restrain the raging warrior single-handedly, but it is futile. Just a glance at the newcomer tells enough. If he wills it, he could kill the Phthian lord right here.

'*ENOUGH!*' the Allslayer roars, at the top of his demigod voice. 'What madness is this? What is your quarrel w—'

Only for that voice of his to catch in his throat, awed and afraid in equal measure, as a sound no less primal, no less divine, fills all their senses.

VII
CONSEQUENCES

It is the most beautiful thing he has ever heard. But it is so much more than beautiful. It is desolation. It is beguilement. It lingers in the heart like a first love. Or a haunting.

Herakles is no longer in Thessaly, standing instead in the pastures of Tiryns one youthful summer evening. Then in the toxic swamps of Lerna. Then the banks of a river of black blindness, where a boatman with no face awaits his toll.

The others around him are similarly stunned, and the Allslayer knows the music is showing something different to each of them. Meleager is captivated, utterly so, on the verge of weeping. Actual tears are pouring down Idmon's sallow cheeks, while Nestor seems incapable of even moving.

And most crucially of all, Theseus' two attackers are utterly mollified, their rage gone as if never there. The longer-haired one wilts in Telamon's embrace, even as the Phthian prince's arms around him slacken and fall away. The other one halts where he has broken free of Peleus, on the verge of falling to his knees.

All at the touch of fingers on lyre strings.

And then he appears, as human and unassuming as his music is divine. A dark-skinned man of slight build and little pretence, picking his way down the path into the circle. His fingers twitch and quiver over the lyre as he rounds his song to a close. But the falling silence doesn't feel like deprivation. It feels right, and natural, as if the flowing melody is simply going where it is needed next.

'My, my, my…' The little newcomer betrays his serenity with his smile. 'All this fighting, wrestling, running around. Is it not exhausting? Really, my Spartan friends. Isn't this better by far?'

'Who are you?' Meleager gasps, his senses gradually returning in the music's wake. 'And what… was that?'

The newcomer smiles. 'I am Orpheus, my young friend. I come from Pieria in answer to this summons. Just as you have, evidently.'

'And… what are you?'

Orpheus smiles once more, teeth of gleaming ivory in a tanned worn face. 'You could perhaps call me a bard, Prince Meleager. Though I rarely take payment for my craft. I would rather call myself a man of the world.'

Herakles doesn't seem especially satisfied with that answer, as the puny 'bard' falls into his shadow.

'Is this your doing?' the Allslayer growls, waving a hand at their two subdued attackers.

'Olympus, no.' Orpheus' air of giddy contentment isn't at all shaken. 'These Spartan kinglets are here for the same reasons we all are. Although I can't say I begrudge them their anger, to be honest.'

Behind them, Peleus and Telamon have shaken their befuddlement loose. Peleus squares up to the first attacker as Nestor tears the man's helmet off. The stubbly short-haired face he reveals is belligerent, but long weary of chasing grudges.

'Why were you attacking us?' Peleus growls.

The shaggy Spartan matches malice with malice, and a dash of haughtiness to boot.

'The pair of you merely got in our way. It is *him* we came here for, not any of you.'

He jabs a thumb over Telamon and Herakles' shoulders. To the other man in their party, still slumped in the bracken, nursing his wounds.

'Well, Theseus?' the other assailant cuts in, a twin in every respect to the first, but for his unshorn face and flowing locks. 'Are you going to tell them how you shamed us? Or shall I?'

The King of Athens recovers his poise, returning slowly to his feet. The Allslayer has never seen such a look upon Theseus' face, and never wants to see it again.

A sudden surge of suspicion wells up in his chest, brewing since his first encounter with Theseus on the road. 'What shame?' he growls. His temper is on the verge of erupting, stoked by gut instinct and spilt blood.

'He tried to carry off our sister.' This from the longer-haired twin, less rageful than his brother but no less zealous. 'Helen. He tried to abduct her as a battle bride. Even after our father rebuffed his advances, making it clear Helen was not yet ready for suitors. We hunted them down, my brother and me. We put an end to it.'

'And he's fled from our justice ever since,' Castor snarls. 'Why do you think he's jumping on this summons now, Allslayer? To keep running, the coward. He hopes whatever quest this Jason has planned will take him far from our shores. Somewhere Polydeuces and I won't find him!'

The Allslayer takes a moment to process these words. He thinks of the Theseus he once knew, a young man of strength and passion. Born to greatness, raised humbly, elevated by deeds rather than blood to the Fate of his future. A braggart among weaklings, a captain among followers, who rules men as deftly as he slays monsters. If it weren't for Herakles' presence, it might well be Theseus these other men look to for leadership and example.

Of all things that could have changed in his exile, of all the unwelcome truths he could come home to…

Behind him, Orpheus is laughing melodically. The Spartan twins continue arguing with Peleus and Telamon, pressing them to give the King of Athens over to them. And their untender mercies, no doubt.

Herakles has no time for any of that. His gaze remains fixed on Theseus, and the pleading look in his eyes is the most distasteful thing the Allslayer has ever seen.

'With me, boy. Now.'

There is no wind tonight, but the barest whispers of lyre music somehow carry to them all the same. The Pierian is playing another melody, not the same heart-stopping motif from before, but a gentler, more restrained reverie. From the way laughter and applause bubbles up from the others – Peleus, Meleager and Idmon in particular – it appears to be doing the trick.

A little way off, further still down the rugged path from Iolchus, Herakles strives to understand just how far his former acolyte has fallen.

It is all he can do not to scream in his face.

'Why, Theseus? Just *why?*'

The Athenian king's remorse appears to have fallen a notch now they are alone. That on its own is enough to sink Herakles' spirits. Shame is one thing, but guilt is quite another.

'I had no wish to offend the princes,' Theseus growls. 'And I regret that they took my overtures so poorly—'

'Overtures?' the Allslayer repeats. '*Overtures?* King Tyndareus all but outright barred Helen from nuptial claim! How could you have made *overtures* to a girl not fit for marriage?'

'Oh, she was ready in all but name!' Theseus can't help but let his petulance slip through the mask. 'She *was* ready, no matter what her idiot father claimed. How is it any different to you, Allslayer? I remember the stories the Phthians told me, of your war against King Laomedon. You seized Troy by the throat when they barred you from *your* bride!'

The sun is beginning to dip, casting the looming shape of Pelion into stark relief.

'If you cannot see the difference, boy, then I taught you even less than I thought.' Herakles growls his words through gritted teeth. His rage is simmering now, cooling into something far, far worse. 'Hesione was *promised* to me, fool! On holy oath! She was *kept* from me against her will. And she was of age to be married! She was no child in poorly fitted hems, awaiting her first bleed!'

Theseus has no answer to that, but the Allslayer senses no capitulation. He presses on, even more frustrated than before.

'Did the Spartans promise Helen's hand to you?'

Once again, a pause. But more pregnant this time. Silent submission is not the way of heroes.

'They did not,' Theseus concedes at last.

The Allslayer's eyes slam shut, exasperation plain all over him. How perversely skilled he is at excoriating his loved ones' secret shames.

'You abducted their sister, Theseus. Their *maiden* sister, after you heard their "no" and chose to ignore it. You fled restitution and tried to bury the truth. And now comeuppance catches you at last, you seek to shake it free.

They are within their rights to take your head for this, boy. And none of us have a noble or honest enough reason to stop them! Not without inciting war between the kingdoms!'

From the stony look on his face, the King of Athens has clearly grappled with these truths already. And for whatever it is worth — whatever in the rankest pits of Hades it is worth — he makes no further entreaty. No pleas to save him, or stand between him and the Spartan twins.

Herakles shakes his head, this time in surrender, as he looks Theseus up and down once more.

'I cannot believe you. You have known love, Theseus. You haven't wanted for it. Not from your father, not from Ariadne, and not from Phaedra now. What manner of *daimon* could possess you to do this thing?'

The Athenian hesitates. How unlike him. The Theseus of yore would never have shrank from difficult truths so cravenly. But then, that younger Theseus would never have found himself in a position like this. Let alone have been the one to light the fire.

Which narrows down the source of the malaise quite adroitly. Herakles spits, chiding himself for not making the leap more quickly.

'*Pirithous*,' he curses. 'That damned Lapith. This was his doing, wasn't it? What honeyed poison did he pour into your ear, that you would lose your balance so utterly?'

'He made me see... see what I was worth.' Theseus pauses again, before tempers can flare once more. 'Do you believe I don't deserve it? Helen is the daughter of Zeus, a child of Thunder just like you! Have I *not* earned the right to take a virgin godling for my bride? *I* rid Crete of the Minotaur. *I* defended Athens from my rabble of treasonous kinsmen, after slaying my way through every brigand and highwayman on the road from Troezen!'

Herakles just watches his younger comrade as he rages. His anger, if anything, has been replaced by a kind of pity. Pity at seeing a man he admired fall so heavily from the path he set him on.

'Theseus,' he gently begins. 'I know you are better than this.'

The Athenian fixes him with a dark look, darker than the fading light around them. He does not answer that claim, or deny it. In that moment, despite the years that have passed since their last meeting, Herakles has never felt the gulf between them so keenly.

And then Theseus turns, walking into the deepening dusk, and the moment is lost.

VIII
BY FORTUNE, BOUND

Heroes, lords and princes now camp beneath the sable sky, passing these long summer nights away by trading sparring blows and campfire stories. Wrestling of all kinds, in the main, much the same as Nestor and Meleager when they'd arrived. Reputation is everything, after all. Renown is the currency on which a hero trades.

Predictably, many of Thessaly's newest arrivals are taken with Orpheus. Every new outlander means someone new to listen and learn from. Before long, the firelit nights are awash with lyre music, owing as much to his listeners' ancestral folklore as it does his own muse.

Those who do not bask in those haunting melodies bask instead in torchlight and fireside warmth. After a few nights, an impromptu set of games arises from their boredom. Boxing, with weighted gloves. The hurling of javelins. The pitting of bicep against bicep.

Idmon's pious and irascible spirit might have had much to say about this – this less than holy merriment on a site where holiness once meant everything – but the wizened seer seems surprisingly to have held his tongue. And more surprisingly still, many of these brash new arrivals seem rather taken with him, warming to his cantankerous old soul instead of chafing at it.

Left briefly alone, Hylas feels a measure of duty and expectation sloughing off his back. He partakes in a little wine and cooked meat, mingling like a minnow among the oceanic leviathans around him.

Many he knows by name and renown, their glory having travelled far across Hellas. A few more he recognises from old quests. He briefly converses with Laertes, king of the storm-wracked isle of Ithaca. Oileus, the gaunt and humourless Locrian, has the dignity to jerk his head at him.

Few of the others dignify Hylas with any time. Calaïs and Zetes, the wing-footed sons of Boreas. Poeas, a young Meliboean with a friendly but solitary manner. A pair of smirking flame-haired giants called Idas and Lyncaeus.

Mopsus. Asterion. Aethalides. Eurydamas. Polyphemus. And so many others beyond that. The rest become a melange of faces and names, their impressions too fleeting to lodge in Hylas' memory for long.

The squire finds himself wandering some way from the glade, reflecting on the tumult of the past few nights. Forgiveness is not in his master's nature. And from what little time Hylas spent with the King of Athens, accounting for one's faults does not appear to be in Theseus'.

It is not a promising pairing, all things considered.

The servant's left sandal snaps something wooden underfoot, something wooden and not particularly strong. And then he is falling, tumbling end over end down the shallow slope he really ought to have seen coming.

He crashes to a mulchy, grassy halt, the only real damage done to his dignity. It isn't till he shifts position, craning his gaze across the gully in which he finds himself, that he realises he is not in fact alone.

A plainly dressed maiden is waiting for him, leaning rakishly against a fallen log, quietly tucking into some figs picked from the low-hanging trees that dot the mountainside. Her face is youthful, softened by self-reliance instead of meekness. As if out here, on the frontier of the wilds, far from any man and with only her hunting bow for company, is the most natural place in the world you could find her.

'Evening,' she greets him, reaching for another of her foraged figs. She does not offer him any.

'I am not asking you for mercy. Merely a stay of execution.'

Herakles cannot bring himself to couch the truth in honeyed words. His sense of honour – bruised and battered and torqued as it is – won't allow it. And in truth, the Spartans would doubtless see through such a craven entreaty anyway.

'I mean it,' he presses. 'I am not saying that your anger isn't just. Nor that Theseus does not deserve whatever end you have planned for him. I am simply asking you to remember where we are, and what is about to happen.'

Before him, the Spartan twins face him with silent frowns and folded arms. The odd cheer and clash of blade on armour echoes up the mountain path, reminding the three heroes of just what is waiting for them down below.

'Go on,' Castor growls, the words a command and not an encouragement.

'I don't know this Jason of Pelion,' Herakles begins. 'But this fool's crusade he has in mind for us… whatever would warrant him calling so many of our kind to this place, do you truly wish to start spilling each other's blood before we even take the first step?'

Neither of the twins say anything. Not because they agree, far from it. They are Spartans, and Spartans rarely care about the odds ranged against them.

'And what of the message it would send?' Herakles risks pressing the matter further. 'There are heroes here from all across the kingdoms, those that make war on one another and those bound by treaties and marriage. And yet men from each city and state prepare to swear bonds of tenuous brotherhood, putting feuds and rivalries aside to fight shoulder to shoulder. Think on that, my friends.'

Polydeuces seems to be gradually ceding ground. Though the same cannot be said for his brother.

'You would have us ignore the slight on our honour for the whole duration of this quest?' Castor can't even keep the bitterness from his voice. 'This was the only reason we came here, Herakles. Sparta has no interest in the family squabbles of Thessaly. And news of Theseus' crimes spread far from our shores, I can tell you. The others will have wind of it. So how, by the black sands of Hades, are we meant to stand before all those men and somehow pretend we let this outrage slide?'

'Brother...' Polydeuces begins. 'Perhaps he has a point.'

'Don't you start, Pol.'

'I mean it, Cas! The Allslayer speaks the truth. No matter what prize this Jason dangles before us, this quest will hang upon a blade's edge. Even before the trials and hardships begin. To slaughter a comrade in arms before we even set sail...' Polydeuces isn't so willing to finish the thought.

Sensing his moment, Herakles pushes on once last time.

'I am not asking you to abandon your grudge, Spartans. But I have known Theseus a long time. There are other sides to him, besides the less savoury ones he has shown you. Wherever Jason would have us go... what harm can there be in giving him the doubt, just for now? Perhaps he can even redeem himself in your eyes. Or at least, earn back the trust and respect he forfeited with his rashness.'

Polydeuces' eyes seem to brighten at the prospect of a compromise.

'And if not?' Herakles continues. 'If we return to Iolchus clad in glory and gold, and the Athenian has failed to rise in your esteem... then do with him as you will.'

The glade is still in fine voice when they return, boisterous showboating still unfolding around them.

Theseus is rarely a difficult man to find, these nights. The camp still rings with wrestling matches, and the Athenian is busy drinking in the prestige of putting so many rivals to shame with his prowess. But no more.

Herakles shoves him against a broken wall with no effort whatsoever. He speaks in dark tones, all bile and snarls instead of the pleading passion he used up on Castor.

'You have a chance here, boy. A chance to show that Spartan zealot you are more than a lickspittle thief of girls and honour.'

The King of Athens looks back at him, shamed but not without defiance.

'Prove to them, Allslayer? Or to you?'

IX
AESON'S HEIR

'I suppose it is finally time!' Jason announces, a handful of humid nights later. 'Time to tell you why you are all here!'

The lost heir had raised few eyebrows when he'd arrived. A shepherd boy, stern of build yet soft of eye, the boy could ostensibly pass as well-to-do once you wiped the dirt off him. Hands that were never born for working in fields have toughened, grown gnarly, and moulded to poor circumstance quite respectably. This Jason was an easy man to like, to Herakles' eye, and he wasn't even a man yet.

But that wasn't all the Allslayer had sensed in that first fleeting moment. There, in the light of his gaze, and the pull at the corner of his smile. There, in the way his amusement and bonhomie spread like a plague. The favour of a goddess, lightly worn but undeniably there. A goddess Herakles knows all too well and has little wish to encounter again.

To the rest of Hellas, this orphaned prince has only existed for a matter of weeks. Every man he has summoned, by contrast, has a twisting saga of deeds to enthral and horrify. Sizing these men up, playing the proud hero, would have absolutely sent the wrong message.

So Jason opted for a wholly different tack.

A night or two of easy banter and conversation, skirting round the topics of King Pelias, or quite how the shepherd boy escaped from the dungeons at Iolchus, passed by quite agreeably. Heroes, on the whole, are used to having their worlds revolve around them. Whatever grandiose tidings this Thessalian child bore with him could wait a little while.

Until now.

'I hope you know what you're about, boy!' another voice calls out over the throng. Echion. Herakles remembers him from an old battle. 'No-one ever, ever calls this many of us together like this. Not without a damn fine reason.'

Herakles almost expected a crowd of raging voices, pressing Jason to spill his secrets like a mob demanding justice. The truth hasn't quite lived up to that expectation, but for the moment, all eyes are on Jason. There is a great deal riding on this moment, and it cannot be delayed any longer.

'Well?' Echion continues. 'We're waiting. What lies behind the greatest muster of valour that any of us have ever seen?'

Behind her protective thicket of trees, the huntress winces. Since being stumbled upon by Hylas the other night, she has made no effort to join the throng of men, or even to stir too far from her spot. These heroes do not strike her as savoury company, and she can hear all she needs to from here.

But right now, what she hears is a lack of pliancy. A lack that somehow, against all rhyme and reason, Jason did not expect.

This should not be a trial for him. He should be able to do this on his own.

'I called you here,' Jason finally replies, 'to avenge an injustice!'

The fires have mostly faded to embers now. Dawn is making her rosy-fingered way across the sky, banishing the worst of the dark and the shadows.

'A grave injustice!' Jason continues. 'The rule of Iolchus, the rule of all Thessaly, is based on a lie! My father was Aeson. *King* Aeson. The rightful ruler of this land! Only to be murdered, alongside his queen, by the man he called brother. And for the last two decades, that treacherous dog Pelias has enjoyed what he has stolen!'

He takes a tentative step forward, his hands beginning to animate themselves as his fervour rises. The young man is no orator, but boyish passion, at least, is easy to trust. Will his wrath be more infectious than his idealism?

'Until now! For years, none believed Aeson's true heir survived that fateful night. How could he? The babe in arms was stolen away from the *megaron*, taken to Mount Pelion, and raised far from Pelias' eyes. Raised simply as a man, without the truth of who he was.'

Jason pauses once again, and this time, the moment feels more earned. 'The truth of who *I* was.'

The huntress smiles, and her smile hides more than it reveals.

'It was Hera!' Jason declares. 'The Consort of Zeus showed me the truth of my inheritance. It was at *her* behest that I came to Iolchus. That I forsook my life on the Mountain, and claimed what was rightfully mine!'

The Allslayer's eyes narrow, at the crowd's edge. He needs no enlightening about Hera's myriad wiles, and the idea of risking life and limb for an Olympian raises the hackles on his neck. Outside of songs and fireside tales, the gods are rarely ever this altruistic.

'This is it, my noble friends! You dauntless few, who have answered my call and made your way to me!'

Jason sweeps his arms out, taking in the throng of heroes he doubtless believes he belongs among. Does he truly expect them to share his zeal? Is this the truth behind the greatest call to arms in a generation?

'Here is your chance to be on the right side of destiny. Join my sacred quest to see the throne of Thessaly returned to honour! Write your place in legend and fable at my side!'

Wind billows. Trees murmur. Dawn's light climbs higher into the morning air. None of the spectators begin to cheer, or applaud, or salute the young shepherd for his audaciousness.

Because that is, after all, what he is. No amount of divine providence or quirk of birth can rewrite the truth of who you are. This boy is no ruler, no warrior, no iconoclast. He is just a shepherd from Mount Pelion who believes he can court the will of heroes.

And that, clearly, is only one thing he has misjudged in this moment.

Orpheus of Pieria is the first man to recover his wits, breaking the silence in the most unlikely and unwelcome way.

'In the gods' names, Jason of Pelion… is *this* why you summoned us all here?'

For a moment, Aeson's son can barely comprehend the question.

'I have told you why, Bard. Hera has decreed I must take back my throne, after fulfilling a mighty quest. And I cannot do that without your help!'

'Is that so?' answers Oileus' irreverent voice.

The effect is spreading. The heroes are now murmuring and cursing among themselves. Peleus and Telamon are deriding their own judgement for answering the call. Laertes is incredulous he was even summoned, while Eurydamas is already counselling the others to leave already.

A few of them, younger men like Meleager and Idas, seem simply dumfounded, their expectations either shattered or deflated. Several of them look ready to leave this very moment, and the discontent of a few is already boiling into anger.

For his part, Jason looks savaged. He came here to rally men together, not to debate his position. It seems, in hindsight, he was ill-prepared to do either.

'Will none of you stand with me? Truly? Will no man here help me unseat this tyrant?'

A hunched crone of a man rears himself up from his seat. Idmon, the aged prophet, finally has something to add.

'Such talk of tyranny and freedom, young Jason. But was your father any less of a tyrant?'

'You, shameless—'

Only for the conviction to drain from the shepherd boy's words. It is clear, in a heartbeat, that this is yet another point he has never even considered. He tries to recover lost ground.

'Whatever you may say about my father, the throne was his by right. *He* was no usurper, at any rate! He was not like Pelias!'

Another voice cuts over his entreaty. Poeas, the lonesome Meliboean.

'Perhaps not, boy. But whatever the truth, what concern would your father's ills be of ours?'

And this, perhaps, is the meat of the matter. This is what Jason has failed so completely to understand.

Injustice is injustice, and its sting never fades. But lives end. Blades are bloodied. Thrones are stolen. There is only so much these facts of life can move a soul, even a hero, when avenging every sin would be the work of too many lifetimes. And sometimes there is more glory in committing wrongs than righting them.

Unless the ousting of King Aeson affected any of their lives, why would any of them care enough to put it right?

'My friends, please! Let me explain the rest!'

Jason is tenacious, that must be said. Still clinging on to the future he believes he is owed.

But perhaps this is unsurprising. Scant days ago he was a mountain boy, with no concerns beyond winter's bite and bad harvests. And now he is made anew, by truth and gods and heritage unveiled, and cast out onto this throw-board of kings and champions.

It must be hard, to not let truths like that intoxicate you.

'The bargain!' Jason he tries. 'Let me explain the bargain!'

Behind him, Meleager scoffs with naked disdain.

'Oh, so there is a bargain now? A bargain with who? Gods of Olympus, are you a liar as well as a fool?'

'Who are *you*, to dishonour *me?*' Jason rounds on the Calydonian prince – a prince younger, and smaller, than him. 'Pampered cur. Call me that again!'

Meleager's gaze darkens, his temper lit. His sword is already leaving its sheath.

The air sharpens. The world holds its breath.

The huntress springs from their hiding place, shortbow raised. She is a blur. She is an arrow herself, loosed by a vengeful archer at their unlucky target.

Metal strikes metal as the deadly shaft hits its mark.

X
COLCHIS' CALL

Meleager is dazed. He simply stares at his open hand, the hand that moments ago clasped his royal blade. That blade now lies in the mud and thickets, shot from his grip by an arrow so unerring it had no right leaving a mortal quiver.

The others have wound back its trajectory with their eyes, right back to this new threat approaching from the hill.

Herakles sees her first of all, among the plinths and the stones and the shrubbery, though through luck or artifice the heroes have only just noticed her. That is the degree to which the lady exists beneath mortal notice.

Her garb and bearing run contrary to her onlookers' expectations. There is nothing ornamental, subservient or nubile in the knee-length skirt and chiton she wears, hemmed and slit to let her move more freely. Barley hair falls just shy of her shoulders, bound and knotted not for the gaze of others, but simply to keep it from her face.

Presumably to not impede her deadly marksmanship.

Meleager is still dumbfounded, either at the shot, or the woman it came from.

'Was that… you?'

The huntress doesn't answer, doesn't even acknowledge him as she passes. She gives Jason the barest brush of eye contact as she reaches to retrieve her arrow.

And then, with a lack of reverence that would make any Achaean gasp, she tosses Meleager's ceremonial sword back to him.

None of the gathered heroes can even find their words, though many of them are clearly on edge. The only one of them truly at ease is Jason himself, and the lack of surprise in his eyes is explanation enough.

'How timely of you, Atalanta.' Self-assurance pours back into his face. 'I was beginning to think you weren't coming.'

The mention of that name elicits an intake of breath. It is a rare hero in these lands who has understanding, or patience, for other ways of living a life. But the legend of Atalanta the Arcadian, the maiden huntress of Artemis, daughter of King Iasus by blood if not by loyalty, is a story that holds tongues still across the kingdoms.

From respect, if not necessarily admiration. She walks an eerily similar path to many men here, though in pursuit of wildly different ends.

'Join my friend's endeavour if it pleases you, Prince of Calydon. Or go back home to your kingdom.' She turns back to look at Meleager, her eyes soft and yet hard to meet. 'But slaying an unarmed man, for merely begging your help? A poor way to begin your legend, no? Especially for someone who's clearly never taken a life.'

To his credit, Meleager doesn't shrink from the huntress' gaze. A few of the older men are sniggering at his expense, watching this unblooded royal kinglet brought down to earth by an unwed girl.

For whatever it is worth, he nods his head with deference, deflated but not fully unbowed.

'My apologies, Princess. I merely believed my honour slighted, and—'

His words are wasted, for Atalanta cares nothing for his excuses. She hasn't been a princess of Arcadia for some time, and years of watching men hack each other into ribbons has inured her to the laughable virtue of honour.

She spares Jason the barest comradely smile before taking her place at his left hand. Behind her, Meleager of Calydon glowers at her retreating form, as if still struggling to process what just happened.

Then his frown shifts, like silt in a flowing river, to an emotion he is less familiar with. Not quite bewilderment, not quite admiration, but some new and unwelcome meld of the two.

Only to return, once again, to his earlier surliness. That is enough introspection for one day.

'Atalanta here knows a little of my plans,' Jason confesses, risking a fraternal hand upon the huntress' shoulder. 'While last to arrive, she has the privilege of being the first I summoned. Which is why you can trust her to vouch for the truth of what I'm telling you.'

At his side, the huntress confirms nothing, denies nothing. Calmness, fairness, neutrality: these things radiate from her in a soothing wave. The Arcadian is more than just another wanderer summoned to this shore. She is clearly in Jason's confidence, or at least knows more than the others of what he plans. Meaning she has just as much to gain or lose from this as he does.

'I spoke to you of a bargain.' Jason lets go of her shoulder, perhaps sensing she is leaving him to do this himself. Now, or never. He won't get another chance at seizing the day. Now, or he might as well die here, as ignominious and ignorable as the shepherds he left on Pelion.

'You have asked me how I am at liberty to make entreaties to you. Why I am here with you, and not lying dead on the floor of King Pelias' throne room.'

There is no answer forthcoming from the crowd, beyond an uncertain murmuration. It is just as well.

'I do desire to unseat my treacherous uncle,' Jason finally admits. 'That, I grant you. But not in the way you think, my noble friends. King Pelias and I struck a bargain. We swore a vow, him and I, in the blood that we begrudgingly share, and in the name of Hera herself.'

He takes a slow, unsteady breath, trying to find the right words to follow. A flicker of silent eye contact is all the support Atalanta lends him. It is only right that Jason does this on his own.

'If I uphold my side – with you here, specifically, *to help me* uphold my side – my father's brother has agreed he will cede the throne of Iolchus to me. He'll invest me, and not his own son, as the ruler of all Thessaly.'

For a moment, nobody seems willing to speak. Which is just as well. Jason's next words are going to change the path of all their lives, and so many others beyond.

'And all I have to do is sail eastward. Sail past the point where maps and gazes end, and bring back the Golden Fleece from Colchis.'

XI
HEART OF THE QUEST

You drift at anchor in the gentle waves, no less menacing for being dormant. But then dormancy is all you have known; you were born not far from here, in the dry darkness of a carpenter's crypt, though you never knew life until they put you in the water.

Though perhaps *born* is not the right word. *Crafted*, or maybe *hewn*. Or is *grown* more apt? You were called forth from Dodonian oak, not by whim of nature but the will of man, to meet a man's vision.

None of this matters, for you have no grasp of language or intent. Sensation, if you can even call it that, trickles down through your oaken bones in a watering of murky awareness. You feel the waves — feeble and pathetic and insidiously gentle — lapping softly against your flanks and hull. Without knowing what they are, or what it means, you know instinctively that you are made for more than this.

To plough the brine and foam, to face down storm swells that crash against your bow, to churn the waves in your wake like tilled soil… this is why you were given this form.

So you wait, letting the water caress your hide. You are good at waiting. Waiting is all you know.

Argus sets the mallet down at last, resigned to his lack of progress. He wipes perspiration off his brow with one tattered overall sleeve, and glares balefully at the decking he has spent all morning trying to mend.

Oak from the sacred groves at Dodona has properties far beyond the ken of mortal men. But for all those mystic qualities, it is a craftsman's nightmare. Argus and his deckhands have had to rehammer several sections along the aft and stern, sending pleading missives to Dodona to have more oak cut to size, each message promising to be the last. The gold and favour of Iolchus will only go so far.

Every night since the commission began, Argus walks the length of the deck, noting where the day's work has come inexplicably undone. Nails of iron and bronze, meticulously hammered in by unwavering hands, appear strewn across the decking or sunk in the harbour shallows. The craftsman's trained eyes spot the lattices of holes where nails once rested, gaping wounds in miniature that have no right lying open. In the first weeks of the commission, one of his younger apprentices swore the wood spat them out before his very eyes, like a newborn babe egesting peppercorns.

Argus dismissed the boy from service with a strike across the face. And then he inspected another oaken panel amidships. Almost a hundred metal tacks he painstakingly drove into the wood were gone. Utterly gone. The panelling was spotless, unspoilt like virgin snow.

And then Argus looked up, and saw those hundred nails crisscrossing the meat of the ship's mast, too high for any of the carpenters to reach.

Putting her in the water went some way to easing the troubles. When the ship was drydocked, slowly taking form, all of this was so much worse. Tiphys, at the time, remarked that it was as if she *wanted* to taste the sea she was destined to sail, no matter how far she was from being seaworthy. Like a child, yearning for what they craved, spurning what they actually needed, lashing out against any guiding hand in the meantime.

Footsteps climbing the companionway jolt Argus back to the present. As if his thoughts can summon him into being, Tiphys ascends from the lower cabin to join him on the deck.

'Shipwright.'

'Helmsman.'

Each title is a misnomer of sorts, though neither can be bothered to address it. As chief craftsman and carpenter of the court of Iolchus, building ships is far from Argus' area of expertise. And Tiphys is only a helmsman in the loosest sense of the word. A young novitiate from Dodona's oracular cult, he understands the blessed oak far better than any Thessalian.

This was made clear to Argus, back when King Pelias tasked them with this endeavour. Simply *steering* such a vessel across the sea would not be enough. Any navigator worth his salt would have to *commune* with her, in a way that went beyond a sailor's grasp of such things.

'How goes the work, shipwright?' Tiphys breaks the uneasy silence. 'The king's counsellors grow impatient, I hear. They say that Jason has already made his gathering of might.'

Argus smiles wryly, dragging greasy wisps of white hair out of his face. In another life his skills earnt the praise of Daedalus himself, and now here he is, explaining to a man half his age why he can't even hammer a boat together.

'Then you have it wrong, helmsman. From what I gather, our friend Jason's little conclave didn't quite go to plan.' He picks up his mallet once more, not for dramatic effect, but simply because he wishes to be left to work in peace. 'And King Pelias knows full well the difficulties we face, I assure you. As well as the progress I have made.'

Tiphys joins Argus on the topmost deck, inspecting the craftsman's work in progress. This high above the water, both men have an enviable view of the noonday sun as it catches the shifting waves of the gulf. And inland beyond that, the city port of Pagasa, Thessaly's great mouth into the Aegean.

'The vessel is seaworthy, yes?'

Argus' brow furrows. 'She is far from finished. This is the mightiest vessel that King Pelias has ever commissioned. It is to be the jewel in our kingdom's crown, and must—'

'That is not what I asked, old man. If this ship of yours raised its anchor stones and made for the open water, would she hold together well enough to make the journey?'

The beating of seagull wings forestalls Argus' response. The flying pest alights on the wooden deck rail, doubtless smelling something vaguely edible. It fixes Tiphys with one beady little eye for a few moments, before abruptly taking flight once more.

'You ask me to quantify the stuff of legends,' Argus berates him. 'Who among us even knows where Colchis truly is?'

'We know where it is *meant* to lie,' Tiphys retorts. 'Where song and fable place it.'

Argus tosses his mallet aside, knowing a losing battle when he senses one. Beneath his feet, the deck is hard and stable. And beneath that, the almost subliminal pitching of the boat in the current's ebb and flow.

'And do those fables mention anyone making it home, helmsman? Does anyone seeking the City of Dawn ever tell the tale themselves?'

That shuts Tiphys up, for the time being at least. But his silence is not a submissive one.

'I will have to,' he finally replies. 'The lives of a great many heroes will rest on it.'

Argus laughs, turning away from the younger man to give the boat another inspection.

'A great many heroes will be going their separate ways, I think. Unless Jason can pull his crook from his crease.'

The boy who would be king would probably resent that term of phrase, but Argus' appraisal is far from unfair. Further inland, on a rolling hillside overlooking Pelion's slopes, Jason considers his unravelling plans.

He has been doing so for quite some time. It has not been a productive morning.

'They laughed at me, Atalanta. They laughed themselves hoarse.'

Beside him, the huntress of Arcadia buries the urge to wince. She has listened to enough of Jason's self-pity already in the hours since his gathering dissolved in disaster. She has indulged him far enough.

'They laughed at you, my friend, because they believed you tried to make fools of them. And they believe Pelias has done the same to you.'

Jason pouts, unabashedly and unguardedly boyish. Years of shared isolation on Pelion's slopes have inured Atalanta to the swinging of Jason's moods. There is a good man in there, somewhere. A man lacking the pretension and presumption common to those of higher birth.

But many flaws of man transcend walks of life.

'They laughed at you because you didn't give them enough, Jason. Because you didn't trust them with enough of the truth. That would have gotten you—'

'Killed,' Jason spits at her, indignant that the world cannot see things from his perspective. 'With my Fleece, and my glory, in the hands of other men. Where would my quest be then?'

Atalanta needs a moment to process that. The Jason she grew up with, the flock-tender she has known since girlhood, never had any grasp or use of glory. How much can one night of divine augury change a human soul? How completely can ambition rewrite a heart?

But unlike Jason, dwelling is not the huntress' way.

'It is a risk, yes. But how else would you persuade them that you know your course? That they have any reason to believe they are chasing more than a whispered myth?'

'The Fleece *is* more than myth, Atalanta!'

'So *tell* them that. Tell them that the Iolchans have sold you more than just a fireside fable. That King Pelias truly wishes you to succeed, and is not simply sponsoring your death.'

For a moment, Jason says nothing. Because he knows, in his heart, that his treacherous uncle has outplayed him either way. Whether the shepherd boy and his erstwhile comrades succeed in bringing their treasure back to Thessaly, or collectively perish in the first storm, Pelias wins.

'The more you tell them,' Atalanta gently presses him, 'the easier it will be to win them over.'

Jason's eyes are distant as he replies. 'The more I tell them, the harder it will be to control them.'

He has no need to follow that worrying thought. Atalanta is no fool. She knows full well what she is hearing.

'The Fleece is—'

'A weapon, in the right hands. All that power, Huntress. All that magic, there for the taking. What is to stop one of them, *any* of them, taking it for themselves? Could even Herakles resist such a lure?'

Atalanta swallows, reaching up to retie her hair. It gratifies her a touch to see Jason actually thinking of the future, beyond the siren call of his own ambition. But all the same... how much truth to tell him?

'To join your crew, they will have to swear an oath. To help you take the Fleece.'

'To help me *find* the Fleece.' Jason smiles ruefully. 'We'll get no more from them than that. What finer plan, than slaying the seeker in his moment of triumph?'

Atalanta's mind flickers back to the morning's tumultuous events. To the heroes bodily kicking apart their makeshift camp, going their separate ways, still fuming that they were foolish enough to even answer Jason's hails. Theseus' curses still ring in her ears, as does Eurydamas' bitter vow against chasing a traveller's tale to the world's edge.

Poor winds and the backlog of ships still arriving have stopped anyone from leaving at once. But unless Jason commits to the course and does the unthinkable, it will soon be a different story.

Right here, right now, Atalanta senses it might be time for him to do just that.

'Tell them what Pelias truly wants,' the huntress urges. 'And what *you* truly want.'

'Ready the ship, helots.'

The central harbour is in even finer voice than normal, and it gratifies Castor no end to know he'll soon be rid of it.

'Come the morrow we are returning to Sparta,' he continues. 'There is nothing for us here.'

Polydeuces is already waiting for him on board. For once, he is not trailing in his twin's shadow.

'This is quite the change of heart, brother. Are you really so eager to leave this place behind?'

'We'll have another chance at Theseus, Pol.' Castor spits overboard, as if warding away some spiritual malaise. 'You mark my words. But it isn't worth getting caught up in this madness. Blood of Olympus, can you *believe* that boy's delusion? I'd rather wage a war against his uncle.'

Polydeuces just watches him, his feigned disinterest as sharp as a blade. Castor ploughs on, heedless.

'I mean it. A *shepherd boy* would unite a ship full of heroes, men sired from *gods*, and lead them to a city of myth and magic? And somehow *steal* their most jealously guarded relic?'

Polydeuces' lips are sealed. He knows his brother well, knows just how to unravel his conviction.

'Alright,' Castor concedes. 'There was a time, brother, when such a story would have stirred my daring. But not anymore.'

'No?' Polydeuces risks a crooked smile. 'Beneath those statesman's robes and soldier's breastplate beats a hero's heart, Cas. I'll admit it if you won't.'

'We are princes of Sparta, Pol.' Castor waves his flippancy aside. 'First, last and always. Our loyalty is to our kingdom. Not to ourselves, nor the legacies we'll leave behind us.'

Above them, the deck is abustle with their attendants. They will be ready to leave as soon as the seaborne traffic lets them.

Polydeuces cocks his head to one side, as if pretending his thoughts have only just struck him now.

'Perhaps you should regard this with a prince's eye then, brother? You say you have no interest throwing in your lot with Jason.'

'Aye, I don't. And I fancy the others will say the same. Even if any of them believe his fancies, they are all too proud to be first to commit.'

'But what if someone does, brother?' Polydeuces' smile is far too knowing for Castor's liking. 'What if one of the others throws down the gauntlet, against all odds? Would that change your mind?'

Castor draws in a heavy breath. *Damn you.* He knows full well where his brother's questions lead.

'You see?' Polydeuces chides him. 'You may not believe in Jason's fantasy, but what if he turns out to be right? What if the Golden Fleece really does lie at journey's end?'

Castor finally matches his brother's cruel smile. If this witless shepherd from the Mountain really can lead them all to such a treasure... what chance does he have of holding it, when set against the mightiest heroes across the kingdoms?

'If the Fleece is truly there for the taking...' he growls, 'then it must come back with us to Sparta. Its power will be the prosperity of our people.'

'And that is the heart of it, brother.' Polydeuces nods. That is what will make this happen. Because no matter how many of us risk our lives for such a prize... could any of us stand to see *another* kingdom take it?'

And just like that, revelation burns behind Castor's eyes. It is not a pleasant shade.

'We join him, then. We join this fool's crusade, and we bring home the power of Colchis.'

'Or the head of Theseus.'

'Oh, brother... do you think I would take one and not the other?'

With noonday's passing, Laertes has ventured further inland. Holding court in a Iolchan saloon forcibly emptied by his royal guards, the Ithacan has the luxury of a little solitude.

He certainly has enough to reflect upon.

The other men who answered this call are heroes of war, many of them sons of divine blood. And here he is, a humble king of a lowly island rock. Would he have the measure of any of them, if blood came to be spilled over the Fleece? How would barren little Ithaca fare against a larger kingdom if the power of the Fleece protected her? How would Ithaca resist the plundering hands of a kingdom holding the Fleece for itself?

His thoughts then drift even closer to home. The rugged royal hall standing on the ocean promontory. Little Odysseus chasing seabirds up and down the stony headland. His son is growing up so fast, half Laertes' height already and still shy of his eleventh year.

What a story for Odysseus this quest would make. What a legacy for him, to rule the isle that holds the Fleece.

'My king.' The new arrival breaks Laertes' reverie. His herald, Alcaeon, who from his dust-covered sandals has clearly travelled with some haste. 'Another missive for you, my lord. You are summoned to the coast. To Pagasa.'

Laertes raises a wisp-thin eyebrow. 'Summoned by Jason?'

'Indeed, my liege.'

The king chuckles, taking one last draught from his goblet of spring water.

'I had best make haste, then. I fancy I will not be the only one.'

A little deeper into Iolchus, yet more princes of Hellas are hardening their hearts to the reality of this gambit. Though some are more naïve, or idealistic, than others.

On the balcony of the royal hall granted for his stay, Meleager of Calydon weighs up the honour in his soul against the ambition.

'I understand the boy's anger, Nestor. No matter how deluded it is. Every man has the right to *try* salvaging their family's honour. I may well have done the same if our places were traded.'

In the chamber behind him, Nestor of Pylos lies prostrate upon an oaken bench, utterly free of care and conscience, as a pair of supplicant women oil and massage his torso.

'I'd fancy every royal house in every kingdom has its dramas and quarrels to untangle. Plenty closer to Calydon than here. If you hunger for a cause, dear boy, you needn't have come all this way.'

Meleager turns from the hillside view to eye the older prince derisively. 'Oh, so you think me some guileless little lost boy, Pylian?'

'My dear Meleager, the only person I've seen strip you of your guile today is that Arcadian girl. Goddess of the Hearth, I can't remember the last time I saw you quite so flustered!'

Meleager screws his face up in the general manner of youth. It rankles him. It rankles him to feel so rankled. Why *does* he feel so rankled?

'My sense of honour calls to me,' he finally admits. 'No matter what my good sense counsels.'

'If you say so, Prince of Calydon. If you say so.'

In truth, Nestor has little desire to claim the Golden Fleece. Such an artefact could make Pylos mighty indeed, but it could make it just as enviable a target. Nestor has some ideas about who *might* try to take it, and whose hands he'd rather not see it fall into.

It won't hurt matters, the Pylian reasons, if the huntress puts Meleager's head into a spin. One less player to contend with at journey's end — when Jason's high-minded plan is inevitably spat upon, and the real business of who takes the prize is settled — is something to be thankful for. Not least a man like Meleager. A man naïve and idealistic enough to truly believe in Jason's cause.

As much affection as Nestor has for the Calydonian and his bloodline… what place could he have in this madman's dream?

'Another summons?' Theseus repeats. 'From Jason?'

The slave is already scurrying away before Theseus can even read the scrawled message. The King of Athens digests its contents for a moment, before crumpling the parchment in one fist.

Behind him, one of Iolchus' less reputable pleasure houses squats, proud and shameless, in the heart of the seedy little shantytown. Pirithous has already made his way inside, enough gold in hand to degrade the self-respect of all within. Theseus can hardly take such a judging view, knowing full well he was about to join him.

Possibilities play out behind his eyes. Spartans laughing as they kick him from the gallows. One last disgusted shake of Herakles' head. Ariadne's damning gaze boring into him whichever way he turns.

The Fleece, in his golden hands. Heroes and princes, chanting his name, sorry they ever doubted him. Athens standing tall and proud, her enemies burnt to cinders.

To his left, the pleasure house awaits him, enticing yet unwelcoming. To his right, the winding alley that will take him back within the palace walls.

'Are you coming?' Pirithous' reedy voice drifts out to him.

XII
UNWANTED TRUTH

'Will you not eat, master?'

This war of attrition is something Hylas has come to dread, its motions bleakly familiar to both of them. The Allslayer has little compassion for himself at the best of times, and the weeks since his lonely pilgrimage to Thebes have been no exception. Nothing that has transpired here in Iolchus has helped matters.

'Master, please. While it's hot. You haven't eaten since we arrived.'

Herakles looks up at last, as if only now aware of the Phthian encampment around them, out beyond Iolchus' outer walls. Peleus and Telamon have had their share of royal hospitality, and a handful of nights within their own tents won't do them any harm.

Not while they consider their path ahead.

A wordless glance passes between master and servant, and then Herakles finally takes the proffered bowl, helping himself to a few mouthfuls of broth.

This gratifies Hylas, for now at least. He is yet to risk asking the outright question, but he knows Herakles far too well to let the matter lie. Thrall he may be, but fool he is not. From what fragments the Allslayer gave him after his return from Thebes, Hylas can piece together the bones of his master's unease.

'It was the Fleece, wasn't it? That was what you dreamt of, all those months ago. You dreamt of Jason's prize.'

Herakles swallows his mouthful, letting it warm his insides. For a moment, he hears Tiresias' knowing laughter in his ear. But of course, it is the wind. Just the wind.

'I did, Hylas. Long before Jason accepted this mad bargain, before Pelias even decided to make it. I dreamt of the ram that bore Phrixus to Colchis, and its fleece of molten sunlit fur.'

'The Golden Fleece.'

'The very same. That is where it came from, all those years ago. The godly beast is long dead, but the Fleece remains there still.'

Hylas is rapt by this confession. It is a rare day indeed that the Allslayer speaks this openly, this intimately, to anyone.

'So Colchis is real, master? Not just a traveller's tale?'

Herakles smiles ruefully. 'Oh, the City of Dawn is real enough. That doesn't make it a place I'd like to visit.'

A flurry of raised voices drifts in from the neighbouring tent; Peleus and Telamon, back from the *megaron* once again. Peleus is boasting about something. Hylas picks up a handful of unfamiliar words.

Argus. Pagasa. Dodona.

'They will want to go,' Herakles confesses.

'Master?'

'To join Jason. This is a story my Phthian friends won't resist. To help the shepherd boy, or take his glory for themselves. Nothing in the world could keep them away.'

Hylas' heart beats a further six times in the silence that ensues, before he builds up the courage to say his next words.

'And what do you want, master? Do you want to join Jason's travelling band? Do you wish to take the Fleece from Colchis?'

Herakles looks at him, in that moment. The most foreboding pair of eyes Hylas has ever seen, or reckons he ever will, bores into the servant's soul for just a moment. In Hylas' opinion, it is a moment too long.

'What I want, boy, doesn't come into it. What will happen if I don't go? What am I prepared to let happen?'

Whatever he means by that is anyone's guess. Telamon's raucous arrival shatters the moment, and though nothing outwardly changes, Hylas feels the armour around his master's soul seal itself.

'He's walked the World Beneath, for Olympus' sake!' Peleus' hands clasp the seated Telamon's shoulders, as if he has just proved his brother wrong. 'The *World Beneath*, Tel! The realm of *Hades!* What is the City of Dawn compared with that?'

Telamon has the good grace to laugh it off. 'I knew you wouldn't let us down, Allslayer. It wouldn't have been the same without you!'

Herakles cocks his head wryly. 'No?'

'Or course not, kinsman! Who else better than the three of us to babysit this drove of dewy-eyed princelings? One week on that ship and Jason will have shat out his guts!'

'Ship?' Hylas asks.

'We're being called together again at the port of Pagasa,' Telamon explains. 'Jason must have a ship to court us with, I tell you. Why else would he presume to meet us there?'

'You mark my words, friend.' Peleus moves to stand by Herakles, giving his shoulder a conspiratorial nudge. 'That shepherd is no seafarer, or fighter. And if this day is much to go by, he's not much of a leader to boot. We won't even have to take anything from anyone. Come the end, we'll be the only men of mettle left standing!'

Telamon smirks, without malice, but still a little dangerously.

'Know it well, Allslayer! That Fleece of theirs will make its way to Phthia. And all the kingdoms will know that it was the three of us who made it happen!'

They all begin to laugh, toasting a victory not yet theirs. Herakles tries his best to join it. It is the easiest way to hide his unease.

A handful of hours later, he finds himself alone once more.

Alone, but not particularly lonely. The Phthians always have this effect on him, and for a little while, he can drink in the fading warmth of their bond. Today, at least, can be spared the worries of tomorrow.

The Allslayer's wandering brings him to the camp's outer limits, far enough to afford a little privacy. Hylas is here, tending to their beds and their belongings, because what else would he be doing? What facet of his life doesn't revolve around his master?

For a few moments, Herakles is content to simply watch him, this boy who is edging closer each day to manhood. How swiftly time passes, when you cease looking. Hylas was barely a child when he came to him. He has changed so much since then, in more ways than just the obvious.

'Diligence incarnate, boy. You should take some time for yourself before we make for Pagasa.'

Hylas' youthful features colour a little as he looks up. Either in pleasure at a rare moment of praise, or simple contentment to see the Allslayer's mood lightening.

'I'll rest, master, when you've gotten another proper meal down you.'

Herakles tries to hide his smile, turning to look at the mass of unpacked provisions being cleaned and stored away.

'Gods above, how many weapons did you bring?'

Hylas swallows. 'I'd rather you weren't caught unawares, master. As our journey here proved.'

Herakles chuckles, the sound so soft Hylas barely hears it. His eyes take in a host of sheathed blades, several of them no longer than sparring knives. The immense wooden club that has become such a symbol across the Achaean kingdoms lies alongside the Nemean lionskin, still strong enough to stop a blade or arrow.

And more, so many more, so many tools of the Allslayer's bloody trade. Flails, spears, throwing blades…

And something else. It is still wrapped in its travelling sack, to protect its craftsmanship from the elements. Or maybe just to hide it from view.

Hylas takes a fearful step forward, placing himself between the Allslayer and his target.

He has seen that look in his master's eyes before. Oh, yes. He knows what it portends.

This is his fault. He shouldn't have left it out, not where Herakles could find it at any time. Why in Tartarus' name did he even *bring* the accursed thing, because it's a weapon, because his master needs weapons, because it's the one damn thing that can slay any foe no matter how he feels when he wields it but how must it feel to even see it to hold it to feel its heft in his hands the thing that brought him ruin and madness the screams the cries the begging the blood the shame the grief the life unlived shattered torn oh please oh please no I beg you master don't listen to the pain the guilt don't hear it don't move don't hurt me don't kill me please oh please oh pl—

A crushing hand shoves Hylas aside. It feels no different to a kick from a horse.

Herakles moves. He throws weapons and provisions out of his path, standing over it now. Pulling off the sack.

And there it is. His eyes widen, as if nothing could have prepared him for this. A great sweeping arc of cured and lacquered maple – or, at least, wood with the look and feel of maple – as thick as the Allslayer's wrist. Even curved, its span is wider than Hylas is tall. Only the bowstring holds it taut, an immense dried tendon that once belonged to the Nemean Lion.

Even lifting this bow would test most mortal men, let alone drawing back an arrow to fire.

Only none of this is in Herakles' mind. Not now. His breath catches, all sound stuck in his throat.

Hylas snatches up a blanket, throwing it over the bow. But it is far too late now. He knows the signs. The Allslayer's eyes snap left, then right. He isn't seeing the tent, seeing the camp. His mind is somewhere else entirely, at that place it can't ever escape.

Dusk falling across the Theban plains. Toy swords, toy shields, abandoned after weapon practice for another night of playtime.

(Father stop father please what have we done wrong father father PLEASE I BEG YOU)

The shrillest, most piercing scream he has ever heard. Even gored by arrows, bleeding out her last, Megara cries out. But not for herself.

(Our boys our perfect boys our family how could you how could you HOW COULD YOU)

Two fists hammering him, then grabbing him by the throat. Iphicles' first and only moment of bravery.

(Why brother why what ails you what madness is this WHAT HAVE YOU DONE)

An ox-eyed gaze piercing the cloud cover, rimmed with flawless kohl. The goddess who will haunt his every step and breath.

(You are mine son of Zeus never forget this lesson Fate is mine YOU ARE MINE all that you are is all that can serve all that you have is all you can lose remember remember REMEMBER)

Eurystheus' snide laughter as his Theban robes are torn from him, leaving a confession of scars and burns beneath.

(Now now cousin could an enemy wound the Allslayer like this how quaint but if it's pain you seek then have no fear that can be arranged did you think your Labours for me would be easy)

Monsters slain. Foes beaten. A legend of pain and sorrow that stinks of valour and heroism to anyone who skims the words. To anyone who admires the myth and misses the man beneath it.

(The Lion the Hydra the Birds the Mares the Apple the Hellhound but what is the point why do I live why am I here WHAT IS THE POINT OF THIS LIFE WHAT GOOD DOES IT DO MY STRENGTH MY POWER THE BLOOD IN MY VEINS THEY BREAK ME BUT THEY KEEP ME FOR WHAT PURPOSE WHAT COULD BE WORTH ALL THIS)

And the bow. In his hand, every damn time, whenever the club and skinning blades won't suffice. A penance for every time he needs to shoot an enemy dead.

(Will this feeling ever fade)

'Yes it will, master. Of course it will. Breathe for me. I'm here. You are safe here, I promise.'

The Allslayer's eyes open once more. He is back in the tent, Hylas by his side. A symphony of worry and sorrow is etched across the servant's face. The boy is speaking again, and if Herakles' heart stops hammering in his ears quite so loud, he might be able to hear him.

Apropos of nothing, his gaze snaps sideways to the tent entrance. But no. Peleus has heard none of this, nor has Telamon. That at least is something to be glad for. How would he ever begin to explain this to them?

Hylas reaches for a flagon of water, hoping his master will drink something. He is no stranger to this dance of theirs. And he knows just what melancholy move to make next.

'Master…' he begins. 'Will you not tell me…'

He thinks for a moment.

'Tell me of the Birds, master. Tell me of the Sixth Labour.'

XIII
THE STYMPHALIAN BIRDS

They were never called that, not in their time. That name would come long after, from bards and poets weaving mysticism into untender deeds.

At any rate, they had never been native to Stymphalus. If they had been, then the swamp folk and hut-dwellers who dwelt there might have stood a chance. But once the accursed Birds found a hunting ground, that was it. A great many empty villages and settlements across the Doric headlands stand testament to that, even now. They would find a rookery or eyrie to their liking, and any former occupants were picked clean of flesh by beaks and talons. They couldn't be reasoned with or warded against. All a man could do was heed the stories, and pray their shadows never darkened his skies.

At some point, their carnivorous migrations brought them to Stymphalus, finding the bogs and mires rather to their liking, and from that moment they became Arcadia's problem. King Iasus' pride in his kingdom's might took a commendably short time to wane. He only let his soldiers be ravaged three times, their armour and chewier body parts strewn across the swamps they'd failed to scour clean, before petitioning foreigners to rid Arcadia of this menace.

In time, news reached Tiryns, and the keen ears of Eurystheus. He always had a stomach for other men's misfortune, even in those early days. Moreso than ever when it came to the Fates of other kingdoms.

He stepped in to solve Arcadia's little problem. Whyever should he not? He was a reasonable man, after all, when the price was right. A tithe — of gold, flesh or favour — was always paid. Not always willingly, mind you, but few who fell upon Eurystheus' dubious mercy had the luxury of haggling over terms. Not when they needed the Gods' Last Son to deliver them from peril.

And thus were many of the Allslayer's early Labours devised. The King of Tiryns would never miss a trick, not when it came to his coffers, or his cousin. If he could debase Herakles in a manner befitting his remit, and indebt another kingdom to his appetites, then that was all to the good.

But none of that mattered, not on that distant day, as the Allslayer walked alone into another fight no man could win.

Just a little further now. The air curdles, with a hint of faraway spoilt meat. Which means he is heading in the right direction.

His sandaled feet splash through the muck, staining him with filth up to the shins. He feels the occasional solid mass beneath his muddied tread, their outlines unmistakeable though caked by mud. Some of them crack and shatter beneath his step, and some do not. He tries not to think about them as he passes.

The swampland around him is far from silent, but quiet enough to feel like it is watching him. Every so often a metallic braying caw cuts through the air above him. No sound like that ever came from a natural throat.

Not long to go now. Not much further.

The bards always make it sound so tidy. The grim business of rescuing kingdoms and monster-slaying.

Of all the tales that sprung from this day, the Allslayer's favourite is the castanets. Forged in bronze by Hephaestus himself, smelted through with ichor from his very own veins, and borne down from Olympus by Athena's obliging hands.

That story amuses Herakles even now. He has met the Goddess of Wisdom and War before, and perhaps he will again. But she gave no divine help in that long ago trial.

The ground beneath his sandals has hardened, and the foetid groves and bowers around him are sparser. Most crucially, the air is thinner now, and clearer. It stinks of decay, rather than death.

Herakles takes one final step, seeing the perfect place to begin the work. It is not a comforting realisation, but he cannot put this off any longer. It is too late, anyway. He has walked too far into danger.

The bow – that gods-cursed, damnable bow that he will never claw from his mind – is strung across his back, ready to be drawn in extremis. His club is belted to his hip, as are several smaller, subtler weapons. One of these he draws now, a flensing knife with jagged teeth and a handle of aged bone.

The blade of iron catches the sick, fading sunlight. The Allslayer glimpses his own grimy reflection for one lingering moment.

And then he slashes it across his forearm, spilling the blood of gods in a cascade of crimson rain.

And with that moment of self-destructive courage, the die is cast.

The Birds have grown to love the scent of human blood. But the wine running through a demigod's veins? That is a vintage they will not be able to resist. Fresh meat and warm blood will make a far finer feast than the dead and decaying of Arcadia.

Herakles is not left waiting long. The first Bird crashes through the canopy of petrified trees, broader than the Allslayer before it even stretches its wings. It screeches its sonorous hunger-cry, cocking its shining head and smelling wounded prey.

Blood of Olympus... these monsters are a breed apart. Herakles has killed a hydra that breathed poison for air, and skinned a lion that fell from the moon. But nothing, *nothing*, could have prepared him for this.

The Birds are bronze. This is no metaphor, no strained attempt at poetry. The Birds are *made of bronze*, still living, still breathing, from feather to beak to bloodstained talon. King Iasus' frenzied stories were true, after all.

The Bird fires its feathers. A score of deadly brazen spines stab into the Nemean Lion's pelt, transfixing its throat and one of its ears. Not quite enough to pierce the hide, but enough to break demigod bone beneath.

Herakles rolls aside with a snarl, throwing himself into the hardening mud. Whatever divine whim wrought these monsters into being, he is happy to oblige in their unmaking.

'Come on then!' he snarls. 'Feast on my flesh!'

The Bird shrieks, that scream of abused metal. One crack of brazen wings and it is gone. Its shadow flicks across his vision before it falls upon him once again.

Or more accurately, upon the ground where he'd been standing.

The club is in his hands before he even realises. Down it falls, the immense pine head shattering one wing into fragments of burning brazen viscera. And then the second wing, crushed in much the same way, on the backswing.

'Fly away from that!' he roars. 'You gods-forsaken scourge!'

The beast is downed, but far from finished. The Allslayer grabs it by its neck and scything talons, keeping the dangerous ends out of harm's way. Then he slings the crippled Bird over one shoulder and begins to run. Not away from the danger all around, but deeper into it.

The Birds are not solitary creatures. They hunt in packs.

Even broken, this one is still dangerous. It strains in the Allslayer's vicelike grip, snapping at him with its burnished beak. Copper plumage flexes and dips as it tries in vain to fire more feathers into the Lion's impenetrable pelt.

And through it all, as Herakles keeps on running, it won't stop *screaming*.

That distress cry on its own is a death sentence, a clarion call to its own kind all around them. He can't see them, but he feels them: glimpses of refracted light and shadows from above him, the ringing cries of tortured iron at the edge of hearing. They are coming. It is only a matter of time.

Herakles doesn't stop. He doesn't slow, doesn't turn to look for pursuers, doesn't even change his course. In time, the ground beneath his feet becomes steeper, ever steeper, and harder to climb. But still he runs.

No help is coming, not from men nor the gods they pray to. All he has is the road ahead of him, and the danger snapping at his heels.

It is all he will ever have.

He comes crashing to a halt at last. This is the place he will make his stand. This is where it ends.

The summit gives a kingly view over the lake of Stymphalus and the foetid marshland surrounding it. Further afield, the peaks around the Diagon river rise into the mist and clouds.

And below him, all around him, the bestial thrum of Birdsong grows balefully louder.

The Allslayer takes one last look at the creature still writhing in his grasp. It scrabbles and flails with what remains of its strength, barely able to lift its brazen head anymore. That hasn't stopped it from trying its luck, drawing blood from a hundred minor wounds and gashes.

But no more.

Herakles lifts it, one handed. The Bird screams in that shearing-metal voice, as if sensing what is coming. Breath blasts at him, the odour of sour wine and stomach acid.

Herakles swings his arm around, and with his own cry of more-than-mortal effort, he hurls the Bird down the mountain.

What follows is a little harder to remember. Or perhaps his memory is just fine, and the act of recollection is what fails him. He had the bow in hand, that he knows. It is hard to recall anything while holding the bow.

Two deafening sounds fill his broken memories, intermingled in one cacophony of hell. The almighty percussive *boom* as the Bird strikes the earth, an immense copper missile from a god's own hand. And the rising swell of shrieking rage, an unholy bestial clamour that drowns all of Herakles' senses.

The sound of hundreds of its kin taking flight, in shock and rage and pain.

Poets and revels will add their own trappings and storied flair to what comes next. But in truth, there is little left worthy of retelling. The Allslayer's skill at arms needs no oral embellishment. His bow fires shaft after unerring shaft into the air, and Birds begin falling from the sky in droves. Down they go, crashing to earth, spurting ichor and shattered bronze whenever they hit the ground.

The rest escape, still rising effortlessly into the clouds, but their pack cohesion is broken. Those who evade the Allslayer's wrath will fly their separate ways, migrating in the manner of true birds to far-flung corners of the world. They will never congregate to prey upon men again, will never even be seen by mortal eyes.

From this day forth, the Stymphalian Birds will cease to exist as a threat to the Achaean kingdoms.

Herakles lowers his bow at last, sweat and blood running down him in cloying rivulets.

He takes a meagre morsel of pride in another Labour done. Another step closer to atonement, an atonement this younger, more naïve Herakles still believes exists. These days are not quite like the ones that will follow, before Troy and his chosen exile. These are the days when his deeds still matter to him. When he has hopes of a life beyond all this.

He—

He opens his eyes, the mountain and the swamps receding into memory. Hylas is crouched before him, one small hand clutching his shoulder. Around him, the tent quarters are much as he left them, albeit quite a way messier than before.

'Master?' the squire asks, voice wavering.

Herakles says nothing for a moment. The air sawing in and out of his lungs is clean now, not rank with the stench of the Birds' rotting victims. The sounds drifting in and out of earshot are the calls of Phthian retainers waiting on their masters, not clawing crashes of living metal hunger.

'Oh Hylas,' the Allslayer finally replies. 'What a fool I used to be.'

XIV
ARGONAUTS

Pagasa offers little to tempt travellers off the beaten track, little that cannot be found at Iolchus at any rate, but Argus is glad for that now. Building a boat that actively resisted its shipwright's efforts would have been far harder in full view of a thousand citizens and visitors.

Now, however, even with the work all but done, the scrutiny of just one soul is proving just as aggravating.

'The ship will need a name,' Jason decides. The shepherd boy has been pacing up and down the deck, surveying Argus' handiwork as if he knows anything about naval capability, battle prowess, or the daily reality of housing fifty men at arms. 'A name,' Jason continues, 'that should reflect the man who sets it on its course. A name that—'

'*Argo*,' the shipwright cuts in. 'The ship is already named, at King Pelias' behest. *Argo.*'

A shadow passes across Jason's face, so brief it could have easily been imagined.

'I must speak with Tiphys,' Argus continues. 'Farewell.'

Jason watches the old man scuttle off, letting it go. Standing on the deck, feeling its sway in the waveless water, makes it all feel that more real.

'She's quite something,' he ponders aloud. 'So, this is the ship that will bear us to Colchis.'

Behind him he senses a presence that wasn't there before, and smiles.

'This is the most exquisite vessel I have ever boarded,' Atalanta notes. 'She must have bled Thessaly's treasury dry.'

She runs a hand along a wooden trellis, letting her fingers feel the oak. And for a moment, she feels just a little something more. Something tense and whispered, speaking softly between the beats of her heart...

She pulls back her hand with a start. Behind her, Jason has noticed nothing.

'Such expense,' he muses, 'and such artifice. This is a good sign, Huntress. Pelias must truly wish us to survive.'

'To a point,' Atalanta cautions him. 'Once one of us — *any* of us — reaches the prize, your value to him will fall. As long as one soul remains to bring back the Fleece.'

Jason's conviction begins to dissipate. But from his telling glare, this is nothing that hasn't crossed his mind already.

'Can we do this, lady? Can we keep them all in line for long enough? And will we even be enough, if we can?'

The huntress raises a thin eyebrow. Rare are the times that Jason refers to them as *we*, especially since this madness all began.

'We must sway them to our banner first, at any rate. One problem at a time, my friend.'

Only the shepherd boy is no longer listening. He has crossed to *Argo*'s stern, looking out at the open gates leading into the harbour bay.

'What is it?' Atalanta asks. 'Are they coming?'

'It would seem they are.' Jason doesn't turn as he replies. 'Well... some of them, at least.'

They do not arrive at once. Why would they? That would imply a cohesion between the lot of them that does not exist. That will likely never exist, no matter how much the son of Aeson, or the fables that follow, will wish it so.

He awaits them as they arrive, stood at the foot of the moored *Argo*, sandalled toes pressed into the sand. Atalanta is a shadowy presence to one side, while that Dodonian Tiphys waits with them, taking the measure of those who would sail upon his ship.

And to the others' chagrin, Argus has also joined proceedings. Now the ship is built, it would seem his cantankerous remit extends beyond its departure from Pagasa.

The four of them wait, a ragged and unlikely court of nobodies, as the first man who would join the quest draws near.

'There are things I should explain,' Jason tells him. 'There are things you should know, before you make your decision.'

Meleager of Calydon just shakes his head, with a stoicism not in keeping with his youth.

'The end you seek to bring about is noble, Jason of Iolchus. You seek to restore what is rightfully yours. To reclaim your father's honour. I will help you do that, if I can.'

Meleager's gaze drifts then to Atalanta, and to the memory of their first encounter. There is no scowl, no curse or recrimination. If anything, he seems almost ashamed.

And then he draws his royal Calydonian blade, and casts it into the sand at Jason's feet.

'My oath, and my blood, to find the Golden Fleece of Colchis.'

Others begin to arrive hereafter, though not all of them share Meleager's certainty. For them, Jason deigns at last to shed some more of his secrets.

'King Pelias has no intentions of honouring our bargain,' he admits. 'The Fleece has power beyond the limits of man, and my uncle hopes to seize that power. If I bring the Fleece to him, I will not receive my kingdom. I will receive my own destruction.'

Before him, Nestor of Pylos stands resolute, weighing up this information. Orpheus of Pieria hangs back at his side, and from his dreamy little smile, he either has a far looser or far cannier grasp of what this all means.

'Which is fortunate,' Atalanta cuts in. 'Because we will not be bringing the Fleece to Pelias.'

Jason smiles. 'Oh, no, no. Once the Fleece is mine, I will use its power to oust Pelias and his son from Thessaly's throne. And then I will bind my kingdom's Fate to the Fleece.'

Nestor's brow begins to furrow. Orpheus is still smiling, but it is now a little hollower.

Nestor lets his hunting knife fall into the sand. One way or another, it is far too late for them to back down now.

'Our oath, and our blood, to find the Golden Fleece of Colchis.'

'Fine words, shepherd boy.' Peleus folds his arms as he speaks. 'But what makes you the man to lead this quest?'

Beside him, Telamon's eyes bore deep into Jason. Behind them both, Hylas awaits with bated breath. Though his master, curiously, is nowhere to be seen.

'My brother has a point,' Telamon continues. 'We've heard a lot of blather about why you wish Pelias ill. But what makes you the man to shackle the Fleece to your will? We have sons and descendants of gods aboard this crew. Indeed, we have the mightiest demigod to ever walk the land among our number. What sets a mortal prince from a broken line above the likes of them?'

For a minute, Jason says nothing. The harbour breeze pulls at the fronds of his hair, as he shares an enigmatic glance with his huntress.

'What do you know of Colchis, Prince of Phthia?' Atalanta asks them all, apropos of nothing.

'It is a place of magic,' Telamon admits, without much certainty. 'A place of power, old power, that predates the gods of Olympus.'

The huntress nods. 'There is little anyone can say for sure of Colchis, but you have it right. The divinity of our blood, Phthians, may well prove our undoing.'

'Oh?'

Jason smiles, grimly. 'The Fleece is an artefact of age-old power, my friends. It has felt the touch of old gods and old magic. The Olympian Ones are not the oldest powers in this world.' He makes a fleeting gesture of warding, ignoring the urge to look to the sky. 'The mortals cast in their image, moulded from their clay and fire… that heritage may well be a burden, where we're going, rather than a boon.'

None of the other three have any rejoinder. Hylas' gaze remains thoughtful, while Telamon looks as if his deepest suspicions have been vindicated.

'And furthermore,' Atalanta adds, 'such power saturates the very soil and span of Colchis. That kingdom has stood since before Almighty Zeus took his throne. For all we know, those of us sired by gods may scarcely set foot in that accursed land.'

The effect of those words on Peleus isn't hard to predict. He is husband and consort to a nymph of the deeps. He has fathered a child with her. Jason can hardly begrudge him his foreboding.

'So?' he asks. 'Are you ready to follow this mortal youth into the east? Are you ready to watch him bring the power of gods beneath his control?'

Telamon decides against rolling his eyes. He tosses his two-headed war axe into the sand, where it lies among a group of other weapons. And he imagines how it would feel to kill Jason with it, taking his precious prize for Phthia.

'Our oath, and our blood, to find the Golden Fleece of Colchis.'

'Spare me your clumsy oratory, boy. Do you think you're the first fool to try to woo me aboard a ship?'

Idmon lowers his weary bones to the sand, too haggard – or unimpressed – to bother standing in Jason's presence. Around him, Atalanta, Argus and Tiphys regard him with idle detachment, nobody really knowing what to say.

'Noble seer,' Jason begins. 'We would be honoured to h—'

'I said *spare me!*' the old man barks, clutching his staff. 'Have you begun to consider the consequences of what you are doing? What your actions may bring about?'

'I am not afraid to die,' Jason replies. 'But to live with my duty und—'

'*Idiot boy*,' the seer bemoans. 'I speak of the consequences of you *succeeding*. Do you think it is for mortals to take up the power of gods? To throw their own strength back in their faces?'

The shepherd boy says nothing. Nor do Atalanta or the other two.

'You think you merely have your crew to worry about,' Idmon snarls. He spares a venomous glance at the growing line of weapons and keepsakes that are strewn across the sand, evidence of those summoned who have already pledged themselves to the journey. 'But what of immortal attention, hmm? Gods, as well as men, will feel the threat of you taking that thing from Colchis. How do you suppose they will react? To some upstart mortal pup wielding that kind of magic?'

Jason is looking a lot less sure of himself than a moment ago, but that won't stop him from fighting his corner.

'The patronage of gods led me to this moment!' he presses. 'I have the favour of Hera on my side!'

Idmon's smile is utterly mirthless, baring teeth in varied states of decay.

'The favour of Hera, indeed. I'm sure our Allslayer has much to say on that subject.'

But in the ailing seer's heart, he knows this is all futile. No logic, or entreaty, will sway the son of Aeson now. And from that pile of weapons already in the sand, the tide has all but turned in Jason's favour.

Idmon sighs like a last breath, and lets his wooden staff fall among the axes and swords. They will do this with his auguries to keep them pious, or without them.

'My oath, and my blood, to find the Golden Fleece of Colchis.'

Idmon's is not the only voice of dissent, it transpires. Though other concerns are far more prosaic than his.

'Word will travel,' Laertes tries to tell his would-be captain. 'You cannot hope for word of this to stay secret, Jason. The *Argo* will be watched, whichever way it turns. It has doubtless already started.'

At the Ithacan's side, Castor and Polydeuces stand silently, keen to weigh up the shepherd boy's response. Only it is Atalanta who allays their doubts instead.

'You speak the truth, King Laertes. But ours is a small crew, with just one vessel. It will make far quicker progress, with far less pomp and fanfare, than whatever fleets or flotillas seek to chase us, or beat us to our prize.'

'And there speaks the logic of a huntress.' Polydeuces chuckles gently. 'But we princes and warriors may not share your penchant for stealth and subtlety, Arcadian.'

Atalanta smiles thinly. It is rare enough to be memorable. 'If you've recognised your failing, my Spartan friends, then you've taken the first step to correcting it.'

Castor waves their banter aside, still unconvinced. 'And what of our return to Thessaly's shores? What is to stop Pelias sending a fleet or army to butcher us on the journey back, and taking the Fleece straight for himself?'

Jason's resolve doesn't waver this time. But for whatever it is worth, he doesn't brush these concerns aside either.

'I have no comforting answer to give you, princes. I can merely trust in the gods who put me here, and in the arms of my crew.'

Castor takes a moment to consider all this. He has fought wars for his kingdom where the stakes were high and the danger close at hand. And then he thinks of the Fleece, and all it might do for Sparta.

And how pitifully the shepherd boy could stand against him. None of them will deny him. Not with his brother to guard his back.

He casts down his iron falchion at Jason's feet. It lands blade first, spilling a shadow over the other dropped spoils.

'Our oath, and our blood, to find the Golden Fleece of Colchis.'

There is a little longer to wait, this time.

The sun is making its way across Pagasa's sky, and the shadows around the port grow longer. The tide is coming in too, waves lapping against the *Argo*'s hull a little heavier.

Jason shields his gaze from the sun. 'Who is that approaching, Huntress?'

Atalanta peers out towards the gates. The next arrival moves slowly, purposefully, but not without doubt. His regal bearing is unmistakeable, even after trading the royal colours of his kingdom for more practical iron and leather.

'King Theseus…' Jason begins. 'I must confess, I did not expect you to come.'

Theseus glowers down his nose at this boy twenty years his junior. But whatever cutting remark he is brewing goes unsaid.

'Is King Pirithous not with you?' Jason presses. This, too, goes unanswered.

'You are aware,' Atalanta informs him, 'that princes Castor and Polydeuces have pledged themselves to the quest?'

The King of Athens keeps his silence. This is his last chance to turn back. He would lose nothing by doing so, for his honour is too sullied already.

A great bronze battle hammer crashes into the other weapons, scattering smaller ones aside.

'My oath, and my blood, to find the Golden Fleece of Colchis.'

Eleven souls. Eleven converts to Jason's fragile cause. Eleven heroes to man the *Argo*, out of the scores who heeded the first summons.

Thirteen, including Jason and Atalanta. Fifteen, if you factored Argus and Tiphys into the bargain.

He had hoped for so many more, whether that was optimism or vanity. The *Argo* had been built to accommodate fifty. Had that been a show of faith on King Pelias' part? Or just a taunt to the shepherd boy's fledgling hopes?

He still waits, out on the beach where the *Argo* holds at anchor. Atalanta and the others have long since left, as have the eleven who swore the oath. But the huntress bade Jason stay.

One more night, before they sailed. What could be lost by one more night?

And so the son of Aeson stands vigil alone, lit only by torchlight and the moon on the water. Only for one last hero to arrive.

'Herakles?' Jason gasps. 'I thought... we thought you had left. Your retainer threw in his lot with us, but you were not there.'

The Allslayer regards this Thessalian upstart for a few moments, trying to catch the measure of him one last time.

'I thought Hylas deserved the choice.'

As Jason digests the import of those words, Herakles begins to think.

He thinks of his dreams, and what Tiresias had to say of them. He thinks of the Fleece, lying far across the world, its power waiting to be tapped by grasping, unworthy hands. He thinks of the heroes and slayers around him, and just how they would pervert its potential to their own ends.

He thinks of Jason, and of Pelias, and just what each man is truly planning, under all their claims to the contrary. He thinks about their limits, and whether either of them could control the sorcery they would wield. He thinks about the gods that would yearn to see such fire unleashed, and the gods that would bleed like men to stop it happening. He thinks of the goddess who claims to favour Jason, that same goddess who has blighted all of Herakles' life, and wonders if those two goals might ever intersect.

He thinks of what awaits this sorry band if the *Argo* reaches Colchis. He thinks about the perils that lie between them and their quarry, and how the expedition would fragment if any of them came to place their hands on the Fleece. He thinks of the calamity their betrayals could unleash when greed shatters their bonds of honour. He thinks of the horrors that could follow, for gods and for men, when this inevitably comes about.

He thinks of what will happen if he is there, and what will happen if he is not. He thinks about the chances of surviving if he decides to intervene.

He thinks about the forces that encircle him, that have done so since his birth, and what they want for him.

And then he thinks about what he wants, what *he* truly wants, when all of this is said and done. He thinks about how he'd feel if he lived, or died, in the battles to come.

One final weapon falls into the sea-licked sand. It is the mightiest bow Jason has ever seen, too big he fancies for him to even lift, let alone shoot. Even the wood of its arms looks older than Jason himself.

'My oath, and my blood, to find the Golden Fleece of Colchis.'

Across Pagasa, across Iolchus, across all Thessaly, news spreads and preparations are made.

When the following night finally rolls around, the beach beyond the *Argo*'s berth is not so empty as before. Thousands upon thousands of Thessaly's citizens have massed to see the heroes leave. Rumour has spread her feathered wings, and all the kingdom would see these men who will brave the voyage to Colchis.

From the *Argo*'s prow, two souls watch these distant Iolchans. One of them is awed, the other faintly amused. But both have far more pressing issues on their minds.

'Keep your wits about you,' Atalanta cautions. 'Don't be deceived by these half-hearted oaths of kinship. They'll help you find the Fleece, no doubt about it. But do you really suppose they'll let you keep it?'

At her side, Jason says nothing, content to keep his thoughts his own.

'I mean it,' the huntress presses. 'When the moment comes, they will betray you.'

The son of Aeson won't meet her gaze. They have all gathered for him. This is his moment.

'They will try, Atalanta. They will try.'

In the boat's great shadow, sixteen souls congregate in a loose half-ring. There is little order or rank among them, for they will always be a disparate group. Perhaps that will change in the days and trials to come. Perhaps not.

Jason. Atalanta. Tiphys. Argus. Idmon. Orpheus. Meleager. Nestor. Laertes. Castor. Polydeuces. Theseus. Hylas. Peleus. Telamon.

And Herakles. The Allslayer, the Gods' Last Son, a man so weary of the Thunder that sired him. Here they all are at last.

Orpheus' melodic voice carries even above the crowd's adulation.

'This ship was built for far more souls than us, shepherd boy. How exactly do you intend for us to crew it?' He laughs with giddy lyricism. 'I'm no rower. I hardly have the arms.'

Jason doesn't answer. He merely smiles and turns.

Tiphys claps his hands three times. A rush of water draws their gazes down the beach.

Fifty oars shoot out from the empty ship, twenty-five on each side. They cut the water in eerie unison, ready to plough the ocean foam.

'Dodonian oak, my friends.' Argus smiles wanly. 'The gifts of the gods themselves. You will find the *Argo* is not like any ship you've ever sailed. Relish the time you spend aboard her, comrades, for you will never know her like again.'

And so, on that moonlit night, it begins. Those who sail the *Argo* — the Argonauts, as they have already begun to call themselves — set about their duties. The strongest among them take position on the oars, though there is little work for them. The *Argo* herself seems willing to do her bit, and with Tiphys there to interpret her primal will, it seems that sixteen souls will more than suffice.

On the beach beyond them, the throng of Thessalians has already begun to cheer. The cheering continues as the *Argo* rounds the bay, making for the open water.

In the midst of the crowd, from the comfort of his royal bier and seat, King Pelias watches the ship recede from view with hawklike eyes. It has begun, for good or ill.

He will rise higher than ever before. Or he will plunge down to newfound depths.

From his place at the oars, Herakles eyes the slowly shrinking beach. Some among the crowd are carrying totems of fortune and goodwill. The Allslayer picks out the icons and imagoes of more than one divinity among the mass of flesh.

One in particular catches his eye, and he knows exactly why.

It is an icon of Hera, staring regally out from her throne on Olympus. The marble facsimile is crude, the stonework sloppy. And yet her gaze still sends a chill down his spine, even here, even now.

Herakles closes his eyes for a moment, muttering a paean of protection under his breath. He prays to Hera's mercy, invoking her supposed favour of Jason. He prays it will extend to the *Argo*, and all who sail within her.

Or failing that, for Hera's wrath to fall on him, and him alone.

If she wants to take him, she can take him. He will die content, if she spares the rest of them.

Across the water, far beyond the light, something watches. It watches the *Argo* slowly disappear from view, empty eye sockets never leaving it all the while.

ACT II

ALONE ON A WILD, WILD SEA

'Flee then, Jason. Flee these shores if you will, chasing an oath that disgraces the gods it honours. But know this, prince of cattle: the further you run from the mistakes you make. . . the longer the victims of your carelessness will haunt you.'

– Hypsipyle, Queen of Lemnos, in the aftermath of the *Argo*'s departure from her Isle

XV
COMPOSED ON THE DECK OF THE
ARGO

Iolaus, my boy.

I cannot say for certain how long has passed since the Argo *left Thessaly's shores. Weeks, at the very least, piling on one after the other. And yet, no matter what the others assure me, it somehow feels longer.*

I'm always like this when I travel on the open sea. There is no land, no horizon, no routine to mark the ebb and flow of days. We sleep when we must, and rise even when our bodies cry out in protest. We measure time by stints on and off the oars, rather than minutes and hours and days.

Orpheus is the only one of us who maintains his sense of time. He gleefully reminds us, each time the pipes meet his lips and his fingers stroke the lyre. I suspect Atalanta can also follow the passage of days — all those years in the wild, I suppose — but whatever our huntress feels, her thoughts remain her own.

Blood of Olympus… this ship is a marvel. Argus wasn't lying when he told us what to expect. The Argo *rows herself as often as we row her, even when there is no wind to sail by. She is certainly capricious, and has had her moments. Sometimes even Tiphys isn't enough to interpret her will, or steer her on an acceptable course. On some days, she sails and captains herself, permitting us to plough the oars like a parent humouring* her children. On others, she all but refuses to bend to our will, and making her do anything is a trial of strength and patience.

But fickle as she is, the Argo wants the same thing we do. She wants to sail to Colchis, and see this through to the end.

Would that those of us aboard her felt such clarity of purpose.

I won't waste parchment tallying every time we've stopped to raid or trade or let ourselves be men again. Every quest has those lulls, spaces between unforgiving runs across the water, to light fires and burn offal and let loose.

But they have felt different on this voyage. They leave a sour taste in the mouth. They seem to be unravelling what little unity, and cohesion, we had to begin with.

Lemnos was when the rot began, to my mind at least. We lingered there for far too long, even before the island's unwelcome truths became clear. A lost kingdom filled with nothing but women and girls, all yearning for us to play house? By Olympus, the weeks Jason spent dallying in that megaron, under their queen's carnal spell. Never mind the Argonauts who followed his boyish lead.

Atalanta, Idmon and Orpheus were the only ones who didn't take the dubious hospitality on offer, besides Hylas and myself. I had an uneasy feeling it was Meleager's first time. Even Peleus couldn't keep himself away. I wonder what Thetis would think of such a thing.

To this day I do not know what Queen Hypsipyle's true intentions were, and I doubt I ever will. Whether she truly planned her girls to make husbands of every man aboard the Argo, as she ardently claimed to the very end, or wanted us skinned and roasted atop her island's sacrificial altars, as Argus and Nestor claimed to overhear. We will have to live without an answer to that question.

At any rate, Jason seemed to have little difficulty sloughing the Lemnian queen off him, once Atalanta and I finally talked some sense into him. Whatever passed between him and Hypsipyle in those gilded *bedchambers, it wasn't something easily broken. And yet it was something he would rather run from than give closure to.*

I lost a lot of respect for our erstwhile captain in that moment.

And if forgetting our quest bought us one kind of peril, keeping it in mind brought on quite another. After Lemnos came our foray to Scryer's Folly, the desolated isle of Phineas the seer. Even as those accursed harpies swooped down from the clifftops to assail us, the once-king's raving auguries could have put Idmon to shame. We should know. We were obliged to hear enough of them, even before we drove the winged monsters away.

But Jason was convinced, for only the gods knew why, that Phineas' farsight was key to finding our way to Colchis. Whatever actual wisdom the blind old hermit had to impart, we can only guess. Jason was the only one who heard it, and the only soul he shared it with was Tiphys.

And then there was Cyzicus. Poor, noble Cyzicus, who welcomed the Argo into port with open arms, and invited us to share the warmth of his banqueting halls. The newly wed lord of the Doliones had more to offer us than decency, however. While we basked in the warmth of his xenia and his fires, he shared with us the secrets of steering a safe passage through the Hellespont, and evading the savage Earthborn who made their home there. A tainted afterbirth of Gaia's bitter rage against the Olympians, these six-handed monsters were distant cousins of the Titans chained down beneath the earth in Tartarus.

The Doliones had long learnt to give these Titanic neighbours a wide berth. Cyzicus didn't enlist us to rid him of them in return for the help he gave us. He didn't even swallow his regnal pride and beg our aid. He simply gave us what we needed, advised us against crossing their path, and saw us on our way.

And how did we repay him? The Argo was blown off course, at the mercy of volatile winds. We made an urgent landing at the nearest port in the dark. And Jason, brash Jason, young little Jason who had yet to prove himself a warrior, decided not to send out scouts or envoys into the night ahead of us. He ordered us to clad and arm ourselves, and sally out to catch whatever unknown garrison we'd found off guard.

Dawn's fiery fingers revealed the sorry truth. We'd been blown around in a circle, and had landed at the very port we'd left. In our ignorance and our zeal, we had slaughtered the same Doliones who'd made us welcome. King Cyzicus himself lay among the slain, his back pierced right through by a spear.

No amount of funeral games, poured libations, or oaths sworn in tears could undo that damage. The Argo set sail across the Hellespont once more, laden with the knowledge we needed to cross with better fortune.

We didn't need Idmon to tell us these were signs.

The Fates laugh at us once more, at any rate, and they keep on laughing as I write these words. Or maybe there is no mirth involved, and these are simply the dues we must pay for our sins.

The winds Cyzicus warned us about have continued to harry and torment us, first fouling our course once more and then marooning us between clashing currents. The Argo, predictably, has chosen this moment to bridle against Tiphys' will, refusing to help — and sometimes even outright defying — our efforts to row against the waves. And so we wait, becalmed in backwater Hellespont shallows, with no clear way ahead and no future behind us.

Such a predicament cries out for leadership. For someone to rise to the moment. Yet few of my fellow Argonauts, between their frustration, their cynicism, and whatever craven plans they are nursing, seem willing to step into this breach.

Not even Jason appears to have an answer, with or without Atalanta's counsel to keep him canny.

The son of Aeson has changed since we left Pagasa, and not entirely for the better. He didn't buckle and break with the embrace of shipboard life, as many of us predicted. Far from it. His itinerant life on Mount Pelion, if anything, has honed him for the Argo's cramped and closeted existence all too well. These days, he feels neither like a prince nor a shepherd boy. He seems to have a touch of both about him.

But those are not the only changes that matter.

This moment was ripe for Jason to bring us close, to show himself in the thick of the trouble, right here at our side. Yet each day, he sinks deeper into his mistrust of us, however justified. More worryingly still, he seems to believe we haven't noticed. He does not see the mutual foreboding grow amongst his crewmates, or at least he pretends he doesn't.

Maybe he sees me as a threat.

We aboard the Argo are no coalition of equals, and every one of us knows it. None of us have had the gall, or the presumption, to outright challenge Jason's position as leader of this quest. Nothing as overt as that. But more than once, when we have congregated in the ship's sweaty hold, or the latest beach we take respite on, we have raised the topic amongst ourselves. Jason cannot fail to notice this, nor can I. I am the one they have petitioned, several times, in varying levels of seriousness and sobriety, to take the shepherd boy's place.

And in matching levels of sincerity, I have refused. Sometimes I laugh the idea away, while at others I wave it aside with sincerity. It amuses them all, either way, and frustratingly it only seems to deepen their reverence. But I am under no illusions. They see me this way because of my skills as a warrior. Or maybe they sense, on some instinctive level, that I don't share their plans for what comes next. That I am not readying myself for the betrayals to begin.

That in some perverse way, my presence might be the very thing that binds this fractious fellowship together.

Jason must resent this. That, at least, I cannot fault him for. Or maybe there is some small part of him, smothered by pride and unwillingness to renege, that chafes under the leader's mantle. That would actually welcome me taking the reins in his place. That would only fuel the fire of his bitterness, no doubt.

Oh, Iolaus… what am I to do? What would you have done, in my place? You were always the wisest of us, nephew. The wisest and most level-headed. Far more so than I. More so than Iphicles, or any of us. Maybe even more so than your grandfather. My father, Amphitryon, my true father. The man who raised me, not the god who sired me.

You would have made a fine Argonaut.

I cannot even bring myself to tell Hylas these truths, though I am sure he would counsel me as you would. I can still scarcely bring myself to think of what lies ahead. Of what will happen when the Argo finds its way through these straits, when the shadow of the prow falls across Colchian waters.

Of what will come when we reach the City of Dawn. When the taste of our prize corrodes whatever bonds still bind us.

A part of me wonders what I will do then. That was the very reason I followed the Argonauts into this madness, and I am still without an answer. I can't help but wonder if I should simply end this all now, putting my club through the Argo's oaken hull.

Some days I ask myself how I could consider such a thing. On others, I wonder why I haven't done it already.

But I have enough to think about as it is. The ship is going nowhere. The winds show no signs of changing. Each passing day, waiting it out becomes a less appealing option. Jason will somehow have to seize the moment. And he must be leant upon to do so, clearly.

But that isn't all.

I feel something, nephew. In my bones. A feeling I haven't been able to shake since we first set sail. I thought I felt it a handful of times with Hylas before we reached Iolchus. But now I have no such doubts.

Something watches me. Never the others. Something watches me, and me alone. Formless, ephemeral, never seen or tangibly sensed… but I feel it there. Sometimes in the corner of my eye, though in truth it is rarely that oblique.

I do not know what it is, or how it follows me thus. But I know the feel of its baleful gaze.

And that, dear boy, is what disquiets me.

This is a feeling I know well. Though I can't, for the life of me, recall where I last felt it.

XVI
BECALMED

The Allslayer's eyes snap upward, away from the parchment he is writing on. There is nothing out there, in the starlit night beyond the deck trellis. Just the glistening waters with no moonlight to reflect, and the starry, clouded sky.

Two differing shades of black, enveloping the *Argo* on all sides. Nothing more. And yet the hackles on Herakles' neck rise all the same.

He crumples Iolaus' letter in one hand, hearing nothing but the tidal susurrus of his own breath. And then he calls out to the silent sea.

'I am here. Whenever you tire of cowering in the shadows, I am here.'

The water stirs a fraction under the gentlest wind, as black as the ink upon his parchment.

It is scarcely any warmer below decks, even with the lionskin wrapped around him.

He passes Hylas on his way to the prow. The squire is sound asleep, wearied beyond disturbance by a day of shipboard labour. Now he rests, curled in foetal repose over a mattress of hay and old feathers. Only a ragged blanket protects him from the cold, but, as the Allslayer ruefully reflects, this is no less than the boy is used to.

A life on the road with Herakles is not a gentle one.

The Allslayer is about to pass him, but he stops for a moment. He pulls the blanket around, ensuring Hylas is more evenly covered.

And with a gentle kiss on the servant's forehead, he leaves him to his dreams.

His face wrinkles as he emerges up top. The prow is not a pleasant place to find yourself, these nights. Not with the smell.

The harpy's rotting corpse, still nailed to the prow like some perverse totem of favour, has gotten no easier to look at. It seems a crude way to commemorate their time on Scryer's Folly. Herakles can't even remember who killed it. Laertes, perhaps, or maybe Theseus. But it was nailed up there at Jason's command, that he knows. The work of a butcher raised on tales of heroes.

The mouldering remains merely drive the point home, no more than a rotted bag of bones and peeling feathers, held together by tendons and muscle tissue. Even the crows and gulls no longer pick at it.

The Allslayer spits over the edge, warding off evil and washing the taste from his mouth. Only for the night to answer him back with gentle laughter.

'I'm glad to see I'm not alone in hating that wretched thing.'

He turns, smiling a fraction, recognising *this* particular feeling of unease. After all this time at sea, it really oughtn't surprise him anymore.

'Huntress.'

Atalanta detaches herself from the shadows, coming to stand with him as he leans against the prow.

'Is the Slayer of All having trouble sleeping?' she asks with a wry smile.

'Yes and no, lady.' Herakles shakes his head, but not for the reason she thinks. 'I don't do well with being trapped. I never have.'

Atalanta reaches down to the deck, delving into piles of sand and salt-encrusted rope, before rising once again with a smooth pebble in one hand. With a far-too-practiced throw, she skims it out across the dark water, silently pleased to see it bounce, and bounce, and keep on bouncing.

It is the only thing that moves in the stillness of the night.

'Trapped?' she repeats. 'Jason won't hear that word. We are *becalmed*, as he insists. A temporary problem, soon to resolve itself. The weather can't keep us here much longer. Nor can the *Argo*.'

Another gentle gust of wind blows the stench of harpy up Herakles' nostrils. He winces.

'You don't sound convinced,' he observes.

Atalanta closes her eyes, for a moment or so longer than is natural. It is rare to see her any more expressive than that.

'I can't abide it either, Allslayer. I... really can't.'

'Being trapped?'

'Being trapped.'

She fixes him with a pointed look, as she reaches up to retie her hair. It has grown a touch longer in their time aboard the *Argo*.

'I was not made to stay in one place.' Her demeanour hardens once more as she clarifies. 'What good is a huntress who cannot track her quarry?'

'Easy, young one.' Herakles raises a hand in mock-surrender. 'I wasn't about to blast that confession across the ship.'

He feels a half-smile tug at his features. Atalanta is easy to talk to, compared with the other Argonauts at least. The two of them are ungripped by the delusions and self-proclaimed vanity running rampant among their crewmates. The two of them know exactly what they are, for better or worse.

And what they are is similar. Broadly, at least, in the manner of the crudest brushstrokes. Their stories may lead in different directions, but run on similar lines. The open sky is their one true master, the road their unforgiving teacher.

Except that she hearkens to a goddess, and he spends his life running from one.

'Have you tried talking to Jason?' Herakles asks her.

'Do you think I don't get that question from the others?' Atalanta hits back. She has barely raised her voice, but it shocks him all the same. Atalanta never raises her voice. 'I hear this question almost a dozen times a day, Allslayer. From you, from the Spartans, from Peleus, Nestor and all the rest of those kingly fools. Even *Orpheus* tries to corner me. Because, just like you, they all assume I know secrets you don't.'

Herakles lets the huntress have her tirade. He cannot help but sympathise with her in that moment; while the other Argonauts have followed a not-quite-prince and the scent of godhood, Atalanta, alone, is here from loyalty instead of obligation. She follows the Jason who was nothing, a dry and dusty nobody from Pelion's slopes, instead of the Jason who would be king.

She was the first approached by him to join the quest, and the first to know his true intentions. And from that moment of inflamed pride — that an undowried, untamed queenlet held answers that a dozen kings and princes of Hellas did not — her crewmates now lay all the blame they wish to shoulder on Jason at her door.

'Forgive me,' Herakles begins.

'It hardly matters, does it?' Atalanta waves the pointless entreaty aside. 'Because you're right. Jason has had long enough to take action himself. I, more than anyone, wanted to give him the benefit of the doubt. But we have to face truths. It isn't going to happen.'

'No,' Herakles concedes, drawing a hand through his greasy, greying curls. 'What do you propose, then?'

'We are becalmed,' the huntress softly asserts. 'We are alone, save for each other. There is no question of turning on our captain. If we go down that path, then we are all as good as dead. The Argonauts will fracture like porcelain.'

The Allslayer's silence invites her to continue.

'It has to come from Jason,' Atalanta presses on. 'In other words, *we will have to make it* come from Jason. We managed it on Lemnos, you and I. We can manage it again, surely?'

Herakles doesn't shake his head, but his furrowing brow invites caution. To Atalanta's eyes, that is the most craven expression a man can wear.

'Lemnos was different,' Herakles warns her. 'That was persuading him to run from a difficult choice. This time we are trying to make him face one.'

For a moment, Atalanta looks pensive... and then, without warning, coldly territorial. Like a mother pantheress, sizing up a threat to her cubs, or a bird defending its brood.

'You don't know Jason like I do. What he may lack as a captain, he does not lack as a man.'

A voice chuckles from behind them at that sentimental judgement.

Jason's voice.

'How touching, Huntress. You always had a way with double-edged blades.'

Down below, within the cloistered wooden cabin that serves as the captain's quarters, the Gods' Last Son and the Huntress of Arcadia try their best to steer their erstwhile leader's course.

'We have waited,' Atalanta presses him. 'We have waited, for as long as was sensible. And the time for waiting has passed. You know it, my friend.'

Herakles is less conciliatory. 'Make a choice,' he growls. 'The longer you leave it, the weaker you look, and right now you can't afford to look weak.'

Jason snorts from behind his table, too emphatic for even the halfway sincere.

'Before one of my noble Argonauts kills me, you mean? Before one of you makes good on all your beachside talks, and decides the *Argo* needs a new captain?'

It is a depressing truth the Allslayer has faced more than once on this voyage already; that Jason is not a man without self-awareness. Though that awareness rarely extends *beyond* his self. Even now, his own precariousness fills his mind, not that of the quest, or the men who now follow him.

'Another route through the Hellespont?' the huntress suggests. 'Or perhaps a way to assuage the gods driving these winds? A sacrifice, some other act of piety, perhaps.'

Jason looks noticeably less comfortable now, even with so little moonlight to pick his face out. The *Argo*'s captain can already guess where this is going.

Herakles thumps a gentle fist on the table, catching his focus.

'You know of what we speak, Jason. The Earthborn that King Cyzicus told us about. That monstrous blight that he sought to spare us from.'

Jason eyes the Allslayer with unfeigned suspicion. 'You would have us fall upon those... those things? Do you hunger for your own death so badly?'

'But *think* of it, Jason!' This from Atalanta. 'We angered the Olympian Ones when we slew Cyzicus. He spoke of how the Earthborn were darkening his people's lives. What better way to wipe away our blood debt? If you want kindlier attention from the gods, than slaying just one of those leviathans is the clearest way forward.'

At her side, the Allslayer holds his tongue. He is privately less convinced that their salvation lies with the gods, but the sea routes infested by Earthborn are the only ones they've yet to try. And giving the Argonauts a common enemy, or at least some travail to bind them closer together, doesn't feel like the worst idea either.

Atalanta risks placing a comradely hand on Jason's shoulder. Such a gesture once came easily to her, but the Jason who dwells aboard the *Argo* has been set off by less.

'Allslayer?' the huntress gently asks. 'May I speak to our captain alone?'

'I can feel him judging me,' Jason confesses, when Herakles has taken his leave. 'All of them do, Arcadian. But he is the worst.'

It has been a trying few days, and even the huntress' legendary patience is starting to erode. Coaxing prey and awaiting the right moment comes naturally to her, but she has yet to encounter a target as stubborn and unmalleable as this one.

'This self-pity, my friend, masquerading as vanity… the Allslayer and the others don't know you. They don't know that this isn't who you are.'

'I am well aware of all the things I'm *not*, Huntress, without you reminding me. The gap between us and our quarry is narrow enough, and I am running out of chances to prove myself.'

And Atalanta can see the truth of that, as well as what it costs him to admit it. The boy is afraid, not just for himself, but for all of them, if they dare to risk the giants' wrath. It is plain to see to every Argonaut, even if he stubbornly refuses to give it voice.

The huntress is reminded of the statues adorning the palatial colonnades of Arcadia, the home she left so long ago. On some days, Jason could easily pass for one of those chiselled and curated heroes.

Perhaps a half-carved one. Where the sculptor gave him power, but forgot to make him fearless.

Atalanta folds her arms, unable to entertain this any longer. 'Then *do* something, as our captain. Convene the others. Make for the straits of the Earthborn. Plot another route out of here.'

Her hopes for the expedition are sinking, even now, like the stone she skimmed out to sea.

'But by the spires of Olympus, Jason. Just do *something*.'

Far beneath the *Argo*'s shadow, that very stone is still sinking, ever deeper into the cold black depths. Down, it falls, slowly, sedately. Down, down, down.

Until it hits the bottom, gently striking the seabed with a thump of muffled noise.

And then an impossibly vast eye opens, lava red within a rocky, bony carapace.

XVII
INTO THE MAW

A thin mist hangs over the water the following morning, as it often does before rain comes. Idmon, rising before any other soul, spends the early hours braving chill to scry omens from passing birds, rewarded with nothing but cloud cover and seagull droppings for his troubles. Hylas buries himself in sailors' chores. Peleus and Telamon resign themselves to wrestling, as they have already beaten most of their crewmates. Nobody wishes to gamble away more spoils on their hopes of besting them.

A few men try their luck at fishing overboard, but what scraps they scavenge do little to fill their idling bellies. Even the *Argo*'s expansive stores are starting to dry up, and the last port stops before her becalming gave the crew little prospect of restocking.

None of this improves the fraying atmosphere below decks, and not even Orpheus' silken lyre can melt the tension between the Argonauts. His appetite for music-making has waned since their marooning, anyway, the Pierian's customary glee weighed down by a burden he chooses not to share.

Few of the others have noticed, because they are too busy at one another's throats. Without any direction from their absentee captain, these proud and august warlords need little provocation to let themselves loose. One spiteful remark from Theseus, and a retaliatory black eye from Castor, is all it takes to break the dam. Most days, dwindling wine and water are enough to kindle fights or squabbles.

Those with leveller heads try their best to smooth the damage, Atalanta among them. The Arcadian, more than any other, attracts an unfair deluge of scorn for these efforts. They curse her as a cold-blooded succubus, a simpering maiden who has no place among the crew.

For her part, the huntress lets these charges slide off her in silence. Knowing most of this vitriol is meant for Jason doesn't make it sting any less.

Such is the atmosphere aboard the *Argo*, the morning things begin to change.

At the stern of the ship, the helmsman and the shipwright are bracing themselves for another day of fruitless effort and disappointment.

'Is there truly nothing to be done?' Argus asks, mainly out of habit.

At his side, Tiphys looks up from his dubious labours. These last few weeks have put paid to what little faith he had in his own abilities. Interpreting the vessel's refusal to move is one thing. Influencing that ironclad wall of stubbornness is quite another.

The evidence of this truth is strewn about him. Resting his hands on the decks and mast, and feeling the *Argo* speak to him in spurts and whispers of touch, is no longer enough. Meditative chanting and Dodonian paeans no longer rouse her spirit, with or without the lighting of holy incense. Water from the blessed spring at Tmolus does little when anointing the wood beneath the hold, and the dripping of sacrificial heifer blood over the prow yields no better result.

In the days preceding this one, Tiphys even resorted to starker, darker means. He watered the deck with his own blood, cutting a vein in the hopes that a fellow Dodonian's essence might be the glut the *Argo* craved. When that came to naught, he managed to talk Jason into following suit, nicking him with the sacrificial blade after appealing to the divine favour doubtless flowing through the captain's veins.

And to all this mystic dabbling... no response. Not then, and not now. The *Argo* is having none of it.

Tiphys draws a weary breath to remind Argus of all this. And then the entire ship beneath them stirs. It lasts little longer than a second, but that is enough. The water churns and whitens. And then it splits, as the oars of the mighty *Argo* suddenly return to the sea's surface. None of them are grasped by human hands.

And at the stern, every single one of Tiphys' incense sticks and candles snuff themselves out, without any change coming from the wind.

'Blood of the Styx, Argus...' the helmsman looks about him, relief entwined with disbelief. 'I think she's ready to move again!'

Jason's weary summons comes an hour later.

The Argonauts congregate on deck with an aura of surprise, suspicion and adulterated hope. Few of them have had a chance to talk with their captain, man to man, but that is not something they'll let continue. The shepherd boy cannot shrink back from fifteen men at once.

Jason is waiting as they arrive, leaning against the great mast. The first surprise is that Atalanta is not with him, the huntress filing in behind Orpheus and Meleager. This time, she knows no more than any of them.

They all arrive, soon enough.

Herakles and Tiphys come last, joining the half-ring facing Jason as they did that very first night in Iolchus. Somewhere far above, a seabird cries. The mist steals all hope of seeing it.

'My friends.' Jason spreads his arms wide in a gesture of magnanimity, if not beneficence. 'I hope you've enjoyed this unexpected respite! I was sure that after Lemnos, we would all need time to find our strength again.'

A fair few of them chuckle at that, rising to the obvious bait, and even Herakles feels a smile pulling at his lips.

'But our friends at the helm have some news for us. Tiphys?'

The young Dodonian takes a slight step forward, less used than Jason is to his crewmates' attention.

'After much coaxing and persistence with the rites, Argus and I have lifted the spiritual malaise afflicting the ship. It may not be an easy passage, or a gentle one, but the *Argo* is willing to sail once more.'

The effect of these words is not hard to guess. Several man whoop and cheer, crying out their gratitude to the gods above. A more reserved few sink to their knees, their thanks more personal, more genuine.

Jason holds up a hand for silence.

'And that is not all, my dauntless ones. For not only is our path now open to us, but I know precisely where we will follow it to!'

'Colchis?' Meleager chips in. Another peal of laughter follows, more subdued but more honest. Just what it is aimed at — Meleager's folly, or Jason's loftiness — isn't clear.

'All in good time, my dear Calydonian. All in good time.'

It is difficult to label the emotion curdling in Jason's eyes. Is that a resurgence of hope and vigour? Or is this simply the last flailing move of a condemned man who no longer has a refuge in inaction? Who indeed can say.

The shepherd boy reaches for something hanging by his waist, something dry and papery and bound in old leather. He unwinds the string of flax holding it closed, letting his seafarer's map fall open to the deck and giving the Argonauts a fleeting view from where they stand. He points to a long narrow of seawater stretching out into a bay.

'We have been trapped in these shallows long enough, my comrades. Even without the *Argo*'s meddlesome temper to deal with—' He touches the oaken trellis respectfully with a gesture of warding, the movement suggestive of placating an errant pet. '—we were hemmed in with no obvious way to escape the Hellespont. The only way Tiphys could have steered us would have been down the straits Cyzicus warned us not to take. Against the *Argo*'s own will, no less. Hardly a pleasant journey, I'm sure you would appreciate, and one we'd have scant hopes of surviving.'

Jason takes a moment to check himself, as if sensing the import of his next words. Across the ring of men, Atalanta's eyes narrow intently.

'Many of you have believed that the gods forsook this quest by stranding us here. That our becalming was at their behest.'

Idmon, apropos of nothing, looks on the edge of saying something. But one manic glance from Jason is enough to shut that down.

'Perhaps you were right,' he continues. 'Perhaps the favour lavished on me by Hera has waned in light of our deeds since leaving Pagasa. Perhaps, despite our ministrations and our piety, we truly have profaned the gods with our actions. We left the altars on Lemnos unblooded. We slew noble Cyzicus and his kinsmen in error, breaking the rites of *xenia*. We are polluted, my friends. *Miasma* haloes us like a carrion stench. It is our mistakes that have brought us to this place.'

At Nestor's side, Herakles' brow furrows, as he realises where this is going. By posing impiety as root of their ills, Jason can suggest purgation as a route out of them.

Now, what idea might he have for such purgation?

'The Earthborn!' the shepherd boy declares. 'The bane of Cyzicus' people! They may be all that stands in our way, but we shall take the fight to them. What better way of righting our wrongs, than of ridding the Doliones of their monstrous oppressors? This is our time, my friends. This is our fight!'

How very inflammatory of him. Jason had gambled on this suggestion stirring his crew into a state, and he is far from disappointed.

'I'm all for killing monsters, boy, but what are the Earthborn to us?' Theseus calls out over the din of clamouring warriors. 'If the *Argo* is ready to leave, we could take our chances just as easily on the water than against the giants. What will accosting one of those wretched things do for us?'

This resonates predictably poorly. Within moments, the more boisterous Argonauts are deriding the King of Athens for his lack of mettle, Castor inevitably loudest of all. Theseus can't be the only one to harbour such doubts, but only he has spoken them aloud.

'For us?' Jason echoes. 'For *us*? Do you really see the world so narrowly, Athenian? Slaying those fell beasts won't be for *us*. It will be for *them*, the Doliones we failed so badly.

How better to repay their help than by completing the task Cyzicus couldn't bring himself to set us? How better to cleanse our soiled piety than by bringing peace and sanctity to those we made war on?'

The shepherd boy goes on talking – evoking images of Cyzicus' newly wedded queen, Cleite, found hanging from her wedding bower the day after her husband's funeral – believing the Argonauts' cheers are for him, and not for the deeds they all hope to perform. Across the group, the Allslayer's eyes momentarily meet Atalanta's. Of course, they will let the others believe this was Jason's idea. That the leader of their quest truly cares about righting others' wrongs.

His plan, it must be said, is a simple one, and the simplest plans are often the ones that go unfoiled. Even if this heroic endeavour invokes no favour from the gods, there is every chance it will lead them to a strait less blighted by currents.

But often, as Herakles ruefully reflects, is not always.

Somewhere out across the water, he fancies he can hear Tiresias laughing at him.

You move so gracefully when you truly want to. Swift, elegant, dangerously so in both respects. Like the sharks trailing in your inky shadow, it is only on the hunt that you truly come alive.

You feel the Many nestled within your decks and oaken innards, feel the waspish prickle of angst and excitement at what they are sailing into. The two emotions masquerade as one another in several instances. Those feelings sink down into your wooden bones, stirring up your own fiery passions.

One of them in particular, one of the Many who burns like a star. His foreboding runs deeper than most, his doubts more than mortal. Not even the Hellespont's icy depths can cool that particular fire.

You sail onward, heedless of the gently turning tides, paying little notice to the Many working your oars. You scarcely need the help. Your untamed soul wants this as much as they do.

You want to move forward. Or maybe, just maybe, you want to be away from this place.

There are other things that ply these waters, after all.

'Something is wrong.' Tiphys wafts away incense as he looks up from the helm.

A little way off, Jason turns to him with a distracted frown. 'Care to elaborate, steersman?'

If only it were that simple. Tiphys cannot quite put his dirt-stained finger on it, but something feels amiss in the way the *Argo* moves. None of his Dodonian rites or meditative focus can narrow the feeling down. The ship is still moving, but her haste feels a little more… fevered. As if coming from a different place in the *Argo*'s ravening soul.

What has the ship sensed out there? And is she running towards it, or away from it?

'Nothing, my captain. Forget I spoke.'

Jason turns away from Tiphys with a snort, returning to his own personal source of creeping unrest.

'Well, old man? It is quite the moment for you to stop haranguing us with dark truths. What do *you* see out there? What has bound your tongue so?'

Before him, Idmon shifts uncomfortably, wrapped up against the storm winds as tightly as his oracles' robes will stretch. Even with his staff, he appears almost pitifully frail, though his yellowing eyes burn with a surprising zeal.

'It isn't what I can see that bothers me, boy. It's what I can't.'

Further down the *Argo*'s length, the rest of the crew have more prosaic concerns on their hands.

Herakles strains, strains, and strains again. Each strain drags his oaken oar through the waves, splashes of brine cooling his burning arms, salt stinging his eyes. There is something so savagely pure about a sailor's work. All men stand equal before the oars. The more you give to it, the more you get in return.

Theseus occupies the rower's thwart across the walkway from him, the Argonauts' two strongest men manning the middle two oars. The rest have taken places around them, brawn and pride dictating their order. Telamon sits one row behind the Allslayer, the Phthian giant somehow matching Herakles beat for beat. Peleus and Polydeuces do their bit, each of them driven to keep their brothers' pace, if nothing else. And Laertes, too, sits not far behind. His natural affinity at oaring in time — a trait shared by all the seafaring folk of Ithaca — has cemented his place aboard the *Argo*.

The ship may well have her own mind to cross the Hellespont, as is reflected by the many unmanned oars pumping water, but the *Argo* on her own is not enough. Her bestial efforts merely make a task for fifty accomplishable by fifteen, and the blisters and callouses adorning the hands of each crewmate are the most overt reminder of that.

'Harder, Argonauts!' Jason calls from the stern. 'We must reach the strait! Before we lose the light!'

As if such invective will make any difference.

Of all the men who follow Jason's quest, Tiphys is spared the worst of oar duty to navigate the *Argo* and interpret her will. Idmon, similarly, is deemed too feeble for strong man's work, his dubious gift of foresight more valuable to the crew anyway. And whatever strength Orpheus has in his gangly limbs, the Pierian singer is more use with his instruments, lifting his fellows' spirits and inspiring them to row harder.

Even now, the sound of his panpipes carries down ship, throaty and lyrical in equal measure. The waves and storm winds would drown out his lyre music, but Orpheus is far more than just his tools. He can make grown men cry with reeds pressed to his lips.

'Well, Atalanta?' Jason calls out again, having gone a few moments with asserting some will. 'What do you see?'

Far above them, the huntress clings to her perch at half-mast, where her preternatural gaze can see furthest out.

'The mist is growing,' she calls down to him. 'And I don't know why.'

In practice, the thickening air means little for the rowers, for they only need to do, not think about doing. Atalanta finds herself next to powerless in her role as lookout, and such powerlessness comes far from naturally to her. And what good is Tiphys, with no horizon or stars to steer the ship by? How else is he meant to see the way?

And of course, no sky to see means no omens to scry. At the rear of the boat, Idmon closes his eyes, as if this vindicates some suspicion he had all along

For his part, Herakles tries to shut out these gently encroaching doubts, conscious that he has more than enough already. His place is simply to row, to follow orders. This he does with distinction, hoping it is an industrious enough example for the others.

He is aware, at the edge of his strained senses, of Hylas. The servant is scampering up and down the rowers' stations, mopping sweat from brows, dousing others in fresh water. The Allslayer has a half-second to register his ward's wispy, malnourished form before he is gone. Life at sea has not been kind to any of them, but Hylas is no demigod or man of bronze. He has little in the way of strength to lose.

There is fear in the air, real and palpable as the fog. The unknown tends to have that effect. But there is also daring, the prickling static of fiery expectation. The unknown often does that, too.

Right here, right now, in the middle of the restless Hellespont, the quest for the Golden Fleece is truly beginning.

Your disquiet roils in time with the water. The Many feed it with their clashing doubts and worries.

Or maybe your misgivings, your primal nameless fears, are feeding theirs.

Something is coming for you. Something that feels your shadow across the seabed. Something that cares precious little for intruders in its domain.

Mercifully, the Argonauts are not left long in suspense.

'She's speeding up!' Tiphys shouts, forced to grab the deck trellis to keep himself stable. The unmanned oars have, indeed, picked up pace, and there is no mistaking their temperament this time.

In the corner, a damp and huddled Idmon clamps his eyes firmly closed, whispering voiceless words of warding.

'What is it?' Jason shouts, holding on like his helmsman for dear life. The waves show no sign of calming, but their capricious ship is more than compensating.

The aged seer says nothing more, head dipped in an almost foetal curl, as if waiting for the end.

Atalanta's cry of warning cuts over the tumult. Jason looks up in the very same moment, the only other soul aboard who is able and willing to do so.

Just in time to watch it rise.

The sea barely comes up to its ankles. That is the degree to which its scale defies human senses.

It must be half a nautical mile from the ship's prow, and yet it towers high enough for all to see. Men manning the oars look up from their thwarts, sweaty hands sliding free in sheer disbelief. For her part, the *Argo* has never rowed herself quite so hard, though with Tiphys as rapt as the others with disbelief, there is no-one to correct her course.

'*Earthborn!*' Jason cries, as if this leviathan could be anything else. '*It's here!*'

Seawater cascades from its rocky bulk in waterfalls, revealing pillar-legs and a tower-carapace cracked through like parched riverbeds. Fronds of viscous seaweed hang from its rocky corpus, having had aeons to grow among those cracks, knotted and tangled like body hair.

And its eye… even the Hound of Hell's eyes didn't burn quite so hideously red. This solitary eye stretches as wide as the *Argo* is long, with no lid or brow to give it character. Yet it blazes at them with unmistakeable spite and fury.

Six immense hands, each one capable of crushing a ship into matchwood, rise into the air. Even the way it moves is godly. They form colossal fists so stately, so glacially, the way mortals must appear to an anthill. And yet, somehow, still unnervingly swift.

There is no time to steer the *Argo* aside. No time to call out a warning. No time to even brace.

The Earthborn's fists strike the water like the Sea God's own trident, their impact loud enough to split the sky.

XVIII
A Legacy of Beasts

Weeks before, the Argonauts had reflected, over an evening of fire and smouldering offal, on the nature of monsters.

The *Argo* waited at anchor nearby, manned only by a weary Tiphys and a sleeping Idmon. The others congregated down the length of empty beach, seemingly the only souls on this little rock in the Aegean.

With the smoking rites over, the fireside talk steered to tales of monsters. And sure enough, to one slayer of them in particular.

'Herakles!' Nestor urged him with a glinting eye. 'Surely *you* are the authority to speak on god-touched beasts! It should be you talking, and us listening!'

A few of them laughed. For his part, Herakles opted for his usual shield of humble melancholy, hoping the others would cease trying to peer through it. For once.

'I have known a few.'

'Well, what's it to be tonight?' Polydeuces snarkily prompted him. 'How you choked the Hydra of Lerna on its own venom? Or the noble tale of feeding King Diomedes to those flesh-eating mares of his?

At Herakles' side, Hylas tensed, wishing the others weren't quite so intrusive about his master's stories. Or at least, a little more conscious of their weight. But the Allslayer seemed ready to talk tonight.

'I see you prefer your stories less... fantastical, Spartan. I've killed my share of wild creatures. But *monsters?*" He sighed, letting his gaze drift to the fire. 'There are things that dwell upon this earth that did not spring from it. Things that were never... meant. Foul creatures, whose *miasma* you can smell from a league away. The fruit of misbegotten wombs.'

Silence. This clearly wasn't going to be enough.

'The children of Typhon,' he continued with a sigh, 'and the monstrous spawn of Echidna. Some I've met. Others I've simply heard about. Beings scarcely tethered to the mortal, natural world. Invulnerable to human hands. *Monster* is the only word that does them justice.'

Around him, the Argonauts were rapt. All except one.

'And who decides that they deserve that name?' Atalanta pointedly asked. 'Who draws the line between a monster to be killed, and an innocent soul to cherish?'

That actually made the Allslayer chuckle. He wondered, briefly, what the Arcadian would have made of Cerberus. Or the Birds.

'Chiron used to believe they were kin,' he continued. 'The Lion of Nemea, whose hide I wear... Ladon, the dragon of the westmost edge, who guards the Glade of Hesperide... the Boar of Erymanthus, who bore Aphrodite's own divine ward...'

The others around the fire listened, spellbound. Only the Spartan twins stayed unconvinced.

'If the Lion of Nemea was so unworldly,' Castor challenged him, 'then how was it left to terrorise Thebes for so long? Why did none of Cadmus' get think to slay it?'

The Allslayer had looked at him with puzzlement.

'That was the Cithaeron Lion,' he finally explained. 'That was before I began the Labours. I tracked it for forty-nine days, and on the fiftieth day I cornered it in its lair for the kill.'

Castor had no reply to that, and settled for a glower instead.

'I have slain a lot of lions, Spartan.'

XIX
EARTHBORN

When the wave hits the *Argo*, it strikes hard enough to splinter wood.

The prow shatters, as if struck by the Earthborn's own fist. The beams, the dead harpy, shards of priceless Dodonian oak, all are swept away by the Hellespont. The front stretch of deck trellis is ripped away like matchwood.

And the mast... the *Argo*'s mast is one of the most sturdily hewn and fitted of any vessel in the Aegean. It took Argus and his aides nearly three months to correctly craft, even accounting for the ship's mischievous spirit fighting back. Erecting it had been a religious rite and trial of strength all on its own.

It is the finest ship's mast ever seen across the Achaean kingdoms. The finest that will ever be seen.

The storm wave tears it from its mount.

Even Atalanta's preternatural reflexes aren't enough to get her clear, and she pays for it. She can't quite make the jump before the mast breaks away, and it fouls her supposed leap to safety.

She twists. She flies. She cries out.

Pain, effort, uncertainty… and the stinging crash of dampened wood.

The *Argo*'s deck is lurching ever so dangerously downward. That cannot bode well. Atalanta opens eyes stung by saltwater, seeing Idmon lying helplessly on the deck beside her. The seer's glassy gaze meets hers, a wedge of smashed Dodonian wood impaling him through the breast, his blood already diluting into the running water.

He tries to speak, but speaking is hard with ruptured lungs.

Atalanta curses as she tries to pull herself away, her right leg suspiciously painful to move. The deck lurches beneath her once again. The Earthborn's emergence has stirred up the waves, and that is the last damn thing they need right now.

'*Turn us around!*' Jason cries from across the stern. '*Get us out of here, helmsman!*'

The shepherd boy is trapped a little way off, a bruised and bloody mess where a chunk of mast collapsed on him, but more or less unharmed. He appears not to appreciate the unconscious Tiphys pinned beside him, perhaps due to his savaged nerves. Clearly, the idea of slaying a monster of legend is different from the reality.

Jason goes on bawling, shouting inane orders or begging anyone to help him. The crashing waves drown him out either way.

The huntress pulls close to the fallen Idmon, as the last of the old man's strength bleeds away. The hoary old seer strains up to her ear, mouthing breathless, lungless words through drying lips.

Before slumping back, eyes lolling closed. He is the first Argonaut to die on this quest. He will not be the last.

The uprooted mast finally hits the water, taking the sail with it.

Even if the *Argo*'s next landfall yields open arms and a trove of resources, even if Argus' skill and Tiphys' temperament can work more miracles from wood, it will be scarred for the rest of its journey.

If, if, if.

At this present moment, there are two quite pressing problems in the way of these fragile hopes.

The sail, bound not only to the broken mast but to the deck it once stood on, that will soon pull the whole damned ship down with it.

And the Earthborn, drawing inexorably closer, breeding seaquakes with every ponderous step.

Herakles emerges on the topmost deck, Orpheus a gentle weight over one shoulder. With his knee crushed by wooden debris, the Pierian Bard will not be walking unaided any time soon. The rest of the *Argo*'s beleaguered rowers clamber up from their thwarts behind him.

The water keeps on flowing, gushing down gangways and corridors with nowhere to disperse or seep through. Argus' meticulous craftsmanship may now be the doom of them all, if they can't shift it overboard. Assuming there is still an *Argo* left to sail when this is over.

'Gods below.' Meleager makes a sign of warding over Idmon's corpse. Beside him, Theseus and Telamon strain with effort as they shift wreckage off Jason's prone form. The shepherd boy's head lolls back, oblivious while still awake.

'Enough of that.' Theseus throws some broken oak overboard with a snarl. 'Coming this way was a fool's gambit. We can't hope to—'

'Hope to what, Athenian?' Castor hits out. 'Hope to make your way home, tail between?'

'Hope to outpace that behemoth,' Theseus hits back. 'Or even move at all. Not while our mast and sail are pulling us down.'

No-one argues. Even discounting the waves bred from the Earthborn's glacial tread, the deck is listing so alarmingly starboard that even standing straight is becoming a struggle.

'Then what are we waiting for?' Atalanta urges the stupefied men, hunting knife drawn. 'Row me far enough out, one of you, and I can cut us loose.'

'No good, Huntress.' This from Argus, huddled miserable in his drenched shawls and tunic, sodden beard plastered to his face. 'That sail was woven from sacred silk. The strongest, most durable silk this side of Olympus, from the hide of the Boar of Erymanthus. Sacred to Aphrodite, in death as well as life.'

Herakles breathes a guttural curse. A lifetime ago, he was the one to wrangle the blasted Boar and bring it, alive, to the court of King Eurystheus. Another accursed Labour.

The Goddess of Love guards her chosen playthings well. She is as fickle and capricious as any human heart.

'Then we can't cut the sail,' he says. 'But we can unharness it from the broken mast before it sinks.'

Another wave crashes across the deck, soaking souls already soaked to the bone. The waves are growing mightier now, because their abyssal foe is getting closer.

The Allslayer turns away from it, looking at the men all around him. There is no pretension now, no time for cloak and dagger. No Jason to pout and countermand him.

The club is already in his vicelike grasp. The lionskin is leashed around his torso.

'Theseus. Castor. Telamon. You are the strongest among us. Take a rowboat. Get us free of that mast.'

None of the three named men raise any objections, not to being banded together, nor the question of what Herakles — the true, undisputable strongest man aboard the ship — will be doing while they are gone.

If the three of them fail, it won't matter anyway.

A new sensation passes through your blessed frame. Not anticipation, for you know that feeling all too well. This is something else, something far sourer and more potent.

This is relish.

Even as the water hammers your flanks, and your breaks sting and burn, you savour the brutal reckoning you feel coming.

Your oars hang still and lifeless, just as they did before. But not, this time, from fear.

This is fortunate, as the Many taking shelter aboard you — and the One, in particular, who burns brightest of them all — has no intention of running from this fight.

He has something else entirely in mind.

'We're away, master!'

Hylas grips one side as the rowboat casts off. It is a small vessel, barely fit to take a group of men to shore, and it was not crafted to suit a son of Zeus. Even as Herakles rows the puny boat outwards — faster and more steadily than two mortal oarsmen could manage — Hylas feels like little more than a piece of extraneous gear.

As does the rowboat's third and final occupant.

'Are you ready?' the Allslayer calls without looking back. Behind him, Orpheus tends his lyre, sat in a way that relieves his damaged knee of pressure.

'It is a pleasant change to feel needed, Child of Thunder.'

'Enough levity, Pierian. This monster is beyond any of us. If Atalanta fails, your music may be the only weapon we have. We must bring it to battle on our own terms. And I don't wish to journey to the World Beneath again. Not today.'

He still does not turn, keeping on rowing. They are out from beneath the *Argo*'s listing shadow now, and the distant outline of the Earthborn is not looking quite so distant.

'Nor do I, Allslayer.' The Bard's reply is strangely toneless. 'Nor do I.'

Across the way, another small paddleboat has also cast off. This one takes a different path across the waves, almost reflecting the arc of the boat carrying Herakles. Two Argonauts set about rowing the oars, while two more wait at the prow, weapons ready for what is to come.

'Keep your wits close, all of you.' Atalanta has several of her hunting knives to hand, more than her fellow travellers believed she even possessed. But the bow and arrows across her back are her surest chance of surviving this.

That goes for all four of them, not that they have the good sense or humility to acknowledge it.

'We only have to distract it, lady,' Meleager replies. 'We are the bait for the trap. A trap the Allslayer will spring before we come to harm.'

At Atalanta's side, Meleager's grip on the royal blade of Calydon grows tighter. Sweatier. His words are meant to pacify the huntress, but it may not be the huntress who needs pacifying. Behind them, Laertes and Nestor each man an oar with slow, nervous precision. Neither of them tries to think too deeply about what they are rowing towards.

'Don't get complacent, boy.' Atalanta's cold eyes grow flintier, and her tone drops to match. 'We're not chasing hounds on some royal hunt. You're doubtless used to having others suffer on your behalf, so let me be clear, Prince Meleager. If you fall short now, it won't just be you who pays the price.'

The rowboat crests another alarmingly tall wave, tall enough to spray them all with brine. The disturbance is growing. The Earthborn is getting closer, its titanic footsteps falling harder.

'There,' Atalanta announces, apropos of nothing. 'That outcrop to the left of our course. This will have a better chance of working with some solid rock beneath our feet. Set us down there.'

Meleager looks ready to argue this point, still unsure why, out of all the crew aboard the *Argo*, it is always the huntress who has this effect on him.

'Nestor and I are princes, lady,' he gently reminds her. 'And our Ithacan friend is a king. We are not used to being ordered about like barrow boys. Not by a woman with no father or husband.'

Atalanta takes a moment to think on this, as she checks her bow and blades for the umpteenth time. Whether this act keeps her hidden nerves at bay, or betrays her giving in to them, is anyone's guess. None of the Argonauts know her well enough to tell the difference. None of them care enough to ask.

'And I am a huntress, little Meleager. I am not used to having three loud and cumbersome weights hanging off my bow-arm, fouling up my chances of stealth and killing cleanly. But it is an imperfect world we live in, Prince of Calydon.'

Ahead of them, the pale granite outcrop juts out of the Hellespont, eroded smooth by millennia of restless tides.

'Just set us down here, my *kingly* friends. And keep the oars to hand, one of you. We may need to leave in a hurry.'

Theseus hits the foaming water hard. He lets himself plummet, pushing down hard into the icy waters before his muscles can seize up in shock.

The Hellespont is cold. Colder than a corpse's embrace. Colder than the Minotaur's bestial gaze, in the moments before he hacked off its bullish head. But down he swims, letting the brine burn his eyes but refusing to close them nonetheless.

There. Down in the inky, watery dark. The broken mast. Slowly, sedately, drifting down on its inexorable journey to the seabed. The King of Athens would have no issue with this, were it not for the immense sheet of exquisitely woven sailcloth still tied to it.

A sheet that is also still connected to the *Argo*, that will pull the whole damn ship over if nothing is done.

A distant crash of muffled noise draws Theseus' attention briefly upward, all sound made distorted and cavernous by the water. Telamon hitting the water after him, Castor following scarce moments later. Theseus briefly wonders if the Spartan will take this chance to settle their grudge, drowning him with no witnesses beneath the waves, and pinning all blame on the chaos of the storm.

His gaze drifts up over them, to the brightness of the surface. Distant, so very distant. He has swum far deeper than he realised, and only by looking all the way up can he truly appreciate that.

Deep water always has this effect on him. The vastness of it, the emptiness… nothing else highlights his insignificance as adroitly. Nothing else makes him feel quite so small.

The Athenian turns his gaze back downward.

Time to get this done.

'You really don't need to be here,' Atalanta maintains, as level and polite as she can manage. Bow drawn, body still, breath calm. She can hold this stance until the stars go cold.

But with a rather irritating Calydonian prince for company, even her legendary hunter's discipline is beginning to fray.

'The Allslayer told us to help you,' Meleager insists. 'However you are planning to distract that behemoth, Huntress… it will surely take more than just one bow and arrow.'

The two of them are standing side by side on the lonely outcrop of rock, restless waves lapping at them from all sides. A little way off, Laertes and Nestor remain in the rowboat, unwilling or perhaps fearful to join Atalanta on her tenuous little promontory.

And far out ahead, they see the silhouettes of the listing *Argo* and ponderous Earthborn through the mist. One of them is slowly falling from view. The other is growing, inch by inch, in their vision.

'The surest help you can give me is by keeping the boat ready,' Atalanta tries to hint to him. 'As the King of Ithaca and Prince of Pylos clearly understand.'

But Meleager is not to be dissuaded. 'They do not want to be here and cannot bring themselves to argue with you. And when you spring whatever gambit you're planning, I think you're going to need all the help you can get.'

Atalanta buries the urge to roll her eyes. She still has yet to even look at him, or take her eyes and aim off the slowly growing silhouette ahead of them.

'You truly think me so incapable?' Meleager continues, stung by the slight he has imagined into being. 'That because I am younger than the others, I am somehow of no use? I have taken the robe of manhood, woman! I have passed the *ephebe*'s rites!'

'I have no opinion of you at all, Meleager of Calydon.'

The prince takes a second to consider this, if *consider* is truly the right word. He steps forward, taking his Arcadian crewmate by the shoulder and pulling her around to face him.

'I can fight, Huntress. As well as any man aboard the *Argo*. Why won't you let me prove myself? What is it about me you do not trust?'

For a moment, Atalanta is simply too stunned to respond. She does not draw her hunting knife and sever Meleager's fingers for his impudence, though the temptation to do so burns magma hot. She does not laugh in the prince's face, either, because she is rarely ever that expressive with her feelings.

'Why?' she finally answers. 'Because I've seen nothing in you that warrants any trust, Prince of Calydon. Because I see an unblooded princeling who has never drawn a blade in any danger. Because right now, on the most imperilled day of your pitifully short life, *you* don't see a danger that needs to be outthought as well as outfought. All you see is a chance to prove yourself a hero, consequences be damned.'

Now it is Meleager's turn to be stunned. He just stares at her, aghast, though not quite unaware of his hand still on Atalanta's shoulder. The huntress can't have missed it either, though tellingly another long moment passes before she finally shoves it away.

'Dear, dear.' She raises her shortbow and aims it out to sea, checking the shaft is still correctly nocked. 'Heroes, and their ilk. All the s—'

'Why are *you* here, Atalanta?' Meleager cuts in, apropos of nothing. This is not the surliness she was expecting, not the chastised petulance of a snubbed prince. This is curiosity. Stately, thought out and not at all misplaced. 'Why are you here with us, aboard the *Argo*? Why have you thrown in your lot with Jason?'

The huntress does not speak for a moment, soft eyes judging her young companion's seriousness.

'I think it is a fair question,' the prince continues. 'You disavowed your Arcadian lineage long ago. You have no kingdom, no allegiance. What could you want with a relic that can decide the outcome of wars?'

It is a rare day indeed when one of Atalanta's boorish companions can genuinely take her by surprise. She has had long years to practice concealing her emotions, though thankfully Meleager is not canny enough to read her discomfort.

'You know the answer to that, Calydonian. I am here because of loyalty, not some magical golden trinket. I am here to help my friend take back his birthright.'

To that, Meleager can only smile. If not threat, or malice, there is a sureness now that Atalanta has never seen in him before.

'So you told us, lady, when this all began. But if that is truly the case, why would you even entertain the idea of this quest at all? You are the maiden huntress of Artemis. The daughter of the wildlands. If you truly wanted to deliver the crown of Thessaly to Jason, you could have done so with the barest brush of effort. Never mind your bow, or those many butter knives you keep close. You could have slipped past every guard in Iolchus, stolen your way into King

Pelias' boudoir, and slit his and Acastus' throats before anyone even realised you were there.'

For a moment there are no words. No ripostes, denials or dismissals. Just the rushing and roaring of ever-growing storm swell.

'You think me so transparent,' Meleager rounds off. 'So guileless. So perhaps you could illuminate me, Huntress – in a way this brittle mind of mine can actually grasp, mind you – as to what you are really doing on this quest?'

Atalanta finally opens her mouth to reply, but Meleager will never learn what she intends to say. The sound of music, somehow audible above the roaring Hellespont, drifts into their ears.

Orpheus doesn't look out to sea as he blows into his panpipes. Given how close they are to their titanic quarry, this is quite an impressive feat of nerves. He just plays, and plays, and plays.

He pulls ocean air through his Pierian lungs, and pushes a throaty, pastoral melody out through the pipes. The music evokes a simpler, kinder time. A time when he and Eurydice had no greater worries than naming their children. A time that never really existed.

Quite how it carries so far across the waves, Herakles and Hylas cannot grasp. But they are glad for it, nonetheless. The Allslayer feels a measure of peace crawl back to him, the disquiet around his thoughts fading into background noise. Orpheus' sanctified gifts affect even him, a Child of Thunder. The oars feel a little lighter in his hands, and the sea parts a little easier with each stroke.

'Master?' Hylas risks pointing a tentative finger, hopes rising with his tremulous voice. 'I think… I think it's working!'

Sure enough, the Earthborn's lumbering, glacial tread has halted. With stately, agonizing slowness, the immense rocky carapace that serves as its head begins to turn, the giant arterial eye bled briefly dry of fury as it comprehends this new, wondrous sound.

Orpheus' music may not part the giant from its wrath, or even give the broken *Argo* space to escape, should it fail. But right here, right now, it is enough to buy them time.

The rowboat surges forwards, as Herakles' oars propel it across the water yet again.

Just a little further, damn it. Just a little further.

He breaks the stormy surface at last, coughing air back into his insides. It is sweeter than Athens' richest honey, even as he retches up a lungful of seawater.

Castor surfaces to his left, similarly shaken from swimming so far into the deep. Telamon must still be down there, trying to pry loose as much sail as he can before his breath betrays him once again.

Theseus recognises the soothing pipe music from his first meeting with Orpheus, more immediate than even the water gushing from his ears. The very same reverie that stopped the twins from killing him. And here they all are about to die anyway.

'*Not much more!*' Telamon wheezes as he shoots up through a patch of Hellespont. '*Once more! All three of us!*'

Theseus drags in one last gulp of air, ignoring Castor's bladed eye contact. And then the music stops, blasted from the air by a roar of lungless, bestial hunger.

'That… doesn't sound good,' Hylas notes.

Herakles rows harder than he has ever rowed before. The oar shafts are slowly splintering, not even Dodonian wood able to withstand his crushing grasp.

Orpheus keeps on playing, his musical lullaby somehow growing more and more languid the more urgently he plays it. But in vain. The Earthborn is moving again, loosing another storm-shaking roar to the sky. Whatever spell the bard hoped to put on it, figurative or otherwise, has not worked.

The baleful red eye falls upon their boat once more, as seething and enflamed as ever. The Titanic monster doesn't even raise fists, now. A man does not raise fists to an ant, after all.

The giant's left leg rises from the waves, blotting out the misty sky. One more step will crush the three of them together.

'Oh, gods!' Hylas wails. 'Oh, gods, oh gods, *oh gods!*'

Only the leg, towering taller than a small mountain, does not fall. It hovers above them like an executioner's axe, in time for the rowboat to pass beyond its shadow, as an arrow strikes it in the knee.

Atalanta lowers her shortbow in triumph, already reaching over her shoulder for the next shaft. No other archer could have made so precise a shot at distance. But then, no other archer has honed their shooting to Artemis' merciless standards.

'*What?*' Meleager cries. '*Huntress, are you insane?*'

The Calydonian can scarcely hear himself over the rising storm. Winds blast, and waves crash ever harder. Atalanta and Meleager have been unwillingly pushed together, conceding inch after inch of their headland to the surf.

Before long there won't be anything left to stand on.

'*We have its attention!*' she hits back at him. '*If it's on us, then it's not on the* Argo*! Or on Herakles! That is what matters, boy!*'

Meleager risks another glance behind them. Nestor is struggling to keep the rowboat moored in place, and Laertes is clearly urging him to cast off. At any rate, the boat may dash itself against the rocks.

Atalanta has already fired again. Somehow, beyond a shortbow's meagre range, through a mist that defies mortal sight, and a storm fierce enough to throw a meteor off course, she has managed to put another arrow into her quarry.

'*You should go!*' she tells him as she nocks a fresh shaft. '*While you still can!*'

Only Meleager doesn't move. He pulls his princely blade free with sombre ceremony, though what precisely he intends to do with it is unclear.

'*You... vexing... if you think I'm leaving you here, alone, to——*'

A crashing wave cuts his lordly vow short. The Hellespont blasts Meleager off his feet, casting him back down upon the storm-washed rocks.

Headfirst.

The shadow falls like a thunderclap, deafening Hylas' senses just by striking the water behind them.

But water is all it strikes, and the servant cries out in euphoric realisation. The Earthborn's leg plunges down into the deep, sending a wave of foaming sea cascading over the lot of them.

If it hoped to crush the boat beneath its tread, then it has failed. Only that failing has made it even angrier. And deadlier.

'Take the oars,' the Allslayer commands. He is rising from his hunched station, a movement which will doubtless capsize them if he takes another step.

But that is not what he has in mind.

'Master,' Hylas begins. 'What are you g—'

He doesn't bother finishing the sentence. There is no point in addressing empty air.

Herakles hurls himself over the waves. The Nemean lionskin billows around him, casting his profile in start silhouette – a bolt of roaring leonine thunder, loosed from his father's divine hand.

He strikes true, just as Atalanta did. Gnarled hands lock around something knotted, viscous, yet true. More fronds of oceanic weed that have grown among the cracks for epochs.

If the titanic beast is aware of its hanger-on, it gives no sign. Its ponderous legs keep on rising, keep on falling, as it makes its malevolent way eastward.

Towards Atalanta's little outcrop, and the source of its true annoyance.

'In. Now!' Castor barks, as he helps Telamon pull Theseus back aboard. The King of Athens slumps back in the rowboat's well, choking out enough seawater to drown a small child.

The sail is free, and though the mast is still sinking, it won't be dragging the *Argo* down with it. Though it galls Castor to admit it, Theseus might well have helped save all their lives.

And he may die a hero's death in consequence, which galls Castor even more.

'*Breathe*, you bastard!' The Spartan thumps Theseus in the sternum, spurring a fresh round of choking coughs. That is promising. If he can cough, he can breathe.

'Oars,' Telamon wheezes. The Phthian looks scarcely better than Theseus. 'Get... the oars...'

Castor snarls as he adopts the rower's crouch. The storm is more than just a gale now. Rain is hammering down at them, blown at them from every angle by swirling winds.

A shadow in the mist steals his focus. What is that, moving through the gloom?

'Is that...' Theseus breathes, managing to point in the Earthborn's vague direction for a few seconds. 'On its leg...'

Castor follows Theseus' finger, seeing something that cannot possibly be happening.

'No...' he gasps. 'He... he can't be.'

The huntress' curses go unheard as she tries to stem the bleeding. Meleager's face is a mess of diluted blood and water, hair plastered to his scalp by both. The wound to his temple is bleeding with worrying glee. With nowhere to turn and no-one to help, there isn't much that even Atalanta can do. The idiot boy may well have doomed them both.

Atalanta isn't a proud or haughty soul, but the idea of her journey ending here, by Jason's misplaced zeal and Meleager's foolhardy courage, rankles even her well-travelled heart.

She tries to look around, across the booming waves. Nestor and Laertes are nowhere to be seen, as is their boat. The storm has killed them, or driven them too far off to help.

Atalanta closes her eyes, heedless of the deluge tearing at her. Instinct has kept her safe more times than she can count, in the unending dance of predator and prey. Out here, in the Hellespont, the Earthborn has turned their roles. She will turn them back, somehow, or she will die.

Hunter and hunted, as it always is. A cycle that cannot end.

Meleager groans a subliminal groan, unconsciousness not quite able to dim his pain. Atalanta braces his wound as best she can. She then takes up her bow with bloodstained hands.

If the Earthborn keeps on coming, she will die on this rock with Meleager. And the *Argo* will escape.

Or she might be able to slay it. And the *Argo* will escape.

If it leaves her be, it might reach the *Argo* before it escapes. And then she will die whatever happens, as will they all.

These thoughts run through her mind in one blink of her soft eyes. The huntress rises to her feet, Meleager forgotten for the time being. The rain has turned her hair to dreadlocks, plastering it across her sodden back and shoulders, while washing the last of the blood from her arms.

She draws her shortbow, ready to fire again at the encroaching giant.

And then she sees an unmistakeable shape clambering up its midriff.

The Allslayer keeps on climbing. Step by step, inch by inch, he pulls himself up higher up the living shifting mountain.

The storm lashes harder at him the higher he climbs. Every few minutes, he holds fast and mutters a prayer. And then the towering leg crashes down, its foot hammering the seabed far below, as the Earthborn completes yet another step. Each time, the impact nearly throws him clear.

Every so often, as Herakles finds another handhold, he strains his gaze out to sea. Between the rain and the mist, he can't glean much. The *Argo*'s rebalancing silhouette is unmistakeable, and by some favour from the distant gods, his colossal mount is not moving towards her. Atalanta's deadly gambit is paying off.

Hylas and Orpheus still live, for they are still crying out for him to come back. Theseus and the others must also have prevailed in their work, because the *Argo* is no longer on the brink of capsizing, but the Allslayer cannot know if they made it back aboard.

The Earthborn's crashing tread steals his focus once more. Herakles tightens his slipping grasp, like a parasite on a bull's rump. How the titanic fiend hasn't yet sensed his presence, he cannot guess. But this dance is reaching its end.

He pulls himself up, again, and again, and again. He is rewarded, at last, with a place to precariously stand. An immense summit of cavernous, rocky outcrops. On a mortal man, this could be considered a shoulder.

The club is already in Herakles' right fist. He sights his target not far off, and hurls himself at it with a battle cry.

Far beneath, Orpheus cranes his neck to watch.

'Well?' Hylas cries over the storm winds, trying his best with the oars. His master always makes it look so easy.

'You wouldn't believe me if I told you,' the bard replies.

He brings the club down, down, and down again. He pounds the rock until cracks become fissures, and fissures start to widen. Each hammer blow takes all his strength, a feat he believes each time he won't repeat.

Gradually, piece by piece, the Earthborn's enormous head inches towards fracturing.

Herakles raises his club above his own head, screaming with pent up rage and effort.

The clubhead falls, its aim unerring. Only this last blow never connects.

'*Turn it around!*' Telamon bellows, outshouting the storm with his roaring cry. 'We are *not* leaving them!'

Castor grabs him by his chiton, pulling him close. The movement is sharp enough to almost tip the rowboat. 'The *Argo* is *free*, fool. And our way is clear! We have to get back aboard!'

'*Not without them!*' Telamon screams. '*Not without him!*'

It is all Castor can do not to punch his Phthian comrade in the face. The Allslayer's commands were ironclad. With Atalanta and Orpheus distracting the Earthborn, he would try his damnedest to slay the colossus or simply hurt it. All while the others got the *Argo* clear of her mast.

From there, with the giant no longer blocking their way through the Hellespont, it was a matter of getting the ship out with as many of them as possible back on board. If that cost them a few lives along the way, then that was that. Quests tend to do that, and a quest is what they all came for.

But Telamon clearly doesn't plan on leaving Herakles' Fate to chance. Not so soon after he has found him again.

'Do as he says, Castor,' a voice growls from behind him. 'If he's still out there, we'll help him.'

The Spartan prince snatches the oars without turning. The two of them can throw him off the boat if they desire, and they damn well know it.

He begins to row them once again, but this time not back towards the *Argo*.

'Gods Above, Theseus. I didn't expect you to suddenly grow a pair.'

'*No!*' Herakles gasps, as the club flies out of his grasp. He grabs after it with his one free hand, but for naught. It is gone, tumbling down through the mist.

A shadow eclipses his view as the Earthborn tries, once more, to grab at him with one of its many hands. Like a man flailing at gnats, it falls each time slowly, inexorably, yet still somehow faster than the Allslayer can follow.

At the edge of hearing, he picks out a tell-tale sound. A grinding crack of metal within stone. Atalanta's arrows still seem to be landing on target. He wonders how much longer the huntress has before it kills her.

He growls, pulling himself back up. He has one other weapon beside the club, leashed across his back.

He could draw it and end all this now. Even a Titan is no match for an arrow doused in Hydra blood.

The question still remains, however. Let the Earthborn kill him, and tear the *Argo* into shreds. Or take up the bow he killed his children with, and live that memory once again.

Which of those things would he rather do?

Atalanta pushes herself above the frothing waves, clasping the half-drowned Meleager close. The sea has swallowed her rocky islet, and now a thundering storm and unconscious prince seek to pull her underwater.

The huntress fights to keep their heads above the surface, gasping as water leaks into her lungs. Her eyes sting with brine, but if she lets them drift closed… it will already be over.

A roar — draconic, deafening, and owing nothing to the race of men — shakes the air above her. Whatever Herakles is doing to the Earthborn, he isn't doing it quick enough.

It has him. At long last, it has him.

The Allslayer roars defiance into the storm, as the titanic hand pulls him free. Even one of its rocky, articulated digits is taller and wider than his own demigod physique. And here he is, nestled in a giant's stony palm, too small to be trapped between its fingers.

The Earthborn's broken, malformed head slowly falls from view, as it gradually straightens its arm. But its baleful blood-red eye never leaves him, never wavers in its burning hunger, even through the lashing rain. He has seen that emotion in the eyes of gods and monsters. It is an anger he knows all too well.

Whatever it plans to do now — to hurl Herakles into the sea, or simply crush him into gory paste — it is now or never.

A moment of choice. How depressingly rare that is.

Die here, as he is, and cease living for the whims of others. Or go onward, still enslaved to Fate, if it gives his comrades a chance of changing theirs.

The bow is drawn, its arrow nocked. He will never remember doing either, for his mind is lost in another place entirely. Not that the present moment is any less horrific.

One shot, aimed true. One shaft, buried in the wreckage of its shattered stone skull. One cacophonous scream of outrage, loud enough to drown out the storm.

Herakles sees none of this, feels none of it. Faces tumble past him in his torpor – Megara, Tiresias, Cyzicus, and far too many others – that gradually give over to oblivion.

That, and the all-too-welcome feeling of falling.

XX
EXIT WOUNDS

Laying Idmon to rest takes more forethought than they expect. None of them are familiar with Argive funeral rites, those most aloof and insular of a kingdom's rituals. In the end, Orpheus' inspiration delivers them. The Pierian Bard performs a gentle paean of remembrance as the funeral pyre burns to ash, a votive addressed to Apollo the Far-Shooter. He is the son of a Muse, after all, and the Muses are Apollo's concern.

Orpheus' makeshift cane props him upright as he sings. It is nothing more than a splayed plank of *Argo*, broken by the storm, but it is the right size and shape to help him move until his knee recovers.

And here, on a lonely shore that bears no name, the Argonauts make their peace with their fallen comrade. Their grief, while palpable, goes mostly unvoiced. It matters little. Idmon's irascible soul wouldn't have cared either way.

The sky above is blessedly calm, a gentle sea breeze carrying Orpheus' words away with the smoke. The storms wracking the Hellespont have dissipated following the Earthborn's brutal death, and the timing of that doesn't feel like a coincidence.

Somewhere, along the chaos of their voyage from Pagasa, the Argonauts have made the right choice. The gods, for now at least, favour them.

To a point. The *Argo* is bereft of her seer, and that doesn't sit well with any of them. Whose oracular gifts will they rely on now to see them right? Who will scry omens for them from the birds and entrails?

At Orpheus' side stands the very man whose role it is to shoulder these doubts. Jason's injuries, superficial as they were, are healing well. The visible and allegorical scars he took are fading, and though no-one among the crew will admit it, it suits him to look a little rugged.

Herakles watches him from a little way off, where he and Hylas stand behind Tiphys at the gathering's rear. The Allslayer watches Jason take the floor, spreading his hands in what he hopes are gestures of magnanimity as he tries to find words to match the occasion.

Orator the boy is not, but none of his erstwhile followers can bring themselves to shut him up. It was Jason's decision to face the Earthborn, a decision that ultimately delivered them from the Hellespont. The boy was right, after all.

But the *Argo*'s escape does not feel like Jason's victory, and from the halo of frostiness shrouding the assembled heroes, the others certainly don't see it as such.

The shepherd boy finishes his meandering eulogy at last, rounding off with a few flavourless plaudits about keeping their Colchian terminus in mind, and their purpose bound together.

Whatever that means.

And then they are away, trudging back to the beached rowboats, and from there to the *Argo* across the bay. With the funerary ashes scattering in the winds, there will be no monument left to mark Idmon's final resting place.

Nothing except his wooden staff, embedded in the sand, standing sentinel over this nameless stretch of coast where no man will set foot again. The *Argo* is now gone from this place, this lonely little island that has never known life or culture. But the staff will remain, eroded and abraded but never fully buried.

To this day, it stands there still.

He still can't fully remember how they pulled him from the water. Recollection returned in spurts and flashes: the odd impression of pain, of feeling, of awareness rather than acknowledgement. A dull, throbbing ache, pulsing through his back and shoulders. Cold damp air, chilling him to the bone. A coppery tang in his mouth, as bad memories had flashed behind his eyes.

When he'd finally opened them, he'd found himself inside a dark little hold. The only light came through gaps in the beams up above, snatches of sound filtering down to him from above decks. Somewhere quiet. Somewhere calm. Somewhere he could convalesce, for a while at least.

The others would relate the whole sorry tale to him in time. How Theseus and Telamon found him face down in the billowing waves, and struggled to pull him aboard. How the roiling tides blew them into Atalanta's path, the huntress treading water while holding bloodied Meleager's head above the surface. How Laertes and Nestor were swept beneath the waves, only for Hylas to steer his boat over them in time.

They survived, all of them, in time for Peleus and the others to get them back aboard the *Argo*.

All except Idmon.

In that moment of awakening, as the Allslayer's senses crawled back to him, he became aware of three things in the darkness around him.

His Lionskin, hanging from a wooden rafter above his head, looking rather more patched and disfigured than usual while still unmistakeably whole.

Below that, his club of gnarled pinewood, still glossed with enchanted lacquer from Eleusis' long-dried springs. How deceptively common it looked when not flecked with blood and ichor.

And beside it, under one of Hylas' woollen winter shrouds, a certain wide and ovoid presence. His other weapon, one he'd hoped against hope that the storm would sweep out of his life.

The others must have found it floating in the waves, with the rest of him.

As if the Fates are ever that obliging.

The Allslayer nurses that maudlin thought as he follows the others down the beach. He swallows down the urge to look over his shoulder and take one last look behind him. The staff will still be there, and there is nothing more to see.

A little way behind, Atalanta and Meleager are sharing intense whispers as they leave. The huntress appears to be pressing a point, and the prince is seemingly trying his damnedest to ignore it. Atalanta still walks with the ghost of a limp, as subtly as she tries to hide it.

Herakles' preternaturally acute hearing tunes into their words, without really wanting to. It is something different to think about, at any rate.

'Making a mistake is one thing, Calydonian,' Atalanta hisses. 'But not being able to see it in hindsight, even *after* it brings the Furies down upon your head, is something else.'

'I tire of this refrain, Huntress.' Meleager seethes at such unjust scorn. Fresh scars around his temple crease in displeasure. 'I was raised better than to leave a young woman alone to face peril!'

Atalanta actually takes a moment to process this, as taken aback as Meleager had perhaps hoped. But not at all, it transpires, for the right reasons.

'You truly do not get it, do you?' Derision, instead of warmth, seems to briefly thaw her out. 'After all this time, all these months spent crossing the sea, you just don't get where we've all found ourselves. Just what is happening aboard this ship.'

Meleager has stopped, turning half a pace to face her. The others continue their dejected trudge toward the rowboats. Tiphys and Castor pay them no heed as they pass, while Hylas, Nestor and even Telamon all eye them suspiciously for fleeting moments as they follow. Argus even pauses, fixing the huntress with a brazenly beady stare, before Atalanta's narrowed gaze sends him scurrying off once more.

'All you did by defying me, Prince of Calydon,' Atalanta says, 'was nearly get Laertes and Nestor killed. And then, not content with maiming yourself to the point of helplessness, you put *me* in mortal danger too, when I had to drop everything to keep you safe.'

'I *know* that, lady, and I *am* sorry that it came to that,' Meleager protests. 'But it *was* the right choice to make. We gave Herakles the time we needed, and—'

'*No*,' Atalanta cuts him off, her voice rising a handful of notes higher than normal. By this point the other Argonauts are all thankfully out of earshot, or so the huntress thinks.

'You *didn't*. You made *a* choice, which, Fates be thanked, didn't prove the death of us all. *Hindsight*, young man. You cannot take risks like that based on how you think you see the future. If Idmon were still here, he would tell you the same.'

Any hope of hers that the Calydonian might heed this lesson is dashed by his put-upon pout. Life cannot be easy when no-one else around you is capable of righting their wrongs.

'I saw you in danger,' Meleager tries, one last time. 'And I felt I must intervene.'

'You saw a chance to be a hero,' Atalanta counters, gently, perhaps more gently than is warranted. 'And you felt the exaltation that would come from performing a deed worthy of song.'

Far off ahead of them, paddles begin to churn the rippling waves. Peleus has put the first of the little boats out to sea, loaded with Argonauts.

'Is that not what it means to be a hero?' Meleager presses her. He sounds more contemplative than confrontational this time. It is a new, if welcome, colour on him. 'To prove something? To yourself, as much as to the world around you? Is that so very different from you, Huntress of Arcadia?'

Atalanta actually gives that a moment's thought. Under the circumstances, it is only fair. She then begins to move up the beach, following their crewmates' silty footprints, inclining her head for Meleager to follow her once more.

'What I do with my life, boy,' she finally admits when they have walked a few paces, 'is between me and my Olympian patroness. She cares nothing for what is witnessed, or enshrined in legend. What outsiders think of her followers is nothing to her. Only the deeds, the commitments, matter. What I do.' She glances at him feyly. 'And what I refrain from doing.'

Meleager holds her gaze for a second as he follows, not quite emboldened enough to ask what that is supposed to mean. The moment passes.

'Heroism, Calydonian,' the huntress continues, her tone growing colder once more, 'is little more than shattering the world around you, and piecing together the rubble in whatever way pleases you. There is no deed too savage, too barbarous, if you can muster a righteous enough reason for doing it. Not *right*, Meleager. *Righteous.*'

She keeps on walking, sandaled toes marring the soggy sand, until she realises that Meleager is not following her.

'I don't believe that,' he says as she turns, a handful of steps behind her. 'This quest, this journey to Colchis, is a noble undertaking. We are risking our lives to right a grave wrong, and all Thessaly will be the better for it.'

Atalanta shakes her head, the exasperation too much for even her inexpressiveness to mask.

'We are risking our lives, Meleager, to steal an artefact we have no rightful claim on, *in the hope* it rights a wrong. And do you really think that is what matters to our *heroic* friends?' She sweeps a hand out to sea, where the first few paddle boats are already trailing foam across the bay. 'Do you really believe our companions changed their minds out of the goodness of their hearts? Because they *care* about putting a mountain boy on a distant throne, instead of laying their hands on that accursed Fleece the first chance they get? Do you think any of them will *care* about who gets hurt, if it means they can get what they want?'

Meleager's pained silence is an eloquent enough answer.

'Actaeon's Bed…' the huntress softly swears, drawing closer once more. 'Every time I think you're finally getting somewhere, boy… You truly have no idea what you have leashed yourself to, do you? No idea what seeing this to the end will mean.'

The Prince of Calydon is still silent, this young untested traveller who has never tasted combat. And had, until this moment, genuinely believed in his comrades' good intentions.

Atalanta recognises that distant look in his eyes, and against her better judgement, she feels a silken stab of empathy. It is a look she knows all too well, for her past self wore it more than once.

Innocence, untenderly stripped, that can never again grow back.

You have tasted your own blood.

Pain is nothing new to you. Life is pain, and pain means life. You were wrought into this form by pain, after all, your wooden bones and timber flesh unshaped from their natural state by the Many. You have known heat, with the merciless sun bleaching your sails clean of colour. And you have known cold, with the ocean's dark waves licking your hull with ice.

But if anything, they galvanise you. They pierce through your mercurial moods, reminding you that you still live.

This has been different. Your wounds are new and unwelcome gifts, not enough to cripple you, but enough to make you wary.

The brine makes them sting and burn, like salt in a bloodied cut. But your innards are already awash with pain. Here, today, that irritant merely gluts the fire of your temper.

But pain can do more than destroy. Igneous torment crackles through your bones, weaving around the wood now displaced or unmade. You lack the cognisance or eloquence to interpret such torment, so you cannot quite know it for what it is.

Growing pains.

'Gods of Olympus.' Peleus claps his hands together in appreciation of what he is seeing. 'You've worked a dark wonder here, Argus.'

Sat further back in the communal hold, the shipwright leers. All his smiles seem to come out as leers. 'It's nothing I haven't already told you, Lord Peleus. Dodonian oak. A fine material, in more ways than one.'

'I'll say,' the Phthian hero muses. He draws a grubby fingertip along the wooden walls, tracing the echoes of damage threaded through the *Argo*'s innards.

A lattice of hairline fractures, spread through the hull like the branches of a hand drawn familial map. Branches that are now growing in reverse.

'The breaks…' Peleus breathes in unfeigned awe. 'They are repairing themselves.'

'Not the right word, my friend.' Argus takes a long draught of wine, pausing only to wipe the spillage from his beard. 'She's *healing*. That chthonic beast wasn't enough to knock the life out of her. Or the fight, I should think.'

The shipwright and Peleus share a low chuckle, and they are not alone in doing so. In one corner, Theseus of Athens grunts with similarly grimy mirth, and to one side of him Nestor of Pylos grins a toothful grin.

To the other, Herakles the Allslayer listens to their glee without joining it. Reclined against the corner of the hold, back hunched, forefingers propping up his right temple, the Gods' Last Son could well be taken for a statue at rest.

The others talk for some time, lauding each other's deeds in their recent struggle against the Earthborn, and deriding absent comrades for their apparent lack of *andreia*. Jason, predictably, attracts a fair deluge of scorn, though the Huntress of Arcadia is a predictable close second.

Hours pass, and the slivers of sun through the deck cracks lower. The others are gone, taking the life from the chamber with them, heedless of the one remaining soul they scarcely even noticed to begin with.

And then something moves, in the dark of the corner. A large, muscular hand reaches from the gloom, pulling close Argus' forsaken wine before taking a long and languid swig.

When the intruder comes for him, Hylas does not look up. This is not an act of courage. Far from it. The new arrival has stealth on their side, and he is far too engrossed in his work to see them coming.

His master's gear needs tending, as it always does. The daggers and blades need a little whetstone, keeping points sharp and edges keen. Some of their handles need the leather rebound and rewaxed, for the Allslayer likes to grip them tightly. Then there is the club, of course, still marked by Titan blood. Hylas delicately brushes more Eleusinian lacquer over its spiked and knotted head, murmuring the appropriate half-remembered rites as he does so.

The lionskin is always the hardest part. Its hide is impenetrable to any blade, as the legend goes, any blade except the beast's own damn claw. Herakles resorted to killing it without spilling its blood, crushing the beast's skull with hammer blow after hammer blow until such mythic foibles ceased to matter.

And yet, as has been proved time and time again, it is not indestructible. Not to the fell beings the Allslayer faces. Hylas resorts to gentler means, now. His threaded needle slowly yet surely repairs the damage to the gods-touched pelt. The needle is whittled from the Lion's last unbroken fang. A gift from Daedalus, as a long ago mark of favour.

Hylas has more or less finished his darning for the night when he feels the hand upon his shoulder. Too small to be his master's, and too tender. But not a grip he could pull free.

'Mistress,' he murmurs aloud, forcing himself to untense.

'Not so formal, please.' Atalanta steps around to face him, plucking the needle from his hands and setting it down. She gives the Allslayer's other personal effects a cursory glance. 'A lot to do tonight, I take it?'

He takes a moment to think before replying. He may not have a hero's pride or backbone, but Hylas can be perceptive in his own way. Just as Herakles can be wilfully blind in his.

'Lady...' He risks a moment of eye contact. 'Is there something on your mind?'

There is little natural light this late. Littler still that makes it this far down, through the gaps in deck and floorboard. Hylas' eyes are far from sharp, but what is that he sees in the pallid moonlight? What is that expression, passing over Atalanta's face so briefly?

'You weren't there, were you?' the huntress suddenly asks. 'You weren't on deck when Idmon died.'

Hylas swallows. On the rare occasions the Argonauts have any truck with him, it is usually to chide or slight him. This is a new and unexpected avenue of attack.

'I was not,' he confirms. 'May the gods rest his blessed soul. I was with the bard, helping the others carry him aloft.'

Another pause. In Hylas' limited experience, Atalanta does not struggle with speaking her thoughts. Hers is a tranquil soul, but reticence doesn't come into it. She may value her own peace, but she is unafraid to risk it.

'No, I shouldn't think so,' she finally replies, more to herself than to him. 'It was just me with the seer when his life bled away. I was the only one there, Hylas, when he spoke his dying words. I was the only one to hear his last prophecy.'

A clutch of miles behind them, on the stretch of twilit shore, a coiling shadow falls across Idmon's staff. Nothing remains on the island to witness it, but some things that cannot be seen with mortal eyes.

A ragged dark cloak, billowing in an utterly silent unwind. A purring rasp, through arid teeth — not breath, nothing so warm, but the hiss of foetid air escaping a broken tomb.

Far across the bay, in the hold of the creaking *Argo*, Herakles opens his rheumy eyes.

'He used the bow, didn't he?' Atalanta asks, as if she hadn't seen it happen. 'To finish off the Earthborn. He used the bow that slew his sons.'

That very weapon lies in the corner of the cabin, covered by its traveling sack. Even speaking of it draws their gazes its way, and pulling them back takes more effort than is natural.

'Idmon foresaw as much,' the huntress says. 'That he'd draw it, with no other choice. No matter how deeply it would wound him to do it.' She takes a slow and unsteady breath, still hesitant.

'Idmon saw it...' she repeats, 'and he saw what would happen, if he did.'

Far above them, on the topmost deck perhaps, something creaks. Life aboard a ship is never silent. The *Argo* has her own aches and pains, just like any vessel that plies the sea.

'Watch him, Hylas.' Atalanta's eyes curdle with something the squire cannot describe. 'I don't know him like you do, and I have enough to worry about with Jason. But from now on, boy, keep your master close.' She swallows. 'All our Fates may depend on it.'

She is already leaving before Hylas can answer, returning to the shadows she seems to find refuge in. It takes the slave a moment of thought to name the feeling in her eyes. In all their time together aboard, he has never seen it in Atalanta till now.

Terror.

'The damned Hellespont, behind us at last!'

Jason's knife skewers the table, and the yellowing nautical map lain over it. There are far less emphatic and destructive ways to mark one's seaborne process, but as Tiphys has observed these last weeks, their captain can rarely resist an empty gesture.

'And dare I say the journey's hardest stage,' Jason adds. 'With blessed Hera in our favour, and the winds running smooth—' He points to the hand drawn tidemarks on the map, as if he has any real knowledge of such things. '—then the route to Colchis can't elude us much longer.'

Tiphys rolls his two-point compass in gentle arcs across the parchment, tracing out a more convoluted yet more realistic route. One the *Argo* has an actual chance of sailing.

'We have come far, Captain,' the young Dodonian begins. 'But our travails may not be over. Our safest path to the City of Dawn lies down the River Thermodon, from its mouth near the Isle of Ares. And to get there—' He dots a slim passage of water with his compass tip, the gap scarcely visible between two peninsulas that clasp it tight. '—we must take the pass at Cyanea.'

'Cyanea...' Jason echoes, tasting the word. 'I have heard that name before.'

'As have I, my captain.' Tiphys snaps the compass blades shut. 'Though I have not seen the headlands, and I don't know any soul who has. They have... a reputation, among those who ply the sea. Folk call them the Clashing Rocks.'

XXI
THE STORM'S SUMMIT

Before long, they come across the wreckage.

The *Argo*'s cattish wariness was the first warning sign. Neither Tiphys' foreboding, nor Jason's scepticism, entirely prepared them for what they'd found. But like any predator of the seas, the *Argo* knows the taste of blood in the water. Somehow, she has sensed what she has sailed into. That does not bode well.

The torn and tattered detritus surround her. These are not just shipwrecks. Not merely the cold, abandoned carcasses of vessels that never made it home. These shredded, excoriated remains of slain ships drift silently around the *Argo*. Nature's warning to the curious, perhaps. Or its entreaty to other travellers, begging them not to make the same mistakes.

The Argonauts don't need to share their helmsman's insight, or their own vessel's unease, to see this dark omen for what it is. What manner of thing could do this to so many mighty ships of Hellas? And how mad, how foolhardy must they be to even countenance running that same gauntlet?

The only soul not particularly disturbed by this development is Argus, who wiles away the hours on deck by naming the kingdoms each shattered wreck hails from.

Doubtless the Thessalian shipwright believes these insights endear him to the others, earning their rugged respect. It doesn't occur to him how loathe they are to listen, his words only flaying their ragged nerves further.

Mind you, the *Argo* was only drifting through dead wood at this point. When they find the first body, even Argus has little to say.

'Pay them no heed, my Argonauts.' Jason paces up and down the length of the rowers' thwarts, shouting commands and exhortations that aren't quite landing. 'Ignore the dead you see around us. They were not chosen for our Fate. They were not the favoured of Hera!'

As Jason passes him midstride, Herakles tries not to reflect on how easily he fits that shoe. Something strikes his oar mid-stroke, and he makes a conscious effort not to look. Just another piece of naval debris, or another corpse long dry of blood. The sight of the first bulbous, shrivelled body was enough. As was the smell of it, the carrion stench carrying over the *Argo*'s customary reek of sweat and voided bowels. Wondrous, what saltwater can do with endless time.

Jason's sandalled tread breaks the Allslayer's reverie. Herakles gives his oar another steady tug, glancing up as the captain slows to a halt beside him.

And then the shepherd boy does something most unexpected. He doesn't shout another empty entreaty, another vain and venal plea to the gods above. He steps over Herakles' hunched form, sliding past onto the remaining sliver of bench beside him. On larger boats, each oar might be pulled by two or three rowers a side, but the Allslayer has no need of other men's strength. And the *Argo* seems more than happy to do her part, for now.

Herakles does not look up from his labour. And Jason, curiously, does not prompt him. He simply lays his own hands further down the oar – dainty, unscarred and dwarfed by the Allslayer's – and begins to gently help him row.

This goes unremarked among the ship's other crew. With the *Argo*'s newfound zeal for reaching Cyanea – or, at least, its desire to be rid of this nautical graveyard – only a handful of the strongest heroes are doing their time on the oars. Peleus works his blistered hands bloody a score of seats up ahead, while Theseus and Telamon do their bit on the port and starboard sides. The others are up top, or down below.

For a moment, the Gods' Last Son and the man who would be king can speak alone, unjudged by others.

'You are worried, aren't you?' Jason breaks the sweaty silence. 'You are worried we aren't ready for what comes next.'

At his side, Herakles grunts. The oar smashes through another long-dead hull without slowing. 'We have done well to make it this far,' he concedes. 'I'd sooner have Idmon with us, to keep us in the gods' good graces. But… we have done well, so far.' He feels himself loosen, despite everything. It is as if the words surprise himself.

'My dauntless Allslayer.' Jason is actually smiling. How rare that is these days. 'How literal you are. I meant what happens once we're past all that. Once the Thermodon is behind us, and Colchis is open to our hands. You're worried about what will happen to me when we come upon the Fleece. When your oaths to me are finally voided.'

Oars heave. Brine crashes. Growing winds pound the air where their sail used to be.

'You sound… calm,' Herakles finally manages. He has slowed his rowing a fraction to keep in time with Jason's. 'I doubted you even thought about it.'

'About the others, you mean?' Jason shifts position, grasping the oar with an unfamiliar grip. 'And just how far they're willing to follow me? Atalanta was… well, Atalanta… about it, from that very first night in the glade.' He lets out breath through gritted teeth. His arms were never meant for plying the seas. 'But I've come to accept it, these last weeks. They will kill me once the Fleece is mine. Or at the very least, they will try.'

The Allslayer has no ready answer to that. Is it pleasantly surprising, to hear the leader of their quest is so much less oblivious than they all believed? Or even more worrying, that he has let things get this far?

How by the Styx does the boy keep doing this? Keep plumbing some new hidden depth to surprise him, for better or worse, each time Herakles believes he has his measure?

'But not you, I don't think.' The shepherd boy smiles at him tenderly as he gives the oar another hoist. Sweat and splashes of water now mar his face and clothes, and in truth it is no intrusion. It paints him more like the men he leads. 'Not you, Slayer of All. No, I don't think you're brewing up a betrayal. You haven't got it in you, have you?'

Is that a joke? A double-edged one, perhaps. Every joke is half-meant, as Chiron always used to say. That was what made a joke humorous.

'To not sink a blade into my back is one thing,' Jason wheezes, between oar-strokes. 'But would you bring yourself to ward them off? When the daggers are finally drawn, son of Zeus… would you put yourself between me and them?'

Heave. Heave. Heave. The oar churns waves, spreads foam, sprays salt. The Allslayer realises, with cold and sobering clarity, that this is the longest and most meaningful conversation he and Jason have ever shared. The longest time they have ever even spent together.

He thinks of Tiresias' laughing, jaundiced face. Of the golden fire that burns his dreams to ashes. And the dark, foetid shadow he doesn't know how he senses. They are coming, one way or another. No matter what choice he makes.

'There is more at stake in Colchis than your destiny,' Herakles finally replies. 'More than a falling out among heroes. I did not come here to see you all take sides, son of Aeson.'

Then why did you come here, Uncle? he can almost imagine Iolaus asking. Or maybe Megara. *Why did you throw in your lot with this madness? Did you ever even know for sure?*

The oar catches a cresting wave, splashing Allslayer and shepherd boy with a burst of cold Propontis. A rather fitting way for their moment to end.

'Nor to join one,' he finally adds.

Jason leaves him rather curtly after that, with as little grace and subtlety as his arrival. No words are spoken, nor need be. His surliness and stung pride are plain to see, every inch the tempestuous, woundable Jason the Argonauts have come to loathe.

He never mentions these thoughts to Herakles again. The Allslayer will dwell on them a great deal in the coming days, but no further clarity will come.

Looking back, he almost wonders if he imagined it.

He is still wondering this hours later, when the *Argo* and her crewmates are taking a collective rest. The water is open but calm, judged safe enough by Tiphys to briefly let them drift on their earlier momentum. The sky is bare of the mist that dogged them through the Hellespont, but still darker all the same. Even Atalanta's hawklike eyes can't penetrate the gloom, and the others soon learn better than to ask her. For now, all is still, and all is eerily quiet.

Except for the birds. The *Argo* has left most of the murdered wrecks behind her, if not the long-dead sailors. But where carrion is found, it seldom goes to waste. Cawing gulls and terns make the most of the remaining bloated carcasses, swollen and salted to a seabird's ideal taste.

A gaggle of them even harry the ship's topmost deck, doubtless smelling something vaguely fit to eat. Telamon swings his immense bronze shield in upward arcs, trying to smack any low fliers out of the air. The shield is heavy, however, and cumbersome. All the Phthian manages is scatter them a handful of times. And then he puts a hole in the deck with its pewter-edged rim.

Telamon curses, loudly and without shame, dropping the shield to cradle his bruised foot. None of the Argonauts feel like laughing, however. They have defied storms and monsters with heads unbowed and spirits undimmed. But this lifeless, lightless expanse of water, with only the slain and their broken sanctuaries for company, is enough to unnerve even them.

Even Orpheus' usual bonhomie has evaporated. The singer has spent the morning cursing at the gulls and ocean birds that seem to single him out, flying close to perch on the deck or ambling after him on webbed feet. The more he tries to shoo them away, the more determined they become.

Even disregarding the pain of his healing knee, Herakles hasn't seen the man this perturbed since Pagasa. What about this place has got under the Pierian's skin so? The multitude of unburned, unmourned dead?

'Can't you do something about them?' Jason snaps at him at one point.

'And what would you have me do, my captain?' the bard somehow sneers without sneering. 'Call down a flock of doves with my lyre to see them off? Would that please you?'

The shepherd boy just snarls at him wordlessly and marches off to air his temper somewhere else. Herakles watches him descend below decks, before stepping forward to see if he can be of any use.

'Bard,' he begins. 'Are you—'

'*Enough* with it, Child of Thunder!' Orpheus snaps with a zeal his crewmates have never yet heard. 'Just *let* it *lie*, please.'

Herakles actually flinches at the younger man's vehemence. It should take a great deal more to make a man like Herakles flinch.

'Can't you feel it?' the bard whispers. '*Death*, Herakles. Death is right here, all around us.'

Something clenches tight in the Allslayer's stomach. He fights the urge to look out across the water. He does not wish to appear craven, not with Orpheus so close. But a small part of him is afraid of what he might see.

You finally rouse yourself to move again, your oars sweeping flotsam from your path. You propel herself across the cloudy sea, unaided by the Many, with a grace that is almost unnerving.

Once more, your bestial heart seems to sense what lies ahead before they do. Your sacred Dodonian bones live up to their reputation. The hearsay of your prophetic gifts is well begotten.

You have risen above your wounds at last. Your mast is gone, now lying on a long-forsaken seabed. Your prow, likewise, is fractured by a Titan's wrath. But the clefts and fractures that bit into your hull — in short, those wounds that could have truly ended your voyage — are slowly but surely healing over, like moats in the sand when the tide comes in. Fissures are regressing into creases. Rents are coming together as furrows. Before long, the Many won't even know where the breaks used to be.

You broke, but are no longer broken. You still have the strength to hold yourself together, in soul as well as body.

It is not quite the same story for the Many.

Jason's eyes snap upward at the knocking on his door. The shepherd boy has retreated to his cabin, no longer working the oars as no-one remains to watch him do so. Leadership is showmanship, after all. The right act witnessed at the right time by the right souls. That is one thing, at least, he has learnt from his uncle in Iolchus.

'Come in,' he replies evenly. The knock is too heavy to be Atalanta's, but if it isn't the huntress behind the door, then w—

'I do hope we aren't intruding,' Nestor greets him. He steps into the small cabin, lit only by fading lanternlight. Laertes ducks his gangly frame as he follows, his greying head still scraping the wooden rafters, with Argus' squat, potted figure trailing in his shadow.

'Pylian?' the *Argo*'s captain begins. 'You have something to say to me? Something that requires a bodyguard?'

This as a joke, of course. Another doubled-edged, half-meant joke. It is a markedly unsubtle test of the waters, but under the circumstances, Jason feels it is warranted. Three of his 'followers' have appeared in his sanctum, unheralded and unexpected. They have chanced upon him at an inopportune time, when Atalanta isn't here to lend him any weight. That is worrying.

Or they have deliberately picked this moment for that reason, which is more worrying still.

'My friend.' Nestor clasps his hands together with laboured sincerity. A rather wily one is Nestor. 'I know you've had much on your mind, these last weeks. Truthfully, I'm awed by how much is on your shoulders, and how you've refused to let it break you.'

Something flickers across Laertes' face at those words, something that he manages to supress. Almost.

'But as our leader,' Nestor continues, 'it is only right you hear our concerns. It would be dishonest for us to hide them from you.'

Jason feels the faintest stirrings through the deck beneath his feet. The gentlest susurrus, as the *Argo* sedately ploughs the ocean. He waves an assenting hand at Nestor, only for someone else to answer.

'Cyanea,' Laertes interjects. 'The Pass, my captain. You would have the *Argo* take the quickest route to the mouth of the Thermodon, over the shortest stretch of sea. It is a shrewd strategy, I'll mark you. We've had enough ill luck with storms and sea-dwellers as it is.'

Jason decides against raising an eyebrow. 'But?'

'But these waters bear a fell legacy, Thessalian. The mountainfolk of Pelion may be ignorant of such things, but to us Ithacans it is more than folklore. Most of us aboard know the stories, but only now we see the evidence strewn around our—'

'The Pass is cursed,' Argus cuts in, startling the others. '*Something* destroyed those ships, son of Aeson. Something spelled the deaths of all those sailors. The Clashing Rocks bear their legend for good reason, Captain. This is just the sort of unneeded risk that Idmon would c—'

'Don't.' Jason kills that line of thought with a pronated palm. 'Don't bring Idmon into this, shipwright. If you've made your point, we've heard it. Don't hide behind a dead seer's frock.'

He is rising to his feet now, his spirits rising with him.

'I am not doing this lightly, my comrades.' The shepherd boy shoves a pile of detritus off his desk, revealing the unbound seafarers' map once more. The puncture marks from Tiphys' compass blades are still visible across the vellum. Jason points to the long promontories of land either side of Cyanea, and the long and tortuous path a ship would have to take to circumvent them.

'If we refuse to dare the Pass,' he tells them, 'then following the coastline to the Thermodon could take months. *Months.* And every day of that time is a day we could encounter another gods-cursed leviathan to drag us to the depths. A day when another crew of sell-swords could beat us to our goal.'

He turns his beseeching gaze back on Laertes. 'Those are your words, King of Ithaca. It was you who made me see that, right when you pledged your word to me. Word of our endeavour has long left Pagasa by now. Maybe even Thessaly. This is no longer simply about reaching the City of Dawn, my friends. We have to reach it before anyone else.'

'Really?' Argus sneers through jagged teeth. They have never been a picture of health or beauty, but his recent defacement hasn't helped. None of the other Argonauts know what exactly he said to Atalanta, back before the *Argo* left the Doliones' shores. Though they could probably guess the general essence of what he wanted, since that exchange ended with a bleeding mouth and smashed nose, neither belonging to the huntress.

'Is that really the case, *Captain?*' the shipwright continues. 'I thought whatever that withered old stick Phineas told you on Scryer's Folly was the key to our final leg of voyage.' He furrows his brow, trying to affect an air of dissidence. 'Assuming you were telling the truth about that whole sorry business. Or were you just looking for another chance to play pirate?'

Jason glares at him for a moment, wondering why he has to suffer the old coot's presence on his ship. And, not for the first time, what the white-haired malcontent is even doing here anyway.

'Argus' words are rashly chosen,' Nestor concedes. The Pylian's forked tongue is getting quite the airing tonight. 'But his point is true. Passing between the Rocks may be an understandable choice, but it isn't the only option.'

At first, the shepherd boy says nothing, thoughts shifting to this change of tack. Before him, Nestor and Laertes seem deceptively at ease, while Argus hangs back, leaning against the open doorway.

Blocking the door...

He shakes the treacherous thought from his head.

'Please, my friend. Hear us out first.' Laertes moves back over to the sea map, misreading the moment. 'Perhaps we don't even have to make this next crossing by water at all.'

'What?' Jason asks. Did he hear that right? 'You would have us abandon the *Argo?*'

'Perhaps, if it comes down to it.' The Ithacan points to the thin stretch of land through which the Pass of Cyanea lies. 'The isthmus is hardly a long way to go on foot. No matter how woody or mountainous the ground. What is to stop us clambering over to the other side, and then chartering another ship once we return to the shore? Or even taking one for ourselves? Ships do wander these parts, this time of year. More likely lonely message carriers and trade flotillas than fleets or bands of warriors.'

Jason smiles, ruefully. 'And you accuse me of playing pirate.'

'Always, always, the race for your blades.' Nestor pretends to chide the others. 'We have some of the strongest men among the kingdoms with us, my friends. Gods Above and Gods Below, we have the *Allslayer*. As you said, crossing that strip of land would be little challenge for any of us. Orpheus might need a little help, but aside from that, we could even drag the damned *Argo* overground, and put her back in the water on the other side. Then we still have our ship, our path, and time on our side. And the Clashing Rocks are left well alone.'

This... this could be wisdom. The *Argo* has had one tempestuous brush with the numinous already, and that was nearly enough for all of them. Does Jason truly wish to dare another?

The moment seems to stretch; the Argonauts stood before their captain's table, and the young, petulant soul looking back at them. Truthfully, Jason and his erstwhile uncle are not wholly unalike, in mettle as well as face. Though no soul knows either man well enough to see it clearly, there is no shortage of Pelias in the shepherd boy's heart, beneath that misplaced sense of right.

Just as with Pelias, two wolves inside Jason jockey for favour. There is the pragmatism, the lack of pomp and pretence, the ego hammered out by years of mountain life. The part of him Atalanta grew to respect, that she sees in him still.

And then there is the need, the hunger. *Want* is too weak a word for it. The molten urge to take back what was denied him all these years, what belongs to him by right.

The urge to push these 'heroes' away and take no counsel but his own.

Lately, one of those wolves has begun to eclipse the other. It can hardly be helped. A goddess whispers into his dreams, mingling her wants with his own, and the men he shares the *Argo* with do little to shake his lack of trust. The need that drives him, drives them all, is also eating him alive.

Jason looks across their faces for a moment. A diminutive, silver-tongued prince. An unimpressive king of nowhere. And a builder of tricks and trinkets who has long outstayed his welcome.

The weak ones.

The thought strikes Jason so hard, it doesn't feel like his own. On any other ship, before any other captain of a quest, the prospect of crewmates taking their discontent this far would shake their leader's resolve apart. But not here. Not for Jason of Pelion, the destined heir to Thessaly's throne. Not for the chosen champion of Hera.

'Where are your comrades?' he suddenly asks. There is no imagining the sting in his words this time.

'I beg your pardon?' Nestor repeats.

'You heard me,' Jason snaps, snatching up his goblet of water. Something creaks in the *Argo*'s wooden bones, either far above, or far below. 'I can't help noticing we are spare a few souls, Prince of Pylos. Where is King Theseus? Where are the Spartan twins, or the brother-lords of Phthia? Where is *Herakles?* Why are the mightiest and most august men among our fellowship not at your back, adding their doubts to yours? Hm?'

No-one answers.

'I think it is a fair question.' Jason drains the goblet and slams it back down. 'Why do you three skulk below decks, picking your moment to accost me, away from sun and scrutiny? Why are the others – *the strong ones*, the *truly* dangerous ones* – not with you?'

'Jason…' Laertes risks raising a warding hand. A feeble attempt to placate. 'You misread our intent. We are not here to undermine you, my captain. We—'

'We what?' the shepherd boy hits back. '*What?* You finally sense your time has come, as we draw close on Colchis? You finally scent my blood in the water? I can't say I blame you. With so many mightier men aboard the ship, you feel the safest time to strike is now? Is that it? Is stretching the oath you swore worth the risk, if it gets you closer to the Fleece?'

More silence, either wondrous or capitulated. He does not care which.

'Of course, you do.' Jason smiles ruefully, a smile that does not remotely reach his eyes. 'Of course, you do not dare to challenge me above deck, where the others could dare to contradict you. You know that you will have to betray me – betray *each other* – before this quest is over. But none of you are man enough to be the first. None of you wish to start the avalanche.'

Nestor steps forward again, drawing breath for one last try. One last attempt at steering them from this perilous course.

'Save it.' Jason isn't even looking at him now. Kings, slayers and heroes earn their victories alone, after all. That is the scope of his experience, and what examples has he ever had? Only his uncle, whose guile and lack of conscience brought him everything. And his father, whose trust and sense of honour cost it all.

'You think by robbing me of chances to prove myself, you will show me to be unworthy of the Fleece? To be an easy captain to overthrow? I hate to disappoint you, Argonauts. We're not abandoning the *Argo* on some gods-forsaken coastline. We are not pulling her from the water, and enraging her untrammelled spirit even further. We are not dragging her across a rocky headland, and exposing her to attack.'

He thumps a fist down on the ageing map. A gesture that would have been comical indeed if it had followed any other tirade.

'We will sail through the gap at Cyanea, and cease listening to our own yammering doubts. We will pass the Clashing Rocks.'

Night finally falls, but there is little rest to be had aboard the *Argo*.

On the lightless deck, Orpheus of Pieria huddles within his robes where the ship's prow once lay. Ocean life has not ceased flowing with the sunset, however, and seabirds are still taking the time to harass him.

Too tired to even move from his spot, he blows dry air through his panpipes. The birds scatter, taking off across the dark. One of them flies forward. Up, past the broken prow, and out into the night.

There is no land beneath its shadow to mark, no wind to gauge the waves' pull. Not that its cold, crude mind can heed such things. The winged pest flies on. And on. And on.

Wherever its avian instinct hopes to lead it won't matter, not before long. Black, beady eyes do little to penetrate the deeper darkness around it. A darkness that, though the gull has neither the senses nor intellect to notice, is now closing in.

The seabird tries to fly upward, sensing at long last that something is wrong. But its pitiful Fate has long been sealed.

It was sealed the minute it chose to fly this way.

The darkness crashes together. And the bird, like every other soul that dares to pass the Clashing Rocks, is smeared from the face of existence.

XXII
HAMARTIA

The crash does not go unheard. Not quite.

You hear it, *feel* it, in your wooden innards. You feel the ghost of a shockwave through the icy water, scarcely stronger than the waves lapping against your hull. It is a gentle change, nigh on impossible to feel. But feel it you do.

A tremor passes through your oaken frame, the way a creature of flesh and blood would shiver against a sudden chill. None of the Many aboard you feel this, but then none of the Many have sensed what brought this on.

Except for one of them. Not *the* One, sadly. But the one among them with the sharpest senses. The one who earnt those attributes the hard way.

Atalanta's eyes snap open, alert and devoid of rheum.

What has woken her?

Few of her unlikely cohort choose to sleep on the open decks, even when the weather is kinder to them. Ocean winds, with no trees or landscapes to break their flow, can make for cold and salty nights indeed.

But the huntress always rests easier beneath open skies, and her soul was never made to be within walls. Her fellow

Argonauts are hardly pleasant company, not when the sun goes down.

What has woken her?

She stands at the stern of the immense vessel, scanning the horizon while drawing a hand through her uncombed, brine-smelling hair. It has lost little of its lustre, but hasn't felt clean or gentle to the touch in some time. Washing in seawater will do that to you.

The huntress has seldom truly cared about such matters. A life lived in the wild, on the road, allows little time for laxity or luxury. But right now, the freshwater glades and pools of Arcadia's hillsides feel more than a little inviting. What she wouldn't give to bathe away a summer's evening there, the way she and the nymphs used to do as girls.

What has woken her?

She doesn't speak the question aloud, for she has no-one to ask it to. The *Argo* continued to row herself as the sun went down, following whatever course Tiphys tried to impress on her. But night rolled in, the currents flowed in support of her, and she's shown no signs of letting up. They were far from land in any direction, and with no other ships for miles around that weren't floating wreckage, the Argonauts one by one dropped the pretence of lookout duty. Even Tiphys left his station in the end, finally allowing himself to rest and trusting in the ship's bestial heart to keep them on course.

So here Atalanta is, awake, alone, and the only soul aboard whose eyes have any hope of peering through the moonlit night. The *Argo* has not been idle in the hours her crew slept. The most obvious indicator of that is out ahead of them. A line on the far horizon, dividing two slightly differing shades of black.

Cyanea. They have finally crossed the gulf.

So what has woken her?

She closes her eyes momentarily, trying to recall what made her open them. What filled her ears when consciousness had returned?

She pauses. She focuses. She breathes.

It was... a thunderclap. Solitary, muffled, almost restrained. Like a peal of Zeus's own thunder, but closer.

Much, much closer.

Waking the others is an unchallenging but thankless feat. Only Tiphys comes to wakefulness with any real grace, the *Argo's* steersman and interpreter long used by this point to being roused without warning or notice.

Atalanta's efforts receive an unjust share of curses and resistance from the others. Heroes and warriors whose names ring out across the kingdoms, they are ready and willing to give their all while awake. But they do very much cherish their sleep, it transpires.

'What is the meaning of this, girl?' Theseus snarls at her. 'Are we attacked? Why is no-one donning weapons?'

'We are safe for now, King of Athens,' she replies evenly, stepping back to let him stand. 'But we arrive, quicker than is natural, and I believe danger is near.'

She isn't deaf to the uncertainty in her voice, but for all their anaemic anger, the Argonauts don't seem to need more prodding. Hylas and Tiphys scamper down the lengths of their quarters, knocking on low-hanging ceilings, pulling away sheets, and picking at aching tempers. Before long, they are all on their feet, trudging up above the deck with laughably heavy steps. Even Jason is here, leading by sullen example, once someone finally manages to dig him out of his cabin.

Atalanta is readying herself for the inevitable battle of convincing them that a woman senses a peril they don't. Only for a red-eyed, uncombed youth to gently pull her aside.

'What is it?' Meleager asks her. The sound of feet on deck echoes above them. 'What has happened?'

'I can't be sure,' the huntress replies. This is not the first time she has shared a doubt with another Argonaut, but this time feels the most honest. 'But I think I heard something, Calydonian. When we came within sight of the Pass. What if Jason made the wrong choice by bringing us this way? What if the Clashing Rocks are more than a sailor's story?'

'She's no longer rowing,' Argus quietly observes, looking down at the gentle starlit waves.

'Tiphys?' Jason barks, crossing the deck.

The Dodonian screws up his youthful face, evading scrutiny. 'I have no insight to give, my captain. These last days she has been agitated by the slain ships we sailed through. I can't explain her eagerness to move forward this night, nor why she has decided to halt now.'

Behind him, Castor and a handful of the others are muttering. *Omens. Bad omens, mark my words. Idmon would agree.*

Jason pretends not to hear them, spitting overboard, and grimacing as if this only confirms Tiphys' uselessness. But tellingly, it isn't the helmsman who feels the weight of regard upon his shoulders now. The shepherd boy glances around him, seeing Argonauts looking on at him with unforgiving eyes. None of them seem keen to give him the benefit of doubt.

'Well?' Peleus asks, unsubtle threat beneath his words. 'We stand upon the cusp, *Captain*. What would you have us do?'

Jason thinks for a moment, stumbling over the break from Telamon's shield and looking out at the encroaching stretch of cliff.

'We are this close to Cyanea,' he finally stammers. '*Argo* or no *Argo*, we don't have an abundance of time.'

Not that it even particularly matters. The *Argo*'s oars may have fallen ominously silent, but the current at her back doesn't even need a sail to be harnessed. Momentum, and strong wind, are carrying the ship slowly but ominously closer to land.

That same wind now whistles across the open deck. It pulls at robes and loose hair. Atalanta's unbound locks billow in the breeze, as do Jason, Polydeuces and Herakles' manes. Even Argus' wispy white remnants blow back against his face and make him curse.

The breeze smells of brine, old stone… and something else. Something natural, but no longer living.

'Jason.' Atalanta steps back, eyes wide. As usual, her hunter's instincts bring her insight before the others. 'Jason, please. We should turn back, now. We can sail around the peninsula. We can even take the *Argo* acr—'

'No.' The shepherd boy won't even look at her, already walking the other way down the deck.

'*Please,* Jason! The Rocks are not just legend. Think of all the wreckage we've sailed through!'

This is shocking enough for the others, at least. None of them have ever heard the huntress beg for anything.

'I said *no*, Arcadian!' Jason turns back to face her in a rage. 'Does Artemis favour those whose nerves flounder so?'

Atalanta breathes her desperation out, her anxieties ebbing. The face that settles on her is no less unsettling. She knows, of course. She knows the mistake she has made, challenging Jason in full view of the others, these heroes-turned-wolves with their last vestiges of loyalty.

She would defy a ship full of legends if their roles were reversed. If Jason truly needed her to. Seeing her friend not willing to do the same… it wounds her.

Though she wipes all pain from her expression, it wounds her deeply.

'We have the greatest, swiftest vessel in all the kingdoms,' the shepherd boy pronounces, not even looking at Atalanta now. 'And the mightiest of Achaeans crewing it.'

He looks out across the dark water, to the distant line of land. And the gap of night-lit sky, cleaving it in two like a wound. The Pass of Cyanea. The Clashing Rocks.

'To your oars, my Argonauts. Every last one of you. Tiphys, Argus, Orpheus… none of you are spared. Every soul aboard the *Argo*, take an oar. It is time.'

XXIII
THE DARK ROCKS

The Pass stretches in both dimensions. Cliff walls of old, pale stone rise into the sky, higher than a human gaze can follow. This is not simply due to cloud cover. The lands the *Argo* will soon pass through are high. High indeed.

Its breadth is scarcely less astonishing. Any complaints Tiphys has about being relieved of duty are voided once the scale of it becomes apparent. A ship five times the *Argo's* size could make a complete turn, and still have room to spare on both sides. Rowing through the Pass will be no hardship.

If 'Pass' is even the right word to use. As the Argonauts row themselves closer upon placid water, the nature of the place reveals itself. It doesn't resemble two promontories of land, meeting in the middle to leave one meagre passageway. The earth has seemingly parted, willingly or otherwise, at the whim of some fearful power.

What manner of god could do this? Has Ares split the land in two with a blow from his brazen spear? Has Gaia herself, the Mother Of Them All, opened her rock-fanged maw on some divine whim?

And what could a boat full of mortals – malleable, breakable flesh and blood – do in the face of such power?

The Argonauts row at Jason's command. Every hand grasps an oar. Every palm sports sores and blisters. Every back hunches in the oarsman's crouch.

The mouth of the Pass looms closer, the lips of the so-called Clashing Rocks. They stand sedately, stately, over the waves that lap and brush against their feet. They have done so for thousands of years already, and will do so for a thousand more.

Cliffs do not move. They do not crush and mangle sailors into ruin. These are facts, plain and simple. The Argonauts, experienced seafarers many of them, know this.

But none of these truths can coax the recalcitrant *Argo* into helping her crew. Or stop the chills running down any of their spines.

A handful of them – Hylas, Nestor and Argus in particular, struggling with the oars their comrades bear with ease – try their best to stopper their dread. The concerns of their stronger, mightier fellows mostly run along more prosaic lines. Some of them think about how inglorious a place this would be to die. They silently lament plans left undone, grudges left unsettled.

From his station near the front, Meleager tries to ignore the doubt rising in his stomach. The doubt over a quest he should never have joined.

Further back, Theseus pulls his oar in time with the men around him. A small, treacherous part of his heart wonders if this honourless death would be payment for his sins. His final Fate, come round at last.

Across the starboard flank, Atalanta finds herself bottling a silent scream of frustration. It has been long since her self-control was tested the way it has on this voyage. But here, in this lightless, godless place, the Huntress of Arcadia may well die. Unmourned, unfulfilled, from nothing but the stubbornness of proud, blind men.

And at the middlemost thwart, Herakles looks out at the crumbling, towering cliffs ahead of him, and feels nothing at all.

Once they enter, the passage between the cliffs seems even wider. Wide enough to make the *Argo*, vast and mighty as she is, feel insignificant. Not to mention the fifteen souls still aboard her.

Theseus is put in mind of the Earthborn's attack, and his underwater sortie to rid them of the vessel's broken mast. The uncomfortable vastness of the Hellespont's depths feels almost trivial, here. Here, at least, he is not the only one to feel diminutive.

Whatever force broke the cliffs apart did not do so cleanly. It left jagged dips and outcrops in the stone that would look more natural together than apart. These stalactites in repose dot each wall, profusions of rock and calcified dirt, like Great Mother Gaia's very own teeth.

'Great gods...' mutters Hylas from his thwart. The inner cliff walls, distant as they are, have a hideous truth of their own, picked out by the lamentably clear moonlight.

Things hang from the ragged, jagged crags, wedged between them or simply impaled. Pieces of ship. Pieces of people. Skeletons, and their fleshier counterparts. Half-rotted. Skewered. Mangled. Dolphins, sharks, in varied states of decay. Old, old blood, so dark it appears more coppery than red, stains the towering walls in long-dried patches.

And that isn't all. Scavengers flock across the uneven crags, taking what they can find. Crows, gulls, even the occasional rat, scrabbling for purchase among the outcrops. Crabs and lobsters, too, or things that look like them.

Some of them are huge, others too small to even see clearly. But their hunger is what unites them, and amid the aptly named Clashing Rocks, there is no shortage of good pickings.

None of the birds fly, that much Hylas notices. They jump, scamper, and scrabble in the way of the rodents that share their precarious perches.

Why don't the birds dare to fly?

The water around the *Argo* is no better off, with more visceral examples of the wreckage out at sea floating down the length of the Pass. The Argonauts' oars bat most of them out of the way. Most, but not all.

Orpheus stifles a gasp as a suit of hoplite armour drifts by. It lies face down, borne aloft on an unintended bier of shredded driftwood, the bronze battle plate covered by green verdigris. But from the gannets fighting each other to dig their beaks into the chinks and grooves, it is far from empty.

He has always assumed Eurydice's loss — and the dark and shadowed place he'd left her in — had inured him to death and dissolution. What horrors can the World Above hold, after all, for one who has walked the World Beneath?

How quaint, to be proven wrong. It seems the dead can be just as horrifying on either side of the ground.

On the *Argo* glides, deeper into this realm of no return.

The sun is rising at last, silhouetted in the fissure behind them. Its arrival brings little joy, however. Shining behind the vessel's stern, it merely casts the carrion horrors around them in a clearer, starker outline.

Like any natural scar or wound, the Pass's width waxes and wanes. Its scale has an ebb and flow, one the Argonauts are already coming to loathe. Sometimes, the gap between the ragged walls is wide enough for twenty *Argo*s to sail side by side. Wide enough that even Atalanta can't pick out the grisly remains adorning each cliff.

At others, the gap is so narrow that their oars can touch each side. At those points, any notion of turning the ship around becomes laughable. Up close, there is barely room to even steer, let alone manoeuvre. And up close, their cadaverous surroundings are no kinder on the eyes. The few intact bodies and bones drifting through the water are bare, picked clean by sharks and dogfish.

An immense crab slips from its perch, far above the *Argo*. It falls a hundred feet or so, before landing on articulated feet in Herakles' rowing thwart. Strings of spoilt human meat drape from its pincers as it regards the Allslayer with stalked, seething eyes. Its shell and carapace are the red of flayed muscle, the brightest, most vibrant thing in this Pass full of decay.

Herakles pulverises it with the fall of one fist. His rowing doesn't even slow.

The hollowness in his chest has not abated, that heartbeat he is no longer sure he can hear. The feeling that has gripped him since facing down the Earthborn has only continued to spread. Is this how the mangled corpses all around him feel? Is this how it is to be one of the unburned and unburied dead? To have your untethered spirit wander the World Between Worlds, while your mortal shell lies shattered and gnawed?

The head and torso of a woman – a Cretan, perhaps, from her storm-washed clothes – bobs in the unnervingly tranquil waves, disturbed only by the Allslayer's oar. Her flesh may be foetid and eroded, but her face, at least, is covered by a gently flowing funeral shroud.

Of sorts. The shroud in question is a shifting carpet of flesh flies, the morning light glinting off their glossy wings and bodies. They take flight in throbbing bursts, revealing a patch of cream-coloured skull each time.

Jason walks the wooden aisle between the banks of toiling rowers, eyes narrowed, ever vigilant for only the gods know what.

He still maintains that this was the right course to steer the *Argo* down, and will maintain that no matter where that choice will lead them. But he isn't blind to the danger here. To the threat that seethes at them from all sides.

Focus, a long-buried inner voice chides him. *Hours of rumination may solve your troubles, but a moment of focus is what will save your life.*

He smiles to himself at the memory. Chiron's quietly growled wisdom. The exasperated commands which shaped his formative years on the Mountain. The old Centaur watched over him on Pelion's slopes, as he'd done for so many heroes in the making. Until Hera fell to earth and changed his life forever, the shepherd boy had never known why.

Focus! the voice scolds him once more, most certainly his own this time. Jason strains his ears for the root of his unease.

The lap and ripple of waves, broken by falling oars. The grunts and growls of his followers, betraying the growing strains of their efforts. The waspish thrum of flies, alighting on corpses. The groaning creak of Dodonian oak, aching and settling under fourteen shifting rowers. The deep, pulsating rattle of something far beneath the waters, almost tectonic, but subtly rising in pitch.

The…

The son of Aeson freezes.

'Atalanta,' he calls. 'Do you hear that?'

The huntress takes this as her cue to forsake her post, stepping up out of her thwart to join her captain.

'Do I hear w—'

Only for her to stop, mid-word, as she comes to understand what he means.

And that is when they finally see it. The pass between the Rocks is almost four times the *Argo*'s port to starboard breadth. Wide enough to leave a gulf of largely tranquil water beyond the oars' reach each side.

Only… not tranquil. Not anymore. The waters hugging the cliff walls are rippling. Undulating. Subtly at first, but growing louder, and more pronounced.

'Huntress…' Jason begins, fear and uncertainty incarnate. 'What… what is happening?'

As if the truth before them isn't plain to see. The cliffs either side of the *Argo*, towering high into the sky, are shaking.

The Clashing Rocks, as fearful seafarers have long called them, sleep no more.

'Row, my Argonauts!' Jason screams. '*Row!*'

As if they need any encouragement. The rowers' thwarts are a flurry of activity. Those still oaring redouble their efforts. Those taking respite snatch up their oaken burdens. All hope and need for keeping rhythm are abandoned, each member of the quest heaving at their oars as madly and as heavily as possible.

It takes a great deal to unite every soul aboard the *Argo*, but the threat of horrific death never fails.

The water is shaking, now, stirring and foaming and seething. A few unmanned oars – those that the *Argo* deigns or declines to animate, depending on how her mood – are even sucked overboard, taken by the restless water. Orpheus of Pieria nearly goes in too, relinquishing his oar in the nick of time before the sudden shift in force can claim him.

The rest of them try their damnedest to row anyway, though this is far from their only concern. The quaking cliff walls have their own gifts to impart, detritus both dead and alive cascading down from where it is dislodged. A monsoon of carrion rain begins to hammer them from above. Bone fragments. Rotten kelp. Body parts, in various states of decay.

A foul-smelling skeleton crashes down upon Hylas, its bones bound together by more than just sinew. The young squire screams as it lands on him, wailing about gods and nightmares and the evil eye. Meleager is the one to finally free him, hurling the ghastly cadaver into the water. But even he has to look to his own defence.

More denizens of the Rocks rain down on them. Crabs and rats, united by their hunger. Foetid, spidery things with fangs and hair instead of eyes. Yet seem to sense their prey well enough.

A gaggle of albino, blood-eyed crows alight on the deck, flitting and hopping and picking their way towards Atalanta. The huntress spits a curse, knocking two of them off the trellis. A pity she doesn't have her bow and blades to hand.

Jason of Pelion sprints down the quaking deck, down the *Argo*'s exposed spine, heedless of the heroes and princes and kings engrossed in their myriad horrors around him. He slides to a gradual halt, sandaled feet clinging to the sodden deck, before the young presence trembling by the ship's rudder.

'Tiphys!' the shepherd boy shouts. 'Coax her! You must rouse her to move!'

'I can't!' the helmsman tries to shout back. The tumult all around them drowns out his pitiable voice, but Jason reads the words on his lips just the same.

'You *must!*' he retorts, and gives the young Dodonian a slap for good measure. There is no-one to stop him, no-one to even see. 'You *must*, Tiphys! Else we all die!'

He points a shaking finger to the distant cliffs. Or, as it transpires, not so distant.

They are doing more than just quaking, now. More than disturbing the waters at their feet.

'The Pass is closing!' Jason bawls. '*Row, all of you! ROW FOR YOUR LIVES!*'

XXIV
HERE, AT THE END OF ALL THINGS

Waves hammer the *Argo*'s aft and flanks, frothed up by the juddering Rocks. They strike harder and more violently than any natural surge or eddy.

Oars are smashed like matchwood. Or torn from grasping hands. Whitecaps break across the deck, drowning the rowers' thwarts in torrents of spiteful brine.

Theseus roars as he beats his oar, hauling it through unpliant water, how has it not broken in his hands, are his fingers breaking instead, is that his own voice shouting or someone else's, oaken detritus, smacking into him on a cresting wave, by the gods, Polydeuces, why aren't you bloody rowing, I don't need your scorn, Athenian cur, but the ship won't stop shaking, don't look left, don't look right, don't think about those cliffs coming to smear him into paste, don't think about the ranks of dead and decayed that wish to make a brother of him, Theseus is no stranger to fighting and rowing, but when has he ever had to row this hard, when has it ever been this bad, when has any of it ever felt so pointless?

The earth herself is groaning, moaning, grinding together. Leagues upon leagues beneath the colossal cliffs, beneath the ocean that laps around their buried roots, the plates of continents are shifting like gnarled, toothy glaciers. They have done this a thousand times before. Never in those times have they let a living soul pass them.

Why would they start now?

Jason splutters out seawater as Tiphys drags him to his feet, this is not his time, it can't be, it can't end like this, the Queen of Heaven promised him so much more, was it all just a game, was Pelias right after all, but what is that look in the helmsman's eyes, by the World Beneath, Tiphys, if I have to slit your throat and hallow the deck with your lifeblood, I'm going to get this damned ship to wake once more, but is a slayer of comrades and kin who he really is, is that what he needs to keep the Argonauts in line, is that what it will take to rise from his uncle's ashes?

The sun is blotted out once more, occluded by the Rocks' overhanging peaks far above.

The *Argo*'s crew can see straight ahead, when straight ahead is unbroken by their neighbours' arched backs, or the hammering fall of waves.

No, it is not their frenzied imagining. The sea's level around them is being gradually pushed upward, compressed by the onset of two closing cliff walls.

Before long, the waves flowing over them won't even need to break.

Hylas cascades down the length of the Argo, *born aloft by a wave of crashing foam, oh please gods let it be quick, somebody grab him, blood across his brow as the deck smacks him in the face, brine that burns his open wounds, help me Herakles, where are you, but deep down the squire knows the answer, knows the Slayer of All is beyond any of their hopes, Nestor's firm hand pulling him upright, help us with this oar, lad, if you want to live, and Atalanta is seated in this thwart, but her other arm is bent and hurt, and dear gods above, the water is so high, and those cliffs are coming closer, and it takes all three of them to even move the oar through the water, I'm scared, Huntress, I've made a mistake, do you think it hurts to die?*

The Pass is narrowing now. The onset of the Rocks is glacial, but inevitable. Like the closing of the earth's own fist.

There is nowhere for the water to go, that which can't escape from the mouth.

The *Argo* is moving. But the Rocks are moving faster.

Orpheus has no tears left to cry with, all breath knocked from his chest from where he fell, was his lyre in his hands a moment ago, the deck is so wet and sodden, where could it be, the shadow falling across him as Peleus slaps him, enough of your caterwauling, Bard, but the Phthian can barely hold his own nerve together at this point, waves hammering the deck like comets from above, how are they meant to even see the oars, but we have to try, Bard, just put your hands on the oar, that's good, just keep going, crashing wood and waves as Telamon and Castor emerge, pulling Argus' screaming form from his thwart between them, we're running out of time, brother, the ship won't help and we won't be enough, where are the others, where is Herakles?

Far, far above, beyond the towering Rocks and the sky that lies over them, she moves in the airless void. Cold, anaemic sunlight pools in the curves of her crested war helm. A helm that hasn't aged a day since its genesis, yet still looks incalculably ancient. A helm that — like its bearer — didn't come into this world by any natural means.

An aegis of creamy, gilded robe billows around her as she descends, moving in some unseen, unfelt current that owes nothing to the natural wind. But is she truly falling, descending through the sky? Or is the world simply rising up to meet her?

No matter. It is not her own whim that draws her to Cyanea, but the behest of the Fates. Loath as she is to admit it, there are some forces that govern even her kind.

There. Down far below, in the glittering foam. A ship with its own oracular heart, peopled with pitiful, sweating mortals. Divination has never been her gift — not least when compared with some of her kith and kin — but narrowing her eyes shows how most of their pathetic Fates play out. She sees battle scars they've yet to earn, lines of age not yet worn in. She hears their final words, spoken or unsaid, feeling the dying embers of their lives' regrets.

Such tiny, fragile little things.

She cares nothing for their flickering lives. Nothing, save for one of them. A not-quite-mortal she is embarrassed to share a bloodline with. But the signs of Fate are clear; this one has a part to play. A part that shapes all their futures.

A part that cannot end here, at the Clashing Rocks.

She plummets like a blade through the cloud cover, sunrays glinting from the head of her war spear.

The Allslayer rows, and rows, and rows.

The chaos all around him crashes and unfolds, throwing up walls of water that shroud his sight. The roars of grinding cliffs and crying men smother his thoughts, his powers to weigh and reason. And still he rows, no faster than usual, as passionless and stately as a percussive drum.

Another mighty wave breaks over him, drowning his thwart, burning his eyes and filling his ears. He scarcely notices it. Before him, around him, behind him, his fellow Argonauts are fighting to survive. Several of them are hurt. He barely notices that either.

Still, he rows. His back arches and shifts, never breaking poise for a second. The oar heaves and pulls. Heaves and pulls. But that steady, loveless tempo never changes. Despite the driven, frenzied efforts all around him, if anything his oaring begins to slow.

The rising, thickening emptiness *(Herakles my friend my kinsman what are you doing)* inside his soul, the tumour that took root when they scraped him off the Earthborn's broken carcass, is finally breaking free. Free to be witnessed at last.

They have striven with all their might, these dauntless Argonauts, and they haven't been enough. Their best has not been enough. The Rocks are about to clash, and they will take the *Argo* with them.

If the Fates of all aboard *(Allslayer why are you slowing are you insane what ails you)* are banded together with his own, then his conscience is clear. Here, at last, he can let go of a lifetime of shameful memory. A life of oh-so-heroic deeds, lauded by onlookers, who see his legacy as something to emulate, and miss the damned point behind it all.

His back keeps arching, arms still bracing and bending. His oar ploughs the watery tumult, losing haste and power with each stroke.

There will be no falling out among thieves over the Fleece, it would seem. There will be no more tests from the gods, breaking him while preserving him, taking away every last thing he holds dear, honing his body and soul for a conflict that may never come. There will be no day of divine judgement, when he saves his Olympian forebears and discharges the duty he was bred for.

It will end here, at the Dark Rocks, with a death that *(Herakles can you hear me you must up your stroke else we all die none of us are as strong as you)* will be as honourless as it is mercifully swift. Not quite the heroic ending his comrades envisaged, no doubt, but such is the lot of those who walk this path.

Slower, his oar moves. And slower.

The faintest pang of pity ripples beneath his thoughts, that the others will share this grisly Fate with him. Shielding his friends from harm was half the reason he threw in with this sorry quest in the first place, but right here, right now *(Idmon said this would happen if you drew the bow again Child of Thunder please don't give up on us now)* it would seem that his presence isn't going to make a damn jot of difference. How refreshing it feels to finally admit that. What a weight off his shoulders at last. He is the Gods' Last Son, the mightiest mortal to ever walk the earth, and he can do nothing to prevent what is coming.

Waves crash around him, the tectonic grinding practically deafening now. The cliffs have swallowed the sun. Shapes fly and scamper past him, his crewmates cajoling him, urging him, begging him. They have minutes left at best. Seconds.

So much of the Allslayer's life *(Master please think of your friends think of me I know you want to go but not here not like this I beg of you)* has been decided by others, be it gods or kings or the weavers of Fate. But he can, at least, choose not to fight this. He can choose how he leaves the World Above.

His rowing slows. And slows. And stops. The oar is pulled out into the raging current from hands that no longer even try to grasp it.

Fate, as Idmon and Tiresias and Phineas all claim, may well be inexorable. But just this once *(by the gods what is wrong with him Herakles Herakles HERAKLES BY THE STYX WILL YOU NOT HELP US)* the Allslayer is content to let it unfold.

One last twist of the blade, on his own terms. And then it will all be over.

XXV
ANGEL OF FIRE

She falls from on high, as radiant and vengeful as the angel later cultures will revere her as. Time is an underwhelming concept to her senses; she has spent entire epochs watching her siblings and ancestors play with it, unwind it, and slave it to their ends.

But mortal men live stunted lives, their perspectives cripplingly narrow. Time matters to them, because they are shackled by it, boxed up in it, and so she wastes none.

Molten light burns across Tiphys' retinas, the scars still prominent when he clamps his eyes shut.

But he has seen enough already. The silhouette flash-flamed across his vision is one he knows all too well: a helmed, spear-wielding goddess of vengeance, the subject of every desperate entreaty and fearful prayer he has ever made.

If she hasn't come to save them, then it would be better to die here than be exposed to her wrath.

Waves continue to buffet him, but now he ignores them. What he has just witnessed scares him even more.

'Athena...' he whispers, hanging onto the trellis for dear life. 'Goddess of Wisdom and War... please don't find us wanting.'

The storm winds curl around her as she descends. Not even elemental forces have the gall to impede her path.

She lifts her burning gaze, only now aware of the paltry threat around her. Shifting stone that she would have barely noticed without focusing. She has lived for aeons, after all. She has spent century after century watching continents drift.

And before her, the vessel of flimsy rotted oak, that is all but broken already. Such a pointless little thing, carrying pointless little lives. It beggars belief, how the Fates of so many rest on so few.

Her gaze bores into several of the screaming, cowering mortals, their stick-thin bodies and hollow destinies. And then she finds him, the One she was led here for. The One who cannot be allowed to die.

Two pairs of eyes meet across the storm. The goddess's, that billow with life. And the mortal's, that want to close for good. The lineage of Zeus, somehow, is still visible in both pairs.

Herakles holds her gaze, dead-eyed, for another handful of moments. Hands continue to grapple and jostle him, and voices continue to plead in his ears. He notices neither.

And then, not for the first time in his life, he turns his back on a god of Olympus.

The Rocks crash together at last, the impact reverberating through the earth. And this time, the Pass of Cyanea is closed for good. It will never open again.

She rises back into the sky, her demeaning task performed at last. This duty was far beneath her dignity, as her father and half-siblings doubtless know. But perform it she has, and she can now rise above the stench of mortal flesh once more.

Olympus awaits. Others of her kind may take umbrage at her tactics — saving a handful of other meaningless lives that rival gods may have designs and claims on — but she cares nothing for such worries. There is little that can threaten her, and any scant punishment is likely to be swift.

The Allslayer sinks back, lying prostrate on the sodden deck. His dead-eyed gaze trails into the sky.

The few uninjured Argonauts are cheering their miraculous luck through raw throats, the sound less brash than it has ever before sounded. Herakles does not join them, for he can scarcely even hear them.

Some punishment is swift. And some, it transpires, is never-ending.

XXVI
THE CHILDREN OF ARES

The ship grows in her vision, its ragged outline gradually sharpening as it draws near. It moves with no particular haste, its oars working without much urgency. Not a war footing, then. Not a raiding party looking to catch its targets off guard.

But from the size and might of the ship itself, not least the hulking half-clad men of war who bestride its decks, this is clearly not a voyage of peace.

She lowers her crudely carved seeing stone, letting it hang on its leather thong. And then, mounting her ageing palomino steed as gracefully as one hand will allow her, she kicks off back down into the valley.

They will have reached the Thermodon in a handful of hours. That is already too far into her domain for comfort.

'A good breeze,' Tiphys remarks, a fairly pointless remark with no audience to even hear it. 'And the *Argo* is in lockstep with our wishes. Even if we stop at the Isle, we'll make good progress down the river before sundown.'

Not that Jason is even listening, for the shepherd boy has brusquely taken his leave some minutes before. He is already gone, leaving the helmsman at the tiller to curse his impudence, descending below decks to one particular corner of the ship.

He is hardly the first to arrive, of course. A dense huddle of his crewmates is already clustered in the dank hold, all readying themselves to shoulder past the two runtish presences in their way. Jason merely joins the back of the group, his herdsman's frame a step shorter than the likes of Castor, Laertes and Argus.

'I told you to step aside, slave.' That is Theseus talking, though from the growls of vague agreement around him he cannot be the first to make that demand. 'It is not your place to come between us. Argonaut or no Argonaut, I'll step over your broken body if I have to.'

In his short life following the Allslayer's maddening quests and exploits, young little Hylas has faced no fair share of beasts and tyrants. Usually from a distance, mind you. But the building rage of so many heroes, pressed close enough to breathe their spite into his face, is more than he knows how to handle.

The same cannot be said for his comrade, however.

'I don't know how many times we can repeat these words,' Atalanta hisses, long past any efforts at soothing tempers. 'The Allslayer has fallen ill, a malady Hylas believes afflicts his soul as well as body. Be it the work of gods or the folly of man, what he needs is rest. Whatever you need to say to him so badly, let it lie. You are not coming past this door.'

Theseus' growl rises into a snarl, little gentler than a stray dog. 'The gods *favour* us, idiot girl. Half the men among us claim they saw Athena herself! A goddess, descending to help us on a plume of sanctified flame! What ungodly pall could lie over our friend now, of all times?'

The huntress says nothing. Her unblinking gaze bores into the King of Athens, and the vicelike grip on her sheathed knife's pommel only tightens.

'He is my friend.' Theseus takes a threatening step closer. 'My mentor. I will not be kept from him by some Arcadian maenad.' Others growl again in agreement behind him, and for a moment, Atalanta wonders if she'll be the first Argonaut to spill a crewmate's blood.

'She said step back, Theseus.'

It takes Hylas a moment to identify those words as his own. More fool him. He has a half-second to contemplate his imminent death, as Theseus' jawline clenches. Only for unsought aid to push its way through the crowd, with moments to spare.

'Ladies, please!' Peleus shoulders the Spartan twins aside, Telamon's imposing bulk close behind him. 'Do you truly wish to know what happened to the last fool who tried to hurt Hylas? What the dauntless, indomitable Allslayer did to that unfortunate soul?' His smile is lightness enough for the dark beneath the deck. 'I don't think you do, somehow.'

'Something to say, friend?' Polydeuces barks at him, testily. 'For once in my life, I think the Athenian may have a point. We no longer have Idmon to guide us on matters numinous. The Allslayer is bewitched, Phthian. We need to see him.'

Telamon raises a pair of placatory hands. 'And who among you claims to be the judge of that? Long has it been since your path crossed with his, Theseus, as your litany of shames and disgraces attests. And you, sons of Sparta?' He jerks his head at Castor and Polydeuces, irreverent but without malice. 'Your father Tyndareus may owe the Allslayer his kingdom, but don't you two pretend to know him well. How many of you had even met him before we reached Iolchus?'

No-one answers for a moment, and Peleus presses the advantage.

'Look at us, my friends. Look upon your fellow Argonauts, and assuage your doubts. Telamon and I have fought at Herakles' side. More than once. We stood with him at Troy, to bury Laomedon's shame and rescue Hesione's honour. We sailed with him to Themiscyra – the very shores we now approach – and helped him battle Hippolyta's finest bladeswomen. Look on us, my comrades, and tell us if you think we don't know our brother in arms.'

For a moment, no-one speaks. Only for a question to dribble from Argus' lips, as anarchic and insidious as the grubby little shipwright had doubtless hoped it to be.

'Why not let our captain decide?'

Hylas is not tall enough to see over his comrades' shoulders. Once the heroes and noblemen turn their murderous focus backward, away from him, all he can do is listen to their words and extrapolate.

In the moment, all the squire hears are shifting feet, and the shepherd boy's disembodied words of farewell.

'All of this is pointless. Leave the Allslayer be, for now.'

And with that, the lot of them disperse, like silt running when the waters come again. All but the Phthians themselves. Have the huntress and the slave traded one battle for another?

'I know that look, Hylas.' Peleus' gaze scrutinizes him harshly, but this time not without kindness. 'I don't know what it is you're not saying, but please don't try to cover our eyes. I'm not Jason, and my brother is not Theseus.'

'What we said back then.' Telamon gestures to the now-empty corridor. 'Those were not just platitudes. Please, Huntress. We know Herakles of old. Let us see him, and let us swear upon your patroness Artemis. We will not speak of what we see.'

Atalanta looks between these two brother-warriors, weighing up the sincerity of their words with the trouble that giving into them could cause.

'Anyone can hide from a foe, lady.' Peleus' certainty never wavers. 'But no-one can hide from a friend.'

He does not open his eyes when they enter, for he has not closed them since they left him here. He cannot muster the effort to do so.

Phthian musk invades his nostrils before Peleus can even grasp his shoulder. Around him, other presences move about the room, but he does not look up to see them.

'Allslayer,' Telamon breathes. The word carries an intriguing mix of feeling: a man on the edge of worry, holding fast to his love and confidence. 'It is good to see you, kinsman. You... you worried us, back at the Rocks.'

A pregnant pause, that neither party knows how to fill.

'But we made it,' Peleus chips in. 'You gave us enough oar, it turns out. Enough to get by. Tiphys is still babbling about the speed of that final push. Reckons Pallas Athena swooped down from Olympus to save us. And now he has the rest of them parroting the tale too.'

Before them, Herakles still says nothing. Does nothing. The silence ensues once more, filled only by his friends' unsaid worries mounting.

'We are coming upon Themiscyra, my friend.' Telamon broaches this last attempt at reviving him. 'We near the Isle of Ares. That is a saga in need of retelling, no?'

The Allslayer's eyes flick briefly upward, the movement brief enough to be almost imagined.

'Themiscyra,' he repeats. The word is devoid of breath or feeling, almost mouthed.

'Indeed, my friend.' Peleus' hopes are briefly lit. Is he coming back to them? 'Though not from the northern promontory, thankfully. It is the south-eastern bay Tiphys is making for. He is adamant that we stop, no matter what Jason and I tell him. Supplies, he claims, though I think he's too proud to simply ask for a night's rest. Regardless, we'll be far from any of the Isle's cities. With the Fates on our side, we'll be gone before the Amazons know we're there.'

Telamon watches the Allslayer intently as Peleus speaks. None of his brother's words seem to be landing, however. None of these thoughts and observations are ringing in Herakles' ears.

'Themiscyra,' he finally echoes, one last time. His most expansive moment is to pull his legs close to him.

And then to roll on one side, curled in a semi-foetal ball, with nothing else to say or hear.

'A spell,' Peleus reasons, when the three of them are back outside. 'It can only be. Peleus and I have seen its like before, but nothing this potent. Never on one such as *him*.'

He jerks his head toward the chamber they have just left, too unnerved to even breathe his friend's name again.

'You are truly sure of this?' Atalanta asks, arms folded. 'I don't know what or who I saw, when the Rocks started to close… but something does not ring true here.' And indeed, it doesn't. She has walked in the company of nymphs and goddesses, after all. She has seen how perilous a spell can be, up close, and none of them have ever looked like this.

'*Trust us,*' Telamon tells her, a little too forcefully. 'Have you ever walked the slopes of Themiscyra, girl? The Daughters of Ares know many things, lore and secrets between them and their god. Believe me,' he adds, ruefully, 'my brother and I have seen it.'

Atalanta looks at them for a moment, before deciding to let it go. Truthfully, she is not sure which explanation she dreads most.

'We sail in the direction of their Isle,' she surmises, 'and the best of us is laid low by some fell sorcery.'

'Exactly.' Telamon reads her hesitance as capitulation. 'It doesn't bode well, Huntress. However fleeting Jason and Tiphys want our stop to be, we may have to take more from this Isle then raided spoils.'

Atalanta's eyes wonder briefly back to the small hold, where Herakles still rests, then back to her Phthian comrades.

'I had an unwelcome feeling you would say that.'

The huntress' words seep through the walls of Dodonian oak, into the Allslayer's low-ceilinged chamber.

'Master…' Hylas fills the goblet with the *Argo*'s last vestiges of fresh water. Which tale should it be today? 'Will you not tell me, master… tell me of the Tenth Labour. Tell me of the theft of Geryon's Cattle.'

For a moment, nothing moves. Hylas thinks back to what Atalanta told him in the Hellespont, her confession of Idmon's last words. The truth of that secret is playing out now, for all to see.

But then, like an avalanche of tumbling boulders, Herakles rolls back around to face him. Bloodshot eyes hit the slave like a pair of falling comets.

'Leave me,' the words ooze from his half-closed mouth.

Not even Tiphys is foolhardy enough to pull the *Argo* up to beach level. They drop the anchor stones in open water – in the shadow of the Isle's most towering, jutting headland – and the chosen few take a small boat towards land.

No few men among the Argonauts would relish the chance to test themselves against Ares' warrior daughters. But time has abraded these men harshly, their travails in the Pass and their unnerving salvation fraying what little remains of their nerves. There is little on the Isle to tempt many of them from a night of peaceful slumber. This mission of exploration, or more, will comprise of only four souls.

Jason leads them, a role even he cannot slink away from this time. With him comes Atalanta, the most adept of them all at scouting foreign ground. And with them come the brother-lords of Phthia. Peleus and Telamon have been here – and fought their way back – once before. Their presence on such an expedition is invaluable enough, even without Atalanta's insistence that they come.

Meleager pressed them to join, but the huntress hadn't been so willing to oblige.

'You should keep watch over the Allslayer,' she explained at the time, to the Calydonian's deflating hopes. 'The others may try to disturb him again, and Hylas won't be enough to keep them back.'

Meleager nodded, realising the huntress wasn't going to shift on this stance. And then, from nowhere, he clasped her upper arm with surprising tenderness.

'Be careful.'

They leave the rowboat in a wooded hollow, stealing their way across shingle, shrubland and eventually dirt. None of them have Atalanta's wildland gifts, but the huntress' path leads them upcountry by a route as occluded as it is direct.

Before long, the four of them have reached the top of the grassy headland, giving them a treasure of a view in either direction. One side looks out over the boundless sea, wine-dark in the noonday sun. The other leads inland, down a gently falling valley towards a long, dense wood, dotted with islands of clear greenery and lonely marble roofs.

'And not a soul to be seen,' Jason muses aloud to the midday air. 'What are those places?' he asks, pointing. 'Halls?'

'We need to get out of the open,' Peleus growls, instead of answering the question. '*Now*. We are woefully exposed up here.'

Jason shakes his head at the Phthian's testiness. Both brothers have been particularly on edge since their arrival, for reasons the shepherd boy can only guess at. Whatever. Their problem, not his.

'I thought you said they wouldn't hurt us,' he tries protesting, following the others down the slope.

'They won't attack us out of hand,' Telamon explains without turning. 'Not without provocation. But they are their own people, with their own ways. Provocation to them might look like something else to us.'

Jason digests this for a few moments. 'Could you and your brother being here be construed, to them, as provocation?' He is fearfully lucky that his smirk goes unnoticed. 'Your last visit to this isle was hardly a triumph of diplomacy, after a—'

Telamon wheels on him, towering over the shepherd boy while still standing further down the path from him.

'Peleus and I *need* to be here, *Captain*. If you want to survive this day, you would do well to listen to us.'

She watches them squabble and bicker, her flint-sharp eyes following them as they sink into the forest glades. She isn't sure what rankles her more: their impudence, at believing they could strut across her island's southern mesas and somehow escape detection? Or their lack of discipline, too engrossed in their quarrels to move in lockstep or watch the skyline?

Her horse is long forsaken, freed from his bridle and left to make a run for home. He knows the way well enough.

She steals her way down the woody mound, every path and passage known to her like a childhood secret. She'll have a dozen chances to overtake the intruders, or cut them off outright, before she even reaches the bottom.

It is simply a matter of biding her time.

*

'How would they react if they found us?' Atalanta asks, an hour or so into the forest.

Peleus shakes his head, helping the huntress jump down a small gully. 'They are not one people, not in the way outsiders believe. Think of the kingdoms and city-states of the Achaeans, all woven into the tapestry of Hellas, but with their own identities and foibles. The Amazons, from what we saw on our expedition, are much the same.'

A little way behind them, Telamon is picking his way through a clutch of thorns and bramble with little luck. His ursine bulk is not made for exploring dense woodland. Jason, as befitting a child of Pelion, is faring a little better.

'The Themiscyrians are the most prominent,' Peleus continues. 'The largest of the tribes, who rule from their citadel in the north. The first among equals, you could say. The Lycastians hold the Isle's westernmost coast. They are said to be seafarers that put the Ithacans to shame.'

Something snaps, in the depths of the forest. The Phthian freezes, and the huntress' nose wrinkles as she scents the air.

Nothing.

'And then there are the Chadesians,' Peleus finishes. 'They claim no part of the Isle as their own, wandering the plains and lowlands. Even among their own kin, the Chadesians have... a reputation.'

Atalanta vaults a half-fallen oaken log, its verdant moss camouflage the brightest thing in the wooded clearing.

'You are avoiding my question,' the huntress ventures.

Peleus snorts, kicking aside the log rather than jumping it. 'I have no answer you wish to hear, Huntress. We found some among their number to be reasonable. Some were quicker to anger than others, as is the case in any *polis* or kingdom back home. But there isn't a woman on this isle I would want to cross, Arcadian. Not without good reason.'

Only Atalanta's attention, as they near the clearing mouth, is slipping loose. The forest before them is growing deeper once more, though they can just about hear the murmur of waves up ahead. It mingles with the rustling of leaves.

'Who among them are renowned for their witchcraft?' she asks.

His first tentative steps on deck are halting. Listless. He makes his shaky, uncertain voyage to the trellis, feeling the unwelcome tingle of blood pouring back into his legs.

And sure enough, here it is. The Isle of Ares stares back at him across the bay, majestic and mighty and deceptively inviting.

He has not been here in some time. Even looking at its outline from afar evokes bad memories.

'Master?' a hesitant Hylas asks from behind him. His relief at seeing Herakles up and about is subdued, weighed down by what this development could mean.

'Themiscyra has not changed,' the Allslayer muses aloud. And then, sensing Hylas at last, 'When did they leave?'

The slave swallows, unwilling to guess where this is going. 'A handful of hours ago, master.'

Herakles takes a moment to digest that, the calm sea breeze playing with his greying curls. His thoughts, leaden and cumbersome still, begin to turn once more, stately and laborious.

'And the others remain aboard?' he asks, softly.

'They do, master. They rest, all but Orpheus and Meleager.'

The Allslayer steps away from the edge at last. There still seems a sense of dreaminess about him. A haze that won't quite fade.

'Prepare a boat, boy.'

They have finally reached the clearing, leaving the forest and its many unseen eyes behind them. And yet the feeling of being watched isn't so easy to shake.

'I was right,' Jason pronounces, when they draw near the small marble building. 'This must be a fane of some sort. To whatever gods these succubae pray to.'

Atalanta chooses not to challenge that remark, examining the nearest wall of battered white rock. Whatever stone relief was carved into the wall here is long gone, washed clean by years of rain and wind. To her eye, it may indeed have once been an altar. But like every other shard of civilisation on this isle they have passed, it looks to be nothing more than a disused ruin. A forgotten remnant of a happier time.

Even a soul as well-travelled as hers feels a little lost here. It isn't an unwelcome feeling.

'I *saw* it, I'm telling you.' Telamon's hissed entreaties break her reverie, as the two heroes of Phthia catch up at last. 'I think someone, or something, is tracking us. Through the wood, certainly. Perhaps even earlier than that.'

At his side, Peleus suppresses a wry half-smile. 'My brother, if our Arcadian friend sensed no such thing, then I highly doubt our blundering would h—'

He snaps around, dagger drawn, a heartbeat behind the huntress' own reaction. Atalanta's bow is already nocked and battle ready, aimed squarely down the clearing, where Jason stands, dumfounded.

He doesn't move, doesn't speak. And the dagger at his throat doesn't waver.

'Hail, Daughter of Ares.'

Peleus advances step by halting step, hands open to display a lack of weapons, his eyes never leaving the Amazon holding Jason. Telamon stands his ground, not breaking eye contact, not making any movement that can be construed as a threat.

Both men are only wearing leather for armour, their weighty bronze battle plate stowed back aboard the *Argo*. If this meeting ends with blades or arrows, they will find themselves woefully underdressed.

Jason twitches in the newcomer's grip, saying nothing, Adam's apple shifting beneath the shadow of the Amazon's dagger. The lethal point hovers at the base of his lower jaw. One quick thrust will put it through the shepherd boy's brain.

'Not one more movement, any of you.' Even her voice is a bladed threat, a thickly accented barb that carries as much fortitude as malice. 'Weapons on the ground. Now.'

Atalanta briefly bridles under the gaze of both Phthians. If she lowers her bow, then they have nothing to stop Jason's throat being slit.

'Of course, lady.' Peleus reluctantly drops his knife. Telamon does the same. 'You have our apologies for our trespass.'

'*Trespass?*' Jason echoes, as loud as he dares to raise his shaking voice. The warrioress ignores his mewling, keeping her blade pressed firm as she continues her calm demands.

'And you, little maiden. Away with the bow, if you would.'

Atalanta bottles a brewing curse, letting the string snap back and tossing the bow aside. There ends their uneasy stalemate, it seems. Unless Peleus' silver tongue can see them right.

'We have come to these shores in good faith,' the Phthian explains. Though only Atalanta notices, he is inching fractionally forwards again. 'We are a band of heroes and lords who call ourselves the Argonauts, and we are in need of supply and shelter. We have no quarrel with the queendom of the Amazons, nor do we seek one. We come to Themiscyra with open hands and honest hearts. We ask for nothing from your people but fellowship.'

For a moment, nothing moves. The dark-eyed lady of war holds Peleus' imploring gaze a little longer. Between them, Jason continues to hide his mounting fear.

Only to skid to the stony ground, nerves aquiver, as she releases him.

'Am I to trust the word of an Achaean?' the Amazon suddenly asks. Her blade is still pointed at Jason, who now tries his best not to scamper between his Phthian comrades. 'You are not the first men from the mainland to spin such a tale, outlanders. And all men, we have learned, can lie.'

Both Peleus and Jason look ready to reply, one of them measured, the other reckless. But thankfully someone else beats them to it.

'I can vouch for these men,' Atalanta claims, stepping forward towards the warrioress and her drawn blade. 'I, too, sail aboard the *Argo* with them, not as a retainer but an equal. If their word is not sufficient, is mine?'

The Amazon holds her flinty gaze for a moment. And then a knowing smile dawns across her face. She seems no less threatening for it, however, and makes no effort to sheath her dagger.

'I should think so, Ward of Artemis. Many among our people know of Arcadia's little foundling. The orphan of choice, instead of circumstance. Welcome to Themiscyra, Atalanta of the *Argo*.'

The huntress' face creases for a moment, not quite sure how to process such an unfeigned moment of praise.

'We didn't catch your name,' Peleus adds from further back, trying to ignore Jason hiding in his shadow.

The newcomer finally sheathes her dagger, reaching up with the same hand to undo the binds holding her hair in place. It falls, an ungainly mass of braided russet locks, framing a face creased with more than just lines of worry.

It is difficult to guess her age at this distance, but to Atalanta's eye, the Amazon has passed at least her thirtieth winter. Maybe more. Certainly no fewer.

'If you seek *xenia* from my sisters, Achaeans, there are subtler ways to go about it.' She takes a handful of steps forward, now her turn to move slowly and without threat.

'I am Sybele, daughter of Myrrina. Once warlady of the Storm's Eye. Once warrioress in waiting to Queen Hippolyta.'

The Argonauts digest this in silence. None of these titles and accolades mean much to them, but this is clearly no untested youth or novice they have happened upon.

'Once?' Jason pipes up, scenting a baited hook to bite at.

Sybele's shadowed eyes drift to him, before she reaches with her left hand to unpick the glove of cured leather covering her right. With a little effort, she pulls it free at last, revealing an empty space where her palm and digits should be. The severed stump below her wrist joint is covered by long-dried scarring. A sword or axe blow, most likely. Clean enough to take the whole hand in one go.

'Once,' she confirms.

Peleus and Atalanta share a brief look, bewildered — or perhaps amused — at how this Amazon managed to subdue their captain with nothing but a butter knife and no free hand.

Sybele turns her back on them abruptly, walking back down the path to the next stretch of woodland.

'You had best come with me, outlanders. We will see what the word of an Achaean is worth.'

After so many testing hours manning the *Argo* — a task he was never built for at the best of times — even this small paddle boat taxes what little strength Hylas has left. Not least when his passenger seems unwilling to do anything but stare ahead.

Getting off the ship was laughably easy, with most of their fellow travellers too battered or shattered to give a damn. Only Meleager tried to dissuade them, for reasons the young Calydonian was strangely reticent to share. In the end, he stood to one side, more worried about defying the Allslayer than whatever had driven him to impede them.

In time, master and servant reach the lip of shoreline. Runnels of sweat, brought into being by the dipping sun, course down Hylas' back and torso. Herakles, for his part, seems unmoved. He hasn't spoken a word to his slave since they set off. In the short trip across the water, he has scarcely even looked at him.

It isn't immediately obvious which route Jason and his cohort have taken, not that the Allslayer seems particularly bothered in tracing it. Instead, he makes his own way downcoast, towards a point on the horizon where the trees recede and the ground hardens.

Waves softly lap, at the edge of his senses. He is faintly aware of some sound in the air up above, the mumbling murmuration of a distant summer storm. The tidal monotony of his own breathing barely carries above either sound.

'You rarely speak of the Ninth Labour,' Hylas breaks the serenity with his shrill tones, risking a glance at his master's face. 'The one that brought you here before.'

Herakles keeps on gently walking, not stopping or even turning to acknowledge him. Words seem to finally slip from his mouth of their own accord.

'We came upon the Isle by night,' he says to the empty air. 'From the northern reaches, not this coast. We made landing within a stone's throw of Themiscyra herself. We could see the city's evening torches from our boat.'

Behind them, the waves continue to lick away their silty footsteps, the outlines of their passing receding more with every breaking front.

'Telamon and Peleus were with me, as were seven of their chosen warriors. Myrmidons, all. Pledged to die with blades in their hands. Only it didn't matter. We were met before our sandals had even touched the sand. They met with us, champion to champion.'

'Queen Hippolyta?' Hylas risks interrupting.

The Allslayer shakes his head, though Hylas is too far behind to notice.

'She wasn't queen then,' he softly murmurs. 'She'd yet to win the Ruler's Mantle in combat. But she met with us, among a host of her sisters and favoured warrioresses.' He almost smiles a rueful smile, at the distant memory. 'They met us, and we told them what we'd been sent to find. The most pointless of common trinkets. The girdle that the Lady Hippolyta wore around her battle dress. Nothing more, nothing less.'

He has stopped, now, looking up into the sunlight sky, lost in memories he'd hoped never to relive again. Hylas could just as easily not be here, or have never been born.

'And Hippolyta… Hippolyta offered it to us. Blood of Olympus, she *offered* it to us as soon as we'd explained. No exchange of insults and blows. No sense of misplaced pride. She saw the desperation in my face, saw my unwillingness at doing another of my cousin's sordid tasks. And she *offered* me the accursed girdle.' He exhales, the breath low and shaky. 'Only that would have been too easy.'

The Allslayer lapses into another long silence, a silence filled only with his own deafening thoughts. Hylas doesn't need to hear them to guess them. He has served this man long enough.

When it becomes clear that no more insight is coming, he asks what happened next.

Herakles looks at him, as if noting his presence for the first time. As if the diminutive squire has no place appearing in his dream.

'Hera happened,' is all he says.

Sybele leads them to another lonely stone dwelling, its lower storey broad enough to hold almost twenty souls, but its upper spire made for just one. A watch tower, perhaps. Doubtless from where she saw the *Argo* coming in the first place.

Five of them singularly fail to fill its bleak, empty majesty. Five aren't quite enough to dispel the loneliness from its walls.

'You are the only Amazon any of us have seen since we arrived,' Atalanta notes, the words dancing on the edge of a challenge. 'Even accounting for how far south on the Isle we landed.'

Sybele looks at the huntress for a moment, and then at her three companions. Even relieved of their weapons, she cannot quite bring her guard down. Now she weighs up what to reveal, and what to keep hidden.

'The Isle finds itself short of denizens, this season,' the warrioress finally replies. 'My sisters have their own wars to wage. Queen Hippolyta has sailed south, with the Gale's Bite and the Spear's Fall, against the Bebrycians. The Lady Amycla was summoned to Ionia's shores, to answer a debt of honour, and has taken the Night's Ruin with her.'

'But not you?' Peleus pensively asks.

Sybele hesitates, as if bringing herself to keep talking. 'Cleomene, daughter of Lyrelaï, now leads the Storm's Eye in my absence. I've no doubt she'll make as fine a warlady as I.'

Jason can't help himself a little smirk, still smarting from his humbling in the clearing.

'So why have you been forsaken?' he dares.

If looks could kill, the son of Aeson would drop dead this very moment. But Sybele simply raises her truncated arm once more.

'I cannot fight, or shoot, to the standard my queen asks of me. I yearn for *kleos* on the field of battle, same as any of my sisters. But my hunger for glory would only put them in danger. And that, son of the Mountain, is not acceptable.'

Jason blanches a little the Amazon's elegant riposte, or maybe at how deftly she has sussed his heritage.

'And duty is duty, outlanders. Someone must keep watch over the southern shores,' Sybele continues, moving to the slit of window in the chamber's marble wall. 'In case the Fates send us boorish Achaeans across the waves.'

She is facing the sea now, so her smile is something the Argonauts sense rather than see. Telamon tries to latch hold of this moment of levity.

'These boorish Achaeans will gladly leave your shores, Daughter of Ares. As soon as we've had some time to rest. And refill our larders and waterskins, if we may.'

Sybele looks over her shoulder at him, raising a wisp-thin eyebrow. 'Is that so, hero? You truly darken our door to rest and recuperate? Nothing more?'

'Nothing more than that, warrioress.' Telamon studiously holds eye contact, silently hoping the gods will forgive this lie. At his side, Peleus feigns interest in the floor mosaic.

Atalanta, nursing the arm she sprained at the Rocks, says nothing.

They have wandered further inland, now. The sounds of the shoreline are long behind them, the sun's blistering bite blocked in part by ghosts of cloud cover.

The Plain of Doias, Hylas has heard this master call this place. It stretches almost as far as the servant's gaze, hugged by a line of forest on one flank and a steep drop down to sand and sea along the other. There is no sign of any life that Hylas sees. No Amazonian warriors springing from the warrens between the tree trunks. No Atalanta, Jason or Phthians barrelling across the sand towards them.

Just the Allslayer, advancing deeper into this island of secrets and threat, and somehow barely seeing or noticing a thing.

The ground beneath their feet is dirty, but thankfully dry, like a memory of long-ago cultivation. But what lies beneath the dried sediment worries Hylas most.

That, and the fact that Herakles won't admit it. Won't even acknowledge it.

'Master,' the slave says, for the umpteenth time. 'I know what I see. We are walking over—'

'Rocks,' the Allslayer dreamily replies from up ahead. 'Just rocks.'

'*No.*' Hylas is done letting this go. Whatever has called his master to this place, it is time to put a stop to it. For both their sakes. 'These are human remains, master. We walk in a place of death.'

Herakles doesn't respond, doesn't even stop. It is as if he hasn't even heard.

Enough of this.

Hylas drops to his knees, ignoring how the ground stains them. He scrabbles over the nearest patch of uneven earth, pulling away clods of dried dirt, ferreting like a beggarman with no-one to witness his mania.

And sure enough, he finds the one thing he hoped he wouldn't, the one thing that will prove his point. The ridges and bumps that must once have crowned a skull, that once formed the outline of a human face. Left to rot and wither along an Amazonian shore.

And that isn't all. Hylas pulls out a drying, fraying, tendril of weave. All that remains of the dead man's clothes, presumably. All that has withstood the sands of time. Year after year of Themiscyrian sunshine has bleached away the colour, but the faded heraldic outline is one that Hylas would recognise anywhere. For he has seen it so many times before.

Most recently, on the banners carried into Iolchus by Peleus' and Telamon's retinue.

The sigil of the Myrmidons. Phthia's foremost clan of warriors.

Hylas drops the streak of fabric in silent horror, only now looking up from his surroundings. The Plain of Doias stretches off ahead of him, and far into the distance, he can make out Herakles falling to his knees.

He knows this place. Of course he does. How could he have forgotten it?

The Allslayer's lips are moving, something he is scarcely aware or in control of. His preternaturally sharp ears make out the sound of running feet, as Hylas tries in vain to scramble to his side.

'You're here...' Herakles breathes. 'Of course, you're all here... and you've been waiting, all this time...'

'Master?' Hylas hunches down to his level, pulling himself close. The wind is beginning to blow now, making his unwashed clothes shuffle and shake.

'They were unburied, you fool,' Herakles goes on with his murmuring. Exactly who he is talking to isn't clear. 'Unburied and unburned, no libations poured, no funeral games held. No passing down of the *oikos* from father to son. Left here, left to wither, just dust across the Plain. Their last breaths borne upon the sighing wind, unheard, unwitnessed... unremembered.'

And that very wind is growing now, carrying clouds of ashen silt in billowing wisps. Hylas pulls his travelling shawl tight, as a chill owing nothing to the weather strokes his spine.

'It is me,' the Allslayer breathes, the calm and oblivious eye of this brewing storm. 'It is me they want, after all these years. They have waited for my return.'

'Who have?' Hylas practically shouts. Herakles ignores that distraction, answering the more relevant question instead.

'I could not save them,' he whispers. 'I couldn't shield them from Hera's wrath. And here they have waited for me. For the man who left them to die.'

Atalanta's gaze travels subtly to the window, noting the distant change outside.

'Well now,' Jason muses from his end of the table. 'It has grown a little cold for the season, no? And where has the sun gone in so short a time? When we landed there was scarcely a cloud in the sky.'

At his side, Telamon and Peleus' eyes darken a fraction, their faces as unreadable as they can manage.

And at Atalanta's side, something passes over Sybele's face, so quickly the huntress may have imagined it.

Perhaps.

'We should go, master!' Hylas' words are stolen by the roaring wind. 'Back to the ship! The others be damned!'

Even if the Allslayer could hear him, he wouldn't have listened. The gale is tearing at them now. Screaming into their faces. Herakles makes out the blurry outline of faraway trees, bent over by this surge of winds. But that is all he sees.

Great clouds of sand and silt billow around them, tossed up by the howling gale. Master and servant are pelted by silken grit, bent double, shielding eyes from a wind that won't abate. The Nemean lionskin is pulled tight around Herakles' form, its hide scoured by a million grains of sand.

But he opens his eyes, after a time. He knows he must, without grasping how. He knows what dread sight will await him. He does so anyway.

Clouds of wind-wafted dirt fill his vision. Every so often a torrent of it hammers into their faces, but each time they pass the corners of his vision, they form shapes. Impressions.

Faces. Each one a face the Allslayer has long tried to forget.

Autolychus. Deileon. Phlogius. And finally Sthenelus, the indomitable son of Actor. The Phthians who followed Herakles here to seek the girdle, all those years ago. The ones who, unlike Peleus and Telamon, didn't made it back.

They speak to him, in their own way. The sibilant gusts of wind keep on hammering their ears. They sound, if you stop to think about it long enough, a little like human words.

Heraklessssssssss...

The Allslayer is down in the dirt now, blown over by the wrathful winds. He can't see Hylas, can't see his own hands in front of him, can't see which way is up and which is down.

Sssssssssslayerofall...

Somewhere beyond the edge of his hearing, Herakles makes out the sound of Hylas' screaming. It sounds little different from a child in distress.

'I can't find you!' he shouts at the top of his gods-given lungs, unsure if Hylas or the unquiet dead are who the words are for. 'I don't know where you are!'

Wemustfleeeeeeeeee...

Totheboatsssssssss...

Wemustfleetheamazonsssssssss...

The Allslayer gasps as he inhales a cloud of silt. He pushes through the nearest ashen wraith, gale winds bludgeoning him from all sides, and begins to stagger in the direction of Hylas' wails.

Sybele surges to her feet, knife aloft. She knocks her bench to one side with her swiftness.

'What treachery is this?' she snarls. 'What craven sorcery? Is this your doing, Achaeans? Have you brought the *miasma* of your gods to our sanctuary?'

Atalanta is already up, guard raised, though with no weapons to hand the gesture is gallingly futile. Telamon jumps to battle readiness, fists up. Peleus and Jason follow him a moment later, the four Argonauts united at last in facing down their Amazonian host.

And outside, through the slits in the pale stone walls, the sky continues to flicker and darken. The distant winds are still potent enough to shake the stone table.

'I received you in good faith,' Sybele says. 'I gave you the benefit of my doubt, and this is how you repay me.' She smiles, utterly without mirth. 'More fool me, for trusting the word of an outlander. More fool me for letting a filthy Achaean darken our shores. I see your game, Atalanta of the *Argo*. Lift whatever spell you've cast upon Themiscyra, and I will let you leave this place with your bones unbroken.'

The huntress draws a breath to reply. To plead their case, and urge Sybele to see this matter clearly. Only someone else gets there first.

'*Hypocrite!*' Peleus bawls, smashing the table so hard he actually cracks it. 'You talk of *witchery*, of putting a curse on your squalid home, when *you* and your blood-maddened harlots are the ones who have bewitched our comrade!'

Sybele takes a step forward, the ice of her rage growing colder in her veins. 'Breathe another word, hide-clad brute, and I will hack you into ribbons! No man slanders the Daughters of Ares and lives to tell the tale!'

'*Then tell us what you've done!*' Peleus roars, ire and spittle flying from his lips. '*Tell us what you've done to Herakles!*'

Silence greets this explosion of anger. A charged, unmoving silence. Atalanta's only movement is to slowly look into Peleus' eyes. A moment passes, as the Phthian warrior realises what he has just said.

'*Herakles?*' Sybele gasps, barely able to cover her own shock and outrage. 'You Achaeans have brought *Herakles* to our realm?'

Atalanta tenses, ready to fight. It is all she has time to do.

Sybele puts her on the floor.

The huntress must have blacked out for a second, because she is next aware of the wall hitting her head. She is down in one corner as Peleus grapples with a blur of flailing hair and tight robes.

Peleus hits the ground as Telamon attacks. The first brother has at least disarmed her, knocking the serrated shortsword from her grip. Telamon lasts all of seven seconds trying to pummel the warrioress like a prize-fighter, before Sybele rolls onto his back and locks her arms around his windpipe.

'*Hnnh!*' he gurgles, hurling himself backward against the nearest wall, trying in vain to crush the Amazon beneath his bulk.

Sybele replies with the keening, ululating battle cry of her people. Only for it to twist, and caterwaul, into a scream of agony. She slides from Telamon's back like a puppet on severed strings, crumpling to the floor in a listless heap.

Her own battle blade is buried, hilt deep, in the muscled flesh between her neck and her shoulder.

And behind her... Jason, son of Aeson, his face and clothes flecked with a hundred scarlet speckles.

It is over before Atalanta has even processed it.

Telamon pulls his lethargic brother upright, coughing from a bone-dry throat. Jason has frozen in place, unable to move, transfixed by what he has just done.

At their feet, Sybele fails to suppress a groan of pain. A groan that becomes an unashamed cry. Blood slowly pools across the mosaic floor tiles, running in rivulets down the runnels in between.

'You stupid child,' Peleus curses. 'See what you've done? She offered us *refuge*, you bastard! And you stabbed her in the back like some mongrel bitch!'

Jason is talking, but the words make no sense. Shock and shame strangle his tongue, as he launches into a score of muddled sentences to justify so craven an attack.

'Enough bleating,' Telamon grunts, shoving him aside. 'Atalanta? Atalanta! Help me staunch the bleed.'

The huntress' awareness snaps back into place, and she complies, ashamed by her own lack of focus. Peleus has torn a swathe of fabric from his chiton, rolling it into a makeshift bandage. The three of them press it down against Sybele's wound, and press it down hard.

The Amazon half-gasps, half-roars, in reaction to this newfound agony.

'Don't talk,' Telamon growls. Blood is soaking through his fingers, too much to clot cleanly. 'Gods Above, you really are a stubborn broodmare. Stop exerting yourself.'

At his side, Atalanta helps Peleus rip more fabric into swaddle cloth. Sybele's eyes have drifted shut, her face pulled into rictus of pain.

But somehow, through it all, her lips curl in an unlovely smile.

'You… fools…' she rasps through a worryingly hollow breath. 'You've… doomed yourselves…'

'Indeed so,' Peleus replies with a sardonic edge. He risks lifting the bandage to inspect the wound, but it is still bleeding as profusely as ever. 'We've stoked another war with the Daughters of Ares, and we'll likely all water the earth for it. We are quaking in our sandals, the four of us.'

'No…' the broken warrioress rasps. Her lips are inches from Atalanta's ears, and the huntress can hear the fear in her voice all too clearly. 'The blood, they… they'll smell… the War God's… blood…'

Atalanta's eyes meet those of her Phthian comrades. Standing apart, Jason of Pelion has gone pale as ice, folk tale after folk tale flying through his head about what happens to those who break the sacred codes of hospitality.

Beneath them, Sybele smiles the last smile of her life, knowing her slayers are soon to join her in death.

'We… are not… the only children… of Ares…'

And like that, she slackens, all tenseness fleeing from her corpus.

Peleus has the dignity to gently lay her head down, resting it on the bloody marble. He clasps his right shoulder with his bloodstained hand, a warrior's salute to a worthy foe.

'You cur,' Telamon hisses, rising to his considerable height and turning back to face Jason. 'You honourless, wretched, *cur.*'

The shepherd boy says nothing, does nothing, weighing up whether to own his mistake or stand by his actions. But Atalanta raises a finger before any of that can happen, shushing the three of them and turning back to the slitted windows.

'Do you hear that?' she asks. 'The storm outside... I think it's stopped.'

A silent pause, as her companions strain their lesser senses to follow hers.

'So it has,' Peleus concedes. 'But what is *that?*'

Atalanta shakes her head, unsure... and then she hears it. All too well. The noise of battle, of metal striking metal, untold leagues away yet growing closer with each maddening second. Only, no. That isn't quite right. That is not the sound of swords beating shields. Those are...

Wings. Wings made of metal.

Half buried in dirt and nightmares, Herakles hawks up some grimy seawater. He is vaguely aware, through brine-burned eyes, of Hylas' prone form a little way off, gilded in filth and seaweed.

They are gone, then. The shades of his first expedition to the Isle, doomed to haunt the Plain from not being laid to rest. Of course the Allslayer's return to these shores disturbed their peace again. How long had they waited here, for their fearless leader to return for them?

A flicker of overhead shadow ends his maudlin reverie. Then another, then another. Herakles cranes his neck upward, just in time to see them spear through the clouds. Snatches of gleaming, tarnished bronze, shaped like death and braying like beasts. He knows that sound. Oh, gods of Olympus. Of course he does.

They were supposed to be dead. Dead, or at the very least scattered. But where else would they go, anyway? Where would their primitive urges take them?

Here, of course. The Isle sacred to the god who gave them life.

'Hylas…' Herakles croaks through an abused throat, shaking his comatose slave to life. 'Hylas!'

The squire comes to, immediately coughing up some phlegm and sand. 'M-master?'

'We need to get off this isle,' the Allslayer urges him. 'It's the Birds, Hylas. It's the accursed Birds!'

XXVII
A Bronze, Awash with Blood

'My friend,' Orpheus asks, rubbing sleep from his eyes. 'Is something the matter?'

'The *Argo* is growing more restless,' Tiphys replies, fussing about his oracular effects. What has disquieted him so? 'In her soul, I mean. Something has stirred its spirit into unrest.'

'What in the Furies' name does that mean, helmsman?'

'It means,' Tiphys snaps back, finally pulling a wad of bound incense sticks from a stoppered jar, 'that something dire could well be soon to happen. And right now, our captain, huntress and two of our best men are unaccounted for.'

'Not just them,' a voice adds from behind them, making them turn. Meleager has clambered up to join them on the topmost deck, a little out of breath from trying to get here quickly.

'Herakles is gone,' the Calydonian says. 'And Hylas with him. They left while we were sleeping.'

'To the Isle?' Orpheus exclaims. 'Whatever for?'

Only something else answers the bard before Meleager can. A distant shriek of braying, metallic hunger carries on the wind, from the distant Isle of Ares.

'Tell me,' Tiphys says, 'that I was the only one to imagine that.'

'Barricade the doors!' Peleus barks, pulling up Sybele's upturned marble bench to do just that. Telamon helps slide it across the doorframe, while Jason, still half shackled by self-paralysis, pulls a flimsy wooden pallet into place behind it.

Atalanta is in the upstairs tower-chamber, ransacking chests and cupboards for anything useful as weaponry. The tower top has a higher, clearer view of what is coming to kill them.

'They're upon us!' she calls.

Something crashes against the obstructed doors, shaking the makeshift barricade. Something frightfully strong, and from the screams that pierce through marble, frightfully hungry to match.

Several somethings.

'Damn it!' Telamon snarls, grabbing a paralytic Jason by the arm. 'Do something, damn you. Help us brace the d—'

The *d—* in question explodes, the bench and crates hurled across the hall. The Phthians are hurled with them, just two more pieces of refuse smashed aside by their unseen attackers.

Unseen no longer. Jason's eyes can scarcely track the blur of bronze rage that cascades into the room, its tongueless cry deafening and reeking. Another brazen blur follows, and another two after that. Each is just as swift, and just as furious.

The son of Aeson screams, all thoughts of playing to his audience forgotten. He would never have jumped out of harm's way — his reflexes are too dull, and the Birds move far too swiftly – but it doesn't matter. It isn't him they have come for.

The first Bird soars past him, its wings of serrated bronze batting him aside. Jason howls again with pain as the wingtips slice his shoulder, a howl that mingles with the Birds' shrieks of hunger not yet sated. The first Birds alight upon Sybele's bloodied corpse, lying prone across the soiled mosaic tiles. And then, with the frenzy of rabid wolves, they begin to eat her.

That ghastly sight, at last, breaks the crumbling dam of Jason's resolve. He can no longer differentiate the Birds' screams from his own. Terror and exaltation fill his ears with no distinction.

He is still screaming when Atalanta grabs his bleeding shoulder. The huntress pulls him back towards the chiselled steps, Telamon leading the bruised Peleus after her. The first few Birds seem busy, fighting each other over Sybele's butchered remains, but more of them are flying into the hall.

One Amazon won't feed them all, and Sybele's is not the only blood they smell.

'To the tower!' Atalanta urges them, wiping Jason's vitae from her hand onto her tunic.

In truth, 'tower' is too kind a noun for the warlady's topmost chamber. This hollow spire with its cold, empty terraces is no place to make a last stand. Peleus and Atalanta drag their stunned comrades after them, all the way to the upper room where Sybele presumably lived.

And here, in the cold confines of an Amazon's bedchamber, four warriors of the *Argo* prepare to sell their lives dearly.

'Heads down!' the huntress calls, not that she has any need to. Even Jason has the wherewithal not to show his face over the parapet of the balcony, as if the flashing forms of incoming Birds aren't enough.

There are, however, more pressing problems downstairs.

Telamon makes ready to drag the bedframe across the entrance, only for his brother to chide him for the effort.

'You want to brace the door again?' Peleus snarls. 'The bloody walls barely stopped them!'

'Then what, by the gods of Olympus, would you have us do?' Jason snaps, strangely petulant. It cannot end here, not like this. Not when he has survived so much already. The Queen of Heaven foretold of so much gr—

Something bright and bronze and piercing splinters the door. One savage thrust is all it takes, and then the foul fowl is through, beak and talons bloodied, right there in the room with them.

Or not.

'This is insane,' Telamon growls, as he follows the other three on their climb. Crawling up the length of a tower roof is mere child's play to Atalanta, and no shepherd of Pelion is a stranger to a steep scramble either.

For two mighty but cumbersome Phthian warriors, it is a rather different story.

'We can hardly hide!' Peleus hisses, a little way below the huntress. 'They're not exactly going to—'

Blade noise screeches out from the tower chamber below. The Birds are clearly not happy at being cheated of prey.

'We don't have to,' Atalanta hisses back. 'If we can just slip down to the ground without them seeing us…'

She never gets to complete the sentiment, assuming she even wanted to. The tower shakes. Their hearts stop. The Bird is topside, hurling itself through the air. And then crashing into the meat of the tower, buckling wood and scattering stone.

The huntress does not pray to Artemis to deliver her, because Artemis is not that sort of patroness. She rears, and she empowers, but she does not nursemaid. She punishes the predatory, but rarely cherishes the helpless.

Atalanta has a half-second to scream, but events, once more, overtake her. A blur of swarthy skin and filthy hair flashes past. And then the Bird is falling, screaming, as Telamon's immense weight bears it quickly yet gracelessly to the ground. Whatever power lies in its brazen wings can't shake that ballast, not least when that ballast is pounding both its fists into its metal body. These Birds can break, then. They can break and bleed like any mortal.

The throaty screech of Telamon's unwilling steed is heeded well. Suddenly, the Birds are all around them, pouring out through the top of Sybele's tower or just flying in from overhead.

'Drop!' Jason screams, from his precarious perch. *'Drop!'*

And the son of Aeson does just that, his sweaty palms slipping from his hanging point and plunging him to the ground. A mistake that would have gotten him horrifically killed, if Telamon's own reckless fall to earth hadn't scattered the nearest clutch of Birds already. When Jason finally strikes ground, he does not scream. That cannot be a good sign.

Peleus is the next to fall, though his descent isn't quite so voluntary. A Bird hones in on him, mid-flight, sizing up a fresh meal. Brazen feathers cascade from metallic plumage, fired across the air like darts, and the Phthian has little hope of dodging them all.

They strike his midriff, biting deep. Leather is no protection, and neither is human skin. Peleus' roar of agony almost drowns out the Birds as he plummets, and his attacker swoops down on wings of bronze to finish the grisly work.

Oh no, you don't.

Atalanta is the last one hanging from the tower. Her fall is more controlled, more agile, than anyone else's. Her feet hit the mossy earth, as the monster is about to bury its beak in Peleus.

She is alone. Unarmed. She has a second to act.

Her hair spills free as her blade strikes home. It is inches long, whisper-thin, too slight to even see clearly. The hairpin, that has held her growing locks in place these last months aboard the *Argo*. One of the few remaining ties to her Arcadian past.

Driven deep into the Bird's metallic eye socket, it is all the weapon she needs.

The howling scream jolts Peleus back awake, as dark and primal as something out of Tartarus. It is not one scream, he realises, but two.

The Bird's scream, the one that was about to eat him alive, crashing back with something speared in its eye, even as its brazen kin turn on it in cannibalistic fury.

And Atalanta's scream as she tumbles backward, drenched with molten ichor spurting from the wound she just inflicted.

The huntress is down, her valiant deed merely buying them another moment of life. A shadow falls across the sky as another Bird takes wing. It is done eating its own kind. Two wounded mortals are a far finer feast.

And then the Bird explodes, smashed from existence by a bolt of percussive force. Burning pus and crumpled bronze fountain in all directions, as the missile that did the deed plummets end over end back to earth.

It crashes down in the dirt by Peleus' head, a roughly hewn weapon of old, lacquered pine. A weapon that has slain a hundred gods-touched beasts, and will slay a hundred more.

Gods of Olympus, Peleus thinks. *I know that club.*

He hurtles across the clearing like a gold-maned thunderbolt, haloed by the sun's rays shining at his back. They cast his form and outline in auric majesty, blurring his features in Peleus' tearstained eyes.

A man-shaped lion. A lion-shaped man. Or a god wrought in human form, wearing a pelt of honey-coloured fur.

Herakles shatters the first Bird with the fall of one fist, not even stopping to fight it. He spins as he charges onward, taking a swathe of fired feathers to his billowing lionskin, before completing the turn and punching another bronze head clean off. Retrieving the club doesn't even slow him, merely another flowing move in his hurricane of unlife. He pulverises two more monsters with falling blows, kicking a third into the tower hard enough to shatter stone and metal. A tight backswing crushes a fourth attacking his blind spot, before he beheads the fifth, six and seventh with one sweeping, arcing blow.

The flock is taking flight once more, this time to evade as well as encircle. The Stymphalian Birds — for these are, of course, the same numinous fowl the Allslayer drove from

Arcadia's mires — are as ravenous and incensed as ever. But they are wary now, sensing an apex predator in their midst.

Bronze streams down on Herakles like a rain of blood and sinew, shards of shattered metal and torrents of burning ichor. He pays neither any heed, stopping for a moment to pull Telamon to his feet.

'How did you...' Peleus stammers. 'How can you—'

One limping Bird isn't so quick to put to air. Herakles tosses Telamon his club, heaving the brazen menace up like a still living trophy.

Only to slam it into the earth with a meteor's force. What's left isn't even a broken body. It has come apart absolutely, like a flattened beetle.

'We go. *Now*,' he growls, taking back his club a little too forcefully. 'Hylas is dragging our boat round.' He takes one last look upward, to the remaining Birds that are circling, scenting another opportunity to fall on them.

And then, pausing only to scoop up Jason and Atalanta's unmoving forms over each shoulder, the Allslayer leads Telamon and Peleus back into the woods.

Laertes breathes out a curse as his blisters burst again, leaking pain and fluid each time he heaves his oar. He is the best oarsman on the ship behind Herakles and Theseus, as the other Argonauts have come to accept, but not even he can shunt the damn *Argo* this close to a shoreline at speed.

But Ithacans don't complain about such things, not least when they are on the water. Their king is no exception.

Laertes calls out through a hoarse and ragged throat, a drowsy attempt at keeping the other rowers in step. Theseus and Nestor are old hands at this, and the Spartan twins have the decency not to complain. But whatever it was that spooked Tiphys so utterly to begin with, whatever drove him to rouse the others and set them to suddenly row, they are none the wiser.

The Isle of Ares looms ahead of them, growing behind the *Argo*'s splintered prow. Laertes is far too practiced to let his gaze wander – absent minds breed shoddy rowing, you see – but the half-awake murmurings around him are getting a little too worrisome to ignore.

'What the bloody hell is it?' he finally snaps, craning his neck up his thwart to see over Polydeuces' shoulder.

'That patch of sky, above the eastern coves,' Meleager's younger voice answers from somewhere behind him. 'Are those… vultures?'

The gap between them all widens. At first, Telamon and Peleus are simply falling behind. Then, they are barely moving at all. Blood seeps onto the sand from the clutch of metal feathers embedded in Peleus' side. Much more of that and he'll barely be able to stand.

'Come on, brother,' Telamon urges him, clasping Peleus' arm around his own shoulders. 'We're nearly at the beach!'

'Gnnnnh,' is the other Phthian's reply. 'We should… have brought… the bard…'

'Don't talk, you fool. Save your damned strength!'

Telamon spies a break in the treeline ahead of them, that leads to open ground and the shoreline stretch they left their rowboat on.

And behind them, he hears… he hears something best not dwelling on.

The Allslayer sets them down on the earthy ground, sparing Atalanta a curt nod before slapping Jason awake. She pulls him upright as he splutters, and neither comments on their saviour's dirty, dishevelled appearance. Or the trails of tears smearing his weary face.

'Go.' He jabs a thumb down to the beach, where a small figure is pulling a battered paddleboat to shore. 'Hylas will get you to the *Argo*.' And indeed, the ship in question is looming in their sight, gliding at worrying speed far closer to the shoreline than a vessel that size has any right daring.

'What about you?' Atalanta asks, nursing her burned torso with her free hand.

'Telamon and Peleus need more time,' Herakles answers, already striding back upward. 'I will give it to them.'

'But y—'

'*Go!*' the Allslayer roars. '*Get to the gods-damned ship!*'

What sense it makes, in bitter hindsight. What a sick, twisted sort of sense.

The Fate denied him among the Rocks is not so hard to elude, after all. The details may have changed, but the ending will be the same. One last bow, before he leaves the stage on his own terms. One last service he can perform, saving his closest comrades, before the darkness claims its due.

He barely even sees them draw close, one of them clasped in the other's arms, because he is barely even seeing any of it. A brotherly hand grabs his shoulder, urging him to join their flight. One of them might even be pleading with him. He cannot say for sure.

A Bird flies down at him through the canopy. Its beak and claws don't even land, smashed from its flight by the club's fall. Another crashes down to the forest floor, flailing featherless wings and charging him on foot. He clamps its snapping maw closed with one hand, ripping its head from its articulated neck. A flood of blistering magma-blood pisses over his arm and shoulder. It is nothing to him. Nothing at all.

The shorn head makes a fine weapon when hurled with enough force. It spears through the next avian fiend to assail him. The headless body, with less elegance, crushes two more into oblivion.

Peleus and Telamon are gone. They must have made it down to Hylas at the shoreline.

Or maybe they were never really here at all, just a figment of dream. Put on the Isle by his mind's own artifice, to justify what he is about to do.

Hylas' feet bleed and burn as he scampers back through the glade. The others are in the rowboat, and from here their escape is their own.

For most of them, at least. Telamon bounds across the forest at his side, lengthier strides pulling him ahead of the short-legged slave. Peleus is in the boat, with a shepherd boy and huntress to watch over him. Whatever the Allslayer said to them about buying them time, Telamon is not about to let his friend face that nightmare alone.

And both of them are worried enough about him already.

The sounds of cawing, dying Birds fill their ears as they draw closer. But what they hear screamed over it, in an all-too-human voice, chills both of them to their cores.

Another brazen freak dies beneath his club. And another. And another after that. More of them fall upon him from the sky, all trying to make it past him and not one of them succeeding.

They form a blurred melange of copper flesh and death screams, another many-headed Hydra for him to slay. He stops seeing their beaked faces, their burning metal eyes. But has he ever truly seen them, any of the men and monsters Fate has pushed him into battle with? Has he ever truly looked at those he slaughters? All those years of life and Labours, for the whim of bored, petty gods. Did any of it mean a damned thing?

He rips out a brazen feather lodged in his collarbone, crushing it between two fingers. His bow and blades are back aboard the *Argo*, and the club and Lionskin are all he has to keep him safe. The former he casts to one side, hard enough to shatter the next Bird that flies too close. The latter he tears away with one hand, flinging into the dust at his feet.

At last. At long, long last. Long overdue, and not a moment too soon. Shadows fall and flash across him as more Birds circle overhead. More of them are landing, now, sensing the end of their fight for food. Sensing the time for the kill is at hand.

No more quests. No more Labours. No more prophets, singing of his destiny. No more Eurystheus, laughing at his wounds. No more Hera, burning down his life time and time again.

No more. He has paid his due at last. He has given his all. He will choose his Fate, and the Fate he chooses is this one.

'*Kill me, then!*' He shouts, falling to his knees like a broken, drained suppliant. '*Just kill me, you bastard things! JUST KILL ME!*'

XXVIII
ACROSS DARK WATERS

Time passes in a staccato of sights and sounds. They flash across his pained subconscious in a searing tide, devoid of context, jumbled from their order. There is no rhyme or reason to any of it. Just spurts of awareness and oblivion that hit him like boulders.

That, and the roiling undercurrent that ties them together. A twisting, crushing sense of shame.

Get him to the boat, someone is saying. Hylas, perhaps, if Hylas had a raw throat and Phthian accent. *He's bleeding fast. Cover him with the pelt.*

Wetness runs its slippery fingers across his torso, a blazing, agonising wetness. He senses, rather than sees, the sweaty hands that grab him and hold him still. Still from what? Is he thrashing in place, where he has fallen? Is the deck pitching and swaying beneath him?

Or is the world quaking around them all, in outrage at a Fate he tried to change?

Something forces its way out of his throat. It doesn't taste like spit, or feel like sick. It is thick, coppery, and makes his guts heave. It tastes of impiety and guilt.

Please, my friend, his mind pleads. Or is someone else speaking? *Apollo's arts are as your own. Please, do what you can for him.*

It is colder now than before. Colder, and the blindness in his eyes feels more eternal. This does not feel like Hades, those dark shores he has visited once before. This feels much, much worse.

I am a Bard, he hears, or thinks, or feels. *Not a healer.*

Someone, somewhere, is weeping. The voice is subdued, heartbreakingly so. It sounds resigned, almost... funereal.

Somehow, against a lifetime's familiarity, against the intimacy of these last months, he cannot place it. It could be a man's, or a young woman's. It could even be a child's.

I can lose anything, it says, and he doesn't need ears to hear its truth. *Or anyone. But not you. Oh gods... not you.*

A salty breeze. A creaking deck. The sibilance of breaking waves.

Something else fills his senses, and this time it is not silence. A keening, crackling wail, one he knows from the swamps of Stymphalus. A hundred wails, in fact, overlapping without pause.

Bronze glints and flashes all around him, visible even to his unseeing eyes. More human shouts of alarm grow in recompense, and the world's pulse begins to rise.

Tiphys! another familiar voice bellows. *Someone help him! Shoot the damn thing down!*

And then it is too late. A weighty presence crashes to earth beside him, dropped from above by blooded brazen talons.

The presence screams out in pain and terror. The screams sound like rent flesh and pouring blood. Like carrion, being eaten alive.

Row, all of you! the first voice blasts at him. *Or we'll all go the same damn way!*

When the shadows part again, his whole world is on fire. Every nerve, every particle... all of him burns.

A part of him cries out, with no voice. Another part of him welcomes it.

If he thrashes, he'll open his wounds again. Is that Theseus' voice? It cannot be. Theseus is far from here, cleansing Troezen's plains of ne'er-do-wells, slaying beasts that skulk in dark labyrinths. And he's still just a boy, not even an *ephebe* yet, but the young grow up, after all, and time passes swiftly when you don't stop to—

It isn't that, another voice in his head replies. *This is a fever. Whatever the root, all my effort will be for naught if it doesn't break.*

In the midst of his eyeless, earless fugue, he wonders what this means. And if he even cares.

Oh, enough with it, someone adds. *You saw what happened. He's nothing but a mewling coward. Let him perish. The blame for all this rests on him.*

In time – in formless, eventual time – another soul joins him in the emptiness. Without eyes to see, or ears to hear, he is at a loss as to how he senses them. But sense them he does, either way.

Is that Iolaus he feels, out there in the dark? If he could remember Iolaus' face – or who Iolaus is – then perhaps the answer would reveal itself.

But no. Those dark curls of hair, that cold yet nurturing face… Is that Alcmena, his mother? He hasn't seen her for far too many years, has no way of knowing if she even still lives.

But Alcmena's arms have never been quite so pale. Her eyes have never shone so dark, ox-like, ringed with flawless lines of kohl. And she never wore a gleaming diadem like that.

It is not a question of when, son of Zeus, she tells him. *But how…*

XXIX
IN THE NAIAD'S DEN

And here they find themselves, cremating another Argonaut, in another place untouched by man. Congregating once more on a strip of lonely shoreline, the dipping sun framing the moment in their minds forevermore.

Pegae, Laertes believes this peninsula is called, but he cannot be sure if that is true. In their helmsman's absence, the Ithacan has taken up roost at the ship's tiller. Sailor he may be, but the geography of the east eludes him. And with no oracular or mystic insight of his own, he will never command the *Argo* the way Tiphys did.

At least with Idmon they had a proper corpse to burn. There simply isn't enough of Tiphys left for a conventional burial.

The savaged carcass the Birds left of him can scarcely be considered a body. His excoriated, half-eaten remnants are covered by a shroud of royal Thessalian yellow, one last semblance of funereal dignity. That shroud is eaten away by the flames, mingling with the stench of charred fat and flesh. The gods, it is said, glut themselves on that stench.

All that will remain of Tiphys, son of Hagnias, will be his still-warm ashes in the wind. That, and the dried pool of Dodonian blood that gilds the *Argo*'s topmost deck.

Fourteen souls remain of the crew that sailed from Pagasa. Thirteen of them are back aboard their ship, while one remains standing in the sand.

Herakles knows he cannot wait much longer. Soon they will lose the evening light. The *Argo* needs to cast off. There is only so long he can forestall this moment.

Leaden feet carry him back, almost of their own accord. He climbs back up the creaking gangplank as fast as his fading wounds will allow, stepping out onto the deserted deck as dusk reflects off the shallow waves. It always seems so peaceful when they lay the dead to rest.

'Back at last,' notes a voice behind him. The Allslayer turns, slowly, on edge but with no real alarm. Even without recognising the voice, this is a confrontation he has been expecting from the moment they escaped the Birds.

No point in running from it. Not that he even wants to.

'It's a relief to see you up and about, at least,' the newcomer observes, with little warmth or affection. He takes a couple of steps forward, out from the shadows, into the amber light. A giant, almost as big as Herakles himself. He took a fair few scars upon the Isle of Ares, but his injuries weren't as bad as some. And his craggy, stocky features haven't changed.

'Telamon,' the Allslayer begins. 'What you saw, when you came upon me in the woods…'

The Phthian floors him with one punch. Herakles sees it coming, but makes no move to block it, or even to evade it. He lets Telamon knock him down, the deck hammering him in the face as he falls.

'I thought Jason was an honourless mongrel,' Telamon tells him. 'But you…'

The Allslayer opens his mouth to speak again, pink spittle dribbling from his gums. But Telamon pounds him again, fist to cheekbone, sending him sprawling a second time. And he refuses to defend himself a second time. This is what he deserves. This is the *least* of what he deserves.

'How could you?' Telamon is incandescent. '*How could you?* How could the man we've followed have fallen so low? How could your *andreia* have finally run dry after all these years? *How could you do this to us?*'

He doesn't wait for a response this time, nor does he wait for Herakles to rise again. His kick catches the supine Allslayer in the stomach, sending him rolling down the empty rowers' banks.

'We watched you come undone at Cyanea.' Telamon's verbal assault is unrelenting, a litany of accusations that hammer home harder than his fists. 'We saw what happened when the Rocks sought to take us, when your valour unravelled for the first time. And we *defended you!*' His anger continues unabated, this time directed at himself in equal measure. '*We defended you* from the others' bitter words. We thought the Amazons had cast a spell on you. Some foul enchantment, that bewitched your soul and sapped your spirit.'

His face, for a moment, twists with sorrow instead of spite. 'I see now that we were lying to ourselves. Grasping for any other truth, but *this.*' He indicates the fallen Herakles with a nod, drenching that last word in all the disgust he can muster. 'That the Gods' Last Son, the mightiest of us all, the example we all strive towards… that that man is nothing but a broken shell. A hollow wreck of the Herakles we used to know.'

At his feet, the Allslayer risks sitting fractionally up. Dark blood trickles from one nostril, with more spilt from a split in his lip. His left eye is darkening, swollen, only willing to open halfway.

Now you see me, kinsman. Now you see me at last.

'To them, you are just a hero,' Telamon goes on, quieter now but no less threatening. 'The Slayer of All. But you were our *friend*, Herakles. You were the brother we chose for ourselves. We would have followed you. We would have followed you to the World's Edge.'

And he would. The truth is written across the Phthian's dejected face.

'Telamon,' the Allslayer finally says, not moving. 'I am sorr—'

'*I don't want your sorrow!*' the other man roars, burying another kick deep in Herakles' sternum. It is the hardest blow yet, and it knocks him clean across the deck. '*I said! I don't! Want it!*' Spittle flies from his mouth as tears roll down his cheeks. 'Tiphys is *dead*, you honourless wretch! And Peleus teeters on the brink, even now! *I don't want your gods-damned sorrow!*'

Herakles waits for the next attack, but it doesn't come. He lifts his broken face off the deck, expecting Telamon to move in for the kill. If anyone must be the one to do it, there are worse choices.

It occurs to him, with belated clarity, that no-one from below decks has heard Telamon's shouts. Or if they have, then they are choosing to ignore them. He can hardly fault them for that. He is merely surprised that none of them wanted to join in.

'I don't know who you are,' the Phthian lord tells him, his wrath temporarily fading. 'I don't recognise the man before me. By Olympus, I didn't recognise the man who joined us in Iolchus.' He takes a handful of steps forward, not towards the stricken Allslayer, but in the opposite direction.

'Once this quest is done,' he informs him, 'and the Fleece belongs to Phthia, I never want to see you again.'

And then he is gone, leaving his fallen friend to bleed on the deck.

Which is where he is some time later, when Hylas and Atalanta find him.

The former already has cotton and swaddling cloth to hand, which cannot be a coincidence. Like the rest of the Argonauts, he knew what Telamon would do to Herakles once Tiphys' funeral rites were behind them. With his brother still abed, none of the others had tried to collar him, to even reason with him. Not even Jason.

'Can you stand?' Atalanta asks him, her small hand buried in his to help him up. There is no bewilderment in her gaze, just a long-buried fear that has surfaced at last. As if this is the one future she prayed would not transpire.

For his part, Hylas has no words to describe what he feels. Pain. Guilt. Futility. He has spent most of his life managing the eddies of his master's misery. It has never been like this, however. It has never hurt so many people.

Herakles groans as he tries to put weight on one leg. Even for a demigod, some hurts run deep. Wounds that Orpheus bound and burned shut have started to reopen, though he suspects few things would hurt like these last blows. Not the sabre-teeth of Nemea's Lion, nor the Hydra's poison fangs. What can cut deeper than a friend turned foe?

'It's... it's nothing,' he finally growls, gently pushing the squire and huntress away.

'Master, just I—'

'I said it's *nothing*, Hylas.'

And with that, the Gods' Last Son begins to limp below deck, as graceless as he is slow.

Hylas is a patient soul – the gods only know that he has to be – but even his devotion has its limits. The slave tosses the bloody cloths aside, not even bothering to see where they land, before storming off to nurse his grievance elsewhere.

Which leaves Atalanta all alone in the light of the setting sun. Her feelings, for once, are clearly etched upon her face. But there is no-one left to see them.

'There is bounty here,' Jason establishes the following morning. 'We should help ourselves, before we sail. Perhaps a day's respite is what we need.'

It is, the Allslayer has to concede, one of the shepherd boy's more perceptive moments. After the calamities of the previous day, Jason seems to appreciate the need to keep them occupied. Laertes, reading the slackening winds, has the tact to not object. The *Argo* is not at its most cooperative, but they may not need to pit oars against waves just yet.

And like that, it is decided. They will traipse across Pegae, if that is where they even are, to take what they can before moving on. Freshwater from nearby springs and rivers. Livestock from any wild herds that haunt the steppes. Perhaps some newly chopped wood to replace their missing oars.

Telamon isn't going anywhere, to no-one's surprise, not while Peleus is still convalescing. Orpheus is content to stay by the injured Phthian's side, and Nestor agrees to lend him help. Laertes, with Argus' curmudgeonly aid, will try his hand at bonding with the *Argo*'s recalcitrant spirit, and Jason will stay behind with both men to help plot their next nautical steps. Together, the three of them will glean what scraps they can from Tiphys' aborted plans.

That only leaves a few others. Meleager needs little convincing, unnerved at spending any more time near Tiphys' pyre. Castor and Polydeuces volunteer, which invariably leads to Theseus following suit. And Atalanta never foregoes a chance to walk on dry land, or a moment to be alone.

Not one of them pays Herakles any heed as they prepare to launch. Castor bodily shoulders past as he makes his way to the rowboats, the move too aggressive to be an accident.

The Allslayer watches the others follow, as they clamber aboard the little boats. Theseus makes a show of hurrying past him, anything to avoid a brush of eye contact. Meleager spares him a lingering glance as he passes, not long enough to betray any real feeling.

Polydeuces pauses just long enough to spit at Herakles' feet.

'Stay watchful,' Atalanta cautioned them, as they come upon dry land. 'Places like this are haunted by more than just folklore. Naiads, in the streams and pools, dryads among the forest trunks, oreads in mountain caves... such wild, untouched places are seldom left unguarded.'

Though they are a touch less boorish than usual, few of the others seem particularly moved by any of that. Meleager at least narrows his eyes, in curiosity rather than dismissal.

The Allslayer is last to step out of the small boat, and he pays the others as little regard as they do him. They fan out, each soul finding their own way across the steppes and basins. A few of them carry urns and pails, hoping to chance upon water that isn't too foetid.

It doesn't take long for Herakles to find himself alone, and he feels no burning need to remedy that. He picks his way down a gully of mossy slate, the ghost of a limp still in his left leg. The sound of the softly running river tickles the edge of hearing, the shadows of towering peaks keeping the morning sun off his back. Arganthonius, this one is called, if they really are at Pegae. He has never set foot here before, but names travel far enough.

'I just want to know why,' says a soft voice from behind him. 'Why now, after all this time?'

Another day, another ambush, and from an equally aggrieved soul. Once again, Herakles doesn't rush to turn around. This newcomer is no Telamon, but he has no wish to escape this punishment either.

'I knew that us joining this quest was a mistake,' Hylas says, stepping closer. The slave is lugging a pewter urn behind him, which is practically half his height. 'I knew seeing old friends would bring back old pain. And I had a fair idea *that* was what made you come. That you wanted to punish yourself, in some sick and twisted way.'

The Allslayer has nothing to say. Perhaps this, *this* is what he is really owed, after all the jeopardy he has put the Argonauts through. His closest, most loyal follower – a boy he regards as his own – letting out a lifetime of unsaid frustration.

'We nearly all died in the Pass, because of you,' Hylas continues. 'And Tiphys and Peleus have paid dearly. All these years I've followed you, beholden to your will, and you were more than willing to leave me masterless. But why *now*, after all this time? Decades of weathering the spite of gods. Twelve Labours that are sung of across Hellas. And wars that have ground lesser men into dust. But one short trip through the Hellespont? Is that what truly breaks the dragon's back?'

The cadence of the Cius reverberates off the heights around them. The tinkling of freshwater is all that can be heard, as the streams run down the pumice slopes to the deep blue pool at Herakles' feet.

'Hylas...' the Allslayer finally replies. What to say? What to even begin to say? 'It... it isn't like that. If I could make you understand, then—'

'By all means!' the servant suddenly snaps, casting his urn to one side with a stony clang. 'Please, *master*. I'm sure I'm not the only Argonaut who would like to know. Should I fetch Telamon? The others? I'm sure they would dearly wish to hear you. To know what warranted risking all our lives twice!'

Another man might maim a slave for such insolence, but Herakles is no such man. And it is hardly undeserved, anyway.

'All these years I've served you, seeing how deep your wounds run.' Hylas is slowly moving, urn forgotten, tracing a path around the lagoon's rocky edge. 'All this time I've tended your needs, trying to put your broken pieces back together. And you barely even register my presence. Imperilling yourself, that is one thing. But imperilling the people you claim to care about...'

'Not by choice,' Herakles whispers.

'What does it matter?' the slave snaps. It sounds out of place from his soft, delicate voice. 'You still did it. I try to hold you together, and you insist on tearing yourself apart. I try to point you toward the future, and you bury yourself in the past.' He stops, no longer able to even play it gently. 'Why do you even need me anymore, *master?* Is there no-one else who can carry your weapons for you? What is the point of keeping me around, if you are only going to choose self-destruction every time?'

The boy's diatribe echoes oddly across the water. Not the way a sound normally would. Herakles casts the thought aside, pulling back his focus.

'Well?' Hylas takes his master's silence as a victory in itself. 'Why, then? I know you never cared about the Fleece, or about Jason's family feud. You dragged me with you aboard the *Argo* for a reason, and it wasn't for the glory of victory.'

The Allslayer says nothing. No other soul has pressed him this deeply in far too many years. None who know him well enough still live.

'So *what?*' Hylas is the very picture of exasperation now. 'What is it about this quest that finally broke your resolve? Which of our sorry, disastrous landings could the mightiest of mortals not—'

'*Stop it!*' the Allslayer roars, at the top of his lungs. The words reverberate across the valley, refracting from the slopes like a peal of distant thunder. '*Just! Stop it!*'

He pulls his fist, with a moment's effort, out of the great grey boulder he has buried it in. It comes free with force, sending cracks cobwebbing through its mass.

'I am *not* the mightiest of mortals! I have never, *ever*, been the mightiest of mortals! That is simply what they sing about me, in their songs and their folktales. All these years of following me, and you truly buy into that?'

He takes a step forward, the lake's shallow edges tickling his sandalled feet. 'What I am, boy, is the *most favoured* of mortals. The vessel the Olympians poured all their hopes into. All that power, all that strength… it is theirs, Hylas, lent to me for a purpose. Not my own. I was *sired* for that reason, just a means to an end. Zeus seduced my mother under a pall of night, but that was all it was. He had no desire to father another mortal, scarce appetite enough even for Alcmena. She was a vessel to him, nothing more. As I am now.'

Hylas doesn't move, doesn't speak. The silence looks a little surly on his boyish face. But he makes no attempt to interrupt.

'You men,' Herakles continues, not quite managing to laugh. 'You *mortals*. You think that Fate is this unseen, guiding force, plied to an end not even gods can know. That is what Tiresias thinks. That is the belief Idmon took with him to the grave. But your prophets and seers have it wrong. They always have.'

How strange it feels, to spill these private thoughts. This is the first time he has ever articulated them, let alone shared them aloud.

'I have walked in the presence of gods, Hylas. Many times. I have seen behind that curtain, not by esteem, but dire necessity. The Fate that binds us all together… it is them, boy. The gods. Nothing more. They write it for their own needs, their own amusement. Think on my life, if you need proof! Think of my story. All my life, they threw tragedy after tragedy at me. My birth. My exile. My wife and sons. The loss of all those friends and kinsmen. Time and again, the gods broke me down, crushing my hopes, but never quite daring to end me utterly.'

He stares his young servant in the face. Tyrants and foul things have quivered beneath that gaze, but Hylas meets it without blinking.

'Why was that, do you think?' Herakles lets the rhetorical question dangle. 'It was to temper me, of course. Temper me to their own ends. Blow after blow, in a rain without end, all to forge me into a surer, stronger weapon. All to leave me with nothing else to lose.'

The air has fallen stiller now, as if in sympathy with the Allslayer's lament. The wind no longer blows. Yet still the lagoon's inky surface gently ripples as if disturbed.

'It is them, Hylas.' Herakles is murmuring now, lancing this boil he has left to fester for so long. 'It is nothing but them. Their will. They have woven Fate around me, each time I raise my club or throw myself into battle. They do this so I cannot lose. So no foe can contend with the might they have given me, so nothing can come between me and the end they save me for.'

He meets his own flowing reflection in the lake's surface. For a moment, he appears lustrous, monstrous. Made of luminous, divine light, instead of mortal flesh and bone.

'It isn't *for* me, you understand. It is no act of charity, or compassion. It is for *them*. Fate is bent around me, for every travail, Labour and quest I've ever set upon. Not to make them easy. Nothing they give us is ever easy. But to make them *possible*. Possible for one such as me.'

Hylas has still not spoken. He doesn't move an inch. Hardly surprising. How does one respond to the doubts of Herakles?

'Do you not believe me!' the Allslayer exclaims, his wrath rekindled by his own train of thought. 'Blood of Hades, Hylas! Just *look* at the truth of that claim. Look at where we've been! What we've sailed through! Do you think I could break from this path if I *wanted* to? I downed my oar between the Dark Rocks, and a daughter of Zeus descended to deliver us! I threw my club aside on the Isle of Ares, hoping the Birds would finish me off! But Fate put you and Telamon there, in the nick of accursed time! Don't you *see*, Hylas? It *won't* stop, no matter how much I want it to. It won't ever, *ever* stop. The gods won't ever let me go. I am *bound* to this path, this destiny. I am *chained* to it. The King of Olympus whelped me for a purpose, and nothing in this world, or beneath, will free me of it.'

He spares his flawed reflection one last glance, still unnerved by just how ethereal it looks, and how unlike him.

'He wanted us gone, you know.' He chuckles, the sort of bleak, defeated chuckle you make to avoid crying yourself to death. 'Tiresias told me once, from one of his auguries. My divine father, he who rules the sky, wanted to start afresh. To wipe away the race of men.' Another pained, anguished laugh. 'But he couldn't. Because he needed mortals alive, to sire the one half-son the Olympians need so dearly. The one who will win their war for them.'

He pulls the sweaty lionskin off, letting it fall to the dusty ground nearby.

'That is why we still inhabit the earth, Hylas. Why any of us still live. Because one day, a battle will come, that not even the gods can win without my help. That is why Zeus fathered me, why he let Hera burn my life to the ground again, and again, and again. Because they needed me here, and they needed me strong.'

He continues his slow walk, this time letting the club fall from his absent grip. Whatever Hylas expected to hear from him, this is not it.

'All those others, boy. All those heroes and kings who would live up to my deeds. Peleus, Telamon, Meleager… even Jason. That is what they will never understand. They can never be me, Hylas. Never even live up to me. *Because I am not like them.* Whatever the Fates have in store for those men, whatever paths they end up following or falling from… it won't be the same. At some point or other, each one of them will get to choose their destiny.'

What a simple life that would be. How pitifully, beautifully simple.

'I am no god, Hylas,' Herakles says. 'But I am no man, either. I am so much more... and so much less.'

When he looks back across the lagoon, Hylas is still there. The boy's delicate feet rest in the rippling water, toes unmoving.

'Is death what you've been seeking, then?' Hylas asks, after a pause that lasts too long. 'What you've wanted, all these years? Was that what all those Labours were, all those battles and stories? Nothing but a way to die?'

Something flows through Herakles' heart, something pure and molten.

'Haven't I *earned* that right?' he snarls, his anger once more in ascendence. 'I, whose deeds reverberate across the kingdoms? I, who has earned more *kleos* than any man who ever lived? *Haven't I earned it?*'

But Hylas' face does not move, and the Allslayer's wrath begins to drain away. 'I... I can't do this anymore, boy. I just can't. I have nothing more of me left to give. Maybe you were right at Pagasa. Maybe I did pledge my word for the wrong reasons. But that wasn't why... why I did what I did, at Cyanea. On the Isle.'

He wavers. This is the first time he has spoken of such things, to god or man, and he will never be this intimate with any mortal again. But all the same... is he truly going to give it voice? This last truth, at the bottom of this confessional draught?

'I want...' he begins, hoping the tremor in his voice is imagined. 'I just want to choose. To break the chains. And I don't see another way how.'

And there it is, at last. Out in the air, after far too many years. What is said cannot be taken back. This ghost that has haunted him for so long — no less than the unquiet souls of his unburied comrades — has been exposed. But has it been laid to rest?

'And that is all you care about, master?' Hylas finally replies. There is steel in his voice, cold and unforgiving steel, and the Allslayer realises he has made a mistake. 'You're happy to die, and leave the rest of us alone? Leave *me* alone, with nothing in the world?'

'No, boy.' Herakles takes a couple of tentative steps into the water, feet curling over jagged rock. 'That... that is not what I meant.'

'*No?*' Hylas exclaims, wading deeper in to put more distance between them. '*Who* then would I have? My father?' He laughs with matching bleakness. 'You *killed* him, remember? Yet another monster you've slain, another tale the poets sing about. And what about the rest of us, your so-called friends? The souls you couldn't bear to let sail to Colchis without you?'

'Hylas...' the Allslayer begins. Between them, the lagoon is starting to ripple and churn. Something bright and iridescent pierces its inky depths, and something moves in the flickers of that light.

'The Phthians?' the slave continues. 'Theseus? Or what about Admetus, in faraway Pherae? What about old Tyndareus?' He laughs yet again, a mirthless, heartbreaking laugh that only the bitterest of betrayals can induce. 'You were right about one thing, Child of Thunder. You are something more than us mere mortals, and no mistake!'

Behind Hylas' back, the shimmering light beneath the water grows. It shines and fades like a starlit aurora, casting a bioluminescent pall. The young servant seems not to notice, striding further into the lagoon in his zeal to air his anger.

'Gods Below... how could any of us ever compete with any of that? How could any of us even scratch the surface?'

'*Hylas!*' Herakles roars, launching himself right into the glowing water. 'Come out of there, boy! Come ou—'

It all happens so fast.

One moment Hylas is standing there, the lake practically up to his elbows. The next, he is gone, leaving nothing behind but a foaming crash, and an Allslayer still waist deep with hand outstretched.

When the flash of numinous light finally fades, all Herakles can see is the water calming once more.

That, and the fleeting outline of a young, watery maiden, her wintry radiance fading from his retinas.

Atalanta reaches the valley bottom, drawn in by the thundering howls of anguish.

A sodden Herakles stands on the lake's stony verge, at first too distressed to even speak. He pauses only to smash a nearby boulder into rubble with one fall of his fist.

'What is it?' the huntress asks, perplexed. 'What happened?'

'A water nymph, in the lagoon.' The Allslayer jerks his head towards the now-calm lake. 'It took Hylas.'

'It did what?' Atalanta doesn't know to be shocked, or horrified. Naiads can be petty, when pushed to it. Vindictive, even... but this?

More hurried footsteps. Meleager, next to arrive, from the other side of the mountain.

'What will you do?' the huntress asks, ignoring the Calydonian.

Herakles has already taken a handful of steps back in. 'Take a guess, girl.'

'You can't!' Atalanta risks a hand on his great shoulder. 'If that was even what you truly saw... you can't. No good comes of fighting with nymphs, my friend. You know this. If the boy is even still alive, he is lost to us. You cannot help him now! None of us can!'

'What is wrong?' Meleager cuts in, gasping for air after running. No-one answers him.

'I am not leaving him in this place,' Herakles growls, turning back to face the lagoon. The water has grown dark once more. 'He's my... he's Hylas. I won't leave him here.'

'Allslayer! the huntress calls. 'My friend, please! Please think about th—'

Too late. With another calamitous crash of water, the Gods' Last Son takes the plunge.

XXX
PARTING OF WAYS

'Let me untwist this,' Jason growls, without the benefit of any doubt. 'Not only have we lost the Allslayer's little runt to some divine spirit... but the Allslayer himself as well? Have I heard that correctly?'

They have gathered on the beach once more, in the shadow of the *Argo*. The ashes of Tiphys' pyre have already scattered to the breeze, too little left to even mark where they'd cremated him. Atalanta and Meleager face their Thessalian captain, a leader in name only whose authority shows no signs of regaining any potency. Around them, a halo of weary Argonauts await Jason's reaction, saying nothing.

'Herakles was adamant,' the huntress maintains. It is not like her to sound so powerless. 'Whatever truly happened doesn't matter. He was convinced, and none of us could have talked him out of it. He dove in after... after Hylas.'

A murmur goes up around the circle. Few among the remaining crew care a jot about Hylas. Apart from the Phthians, perhaps, or Atalanta herself. But the loss of Herakles, even after the tumult of the last few days, sits well with none of them. This voyage has had enough bad omens already.

'You stupid girl.' This is unforgiving, even by Jason's standards. 'How witless can you be, to just let him go like that?'

'She didn't,' Meleager cuts in before the huntress can stop him. 'It was me, Jason. It was me who let him go. Atalanta didn't get there till after.'

Jason's cold gaze drifts to him, his emotions as crudely transparent as usual.

'Then you're a fool as well as a nobody, Prince of Calydon. Well?' he shouts once more. 'What happened then?'

Atalanta takes in a breath, getting ready to impart more scarcely tolerated truths.

'We waited,' Meleager pre-empts her once again. 'Atalanta didn't leave the lake for almost an hour. Prince Castor and I scoured the rest of the valley in both directions, as well as the slopes around it. Prince Polydeuces followed the river right back to its source, up the crags.'

Eyes bore into the Calydonian youth without much subtlety, waiting for a reassurance he cannot give.

'Nothing,' Meleager concedes, sorrowfully. 'No sign of either of them, or the accursed naiad Herakles claimed he saw.'

'I had no better luck,' Atalanta adds. 'Nothing came in or out of that lagoon after the Allslayer. It was quiet… too quiet. In the end it was enough to unnerve me.'

Jason snorts, refusing to let the thought of spiteful nymphs unman him. Easy indeed, if you haven't encountered one in the flesh.

'Sixteen of us there were,' he muses, abruptly turning his back on them and talking to the air, 'when we set out from Thessaly's shores. The greatest and most renowned souls across the kingdoms, with the sons and wards of gods among our number. And now we scarcely number twelve.'

Scarcely. Telamon's scarred brow darkens at that, quite understandably. Despite the best of Orpheus' and Nestor's ministrations, Peleus still lies close to death's halls. There is little the others can do, beyond trusting in the gods' capricious mercy and the Phthian's own indomitable will.

'We made good on our impiety,' the shepherd boy continues, seemingly unaware of the risk of airing his doubts so publicly. 'We lifted our *miasma* in the Hellespont, when we rid Cyzicus' people of the Earthborn. Yet it seems our Fates aren't yet unsnarled, my friends.'

Atalanta shares an uneasy glance with Meleager. Jason's intuition is a fallible, temperamental thing, and they have long learnt that questioning it is seldom a sound idea.

'Well,' Telamon says, stepping closer into the loose ring. 'You pissed over the sacred law of *xenia* when you stabbed that Amazon in the back. Maybe it is you the gods have taken umbrage with, son of Aeson. Not us.'

A jeer of throaty agreement from the other Argonauts answers this claim. Even Theseus and Laertes join it.

'The gods have taken our strongest warrior, and our peerless helmsman!' Argus sneers through his cracking lips. 'And have almost claimed another of our finest men! I'm sure Idmon would have plenty to say, if he still lived. But no! He cannot! Because the Olympian Ones have cut his thread also!'

As the jeers around him swell, Jason shoots the shipwright a look of unadulterated malice. His fists briefly ball, but he doesn't risk raising them. He has little enough control of this moment as it is.

'I have the Queen of Olympus on my side,' he finally replies, as hollow as it undoubtedly sounds. 'And I didn't bring us to Pegae for soul-searching. We still need more supplies, and my patience runs thinner with each moment. Let us vote, here and now.'

Behind him, Theseus' mouth falls briefly open, as if he has something pressing to say. But the moment passes before he can speak.

'A show of hands!' Jason shouts, trying to sound more formidable than he is. 'How many wish us to forget the Allslayer and his minion, and press onward to the Phasis?'

Abandoning a brother in arms is one thing, not least a brother so many of them – until now – have respected. But forsaking their course, and being beaten to their prize, is quite another.

'A show of hands!' Jason barks at them again, and those that want to finally comply. Their captain counts the raised hands in his head, not pleased, but not disheartened, at the tally.

'And now, the rest of you. Who here would have us continue our search for Herakles?' he growls. 'However long it takes?'

Another pause, and another clutch of hands go up. The shepherd boy counts them once more, his displeasure still evident.

'No abstainers!' he scolds them. 'Everyone takes a side. No exceptions.'

For all the difference it makes. After what happened with the Birds, this vote was only going to go one way.

But not entirely.

'We cannot do this!' Theseus calls out. 'What ails you, comrades? We cannot sail to Colchis without—' He breaks off abruptly, either unwilling or unsure how to go on. 'Without our strongest man,' he finally adds, turning to look at each of the others. 'How can you do this? How can any of you even countenance this?'

A dirty chuckle cuts off his righteousness at the roots.

'Tell that to my brother,' Telamon growls. 'Go down into the *Argo*'s hold, Athenian, and make your case to

Peleus.' He smiles, coldly. 'I speak for him, when I say we've no objections.'

Telamon's laughter is taken up by his less charitable comrades. The righteous snarl catches in Theseus' throat as he realises, in this moment, just how powerless he truly is.

'What's the matter, Labyrinth-Breaker?' mocks Castor, as the Argonauts' cruel mirth echoes into the sky. 'Afraid to lose your sole protector?'

In Jason's eyes, this settles it. They will spend one more day at maybe-Pegae. Not for Herakles, of course. Not even for those still hoping to find him. But for whatever bounty this place has yet to yield.

'You don't have to decide this now,' Atalanta says, when the two of them are alone below decks. She knows it is futile; Jason is still riled by the others' irreverence, pleased only to have channelled it back at Theseus, and he lacks the assurance to change his mind so publicly. But still, she tries.

'The Allslayer was your ally,' she tries. 'And allies are what you'll need when we finally reach the Fleece. Another day or so of waiting might make all the difference.'

For his part, Jason just walks past her, not even sparing her the dignity of a glance.

'This is not a discussion,' is all he says.

'*Why* are you doing this?' the huntress shouts after him. 'I am the only soul on this ship not biding my time?' She laughs, in sheer disbelief. 'Do you think I *don't* know what this is like? To be alone in the wilderness, surrounded by nothing but wolves?'

He walks on without giving her an answer. And why would he? Colchis is calling to him, calling to them all, a little louder each day.

She nurses that dark thought as the sun falls among the trees, hauling her now-full pail of drinking water back through the woods. She is accustomed, by now, to nursing dark thoughts. This quest has given her plenty of practice.

A string of Calydonian curses crashes through her maudlin reverie. A knotted tree root, and one moment of boyish inattention, sends Meleager rolling down the slope to the rocky bottom. His payload of dry timber cascades from his hands.

Fallen still at last, the prince risks touching his forearm with his other hand, the fingers coming away with sanguine smears. More cursing, beneath his breath, softer yet harsher.

'Gracefully done,' Atalanta chides him, setting down her sloshing pail and drawing nearer. 'It doesn't look good, does it?'

Meleager scowls, failing to wipe away blood or muck as he regains his composure. But he has enough dignity left to feel affronted.

'I imagine not,' he neutrally replies. 'But to take Theseus' side would have ended terribly, from what I saw. And I didn't hear you speak up for him, either.'

The huntress steps up to him, fixing him with a long, unimpressed stare.

'I was talking about your arm, Calydonian.'

'Oh. My apologies.'

For a moment, Meleager's gaze drifts across the wood, as if seeking anyone else who might have seen them. But no. They are quite alone here.

Atalanta gently clasps his wrist, lifting his arm to inspect the wound more closely. 'You lied to Jason, earlier. On my behalf.' Her eyes drift back to his. 'You didn't need to do that.'

'I… I didn't think I did. I wanted to, regardless.'

'Meleager...' she gently presses. 'You didn't need to do that.'

He holds eye contact for a moment longer, his wrist still in her hand.

'You're welcome,' he finally replies. Her attention is already elsewhere, as without asking permission, she begins to tend his gashed arm. He is acutely aware of her proximity, uncomfortably so. This is the closest they've been since the Hellespont. Since the two of them huddled on that storm-wracked outcrop, as a monster of myth bore down on them.

'If we're thanking each other,' Meleager finally adds, 'then I suppose I've yet to thank you for saving m—'

She shushes him, her eyes not even moving from her task. Every so often, her lips move soundlessly, in tune with her thoughts. This close, the Prince of Calydon can count the freckles and birth spots on her face. Smell the subtle tang of her hair. See the flecks of barley in the rings of her eyes.

'Something to say?' she finally prompts him, more gently than perhaps is warranted.

Caught off guard, Meleager's mind scrambles. He doesn't plan to say his next words, but has no regret doing so.

'You were right, Huntress.'

'About what?' Atalanta's face has returned, more or less, to its customary inexpressiveness. If anything, after the last few days, that sets Meleager at ease.

'About what you told me, when we laid Idmon to rest. You told me that I had no idea what I'd pledged myself to.' He does not resist as she continues her silent work. 'And here we are, four men down since Pagasa, with the real struggle yet to even begin. Here we are, among a fellowship that seems to deteriorate with every passing moment, following a leader whose honour and authority hang more precariously each day.'

He glances at the gash Atalanta is cleaning, wincing as her fingers find the wound's edges.

'Our comrades, as you claimed, have far bleaker plans than honouring Jason's wishes. And the longer our voyage takes, the less inclined they seem to even hide it.' He smiles a rueful smile, though Atalanta is not looking at it. 'I would be no match for any of them, if it came down to such a thing. Not even Jason.'

And now he laughs, gently, in the sylvan twilight. 'But it wouldn't come to that,' he finally admits, and Atalanta doesn't need a hawk's sight to see what this confession costs him. 'Because none of them would have to bother slaying me. I am no threat to any of them, dead or alive.'

The huntress digests these murmured truths in silence. Now the gash is safely bound, she sets about wiping away the dried blood. She doesn't coddle the Calydonian prince, or soothe him with words that reassure. That is not the way she was raised, not the example that Artemis sets.

But like every soul who sails the *Argo* with her, she is so much more than the sum of her upbringing.

'You were right, too.'

Meleager's eyes narrow. 'About what?'

'About me.' She avoids the prince's gaze as she works. 'About my reasons for joining this quest. I cared...' She halts. 'I care about Jason, and I wanted to help him restore his family's pride. But that isn't the reason I came. Not truly.'

This time, it is Meleager's coy silence that bids her continue.

'I am a huntress, Calydonian. *The* huntress. The chosen champion of Artemis. And here we all are, alone on a wild, wild sea. This is the hunt to end all hunts, and the Fleece of

Colchis is the ultimate prize. I want to see this done, Meleager.'

And with that, she goes on cleaning the wound, waiting for him to nod in understanding. But no nod comes, and she inwardly chides herself. Perhaps some of her perceptiveness is rubbing off on him. Stranger things have happened on this quest, after all.

'I suppose that isn't the whole truth,' she whispers, answering the Calydonian's unspoken question. 'The others call me *Huntress*, and make it sound like a title. Which was never my intention, but...' She pauses, wiping some balm down Meleager's forearm to clean it. What is that, in those gold-flecked eyes of hers? Embarrassment?

'But it is mine,' she finally admits. 'Rightfully earnt, like the reputation that preceded me in Iolchus. The men we share the *Argo* with are used to taking things by force, whatever their intentions. I'd rather... I'd rather some things stayed beyond their reach.'

Atalanta clasps his hand, pulling it closer to expose the last blood left to cleanse. And in that moment of unfeigned honesty, Meleager understands.

The woman stood before him is a woman who stands alone. Even before King Iasus disowned her, even before she forged her own path and legend, Atalanta's life was hamstrung by what she'd chosen to forego in a way no man that made such choices would ever be. Of course she clings to the moniker of Huntress now. She is a woman among kings, with no family, no allegiance. She would rather be defined by what little she has, than the many things she lacks.

In Thessaly, Meleager had assumed she had no stake in the Fate of this voyage. Looking back, he couldn't have been more wrong.

'There.' She breaks his reverie with a gentle word, letting go of his hand at last. 'And that's you done, Calydonian.'

Meleager murmurs his gratitude, flexing his arm.

'I'm afraid,' he suddenly admits. 'I'm afraid I am going to die on this quest, Huntress, at the hands of another Argonaut, and that my death will be for nothing. And that I'll have nobody to blame for it but my deluded, vainglorious self.'

Atalanta has no reply for this, and the prince inwardly curses himself for being so crude. He has said too much, of course he has. Misread the moment. As if she has any patience for his—

The huntress takes his hand in hers again. This time, quite willingly.

'No, Meleager,' she quietly promises him. 'None of them will hurt you. I won't let that happen.'

Miles back by the coast, a dark, ravening blackness spills over the sand where Tiphys was burned. A blackness that becomes a shadow. A shadow that becomes a shape.

It has come to seek the dead, and it has not been disappointed. But the dead, as Fate will tragically transpire, is far from all it seeks.

Not long to go now. Not long at all.

ACT III

CITY OF DAWN

'Show me a hero, and I will write you a tragedy.

Show me a man of peace, and I will write you a bloodbath.

Show me a conqueror, and he will write what he pleases.'

— Ancient Colchian proverb

XXXI
COMPOSED ON THE ROAD FROM PHERAE

Iolaus.

Please do not begrudge my delay, nephew. I have so much to explain and so little time to do it. In truth, I barely grasp most of it myself.

I find myself on another ship, among another crew, and following another captain. Only this time, the circumstances are profoundly different.

Things have changed since last I wrote, and not at all for the better. Mistakes were made, by more than one party. I can dispense a share of blame to other men. To Jason, for his myopia, and to the fraying trust and pride of the Argo's other crewmates.

But the meat of it lies with me, and I won't shirk it. I made choices, many of them bad ones, and I was not the only soul who paid for them. Men have suffered, good men, for the crime of trying to pull me from the brink. Tiphys, torn down like carrion. Perhaps Peleus too, if he fails to rise from the deathbed I helped put him on.

And Hylas... blood of Olympus. Poor, innocent Hylas. I am bereft of my boy, and all he did was try to tell me the truth. Of all the losses I have suffered in my life, I can say that this one was no whim of the Fates. This was my fault, pure and simple. The reaped harvest that my obstinance sowed.

I am lost to them, Iolaus. The Argo *left me behind, as much my fault as theirs. I won't waste time reliving the details, because the details are not what matters. But Jason and the others are still on their chaotic, inexorable way, nearing Colchis with every passing dawn. And I am not with them.*

I see my path now, nephew. How venomously timed was the weight of my epiphany. As my former comrades set sail on their course, leaving me kneeling in the ashes of my mistakes, I felt a clarity that I'd yet to sense on this quest at all.

I had broken my cardinal rule, the rule that had fed me through all these years of strife and exile. I had allowed my pain to spill out, to hurt those who walk in my shadow.

Telamon of Phthia had tried to tell me that, I think, the last time he and I spoke. In his own simple, wrathful way, he had tried to open my eyes. He was one of my oldest friends, Iolaus, a brother of battle I could never imagine parting from. And yet, at any point over these last long months, he could very well have died while cursing my name.

But it was those failures of mine, those mistakes that blew us all apart, that made me see.

It didn't matter if I wanted to see Jason's folly through, or if I truly wanted to wrench my life off the path the gods have made for me. Right here, in this moment, those things do not matter.

My folly put the Argonauts in peril. Two of them are lost as a consequence. I cannot let them walk into any more danger without me. I owe them that much. I owe it to find them again, to save them from another Themiscyra. Another Clashing Rocks.

Once I follow them to Colchis, and once this whole sorry business is dispensed with, I can let myself decide what to live or die for.

But I am getting ahead of myself, boy. You were always the keenest mind among us. You have questions, no doubt, and in your mind's eye I am still at Pegae, with no vessel, no Argonauts, and no Hylas.

Tracing my servant's path took me falling into the inky depths of a mountain lagoon. Do you remember your boyhood, Iolaus? Do you remember those gilded tales Iphicles and I would tell you, when you tired of brawls and playfights?

You always knew that spirits and nymphs were no matter to laugh at. Your mother and matrons saw to it. There are fewer more foolhardy goals than chasing a naiad to her oceanic lair, or coming between her and her prey. I took a tenacious stab at both. I achieved neither.

In truth, I can barely unspool those memories now. Was it the oily black of the ocean deep, farther down than the light of Helios could sink? Was it the lack of breath in my breast, clenched tight by my clamped jaws, as the pressure threatened to split my skull? I swam deeper into that water than a man has any right to, and neither my body nor soul came through it unscathed.

I see flashes of it still when my eyes drift closed. Sea nymphs. Water kine. Dolphin courts, and their ministries of minnows. If my quarry had truly taken Hylas this far down, then one way or another, the boy was truly lost to me.

And then I saw Glaucus, that colossal kelp-bearded vassal of the brine. I remember the slow silhouette, that cetacean tail of his, as immense as the seabed and every bit as dark. The tail fell, shaking the whole sea with its motion... and then I was rocketing up through the depths. Back up into the light, into shallows that were bright and not penumbral. That teemed with mortal life, instead of hiding cold, divine leviathans.

I broke the foaming surface at last, gasping ocean air through lungs that had never craved it so desperately.

And that, with the passing shadow of a nearby trireme, was how King Admetus found me.

My mind, in that moment, was far too addled to think clearly. Too addled to even feel any gratitude. I let the men of Pherae fish me out of the water, tending my body and nursing my pains, as my thoughts slowly, but surely, fell back in line.

Not that there was any real mystery to solve. Admetus' joy at seeing me after so long, and being able to render me service, was incandescent. He barraged me with question after question as soon as I was well enough to hear them. Not to interrogate, but merely to grasp the ebb and flow of my life once more. And from that, I grasped the ebb and flow of his. His kingdom at Pherae, flourishing like never before. His wife, Alcestis, as happy and luminous as the night I'd prised her from Death's clasp.

And the summons he'd received at court, just as every lord across the kingdoms had. A summons calling him to the city of Iolchus, to join Jason's expedition eastward. Only matters of state and wrathful currents had kept him from reaching Thessaly's coast before the Argo left. The two ships had missed each other, it transpired, by a matter of days. And since then, he had been chancing his luck on the open sea, hoping to pick up the Argonauts' trail and join their hunt.

What a find, Iolaus. You always said the gods move in mysterious ways. The Fates may drag you down, and they may exalt you, but they never stop surprising you.

I told Admetus the truth, for I hardly owed him any less. I told him the truth of Jason's quest, and the actual truth that lay behind it. I told him how things had started to erode as the voyage unfolded, and the mistakes I had made that had caused such death and desertion.

I told him the what, nephew, if not the why. Can you blame me? At that point, I had scarcely come to grips with the why, myself.

And without another word or promise needed, the two of us set sail. The scraps I had gleaned while Tiphys lived were a promising enough start, and the Pheraeans were valiant enough upon the water. But as Admetus and I came to finally realise, after several fruitless yet intriguing landings, there was a far simpler truth at play here.

We didn't need to seek the land of Colchis. Not at all. We simply needed to seek the men seeking it.

The Argo *and her crew had cleaved their own unique trail, one that a man who knew the signs could follow. While a traveller on foot or horseback would leave prints or broken fallow in their wake, Jason's band of tenuous brothers left stories. How many vessels that plied these waters had the power to row themselves? How many of them carried enough lords and demigods to rule over half of Hellas?*

We passed the river Acheron, the Dark Mouth, one of the many shadowed tributaries flowing down into the World Beneath. We passed the Isle of Philyra, where my old friend Chiron had been born in secret to the Lord of Titans. We passed lands burned clean of life, when the sun dipped so low each dusk it made it seem the waves had caught fire.

We sailed where the stories took us, and our hunt bore wondrous fruit. In time, we learned of Amycus, the savage Bebyrcian chieftain, slain in combat by a boxer who could only be Polydeuces. We learned of Thynias, and how that island had cracked asunder when our friends' blundering disturbed Apollo's own wanderings. And we learned of Lycus, who had welcomed the Argo *to his Mariandynian shores, only to find his wooded farmsteads pillaged and his plains run amok with wild boar.*

And so, dear nephew, here we are. Each dawn, Admetus and I stand upon his prow. Each day, little by little, I feel us draw upon the Argo. *Perhaps out there, in that feral heart of hers, she feels it too.*

On gentler waters, I sometimes expect to see her stern on the horizon. I wonder how her crew would react, if they saw me on their tail. How Laertes' brow, at the rudder, would crumple and crease. What curses Telamon would growl beneath his breath. What uneasy glance the huntress would share with Meleager. What bottled fears Theseus would fail to admit, even to himself.

In those moments, I find young Hylas coming to mind, all too often. The last words he said to me before the naiad pulled him under echo through my thoughts. I wish I could forget them. I want to forget them, forget the wound they seared into my soul, but I dwell on them. I clasp them tight, letting the pain of recollection burn me.

Because, Iolaus, that is why I do this. That is why this ship of ours has crossed the Inhospitable Sea, sailing down the river Phasis into a realm governed by myth and magic. A realm no Achaean has ever returned from.

I have to undo the damage I have done. I must atone for those mistakes. And more than anything else, I must prove Hylas wrong.

Even if I die trying, even if it tangles and snarls up the Fates of Jason and the gods he seeks to honour, I have to prove Hylas wrong.

That boy knew me better than any man alive, and I have to show that he was wrong about me.

I have to do this, nephew. For all our sakes.

XXXII
WITCHSIGHT

You feel the waters around you boil and roil, sea salt burning at your hull and oars. This is not right. This cannot be.

Your progress halts, midwater, as pain seeps into your oaken bones and cracks. The Many who puppet your oars flounder, fearful. They are every bit as affronted at this newfound change, and every bit as startled.

It worsens, moment by crawling moment. The ocean waves have turned to molten agony, coursing across your wooden skin. Reaching out with your oars becomes impossible, even moving at all. The pain grows, and grows, and grows, its fiery promise delivered and exceeded.

The Many sheltering aboard you learn better than to push their luck. Your oars hold fast in place, locking in the corrosive water, and no force in the world will move them without your assent.

Snatches of words drift their way across your senses, words you have no context or comprehension to interpret.

Ambush. Colchis. Witchcraft.

You feel the insipid scrabbling as the Many rush about, the way a man might imagine spider's legs in half-slumber.

And then you feel something else, out there in the waters that bite at you with every drop.

Other presences, drawing closer, in a slowly tightening gauntlet.

She sees all of this, of course. Not that there is any gain in doing so. She has long transcended the point of not trusting her own abilities. Not trusting herself.

Doubts are for other women, lesser souls, and she is not a lesser soul by any definition.

The hour draws near, and the moment is come. Only now, with the moon's radiant arc taking it right above her chamber's sky hole, can she finally seal her unnatural rite. Her immense bronze font dominates the centre of the tower, filled with dark fluid that glistens in the starlight. A few scraps of crudely joined oak bob about the moving surface. They hold a rough outline, one that it would take some charity to appreciate. The outline of a ship.

That is no accident, and nor is the oak it came from. Dodonian oak, that most sacred and prised of Hellas' treasures. These discarded fragments were taken by deceit from Pagasa, right beneath the nose of Thessaly's ageing shipwright.

This, she insisted upon, though her hand was guided by more than just vanity. Her kingdom's seers had farseen the *Argo*'s rise and eventual terminus, as they had every doomed Achaean vessel foolish enough to chart a course to Colchis, but the toil and guile of taking Argus' table scraps was the vital ritual element. It was hardly a difficult task, and her agent had little trouble parting the white-haired goat from what he needed, but that personal touch gave the stolen wood its resonance.

And here it floats, in her ritual font, as the fluid around it darkens.

She tilts her unstopped vial just as the moonlight touches her golden hands. A cloud of viscous dust pours through the air, landing in the black water like a rain of long-dead snowflakes. This is more than just dust, of course. The ashen dead, those unlucky souls fed to her father's Brazen Bulls, slain without honour or burial. This all that remains of their immolation, another invaluable unguent for her ritual work.

Some of her acolytes would baulk at this, at using such a polluted salve so carelessly. But like any devotee of Hecate, she knows her patroness has no such reservations. It doesn't matter which victims were thrown to them while alive, and whose corpses were left for them as fleshy fodder.

The gods care little for such distinctions, and so the ashen remains of just and unjust dead are of equal use to her.

The fluid in her font begins to boil and effervesce. She sees it in the moonlight, this brief sliver of white she has minutes to make use of, and she is sanguine with what she sees.

Some things in this world cannot be killed. But everything – *everything* – can be bound. It is all a matter of finding the right fetters.

The contents of her font continue to bubble and spit, and she closes her eyes, the incantation finished at last. In her mind's shifting landscape, across those vistas of memory and nightmare, she almost sees them. Those deluded Achaean fools, scurrying about their stricken ship as the sea around them turns into corrosive foam.

And she sees him, in the midst of it all, unaffected by the chaos but powerless to hold back its tides. She sees his pleasant, unimpressive face, and she feels a tickle of hope in her devious soul.

And for Medea, witch-princess of Colchis, hope is a dangerous emotion indeed.

XXXIII
The Court of King Aeëtes

Aeëtes is waiting for her. He is always waiting for her. It is as much a familiarity as a fear.

It is quiet out here in the Colchian lowlands, eerily so to any soul that isn't Medea. Even the her skiff's oars make scarcely a splash as they slide through the water, every stroke in unnerving unison. On board, Medea's attendants mutter their meditative verses, morning light glinting from the swirling mandalas over their skin, and the paddles move of their own accord.

The arid plains and slopes around the skiff begin to change. A part of Medea always dreads this stage of the journey, something that sends a shiver through even her malcontent soul. The first trees appear on each riverbank, their woody limbs parched and vein-thin. There is no greenery about them to admire, however. The witch-princess suppresses a muted shiver as they drift on by, trying not to look at the unnatural fruit hanging from spindly branches.

Bowers, woven from darkened flax and spidersilk. The weave is thick, but not opaque. When the sun shines through, the outlines of mummified human forms are all too clear to see. The Colchian method of burial is visceral enough, even to one brought up in those ways, but Medea knows all too well that death is not always the end. The deceased occupants of these bowers are known to disappear under the cover of night, their cocoons found ripped apart from within come the morning. Always the male deceased, curiously. And never the elderly, or the overly young, either.

Medea has asked Aeëtes about this, more than once, but her kingly father's only response is a wolfish smile. Like all his many secrets, he clings to it like gold, and relishes his daughter's fear.

The skiff is nearing Aea, now. Medea knows this because the rivulet she sails down now runs with golden honey instead of water. Most of the Phasis' streams into the capital are the same, with some that flow with milk and cream, as well as water hot enough to bathe and cleanse in. But the surest sign of their arrival is the daylight, amber and clear but with an unnaturally heavy tint for a summer morning. Night never truly falls in the heart of Colchis, the legacy of the sun god's touch too majestic for time to tame, and it won't get any darker than this before the seasons change.

'Princess.'

The honorific snaps Medea back to the present. A cluster of Colchian guards escort her from the boat across the riverbank's marble-paved boulevard. The pale, pink-veined stone of Aea is in evidence now, towers and walls reaching as high in some places as Medea's mountain fastness. It clashes with the crimson robes and pewter armour of her kingdom's ceremonial warriors.

Ceremonial, Medea reminds herself ruefully. Colchis is protected by far more than just the physical.

'Your arrival is timely, lady.' This from the lead guard. The witch notes the unease in his eyes, still palpable after decades of duty. The king chooses these men for their loyalty, and sometimes, when her second sight is particularly acute, Medea can see the astral chains that bind them to his throne. But this is more than loyalty. These men fear what she is. And who she is. And who her father is, of course.

'The king is most... eager, for your presence, to greet the new arrivals. My lord Aspyrtus, and my lady Chalciope, attend him already.'

Beneath Medea's priestly blouse, she feels embers of distant pain, as the fabric brushes the ghosts of old burns. Aeëtes' veins burn bright with the heat of his Titan father. It sears foe and family alike with little provocation.

'The witchsight proved true,' another guard explains, as throngs of Colchian citizens scurry about their business around the riverside boulevard. 'A band of marauding champions, though their provenance raises troubling questions. We came upon their vessel after your ritual ensnared it, lady. Each man we took hails from a different kingdom of Hellas, and each claims, in an unconvincing tone, to have sailed into our waters for the very same thing.'

The Fleece. What else? Aeëtes' prized possession is a bauble more than one ambitious hero has tried to seize, down the years. Against all her instincts, she feels a flutter of sympathy touch her heart for these latest arrivals. Her father won't be kind to them for their temerity.

That trepidation only deepens as they make their way through Aea, and it becomes disturbingly apparent where they are going.

'The Vault of Hyperion?' Medea asks, as the structure's menacing spires and turrets loom before them. 'The intruders are interred *here?* What warrants this?'

'Our orders only concern you, lady.' The guard's gaze remains studiously forward-facing as he leads them to the gates. The Vault stretches far deeper beneath the earth than above, to a place whose delights Aeëtes only extends to those who truly earn his ire.

'You are to proceed below.' The escort stamps to a halt, a chorus of marching feet that seem alarmingly glad to be going no further. 'Your father is waiting for you.'

Of course he is.

The cool, dank depths of the subterranean citadel are bleakly familiar to her already, for this is a duty she has helped her kindred perform countless times before. Every step she takes deeper into this pit of terrors, every moment she spends in its dark, dripping warmth, is a reminder of what Aeëtes is capable of.

Aspyrtus finds her first, grabbing her forearm by way of greeting. It takes a lot to unsettle her princely brother, but their father never fails.

'*Where have you been?*' he hisses. Medea pulls her hand back, noting the lines of care and bitterness in Aspyrtus' face. The light of Colchis doesn't shine down here, but in the lowest reaches of the Vault, a more primal and more fearful form of radiance rises from below.

'What is so important about this latest band of strays?' she hits back, trying not to notice how fearful her brother seems today. 'Why inter them here? And what about this requires all four of us in concert?'

'A worthy question,' a voice says from behind them, a voice as inviting as molten honey, and just as sickly. Brother and sister turn, a little too quickly, but Medea doesn't even need to recognise the voice. The heat haze that shimmers around him is recognition enough, and that is before her eyes even meet her father's.

It is like staring into a sunbeam, a sunbeam that wears an affably menacing smile. And then King Aeëtes is before them, a golden apotheosis of godhood who wouldn't even think to shield his children from his radiance.

Even looking upon his aura sets Medea's preternaturally attuned gifts atingle. To a witch of her ability, the elements themselves hold power, and the wizard-king of Colchis is as one with the sun's fire and luminance. Medea feels her thoughts bubbling at the seams in his presence, her fevered desire—

'... to meet these men,' her lips move, betraying her. She locks her feet to the grimy floor, refusing to stumble back. By the blood of Tartarus... her father always has this effect on her. There is nothing that stays hidden from his gaze, nothing sacred from his polluting touch.

A knowing, elegant chuckle. That kind that precedes an excoriation.

'Is that so?' he fawns on her with mock sincerity, relishing her daughter's vulnerability in his presence. 'My, my, Aspyrtus. It would seem I was wrong. Does the weakest of my get take after me the most? You've never shared my penchant for Achaean playthings before, daughter. Or do you?'

The witch's body tenses, as subtly as she dares. Don't give anything away. She *won't* give anything away. Not even a stray thought to be read.

Aeëtes takes a slow step closer, unthreatening. How very unthreatening. It is only then, with his aura shifted, that Medea notices her sister in the king's great shadow. Chalciope wears the robes of a Colchian royal, but her bare skin has been freshly inked and daubed. Swirling runic invocations signify chastity, innocence and protection. She always wears them whenever she knows she must appear before Aeëtes.

Medea does not think about why. She *won't* think about why.

'No,' Aeëtes breathes, the word evaporating in her ears like a mirage, or a delirium born of heatstroke. 'No, my dear daughter. I don't think that is it.' His strokes Medea's cheek with his golden hand, running his fingers menacingly, or perhaps lovingly, through her hair.

And then he speaks a word of power, a word no mortal ear can comprehend, and Aspyrtus crumples to the ground, screaming. The glyphs and sigils marking *his* flesh flare with amniotic light, searing their potency into the young man's soul.

'So if I were to do *that*,' Aeëtes' honeyed words somehow carry above his son's pleas for mercy, 'to the crew of intrepid heroes and lords who languish down below, you would take no umbrage with me at all? Hm?'

Aspyrtus goes on thrashing, spittle flying from his lips in burning torment. Medea's eyes flick down to his shaking, rolling form, though her face remains inches from her father's.

Don't break. Don't give in. Don't let him see the damage.

Aeëtes' eyes shine with something, though whether it is divine power or simple human cruelty, who can say?

'Perhaps you've a stronger stomach after all, girl.' The wizard-king whispers another primordial word, and Aspyrtus is finally released from his spell of agony. He sags back at his father's feet, a crumpled pile of sweat and exquisitely woven robes.

'I... I trapped their ship.' Medea overenunciates each word, refusing to let her voice seize up. 'In the straits. Our outrider vessels overwhelmed it easily enough.'

'Indeed, indeed.' Aeëtes rubs his chin indulgently, playing the contented, world-weary, elder as convincingly as a Titan can. 'Quite a feat of witchcraft, from the least powerful of my children. Which leads me to wonder...' He trails off, pretending to have lost his train of thought. 'Why not reduce them to fire and cinders with a simpler spell?

Why not turn the waves around them to lava, and make an offering of screams and smoke to my father?'

Medea clamps her jaw closed, forcing herself not to swallow. Her father is a shark, born to swim dark waters, and if there is one bloodied scent he is drawn to above all others, it is sentiment.

'Their vessel,' she hears herself replying. In her eyeline, Aspyrtus pulls himself back upright. 'It is a marvel of godly craftsmanship. I thought it best preserved.'

'Oh, I agree.' For what it is worth, that feels the most honest thing the wizard-king has said today. 'Oracular oak, from glades sacred to the daughter of Metis.' His beatific lips curl at that last, as if even mentioning Athena by name would make him spit. 'The ship has been moored in a backwater cove. It has secrets and gifts, and I intend to pillage both.'

Medea forces her cheeks to rise into a smile. 'Fortuitous then, my lord, that I was not wasteful.'

Oh, you fool. This time, she forces herself to untense, awaiting the strike or burning blow before it falls. But her father laughs instead, another of his deceptively melodious laughs.

'Perhaps there is hope for you yet, girl.' He turns back to face her, the very image of magnanimity – and then she flies, neck first, into his outstretched hand.

'Because if I thought for one minute, *daughter dearest*, that you had any other reason for preserving those outlanders and their ship...'

He clenches his perfect, porcelain teeth as his pore-free face contorts with rage.

'...That you were contenting yourself with daydreams of being the most dreaded and fell of all Achaeans, instead of the most pathetic and ungifted of all Colchians...'

He unclenches his hand at last, and this time it is Medea's turn to fall to the volcanic earth.

'Well. You are a smart woman, Medea, for all your other failings. I have an elder daughter, and a son. Both of whom command Hecate's gifts with far greater poise than you. You amuse me with your need to impress, girl, but don't imagine that adds to your worth.'

Aeëtes looms in her vision, towering over her, the way the sun's light shines down upon all things. This is her life, this is all their lives, and life with a deathless Titan does not change.

Neither Aspyrtus nor Chalciope say a word, or even move to help her rise. Fear rules them, Medea reflects, as eternally as it rules her. But however fearful her siblings may be, even the lowest and basest of souls need someone to look down upon.

'Come, all of you.' The wizard-king is already gone, his footsteps echoing lower into the Vault's depths. 'You will all play a part in this. Let us see what dregs Hellas has sent to our door this time.'

XXXIV
OUTLANDER

He forces his hanging head to rise, his mouth and eyes so dry they feel fused shut. Pain and a lack of sleep have pissed over his short-term memory, but he knows the voice of cruelty when he hears it.

Here he is, in another dungeon, at the mercy of another foul tyrant. His dead man's journey ending right where it began.

How many more, Queen of Olympus? How many more of your sadistic jokes?

Jason of Pelion wrenches open his eyes at last, and golden pain fills his vision. It is so much more than just light; it is the blindness that smudges across your gaze when you look into the sun. The shimmering haze that lingers over a desert plain. The aura of fractal white that glistens above a sunlit sea.

It fades, and not a moment too soon, leaving the shepherd boy feeling bereft and relieved in equal measure.

'Aeëtes.' That voice is speaking again, the one that filled his soul with dread. 'Aeëtes, son of Helios. Wizard-king of Aea. Lord of the realm of Colchis, and master of the blessed artefact you have come to steal.'

Jason's red-veined gaze begins to roam, his thoughts rolling their groggy way back together. The Colchians took the lot of them alive, hauling them from the *Argo*'s thwarts without a moment wasted. His eyes adjust to the unlit dark around him, as far as they can roam without moving his head.

He has awoken in a chamber of cavernous rock, airy though possessed of a sickly warmth of its own. And lonely, too. The shepherd boy and his godly, kohl-wearing jailer are the only souls here.

Jason's tired, aching mind should be troubled by this development, afraid for what has become of the remaining Argonauts while he slumbered. But right here, right now, he cannot quite bring himself to care.

In this chamber there is enough peril to go around as is.

'A scourge upon your line!' a dust-parched voice rattles. Jason recognises it, belatedly, as his own. 'Colchian scum! You've no… no right to… keep us like this! Where is your shame, warlock? Where is your *xenia?*'

The shepherd boy's eyes have only just adjusted — taken with the forty-year-old god and the radiance suffusing from his being — before he can even truly follow what is happening. Their lordly captor extends a golden hand. And then, somehow, Jason is rising into the air. Rising, but still bound, shoulder to sole, in chains of ember-glowing silver.

'How quaint of you.' The mage lifts his hand, and the son of Aeson with it. 'You think too small, my Thessalian friend. Did you truly believe our people were bound by your customs? By your tangle of honour and obligation?' He lowers his hand once more, and Jason's inert form crashes down to the dungeon floor. 'How very quaint, indeed.'

Jason draws breath for another curse, only for more fetters to fly across his open mouth. They glow, even now, as if eternally freshly smelted.

'Come now,' his captor gently chides him, a finger drifting to his lips. 'Our ways are not your own, outlander. The judgement of your gods does not fall here.'

'We...' Jason's muffled avowal dissolves into a choking fit, as he hawks up first spit, then bile, and then an ominous mouthful of blood. It splatters across his chains, down the ragged remnants of his clothes, sticking to his jutting chin.

'Oh, my.' The wizard-king's face wrinkles in petty disgust, his most expansive expression yet. 'That will be my daughter's work, I believe. You'll have to forgive my dear Medea, outlander. The weakest of my get she may be, though she does sometimes misjudge her own strength.' His face drifts back into its aquiline sneer. 'As if she hasn't enough failings already.'

At his feet, the shepherd boy shifts once more, trying to look a little less helpless. On a whim, the Colchian lord unshackles the chains binding his mouth with a noncommittal wave of his hand.

'I didn't...' Jason splutters. 'We did not come to this place to rob you, Lord of Colchis.'

'No?' Aeëtes raises an immaculately gilded eyebrow, indulging the prisoner's lie for a moment. 'Did you not sail far away from Hellas at the whim of your estranged uncle? Did you not unite the greatest heroes among the Achaeans, and convince them to man that enchanted boat of yours, to bring the Golden Fleece back home to... Pelias? Is that his name?' Aeëtes cocks his head, in mock puzzlement. 'I have to say, *Jason of Pelion*, do you truly wish to compound your disrespect with dishonesty?'

The silence stretches between them, and the wizard-king's spreading smile only adds to it. It is beatific and damning in equal measure, its wearer relishing how it feels to reveal his captive's most intimate shames and secrets.

'Swindling you was never my desire, Lord Aeëtes.' Jason manages to choke back the muck in his throat, this time. 'My uncle charged me with an impossible quest, and I came here simply to play his game. Doing so was my Fate, as the Queen of Heaven revealed to me. Stealing your treasure was the only way I could reclaim my birthright. Reclaim the destiny Pelias stole from me.'

As he speaks, the Lord of Colchis nods along, pretending to humour him.

'Well, well.' He finally adds when it becomes clear no more is coming. 'That is a breath-taking level of trust you place in your kinsman, young man. I suppose, it isn't as if he has proven how untrustworthy he is already... Oh, bother. He has, when he slew your father.'

Aeëtes scoffs in the dark, humid air, turning from Jason as if he actually needs a moment to process how pointless this all is.

And then he spins, in a flash, one elegant finger pointed down at him.

Jason *screams* as a burning vice bites into his ankle. And then he is falling, *upward*, strung up to the cavern's unseen ceiling and hanging upside down like a slain bull being drained of blood.

The chain... how? Is it the same one? How can it hang from above with a moment's thought?

'No,' Aeëtes hisses, as the shepherd boy continues to sway from far above. '*No*. As frightfully pathetic as you seem, I cannot quite believe you would make it to my gates on moronic goodwill alone. *No*,' he draws in an agonisingly long breath, trying to hide his fury behind a magnanimous mask and failing utterly. 'You *had* to have your own designs on my blessed Fleece.'

For a few moments, Jason just hangs, still swaying from his abrupt rise, features slowly reddening as the blood flows to his head. Another dribble of drool worms its way down to earth, this time crawling up his face and brow at gravity's behest.

It is so damn warm in here. This subterranean hellhole feels close to the earth's igneous heart.

'I did,' the son of Aeson wheezes at last. 'I... I hoped to take the Fleece, yes. Destroy my uncle with its power, too. The others... they only came with me, for that reason. They hoped to... to take it for themselves. Their oaths to me merely extend to when we find it.'

For a moment, the wizard-king is unsure if he has heard correctly. He waits some more, for a twist or punchline that isn't coming.

'You really have sailed into dark waters, mountain boy. I'm not sure if I should laugh at you, or light a candle for you.' A malevolent smirk lights his features, barely visible in what little light remains. 'Is *this* the truth behind your claims, Thessalian? Is this the branch you seek to extend to me? That you will take my Fleece in good faith, burn your uncle to ashes with it, and then... what? *Return* it to me, with grateful thanks?'

The shepherd boy sways. And sways. And sways.

'If that is what you want,' he finally murmurs. Upturned eyes lock onto Aeëtes', and the sincerity is painful enough.

'Unbelievable.' The Colchian king's face is creased in astonishment, the most genuine, unfeigned expression he has worn. 'Just... unbelievable. I had so many questions about you,' he admits, taking a threatening step closer, and another, another after that. 'When the scryers in my coven told me what they'd seen, what was crossing the Inhospitable Sea towards us, I almost didn't believe them. So many souls we'd heard stories of, so many preening lords and heroes of Hellas. Godsblood flowing through their veins, half of them. But *you...*'

He is directly beneath Jason's upturned form, where he hangs as helpless as he feels. '*You...* you were the one I was truly wary of. The lost heir, sprung from nowhere, with no *kleos* to his name but able to bind far mightier men to his cause nonetheless. The cattle-prince who truly thought he could challenge one king to dethrone another.'

Aeëtes hisses another of his wretched words of power, and the chain connecting Jason to the rafters begins to grow, like something that has no right being alive. The son of Aeson slowly descends, finally falling into the eyeline of his tormentor.

'And look at you,' the warlock scorns him with a whisper. 'A mountain milksop who can scarcely control his comrades, crying Fate and hiding behind voided promises. Is *this* all the tutelage of Chiron begets? Is *this* the best the Olympians can muster against our power? By the shadows of the sun... I would laugh if it weren't so frightfully pathetic!'

'You would dishonour the gods?' Jason snarls, rage and stupidity blighting his fear for a moment. 'You would dishonour Hera?'

'Alright,' the Lord of Colchis cackles. 'Now I truly am laughing, shepherd boy! You think I give a damn about your precious patrons on Olympus? Drink in the air around you, child. This is Colchis. Your feeble gods don't reign here. This kingdom hearkens to the *old* ways, the *old* gods. The Titans, boy, who reigned when the sky was young.'

Jason hangs, slacker now, his shattered conviction plain to see.

'You must have tasted it,' Aeëtes continues. 'The sickness that suckles at your soul. To even breathe Colchian air is to feel that truth. The Olympian blood running through your veins will avail you nothing. You will take nothing from this kingdom without our behest. You will not wield the Fleece's power against your uncle. Your blood will not be turned to ichor by its magic. And your *Fate*,' he spits the word, looking right up into Jason's reddened eyes, 'will be whatever I damn well choose.'

'You lie…' Jason can only breathily curse his captor, bereft of much of his strength already. 'You *lie*, wretch! My Fate… my Fate is to survive. My Fate is… to *triumph!*'

Aeëtes spares him one last glance, before the chain binding Jason's ankle begins to contract. It has just the effect he desired, as his helpless prisoner begins to rise once more into the shadows.

'Your Fate, if you must know, is to be the latest plaything for my Bulls. You and all your wretched followers, though I think you'll have the honour of being first. We'll see how far your goddess' protection stretches.'

XXXV
A Pact, Infernal

A barren and unknowable span of time later, she comes for him.

There is no mystery to this meeting. Her father sent her, as he always does when he tires of making sport with new playthings. As his magicks and untender words blitz their defences from without, her honeyed lies and false compassion weaken their resolve from within.

So it has played out a thousand times before. And so, King Aeëtes imagines in his divine arrogance, it will do so yet again.

In this respect, the wizard is, and is not, wrong. Medea has slithered her way into Jason's dungeon to do this very thing, it is true. But not quite to the end Aeëtes has in mind.

The shepherd boy – the bruised and broken remains of the shepherd boy – tries to resist her touch, at first. Not that he has much capacity to resist anything. He is far too weak and weary for that.

'Cease struggling,' Medea quietly demands, raising the goblet of water once more. Chained to the cavern walls as he is, all he can do is move his head away, but he has little energy left to do even that. Even the gentlest of her father's mental assaults can carve scars across a psyche, and her father is seldom gentle. But Jason's resistance finally crumbles. He dips his head for some water before recoiling in what would, in any other situation, be considered surliness.

'Do you wish to die before your punishment comes? Is that it?' Medea suddenly snaps, with more venom than she intends. 'Is this your ploy to avoid that Fate?'

That word seems to revive him at last, more so than any water or soothing entreaty. Jason's eyes loll back out from beneath his eyelids, more bloodshot than white, and that head of untended, overgrown Thessalian curls rises uncertainly to meet hers.

'Fate…' he wheezes, 'is a lie.'

'Oh?' The witch pauses for a moment, unsure if this is the blackest of jests or graveside wisdom. 'Such impiety, from an Achaean's mouth. If your Olympian protectress could hear you now…'

'*No.*' The son of Aeson pulls back on his taut chains, relishing what little cool the jagged walls behind him can impart to his inflamed, tarnished body. 'My goddess… my Hera… has betrayed me. Tempted me from my solitude on the Mountain. Thrown me… thrown me into *this.*'

Looming over him just as Aeëtes had done, Medea feels a stabbing need to sigh. Being a direct descendant of divinity – one of the most powerful gods in the firmament, no less – she sometimes forgets how blind and askew the lives of blood-and-clay mortals can be. Just how arbitrary and unknowable the forces of time and destiny can seem to them.

It is pitiful, in its own novel way.

'And what Fate was that?' she asks, archly, giving him a little more water.

'To rule my kingdom,' Jason hoarsely replies between mouthfuls. 'To burn my uncle and his sins from existence. To be the man I was born to be.'

Medea has no rejoinder to any of this. She has heard words like these a wearisome number of times before, from the mouths of other self-proclaimed and Fate-obsessed champions who have tried their luck against Aeëtes.

'I have been blind,' the shepherd boy confesses, without any prompting. 'I have been wrong, for so long... perhaps even from the beginning.' A laugh escapes his desiccated throat, wheezing and with no real breath behind it. 'Perhaps I'm not even of the royal blood after all, and Pelias has nothing to fear from me. Maybe Idmon and all those other preening heroes were right. Perhaps the Queen of Heaven needed a new toy to fight her ennui, another piece to toss across destiny's gameboard. The gathering of the Argonauts, this entire quest... nothing but Hera's cosmic joke.'

Medea keeps on listening, waiting for the boy's self-pity to burn itself out. If Jason had been looking up in that moment, rather than gazing indulgently into space, he would have seen the stately machinations turning behind the Colchian princess' eyes.

'You don't have any faith in the Fates?' She finally breaks the burgeoning silence. 'Any regard for the winding of fortune?'

Their eyes meet for a moment, hers alight with the promise of power, his red and raw with fatigue and pain.

'Not anymore,' he says. This close, he can smell the deceptively pleasant aroma of her body, bewitching yet not quite natural.

'And your brothers in arms?' she persists. 'Those men you have convinced to follow you down this path? You would leave them here to rot, if it meant you could be free of this?'

Jason takes a long moment to find his words, but who exactly he seeks to assuage isn't clear. Medea, or his own long-gagged conscience.

'Those men…' he breathes, ignoring the pain of his wounds, 'are not my comrades. They want the Fleece for their own ends, not mine. And if our places were traded, they would have no qualms about casting me aside. The only one of them who would have truly helped me is gone, marooned behind us at my own damn behest. So no, sorceress. To Hades with the cursed lot of them. They are one more thing I must leave behind.'

And with that bitter confession dripping from his lips, the Fate of several kingdoms shifts on its axis. Possibilities play out behind Medea's eyes, a strange mix of precognition and tentative hope. She looks at the boy chained before her, this pitiful remnant of an adventurer whose wisdom has come too late. She looks at him and sees a dejected, malleable soul, his zeal spent, his hopes doused. A boy who seeks not to strive towards destiny, but to cut himself free of it.

For a minute, Medea hears her father's laughter again. Her neck burns beneath his scalding touch.

'Very well, Achaean,' she finally concurs. Jason's brow arches in confusion. 'If you truly wish to cast your honour and inheritance aside… you shall do so. I will help you do it.'

Jason's silent disbelief is practically audible, but a drowning man cannot pick and choose his raft.

'H—' he falters. 'How? And why?'

'I've served Aeëtes long enough to know what he has in store for you.' The witch laughs without much humour. 'My father is a creature of habit, but therein lies the chink in his defences. I will give you the means to slip through his clutches, and from there, you will be able to escape.'

She rises from her kneeling poise, looming over her Achaean prisoner once more.

'And as for why? I don't think you've the luxury to question my motives right now, little boy. But very well. You are not the only soul who tires of these walls, Jason. I will give you the means to escape from this place, if that is truly your wish, and to make your way back to your kingdom.'

She reaches into her flowing robes, pulling her sacrificial dagger free and holding it up.

'But if you do, Achaean, then you will be bound to me for the duration. It will be my wiles and power that set you free, though it will be your freedom that ensures my own.'

Jason winces as the blade nicks his palm. It is hardly the first hurt he has suffered in this dungeon, or the deepest, but something about this violation pains his soul just as much.

'We will make a pact, you and I.' Medea clasps the shepherd boy's bloodied palm with her own, having drawn her blood with the very same blade. 'A pact infernal.'

XXXVI
CONVERGENCE

'Gods Below...' Admetus murmurs, his words curdling in the honeyed air. 'Is that... Is that blood, flowing in that river?' He strains his gaze around the beached boats and abandoned wagons. The light around them is fading, but it is somehow still bright. Only the weighty weariness pulling at Admetus' eyelids gives the truth away. Night should have fallen. Sleep should have taken him.

'Focus.' Behind him, the Allslayer grimaces as he admonishes him. 'Pull yourself together, my friend. The gazes of our gods do not fall upon this kingdom. This place is not meant to feel our tread.'

Privately, though, he shares the king's revulsion. The not-quite-light that sees all, seeping through every shadow. That aroma in the air, sickly but not sweet, trickling deeper into their lungs with each breath.

Yes, Colchis is a queer enough place, all things considered. Life has grown along a different path here.

Herakles breaks from cover, stealing his silent way up the riverside colonnade. He finds his next refuge behind a plinth of dark quartz, furtive eyes scanning around for any witnesses. Only then does he beckon Admetus forward with a frenetic wave.

This has been their shared life, since the latter's ship delivered them to the Phasis' mouth. Sailing straight into the lion's den was out of the question, whatever the foolhardy crew of the *Argo* had elected to do, so the Allslayer and the king made their clandestine way upriver equipped with nothing but the clothes and arms on their backs. No supplies, no backup of sailing men from Pherae, no herald to clear the way for them. This would be done with guile, or it would not be done at all.

And here they finally are, in this cradle of sorcerers, haggard and hungry after several sleepless un-nights. Quite how they have passed this far undetected is a miracle Herakles is already coming to doubt. Fate can play tricks on you, after all. In the Allslayer's case, it frequently does.

Across the dimly lit stone boulevard, sounds echo oddly from up ahead. The distant patter of marching feet, the murmured cries of toil and effort from the market squares. The rare cadence of laughter.

'Come on, damn it!' Herakles hisses as Admetus draws near. For all the Pheraean's many qualities, subterfuge is most certainly not one of them. How he hasn't given them both away already, the Allslayer has no idea.

'Forgive me,' Admetus blurts as he scurries into cover. 'I think… I think we've been followed.'

'What?' Herakles risks another fevered glance around the pillar's breadth. Nothing. The square is still empty, the only sound the rustling waters. 'By whom?'

'I can't say.' Admetus is clearly pained to disagree with his friend, but he presses the point nonetheless. 'I haven't… I haven't *seen* anything, Allslayer. But I glimpse something, occasionally, in my gaze's corner. It feels like—'

Something swift and robed drops down on him from above, like a spider wrought in silken cloth. Admetus has scarcely a moment to scream before the spider clasps his mouth, righting itself with a moment's notice. One hand grips a sleek little hunting blade, a blade Herakles has come to recognise during his time aboard the *Argo*. The other hand, removed from Admetus' mouth, is open and empty, raised outward to indicate no ill will.

'So, you're here,' the silken spider observes, lowering her knife and pulling down her hood. 'You certainly took your time. You would have been a great boon to us when we arrived, Allslayer.'

Herakles sighs, a weary smile creasing his unshaven features.

'Atalanta,' he greets their new arrival. 'It would appear I've missed a few steps.'

Of course she'd been the only one of them to evade capture. Of course she'd had the wherewithal to survive, utterly alone, in this alien land that hated her with every atom. Of course she had.

And now, as she leads the new arrivals through the few shadowed paths that cross Aea, the Allslayer and the huntress bring each other up to speed on their time apart.

'I leapt from the *Argo*'s deck,' she says, as they cross down through a long-forsaken tunnel that could be considered a sewer. 'The sea… I don't know what they did to the sea. But it burned me, in mind as well as body. I swam beneath the water, far out beyond their gaze, as their outriders stormed the *Argo*.'

She hesitates for a moment, as if the memories aren't quite coming willingly.

'When it was over, I broke the surface beneath the Colchian vessel's stern. I clasped onto the frills on its hull, and let it carry me inland.'

On they travel through the cavern, splashes of unnatural sunlight striating their watery tread. Admetus trails a little way behind them, still a little perturbed, like most men of good birth tend to be, by the huntress' unapologetic coldness.

'And the others?' Herakles asks her. 'Were they all taken?'

'As far as I could see, yes.' Atalanta wipes a backhand across her glistening forehead. At some point since their last meeting, she must have given into her impatience and cut her hair short, for her shoulder-length locks have been quite messily severed by blade strokes. On any other soul it would look crude, but the Arcadian wears her newfound boyishness well.

'I didn't see all their faces as they were hauled overboard, but by my count it was all of them. All ten.'

'Ten?' Herakles echoes, halting in place and making Admetus check his step. A cloying darkness flows into his thoughts. 'But Peleus... did he—'

'Peleus lives.' Atalanta clasps his shoulder with a delicate hand. 'He pulled through his injuries...' A pause. There are some things that not even the huntress wishes to dwell on.

'Argus is dead,' she finally reveals. 'Jason killed him, not long after we sailed from Pegae.'

The Allslayer says nothing. His silence asks the question he cannot.

'Our captain found something,' Atalanta explains, her voice barely carrying over the susurrus of water flowing about their feet. 'At least, he thought he did. He found letters, and gold, in our shipwright's personal effects. Letters that were addressed to King Pelias, keeping him abreast of the *Argo*'s movements.'

Herakles still cannot will his lips to move.

'Jason dragged him above deck,' the huntress continues. 'The more we tried to stop him, the angrier he got. He was ranting about Aeson, and Hera, and Chiron's lessons. Then he rammed his sword through Argus' breast and hurled him overboard.'

Hovering between them, Admetus' patience finally fades.

'Is now really the time for this discussion?' he growls. 'We have to keep moving.'

Atalanta shoots him a look that could stop a centaur's heart. A look that could have transfixed the Ceryneian Hind, whatever its divine protectress would hope to prevent. A look that can bore through a prince or beggarman with equal disregard.

'My friend,' Herakles begins, clapping a hand on the King of Pherae's shoulder. 'Would you do me the honour of scouting the way ahead? The lady needs a moment of my time.'

'As… you wish.' And like that, Admetus is gone, leaving nothing but splashing footfalls and a scowl on Atalanta's face in his wake.

Allslayer and huntress regard each other in the ensuing silence. Water-dappled light flickers across the tunnel walls, casting their faces in mottled shadows.

'Hylas?' she softly asks him. A shaken head is all that answers, and it takes a moment or two before she can finally speak again. When she does, her voice shakes too audibly to be worthy of her patroness. How very unlike her.

'He… he was just a boy, Herakles. I don't know how long I've been here. How long I've been scrabbling through these streets like a rat. I don't know how long the others have languished here, at the mercy of these witches and warlocks. They are strong men, *proud* men. I can't see most of them breaking, but…'

She tears her gaze from his, unwilling for some reason to let Herakles see her face.

'Jason,' the Allslayer breathes. 'Orpheus.'

Atalanta's eyes close, as she slowly bobs her head.

'Meleager,' he adds, finally.

He takes a step forward, not letting her pull away a second time. Hands as broad as supper plates, strong enough to crumble rock, clasp her shoulders with a closeness that is wholly unromantic, but no less tender for it. If anything, it feels fraternal; the comfort of the brother Atalanta won't ever admit she always wanted.

'We'll find them, Arcadian. Your sanctimonious captain will not be dying today, nor will your Calydonian friend. Look at me, Atalanta. Hear what I am saying.'

She meets his gaze unflinching, bloodshot eye to bloodshot eye. The tears are still leaking from her eyes, but these tears are more than just shed sorrow.

'We should go,' she finally whispers.

They find themselves in the unseasonable light once more, as Admetus' guess and Atalanta's gut see them out of the gilded sewer pit. Back beneath the skies of Colchis, the three of them forge an unlikely but unbroken path through the City of Dawn.

But not inland, not any deeper into Aea's urban heart. The trio keep to the southern reaches, hugging the paved and cultivated path that follows the Phasis' reach.

But a river means life, and life means people. The shambolic robed mess of Colchis' citizenry is in more evidence here, as are marauding warriors sworn to Aeëtes' service. The former vastly outweigh the latter, which is something at least. Losing yourself in a crowd of sorrowful peasants is one thing, but evading the watchful gaze of fighting men is quite another.

There are several points of worry along their way. Several times when the alarm is almost sounded. But by some miracle of their absent gods, the three Achaeans manage to fare thankfully well. Whoever Atalanta cannot slip past, Herakles can still silence, and Admetus manages to hide the bodies before any are witnessed.

In time, they find themselves climbing down the river's bank. The squares and avenues around them are beginning to fill with Colchian citizens, but the huntress seems sure that this is the right path to take. Below street level, as risky as it is, the three of them evade notice.

'And who is it who moors here?' Admetus presses her, still not ready to believe her.

'Royalty,' Atalanta replies, 'as I have said. I can't vouch for who, or why they land here without ceremony. But I have watched this skiff come and go enough times since I arrived. The iconography upon its flanks is unmistakeable. The ship belongs to Aeëtes' royal house.'

Aeëtes. Even that name elicits an intake of breath from Admetus. Fearful legends wind their way across Hellas of the sorcerous king of Colchis, son of a Titan's fire, and the fell powers he commands. Fireside tales, most of them, meant to frighten children into behaving. The fact that nothing else is known about him only makes it worse.

'And this is your plan?' Herakles says. The words are no challenge; unlike the Pheraean, what little Atalanta has managed to glean from this place is enough to put his faith in.

'It is.' The huntress has drawn her hunting knife again, her surest weapon since losing her bow on the Isle of Ares. 'Whoever boards this boat cares more for subtlety and solitude than the solace of armed guards. There'll be little they can do once we steal our way aboard. At worst, ransom. At best, information.'

She raises her blade.

'But one way or another, they'll bring us closer to the Argonauts.'

Boarding the ship is almost shamefully easy, a fact that won't resonate with any of them until it is too late. Even accounting for Herakles' and Admetus' lack of clandestine talent, the trio clamber their unsubtle way aboard without a vestige of resistance.

How arrogant the passenger must be to have taken so little precaution against intruders. Or how oracular.

The Allslayer shoulders the rickety doors apart, leading them in with his club raised. Atalanta and Admetus are barely a step behind him, the huntress' knife ready to parry or stab whatever lies within.

Whoever.

'Greetings,' a dreamy, buttery voice greets them. It betrays no surprise at being startled, no unease at facing down three intruders. 'More Achaeans come to grace our shores with their presence, I presume?'

Herakles' rising reply has caught in his throat. He knows this woman, knows every inch of cuneiform that striates her golden face. A face he has seen before, but not with his eyes.

A face he has dreamt about far too many times. A face that drove him to Tiresias.

XXXVII
A Pact, Mundane

For a moment, Medea is almost pleasantly surprised. The unlikely trio of wanderers come aboard are clearly as taken aback as she is. Neither they, nor her, quite expected to see what they are seeing.

'You?' the largest of them guardedly asks, a mountain of muscle and scars with a voice like pacified thunder.

'You seem surprised to see me,' Medea wonders aloud. 'And yet, there isn't a soul in my kingdom you should recognise.' She wills her gaze to stay on him, and not stray to his two strange compatriots – the prim-looking lord with his comically formal wargear, or the young ranger pointing her dagger at Medea's face.

'I have seen you,' the man-mountain insists. 'How did you infiltrate my dreams?'

The sorceress smiles, wanly, enjoying the way this demigod blazes in her witchsight. This can be no mortal man. He is so much more, more than even he realises.

'My farsight can extend a long way,' she confesses, as her irises shimmer with honey-coloured light. 'So I may well have disturbed your sleep, Achaean. I would read little into it, truthfully.'

The towering hero's face clenches, but Medea isn't done.

'Now,' she purrs, feeling her aura flare and making no attempt to dim its potency, 'either this land's mystic defences have been breached for the second time in days, after untold centuries of solitude… or you motley fools are following the son of Aeson.'

'Jason is here?' the hunter girl asks, clutching her knife tighter. 'And the Argonauts? They still live?'

'Don't listen to her!' the third of them urges from behind them. 'This is bewitchment, all of it. Mark my words!'

It is all Medea can do to suppress a chuckle.

'The waifs and strays who rode Jason's coattails still lived when last I saw them. Though I can't say how many draw breath now. My father tends to wear through his playthings quickly.'

The girl – an Arcadian, if Medea's ear for dialects rings true – slashes forward with a feral cry. She is fast, this one. Faster than a mortal, almost too fast for a witch's sight to——

'Enough,' the man-mountain growls, clamping her between his mighty forearms. 'Enough, Atalanta. She can't help us with a slashed throat.'

The Arcadian struggles vainly for a few more moments before finally abandoning her resistance. She lowers her hunting blade without relinquishing it.

'Temper, temper!' Medea pretends to chide her, savouring every moment of this formidable woman's hatred. 'I doubt King Iasus would care for your lack of manners. Or the Daughter of Leto, for that matter.'

Another charged, wrathful silence, but this time Atalanta's rage manifests as ice rather than fire.

'Don't push your luck, warlock.' This from the giant among men, now stalking malevolently closer. 'Keep your sorcerous tendrils out of our heads, or I *will* let her kill you.'

Medea doesn't step back. She won't. Not in one of her havens. But she subtly shifts poise to keep all three in eyeshot. She may well have the measure of them, but this towering one radiates threat with every move.

'Very well, Achaeans. Shall I bite? What help do you think possessing me will avail you?' She laughs again, but there is less of her heart in it this time. 'If you think King Aeëtes will ransom my head from you, then you don't understand who he is. Or who I am.'

'Oh, nothing so crude.' This from Atalanta, who has edged closer even as her hulking comrade stands at Medea's back. 'You are going to use your gifts, sorceress, to help us free Jason and the other Argonauts from your father's clutches.'

'Indeed!' the last member of the trio adds, in an accent that smacks of… Pherae? 'And once that is done, you will help us escape down the Phasis, where my ship awaits.'

The inside of the skiff is not a large space, and three unwanted guests are enough to fill it with threat. The colossal hand, coming to rest on Medea's shoulder from behind her, only drives the point home. It has been a long time – by mortal or godly count – since an outlander has had the gall to menace her like this.

But enough is enough. She is a daughter of Titans, a deaconess of Hecate's darkest arts. She serves a man far more terrifying than this one.

'If you seek to free the son of Aeson,' she informs them, 'then your wisest course of action would be to stay your hand, and allow me to carry out my work.'

Atalanta's face pinches in suspicion, the expression uncharacteristically clear.

'You? *You* seek to free Jason? What a striking, dubious coincidence that is.'

'I make no jest.' Medea raises an open hand, only for the intruders to flinch from it. A moment later, satisfied that no curse or incantation is coming, they peer down at it.

More specifically, at the reddened welt that crosses her palm, half-healed but still infused with amniotic glow.

'We swore a pact, him and I.' The sorceress lowers her hand. 'A binding of lifeforce. Our *Fates*, as you Achaeans understand it. They are entwined. My fortune is his. And his peril is my own.'

On her shoulder, the monstrous hand begins to tighten.

'I can feel the rhythm of your heart,' that thunderous voice rumbles from behind her. 'Tell a single lie, warlock, and I'll crush you like brushwood.'

Medea releases another shaky breath, keeping her eyes on Atalanta's. She won't show any fear. She *won't*.

'Then feel my truth, hero. Feel the honesty in my words. It is every bit as much in my interest to free your friend as it is yours. This place…' She indicates the rest of the boat, and by extension the rest of Aea, with a flicker of eye movement. '… is no longer a stronghold for me, or even a haven. Once Aeëtes realises what I have done, I will be hunted as zealously as you.'

No-one speaks for a moment, and the Colchian can hardly move to see. But she feels the silent exchange above her head. Atalanta and the man-mountain, wordlessly weighing up how much to trust her.

'If we assume, for one moment, that you are telling the truth…' The third man, once again. The young king. 'It isn't merely Jason we want. It is all of them. Every man your lackeys took from the *Argo*'s deck.'

The sorceress is laughing before Admetus has even finished his sentence. It is shrill, hollow, and makes them all start like a howl on the prairie.

'That is *all* you want, Achaeans? Am I to believe you will leave Colchis *without* its most potent of treasures? That you will sail back across the sea *without* the Golden Fleece in your war chest?'

She watches the light fade from Atalanta's eyes. No matter.

'I already have a plan for Jason,' Medea says. 'The means are... complex, but all it takes is preparation. He has his part to play in it, and I have mine.'

Tighter, that mighty hand grips her. Tighter.

'Speak,' Atalanta commands.

'I am to journey downriver,' Medea informs them. 'Which was precisely where I was going before you stole into my ship. The Roots of Iapetus, that grow in the shadow of the Caucasus Mountains. I will come upon them, when the moon has waned enough, and harvest the unguent from those Roots for my ritual.'

And like that, the hand releases her without warning. She can finally move and turn, flexing her pained shoulder a fraction, as the mountain of flesh and power takes a step back.

'The Roots of Iapetus,' he echoes. 'I know of them.' His stony eyes drift back to Atalanta. 'She speaks the truth, Huntress. This can deliver Jason to us.'

For her part, the Arcadian remains unswayed. 'That still leaves the other Argonauts, daughter of Aeëtes. What do you intend to do about them? And even assuming they can be saved...' She actually takes a moment to spit on the creaking deck at Medea's feet. 'What vow do you think you can even swear, that would compel us to let you leave here in your way?'

Medea takes a moment to gaze into the huntress' eyes, eyes so different and yet so like her own. What could the two of them have been, if not for a quirk of birth and circumstance? Could they have ghosted through the Glades of Artemis together like dryads? Have ruled all Colchis between them, using their uninspired brother as a king and figurehead?

The sorceress cares nothing for the other ruffians Jason brought here, and frankly doubts she could sway any more of them to work together with her, even for their escape. She peers down at them with her capricious witchsight, and all she sees are complications. More instability in an already precarious plan. More influences over a prince Medea seeks to puppet alone.

She has not leashed herself to the son of Aeson on a whim, after all. Jason has what she seeks, or soon will have, and the lack of wit or fibre to stop her wielding it for herself.

The most dreaded and fell of all Achaeans, or the most pathetic and ungifted of all Colchians...

But if she can't escape this kingdom, then none of it will matter to begin with. And if she wants to escape this kingdom, then she must escape from within her own skiff first.

'They will have taken Jason to the plain, by now,' Medea finally admits. Her words are meant for all of them, but it is Atalanta she truly seeks to convince. 'The rest of your friends languish in the Vault of Hyperion. I can show you the way, Achaeans, and I can give you the means to overcome their jailors, while I take what I need from the Caucasus.'

The huntress doesn't respond, or move. She doesn't even break eye contact.

'You'll have company then, warlock. I'd hate for you to slip away again, once you're out of my sight.' And with that, Atalanta finally sheathes her hunting knife, letting it hang from the belt around her thigh.

'My friends will kindly escort you to your terminus, Medea of Colchis. Now point me at this Vault of yours.'

Atalanta's eyes flash with something. Nothing as literal as Medea's magic, but every bit as fiery and untameable.

'And pray for your own sake that none of them have perished.'

XXXVIII
THE WARLOCK AND THE WRAITHS

And here it has finally come. Not quite the heroic death he'd dreamt of, a fight for his throne that would fill Chiron with pride, but a man's death, nonetheless.

There are few things more horrific, or intoxicating, than the idea of a man's death.

The red-robed guards march across the sand in stately, soulless precision, their chains of celestial power dragging a filthy, bloodied bundle with them. That bundle was once Jason of Pelion, a simple, good-natured mountain boy, until a centaur taught him the truth of royal bloodlines, and a goddess filled his head with pyrite promises.

Captain, coward, slayer of shipmates, challenger of kings. A boy whose weakness has done what his courage could not: muster the mightiest souls across the kingdoms and bind them to a unified end. Not the end he intended, but an end all the same.

Somewhere, at the edge of his fading senses, he hears jeering. A distant crowd of onlookers, who probably aren't cheering for his survival.

He set out to forge a deathless legacy, and that is precisely what he has done.

In that respect, at least, the Fates have it right.

'A curse on this infernal sky,' Admetus mutters. 'All this light, every damned hour. How can we even judge the day?'

At his side, on the deck of Medea's little boat, Herakles cranes his gaze up to the heavens. The King of Pherae has a point. He could have sworn, twice already, that the sliver of argent light shining down on them was from the moon.

Whether it is even the same moon that looks down upon Hellas isn't clear, but moonlight is what the witch claims to need. So they keep on staring, as the skiff keeps on rowing. Up through the queasy halo of sunlight, trying to make sense of the insensible.

'Come down here, both of you.' Medea's voice, floating above-deck. 'Neither of you could pass as Colchian in a year of perfect harvests, and any single onlooker who recognises you means death for all of us.' And with that, her voice drops to its sepulchral murmuring, the mystic chants that keep the boat's oars about their gentle task.

Admetus moves to heed her command, only for the Allslayer to gently grip his forearm. In their hours of sedately gliding down the Phasis, they have yet to pass another vessel going either way. But that is not why they stay.

'I don't trust her,' Herakles says, his eyes not leaving the skyline. 'She may well be speaking truth about this ritual, but I don't trust her intentions.'

Admetus spits overboard, his wad of spittle curdling in the gloopy waves of milk lapping at their hull. 'The understatement of the age, my kinsman. What can we do if she sells us to some foreign bidder? If we are taken off-guard this far from Aea, will we be able to do anything to help the others?'

The Allslayer lets his eyes fall closed for a moment, drinking in the sounds and smells of this land. Medea is listening, that much he knows. Be it witchsight or all-too-human paranoia, she will be hanging on every word that passes between them.

'The Roots of Iapetus are real enough,' he maintains. 'And they may well hold the key to our escape, if our new friend is as proficient with her spells as she claims to be.'

Admetus lets the silence hang, unsatisfied and unplacated.

'Atalanta may n—'

'Atalanta can take care of herself,' Herakles gently pre-empts him. 'And she is more than equal to the task before her.'

'If you say so,' Admetus finally replies.

Shadows flicker over their faces, the umbral outlines of ghostly tree branches overhanging the riverbank. They look curiously bare, as if some immense fruits had once hung from their spindly limbs.

'Do you trust me, Admetus?' the Allslayer finally asks. 'I believe you do, and I trust the huntress.'

'Oh, *enough* with it!' the Pheraean snaps back at him. 'I trust you more than I trust myself, Child of Thunder. But you're asking me to put too much faith in too little, friend. It wasn't that orphan from Arcadia who pledged to search the lands for Alcestis, no matter what the laws of death and life forbade. It wasn't this Colchian serpent that battled Hades' emissary for her soul.'

Herakles lets that go, considering if his old friend is right after all.

'You came here to be an Argonaut,' is all the reply he can muster. 'This is what that means.'

Admetus snorts, perhaps sensing the Allslayer's lack of conviction. There has been little trust or faith between the crew of the *Argo*, after all.

'We've humoured Medea this far,' Herakles says at last. 'And in honesty, I believe we passed the time for reservations when we cast off from Aea.'

He looks back out over the pale waves, as Hylas' last words press at his thoughts.

The dirt of the arena floor tastes awful. He should know. He has hawked up enough of it so far, and somehow swallowed even more.

How long has he been lying in this filth? How did he even get here in the first place? The questions slide across his consciousness as his eyes flick here and there, trying to bring some order to this madness.

He is… somewhere. The sickeningly sweet light of Colchis surrounds him like an aura, stealing all hope of gauging place or distance. He was in an… an arena? A desert chasm? A plain? Who can tell?

He whirls on his unsteady feet, trying to gain any sense of his surroundings. The radiance around him bleaches the sight from his gaze, but if he strains his eyes hard enough, he fancies he can see…

Faces. Tightly pressed together, baying for his blood with silent lips.

Spectators.

Jason recoils, though there is nothing but oppressively warm air to recoil from.

Take your time, son of Aeson, a voice whispers inside his head. It is Jason's own voice, his inner monologue, slaved to another's will and stolen without shame. Yet another violation to thank Aeëtes for. *Where would be the fun in watching you die quickly?*

He has not walked these valleys in a great many years. It is only natural that they feel different now. His last visit changed the soul of this place quite profoundly.

'The two of you will need to guard me,' Medea insisted upon arrival. From her tone, disobedience wasn't something that had even crossed her mind. 'This is more than about harvesting the right reward. It is about the time, the alignment, the intent in my heart. The summer moon is waning at last, and that leaves little time. This will require all my focus.'

'Do you truly need bodyguards for this task?' Herakles asked, raising a sardonic eyebrow.

'Guard against what?' Admetus cut in. Which was probably the better question.

The witch had deigned to answer neither man. She'd simply gone about her work, with only a hiss of wordless displeasure to dismiss them. There was no preamble, and contrary to her claims, no ritual or ceremony. The Allslayer and the king were left to themselves, alone and unmoored in the uncertainty of this place.

And what a place it is. It ought to remind him of Pegae, but that comparison does little justice to its majesty. The peaks of the Caucasus form an immense, arcing vista above and around them. This far down, at the sloping feet of the mountains, there is little scope for anything natural to grow and thrive. But life always finds a way. Never more so than when the gods are involved.

Along the slanted plains of grass and rocks, immense coils of fleshy sinew grow, quite naturally, from the earth. Their swollen, meandering forms have wound their way among the crags and crevices as if predating the mountainside they cling to. Which may well be true, for anyone old enough to remember.

In the shadow of the nearest sprawling coil, Medea kneels. She clutches a forager's knife in one hand, teasing the translucent meat of the nearest coil with its tip and taking note of the glimmering power beneath its skin. The odd slip of shamanistic murmur escapes her lips, drifting down the mountain slopes. It is the only sound that carries across the twilight.

The Allslayer puts this from his mind as his feet absently carry him. There has been little else for either of them to do since their arrival. Whatever threats the sorceress expected, physical or otherwise, have failed to melt out of the dusk, and Medea hardly needs either of their input for her own task. He glimpses Admetus drawing near, once more.

'This place…' the King of Pherae begins, uncertainly, when their paths finally cross. 'There is something fell and foetid about it.'

'I don't disagree,' Herakles replies. A flash of muted, shrouded light pulls his gaze briefly eastward. That way Aea lies, at the source of the Phasis. Summer lightning, perhaps, the closest thing this kingdom has to weather. Or maybe something less natural.

'These… things.' Admetus inclines his head towards the nearest fleshy growth. 'Are they…'

'The Roots,' Herakles confirms. 'The Roots of Iapetus.'

The stringy, corpulent fronds shiver, as if something deep within them is perturbed by being named. Idly, Admetus wonders how they would taste, to fry and boil and eat.

'Many years ago,' the Allslayer recalls, arching his gaze up to the mountaintops, 'a god was chained to these slopes.

Millenia passed, and he hung from his bonds, at the mercy of every storm and element.'

How odd it feels to speak of all this now. The Eleventh Labour was far from the most arduous he performed for Eurystheus, but few others are seared into his memory as deeply.

'And he bled, Admetus. He bled, as only a god can bleed, from wound upon wound upon wound, each more cruel and ignoble than the last. The violation he suffered in these mountains, I... I can't even begin to understand how it would feel. But the ichor, the vitae that bled from savaged veins, it fell upon the ground on which we stand. And from that priceless blood came all this. The Roots of Iapetus, sprung from the wounds of a Titan in chains.'

Admetus shrinks back from the Root he was moving to inspect, hesitant to even stand near it, as if some of that godly influence could rub off on him.

'How could you know these things, Allslayer? How does any Achaean come to learn of such stories?'

Against Herakles' will, a knowing half-smile tightens his features. As if he could ever forget it.

'Because I came here, my friend. Because I broke the god's fetters, and saved him from his torment.'

Neither man speaks as they each digest that truth. Only for Medea's distant voice to bring them back to themselves. The daughter of Aeëtes hasn't acknowledged them, or even moved from the heart of the Roots, since she began her harvest. But now, she begins to chant. A sibilant, breathless litany of long-buried lore.

The Allslayer has no comprehension of what it means, and no desire to understand. He suspects, in his heart of hearts, that it bears some relation to the ink-etched mandalas that swirl across her arms and face. But some secrets are not for men to know.

Only then does he truly peer down to the valley's deepest recess. Around the sorceress, unstoppered phials and vials have been laid out in undiscernible patterns. Each of them is filled with a suspension of murky violet, an unguent Medea has painstakingly teased from the pores of each Root.

Medea's chant steadily grows in pitch and volume, her arms raised as if dancing to the music of the spheres. It is a music only she can hear, and neither Herakles nor Admetus are any the wiser to her intentions.

'I have a bad feeling about this,' the Pheraean mutters. Herakles doesn't argue as he watches her, the Colchian's tuneless warbling reminding him a little too much of Megara's death cries.

Around the warlock's half-glimpsed ankles, the vials of unsettling liquid begin to glow.

He has to keep moving. That much he knows.

Jason's scabbed feet burn and blister on the hostile sand, yet another incentive not to stand in one place. Exactly where he runs to isn't clear, because the blinding, impenetrable light around him still steals all notion of time and distance. But it isn't long before he feels it, at his back. Or maybe much further away. But feel it he does, nonetheless.

Breath, making the hackles on his neck stand up straight. Slow, bestial, through a mouth without human teeth. Jason is bloodied, broken, with no weapon to hand and shredded clothes. He lacks the luxury of standing his ground and fighting. His only recourse left is to run.

The onlookers' distant eyes burn into his back as he flees. He has no idea where they are, no idea if they are even real. But he feels their gaze upon him, and that is what matters. To them, this is simply art, a pleasing way to stave off divine boredom. What finer sport can there be than watching hapless mortals bleed and break?

And of course, Aeëtes is still watching. His is one pair of eyes the shepherd boy knows he isn't imagining. The wizard-king's hunger for his death is a tangible thing, a whetted blade that doesn't waver from his throat.

My bulls are a curious breed, Aeëtes gleefully informs him at one point, slaving Jason's inner monologue to his own ends once more. *They breathe fire instead of air, and eat flesh instead of grass. Though we have found, only the gods know why, that live flesh makes a finer delicacy for them than carrion. The livelier, the better. I have to do something with all the travelling heroes who come to my door, after all.*

The son of Aeson tries his damnedest to shut this taunting out. But it is hard, though, to ignore a voice that promises your downfall. Particularly when it springs from inside your own head.

As he runs, he passes… things. From his snatches of vision over his shoulder, they remind him of seedpods that hang from the pine tree branches on Pelion. But these are bigger, much bigger, and while organic in appearance, they are clearly shaped by artifice that goes beyond the natural world.

They squat on the parched and featureless ground, too perfect and too aligned to have grown there by chance. As if anything could grow in this place, anyway.

Only Jason has no time to think about any of this. He keeps on running, slowing only when his body forces him to, ignoring his screaming joints and pains for the rest of it.

It doesn't matter that there is nowhere truly safe here. The shepherd boy has a plan, after all. Not *his* plan, of course. If he has learnt one thing on his voyage from Thessaly, it is that crafting plans is not his gift. Tthis plan is Medea's, imparted to him scarce moments after they swore their pact. The burning light in his left palm is only the starkest reminder of that.

Jason reaches into the tattered remains of his tunic, pulling out a small object from its half-torn pocket. A crude, filthy vial of unclean glass, stoppered with bark, carrying a few drops of diluted residue. Peering closely, he can just about make out the vestiges of purple in the liquid.

The timing is everything, or so the witch told him. He has to wait for the right moment. No sooner, no later.

A bestial, bovine groan cuts across the air, a good deal closer than he expects. And then Jason is running again, phial clutched in his sweaty fist, leaving nothing behind him but his doubts.

'I don't like this,' Admetus admits, for the umpteenth time. 'The light keeps fading and rising, Allslayer. How long have we even been here?'

At his side, Herakles is doing little better at hiding his discomfort. The great shadows of the Caucasus are growing wider and deeper, though he can't judge whether or not the sun is moving. Fatigue pulls at his limbs and insides, after being awake for only the gods know how long.

But around them, the Roots of Iapetus are changing. They begin to glow the same burning purple as the vials of their serum arrayed around Medea. Flickering tongues of violet light billow beneath their sinewy skin, as if some infernal fire is eating at them from within.

And at the heart of it all, the sorceress stands. She has not paused to take any breath since her incantation began, but her spoken spell has not halted or changed since then. The glass vessels that surround her brighten with the gathering of her power. A gathering that, by the Allslayer's reckoning, is building to a climax.

And then molten light flares in her eyes, and Medea falls silent at last. Herakles fights the urge to pull his lionskin tighter about him, as the season feels as if it has turned to winter in one passing moment.

'Witch!' he calls, finally giving into his unease and striding down towards the rings. 'We have done what you asked for, and you have taken what you need. Enough delays. You swore this was the way to save Jason!'

Medea's ocular radiance cannot dim her remorseless smile.

'And so I did, Child of Thunder. I will deliver your erstwhile captain from my father's clutches, have no fear. I must thank you for accompanying me this far out of Aea, and standing where I can see you for all this time. My solution is artful, I must say, though I doubt you'll be able to watch it unfold.'

At the Allslayer's shoulder, Admetus tenses as he draws his sword. The witch's words fly mostly over his head, but he understands enough to know the truth. They have been tricked, and Medea has brought them here for her own reasons.

'You filthy succubus!' he cries, rushing past Herakles to close the distance. 'You'll pay for your perfidy, witch!'

Medea's mouth remains closed, but her chuckle carries across both men's minds.

The phial in Jason's hand is now scalding to the touch. The residue within shimmers and smudges with blushing light. It is all he can do to clench it in his hand.

The moment is yet to come. But by the spiteful and distant gods of Olympus, it cannot be long now.

The shepherd boy skids to a halt in the sands, burns and callouses across his body going unheeded. Aeëtes' taunts in his mind have faded to background noise, as have the hungering gazes of the bloodthirsty crowd. For a handful of moments, his breath returns, the thundering pulse in his ears the only sound they hear.

The braying of the Bulls will come again. He still can't see any further than before, but he knows, before long, that he'll feel their breath and hear their hooves across the light. They are coming, and gaining on him with each moment.

It is as Medea said, all of it. She has watched enough Achaeans die this way, after all. He just needs to keep moving, until her ritual reaches fruition.

So held is he by this thought, and the ever-warming phial of potion in his grip, that Jason does not notice what is happening behind him.

The nearest of the colossal pods – a hundred of which he has passed in his flight without incident – begins to crumple and contort. Something is pulling it apart from within. Something with a vaguely humanoid outline, from the way the light seeps through its membrane. But that is where the similarity ends.

A pair of filthy, skeletal hands pull the wooden caul apart, and Jason recoils from its mass with a strangled scream. Not that anywhere else is safe, for the scene is repeating itself all around him. Scores of once-inert organic bowers, hatching like unnatural eggs to birth their hideous cargo.

Ah, so you have finally met my little friends. Aeëtes' faux voice is as cruel in anticipation as it is in victory. Right now, he can taste both feelings at once. *We have curious burial customs, here in Colchis. Preserving our departed in tree bowers affords me many vessels to practice my spellcraft. What do you think of my efforts, shepherd boy? Do they pass muster?*

Jason is too terrified to listen, scrambling back from the nearest shuffling cohort. The newly hatched skeletons are still sluggish from rebirth, but every second of unlife makes them more aware. Many of them still clutch the weapons they had in life, the rotted, ragged remains of red robes still clinging to their bones like gristle. Jason is half-expecting magical fire to burn in their eye sockets, a malevolent reminder of their puppeteer's infernal power, but their hollow lack of self is their most unnerving aspect of all.

The son of Aeson bolts, as fast as his bleeding feet will carry him. The Bulls are gaining on him, but this is hardly a better end.

He feels Aeëtes' desire for his death reach fever pitch. He feels the spectators' patience start to wear thin, trumped by their wish to taste blood.

And he feels Medea's phial, burning through the fabric of his clothes.

Just a little longer, damn it. Just a little longer.

'Traitor!' Admetus roars. He thunders down the ashen slope, blade in hand, hurling himself the last few paces.

Medea's laugh has finally reached her lips. She speaks a single, guttural word of power. A word not meant to be uttered by human tongues. A word that scrapes at the fabric of Herakles' soul, as haggard and bruised as it is.

The light within the Roots of Iapetus burns white-hot, exploding out like the halo of a dying star. Every vial upon the ground shatters and burns, adding their potency.

Medea's laughing face is swallowed by the flames of power, and when the blast fades, she is gone.

When the phial starts screaming with suppressed potency, Jason knows it is time.

The Colchian undead have surrounded him, reaching down at his helpless form with half-rotted hands and fingers. The shepherd boy hurls his phial at the ground with a cry of horror, clamping his eyes shut in the exact same moment.

It shatters. It burns. Bright enough to scar his retinas.

And like dust in the wind, he is gone.

'Gods below...' the King of Pherae gasps, as he scatters a cloud of violet ashes from his hand. 'Where did she go?'

Herakles finally slows to a halt beside him, his club clutched in one tight fist.

'She spoke of Jason, did she not?' he says. 'So she truly did mean to set him free...' The Allslayer's eyes shift back and forth, as the pieces of a rather unpleasant puzzle fall into place.

'What is it?' Admetus asks.

'The Fleece...' Herakles murmurs, before rounding on his friend once more. 'That must be it, Pheraean! If she wanted to free Jason *and* remove us from the picture... it has to be the Fleece. Medea is making her own play for it, and is using Jason to help her.'

'Then why go through this pantomime?' Admetus waves a hand at the nearest Root of Iapetus. Without their unearthly light, they look much the same as ever.

'Because she needed us out of the way.' It is all the Allslayer can do not to hurl his weapon away in frustration. 'She must be back in the city, now, with Jason, and you and I are too far away to stop her. It will take Aeëtes time to even realise what has happened, and those who know what she intends can do nothing about it!'

Admetus snatches up his bejewelled war sword, sheathing it at his hip.

'Atalanta!' he gasps. 'Your huntress could be walking into a trap!'

'Perhaps.' Herakles shakes his head. 'But freeing the Argonauts could be the distraction Medea needs. She certainly cares nothing for their survival, and I doubt Jason will, if the sorceress can give him what he came for. But either way—' He pulls the Lionskin about his shoulders, looking back down the path they walked. '—we have to get back. Now.'

'How long will that take?' The Pheraean seems less convinced. 'If Medea crossed that distance in a blink with her ritual, what hope do we have of catching her?'

'We have to try!' Herakles snarls, trying to channel his volcanic anger back at its rightful target. 'Medea's skiff is still moored at the river's fork. I'm through with all this cloak and dagger, old friend. We'll row. We'll row hard and kill anyone who tries to bar our way. Never mind that cancerous bitch. The others will need us. We have to get to them.'

The skeletal figures freeze, dumfounded. Bereft of their one true target, their scarcely animated forms flounder, as if tormenting their victims is all the purpose they have left.

Through the degraded, rotted remains of their senses, Aeëtes detects the hint of magic in the air, even as the last of the ash disperses.

Which tells him exactly who is responsible for this.

XXXIX
UNBOUND, UNBOWED

'Just keep breathing,' Meleager rasps through a dehydrated throat. 'Look at me, you Pierian bastard. Focus on my eyes. Hearken to my voice. Don't you dare let go.'

A little way across the dark from him, the last vestiges of Orpheus' will are slipping away. The part of his soul that has any fight left — the part that wants to live, and make music, and move beyond his pain — is fading. The part that just wants all this to be over, to hold Eurydice close somewhere the light does not reach, is spreading across his blackening vision.

His wiry, delicate body is failing him. He feels it, moment by slackening moment. It isn't an unpleasant feeling.

'I *mean* it!' Meleager gasps, his gentle voice made brittle by thirst. '*Come on*, Bard! You don't get to leave me now. Not *now*, kinsman. Not like this.' Desperation is all the Calydonian has left. '*Please*, Orpheus. You can do it. Don't... don't leave me in this place.'

A hollow creak of chains pulled tight is all that answers. The Muse's son sags on his fetters, hanging from the towering stone wall beneath the depths of endless black.

Meleager of Calydon hangs a few feet from his side, from an identical chain bound around his torso, suspended from an identically perilous height. The young prince has no idea of anything anymore. Whether the other Argonauts are suspended the same way in nearby chambers. Whether any of them know how long they've even been here, how long since those Colchian devils fell upon the *Argo*.

The pain… the pain of these shackles is excruciating, even when the corrosive metal isn't actively cursing and punishing them for struggling. The act alone of hanging while bent double, for all this indeterminate time, may well have crippled Meleager for life.

And then there is the torture, the way these thrice-damned warlocks taunt and tear at his mind. Meleager isn't sure if this has really happened, or if it is something his warped, starved senses have conjured from the humid dark.

He isn't sure which possibility is worse.

Right here, right now, with no witness but Orpheus' unmoving form, Meleager cannot even cry. There isn't enough moisture in his body to allow it.

So hang he does, alone with his despair. Time unspools and frays in his mind, the chasm's endless black diluting the flow of this thoughts.

He doesn't notice the springing crash of metal above his head, or how the spent arrow flurries down into the gloom. Nor does he feel the world fall away from him, rushing up past and leaving him behind.

Only when his bruised, maltreated body thuds into the uneven ground below does his awareness snap back into place. His blurry vision makes out Orpheus' prone form fall a moment later, his chain also shot apart by an unerringly fired arrow.

Meleager cannot move, not yet. But right here, in this moment, this is all the stricken prince needs to keep on going. An arrow just like that brought her into his life, all those months ago in Iolchus when he'd known so little and been sure of so much. That single accursed arrow, knocking the sword from his grasp and his whole life out of kilter. He'll never be the man he was before that moment, the man Oeneus and Althaea strove to make of him, and he has no wish to be at all.

Because of her. Because of the world he now sees through her eyes.

'We didn't th—' is all his failing voice can manage. He doesn't need his sight to sense who it is standing over him. 'I didn't... I didn't think you—'

Atalanta reaches for him, and they clasp each other's forearms at once.

'I'm where I need to be,' she assures him, pulling him up to a sitting position. 'Can you walk? Orpheus is breathing, but I can't stir him. We'll have to carry him between us.'

Meleager just looks at her, as if trying to memorise every nook and cranny of her face. There is next to no light in this benighted place, but that doesn't stop him trying.

'Oh, enough of that.' The huntress hauls the prince to his feet. 'You Calydonians and your melodrama.'

It transpires there is a world outside his cell after all.

The two of them hoist Orpheus through the rocky passageway, and they are not alone in doing so. The dead and the living are in abundance here. The former as slumped, lifeless Colchian royal guards strewn over the ground. The latter, the menacing yet familiar forms of the *Argo*'s surviving champions, standing at arms. Alone as she was, Atalanta is doubtless responsible for both.

A burnt, grime-coated figure speaks with Theseus' guttural voice. Castor and Polydeuces' haggard forms are scarcely distinguishable anymore, a pair of bearded, longhaired ruffians marked apart only by scars and lesions. Even Telamon's hulking form is hunched over by more than a low ceiling. The Argonauts have been stripped down to their bloodied core in more ways than just the obvious. Bereft of their arms and armour – some of which are as storied as the men who bear them – and relieved of their clothes, strength and pride, they make quite a sight indeed.

'We cannot dally,' Atalanta asserts. She and Nestor, the least ostensibly injured among them, lead the way; a handful of sooty, sweaty bodies pressed tight by narrow walls. Meleager, still hefting Orpheus on his own, feels his feet almost betray him a handful of times, neglected by pain and lack of use. But he forces himself on nonetheless. He needs to prove the equal of these men, now more than ever.

Peleus and Laertes are the last to be freed, after Castor breaks their guard in two and the huntress shoots them down from their jeering, weeping shackles. The King of Ithaca can move well enough, but is still too shocked to speak. The Phthian barely manages a cheap quip about Colchian hospitality, only slightly less jarred by the sight of Telamon among his saviours.

'Where is he, then?' Theseus snarls, through a throat of bloodied phlegm. 'Where in this infernal hellpit is Jason?'

'They took him,' Meleager croaks, before Atalanta can stop him. 'They led him somewhere else when they brought us to this city. I saw Aeëtes and his warlock bitch take him for themselves.'

'The *bastard!*' Polydeuces thunders. 'The two-faced, honourless mongrel! He'll try to sell us out, I know it! Anything to save his own skin. The spineless little cur!'

'Never mind that!' Telamon protests. 'Who's to say he hasn't made some deal for the Fleece? Or even has it already?'

The dungeon promptly erupts in uproar. Speculation billows wildly before Atalanta can put it out.

And like that, clad in nothing but indignation and what scraps of Colchian armour and cloth they can scavenge, the remnants of the Argonauts surge like a tide through the Vault that once entombed them.

He is throwing up his guts before he even fully wakes, having hurled himself through the air and landed in a completely different desert. Retching up the last of the witchery from his system takes longer than planned, and sure enough, his deliverer is standing over him when he finally looks up.

'Graceful,' Medea observes, arms folded across her willowy midriff. She seems to share none of his afflicted weakness, and looks none too impressed with his display of it.

'Wh—' Jason splutters, before fully regaining himself. 'What happened, lady? Where are we?'

They are still in Colchis, as the sickly light and fever-warm air attest. But the unnaturally high, unnaturally pointed peak looming before them owes nothing to Aea's gods-given landscape.

'This, son of Aeson, is where I make my home.' If Medea is aware of how this place must look to an outlander – a towering fastness where covens and shadow-lore would fit in well – than she does not show it. 'I promised to deliver you, Jason, and to help you leave this place with the Fleece. I have done the former, and as for the latter…'

The witch stretches a hennaed arm, indicating the lonely path through more distant mountains extending behind them.

'I have even brought you most of the way. Please don't feel any need to thank me.'

For a moment, Jason can't quite comprehend those words. How close it all suddenly seems. How alarmingly real it feels. He has walked down a Mountain, and bargained his way out of death at Pelias' hand. He has sailed across the world, evading death at monstrous hands and the malice of his own comrades. And now he has slipped through another tyrant's noose, with his eventual goal no more than one last trek away.

'The Fleece,' he stammers, 'the Fleece is fabled to have a guardian. An immense monstress, whose serpentine bulk haloes its grove.'

That makes Medea smile again, showing all of her unnaturally perfect teeth.

'My dear Jason,' she coos to him, as the light seems to wane from Colchis' skies once again. '*I* am the monstress that protects this place. Did you think Aeëtes would entrust the duty to anyone other than blood? But I can assure you, Achaean, that I am not *all* that protects it. If you are worried your erstwhile friends will interrupt us, then don't be. I have taken care of that as well.'

'My friends…' Jason murmurs. What is it that has him in a daze? Medea's magicks, or the approaching summit of his ambitions? 'The Argonauts. They are coming to this place? They are free?'

'They are free,' the sorceress confirms, her finger on Jason's lips forestalling his next gentle protest. 'I gave your Arcadian companion the means to let them loose in Aea, but they will go no further. Your rampant followers will do nothing but draw my father's attention. By the time they are defeated, you and I will be gone.'

'The Arcadian…' Jason echoes. 'Atalanta… my friend. My truest friend.'

'*Focus!*' For the first time in the shepherd boy's presence, Medea's temper surges. The first, but most certainly not the last. 'Forget your bleating entreaties of fellowship. Forget those mewling brutes who snap at your heels! You are *so* close to the end now, my love! It is fortitude that has brought you this far! Not skill. Not sentiment. Don't let it flounder now, not when you are so close to your prize!'

My love. Those words sound good on her tongue, and in his ears. There may have been a time, not too long ago, when the son of Aeson would have seen so unsubtle a trap from a long way off. But not now. Not since Hera. Not since the gathering at Iolchus, and the breaking of honour.

'Show it to me, lady. Show me the way.' He does not even maintain a front now. No pretence of clarity or thought.

'All in good time, my sire.' Medea's only other movement is to clasp his hand with her own… before drawing another flick of his blood with her knife. She repeats the process with her own forearm, allowing their vitae to mingle in droplets on the sand.

'What…' Jason begins.

'I told you,' she replies, between rhythmic murmurs, 'that I was not the only guardian of this place. There is one last line of defence between outlanders and the Fleece, and I am calling it to wakefulness now. By this blade—' she flicks blood drops off its tip. '—do I deaden its senses to our blood. If we want to proceed any further and not be slain, this is the way.'

Jason just watches her, his almond eyes shifting. He isn't sure what troubles him more. Medea's glee, or the lack of unease he feels.

The oar crackles beneath his grasp. It will shatter if he grips it any harder.

'Nothing!' Admetus calls from somewhere up ahead, beyond his sweating eyeline. 'Still nothing! There's no-one on the damned river!'

Between his frenzied strokes, the Allslayer doubts if this is any cause for celebration. It is fortuitous that no soul on the Phasis has challenged them yet – or at least, no soul has had the courage to impede the vessel of Aeëtes' daughter – but this sudden change in fortune does not feel like a boon. What could be happening in Aea right now to stop the river's traffic from flowing?

He rows. He rows. He rows. This skiff is not meant for one oarsman, but the Child of Thunder has arm span enough for the task.

'*Herakles!*' the King of Pherae shouts once more, from above-deck. 'Do you hear me? I think we may make it to the city in time!'

Herakles doesn't bother replying. Making it back to Aea's docks is one thing, but finding their friends, let alone finding some way to get them all out of here alive, is quite another. He shares Admetus' open mind, if not his optimism.

Though the Pheraean can be excused that optimism, all things considered. He has seen death cheated out of far starker odds already, when the Allslayer descended on his kingdom to fight for his—

Herakles freezes, mid-stroke. The skiff continues on its journey, carried on by a demigod's momentum, but the Allslayer pays it no heed.

'My friend?' Admetus calls down, but is not heard. 'Is all well?'

The Allslayer feels himself rise to full height. He observes through his eyes as he strides out to join the young king on deck.

'What's wrong?' Admetus needs no further prompt. 'Talk to me, friend.'

'I have been blind.' The words slip from Herakles' mouth of their own volition. 'All these months, Admetus, I have been blind.'

He grips the Pheraean by both shoulders, tenderly, but not without urgency. 'Don't you see? You would have known, kinsman! If you'd been here from the start, if you'd heard my misgivings, you would have recognised it instantly! Because I told you the whole damned tale, last time!'

'Recognised what?' Admetus cries, but his friend is no longer listening. Memories flare behind Herakles' eyes, memories that, with this new hindsight, make a dark and sickening kind of sense.

'The shadow,' he says. 'The dark pall that has pursued me here, all the way from Thessaly. I sensed it a handful of times, in the corner of my gaze. There, but not there. I knew I'd felt it before *somewhere*. I knew I recognised it. But now I know.' He claps Admetus on the shoulder. 'Now I know exactly what has haunted me, all this way.'

Fate really does have a sense of humour after all, it seems. It shouldn't be a surprise when he thinks about it. He has met gods before, and gods are fond of irony.

'I feel the hand of destiny on my shoulder,' the Allslayer rumbles. He is looking not at Admetus now, but the rocky bank rolling on by. 'You finding me, out there in the endless blue, was no mere happenstance. All this time you think you've thrown off Fate's shackles, and you find out the joke was played on you all along. If you hadn't been there, Pheraean, then I would have made this whole journey without realising.'

'*Herakles!*' the younger man cries out vainly, love and shock written plain across his face. 'You aren't making any sense! We must sail for Aea before it's too late! That is where our path lies!'

'No.' The Allslayer grips Admetus' shoulders once again, firm but this time fraternal. 'That is where *your* path lies, my friend. I need you to ride this boat as far upriver as you can, and be ready for when Atalanta leads the others out of here. There is only so much she'll be able to do for them, and wherever Medea has gone, she won't step in to help. The Argonauts will need an escape down the river. You must be that escape.'

He doesn't even wait for the Pheraean to respond, already stepping up to the topmost wooden gunwale. It is all too obvious what he plans to do.

'Where will you go?' Admetus asks, scarcely even expecting an answer.

What he gets is not expected by either of them. Herakles gives him one last look, and it is the calmest and most serene he has ever given to anyone.

'I think I know why I am here, Admetus. Why I am truly here. Why I was put on this voyage and steered to this moment. All debts and accounts must be settled in the end, boy, and I've been around long enough to accrue a few. For the first time in far too many years, I go toward a fight of my own choosing. A fight, at long gods-damned last, on my own terms.'

He grasps the haft of his club, knuckles whitening with force. In all the years he has borne it, it has never failed him yet. That, he drily reflects, may have been the point. Maybe it, like him, was always heading for this moment.

'Gods be with you, Admetus of Pherae.' The Allslayer turns away from him once more, for what may be the last time in his life. 'Save my friends for me, and give my regards to your wife.'

And then he flings himself overboard, lionskin billowing in his wake.

XL
BEFORE THE STORM

Many long years before that moment, in an age when blood burnt hotter and valour was more novel, a distant traveller came to Pherae.

He didn't know the kingdom or any of its countrymen, and had little desire to acquaint himself with either. But necessity had forced his hand, as it all too often did. He had another infernal Labour to perform for his erstwhile master, another step to take on the painful road to absolution. He was sworn to bring back the horses of King Diomedes, those infamous Thracian mares that ate flesh instead of barley, and to bring them back tamed and docile. But such a heroic feat demanded expertise. Lore not easily sought.

It was the pursuit of such lore that led the traveller to Pherae, where word had spread of the skill and flair of its ostlers and steed-rearers. But he found no answers in that foreign kingdom. What he found was a land in disarray, and a royal house bereft by cruellest circumstance. A girl, on the cusp of maidenhood, snatched away not by disease nor chance, but by the blackest of misfortunes. A pact between god and mortal that went wrong. So very wrong.

The girl was the princess Alcestis, daughter of King Pelias of Thessaly. She had been betrothed to young Admetus, heir to the throne of Pherae.

The royal house received the traveller in good faith, as the bonds between hosts and guests dictated. No honour was spared from him, no obligation neglected. And in a show of magnanimity that would break the traveller's heart when he learnt of it, they entertained their visitor while keeping the truth of their bereavement from him.

Young Admetus, bereft and broken as he was, was insistent on this point. The boy-prince saw to the traveller's warm reception personally, ensuring his needs and requests for knowledge were met, while lapping up his tales of wars and distant lands.

It was only when the traveller wandered the *megaron* passageways at night, happening upon tearstained slaves and scullery girls, that he learnt the truth of the matter.

And in that moment of unplanned revelation, a die was cast.

Here was a chance to perform a deed of heroism, not for the man who held his leash, nor for the gods who wrote his story. Here was a chance to flex his power – a power already described in fearful whispers as 'Herculean' – not for glory, not to prove a painful point, not for anything as crude or vulgar as that.

Here was a chance to be the man he wanted to be, the man in his heart of hearts he truly was. Here was a chance to help someone in pain – someone he'd already come to love, these past days – and right a terrible wrong.

And so, that night, the traveller set out from the palace at Pherae. His nocturnal pilgrimage would take him across the slopes of Mount Othrys, whose olive groves put Athens' to shame, to his sepulchral destination.

There was nothing waiting for him. Nothing living, at least. This shrouded and petrified garden, where the ashes of Pherae's royal scions were interred to rest in peace, was where Alcestis' cold corpse had been laid out for burial, to drink in the wind and moonlight one last time.

And right there, visible only to a demigod's eyes, a shadow waited. This was a rite it had performed several thousand times before, after all. Severing the hair of the recently departed, to shepherd their passage down to the realm of the dead.

But not here. Not this time.

The traveller called out to the shadow, interrupting its sacred task, and issued a challenge. They would wrestle, the son of a deathless god and the avatar of human mortality, and whoever proved stronger would win Alcestis' soul. To lead it to its rightful resting place, or bring it back to the land of the living.

For many years after, every travelling bard from Pherae to Ionia sang of the outcome of that legendary brawl. There were, of course, no living witnesses to what truly transpired in the burial grove that night, but that only helped the legends spread further, growing wilder with each retelling.

And fortune would continue to bless Alcestis. A happy marriage to Admetus, child after fruitful child from their union, and a kingdom unblighted by the wars and worries plaguing the larger, mightier lands around it.

But actions have consequences, no matter how dire the action and how minor the consequence. The laws of time and death are not to be meddled with, no matter how mighty, or gods-touched, the meddler. No matter how straightforward or striated the path, time comes for us all, swallowing up the years as Zeus's Titan father once tried to swallow his infants whole.

And right here, right now, in a land most Olympians would fear to tread, a debt must finally be paid.

Hanging from Meleager's tiring shoulders, Orpheus of Pieria's eyes snap open. Something has changed in the air, a change he can feel. A presence he recognises from long, long ago.

Across the sea in Pherae, Queen Alcestis' angelic face gently contorts in her sleep. She absently pulls the sheets tighter around her, as a dark and foetid presence stalks her dreams.

Far above the Colchian plains, that very same presence spills into reality at last. It has been waiting for this moment for far too long, and its time has finally come.

XLI
A BRAZEN TIDE

Not even Aeëtes' immortal memory could have recalled the last time war came to Colchis. The kingdom has had its fair share of unwanted and unwelcome guests, that is irrefutable. Its borders are protected by sorcery and arrogance in equal measure. What kind of deluded fool would bring battle to this den of vipers, ruled by powers older than the gods of Olympus? Powers who command forces no mortal was ever meant to witness, let alone contend with?

But battle has come, at last, and it has caught the streets of Aea by bloody surprise.

The rabble die first, those too dazed or petrified to defend themselves cut down without remorse or even pause. This only serves their tormentors further, as the remainder panic and flee in all directions. They throng the lattice of streets and avenues in their rout, making those same thoroughfares impossible for anyone else to navigate.

The fighting men of Aeëtes' royal house fare scarcely better, possessing the blades and tactics to at least put up a pitiful fight, but lacking so much more besides. Their foes are cornered, desperate, all too aware that they will either rise to their quest's zenith or plummet to inglorious ends. They fight like heroes, like berserkers, like nightmares, and they have the power to be every last one of those things.

By contrast, all their captor's lapdogs have are their lives. That, and the feverish fear of what happens to those who fail Aeëtes.

The royal warriors of Aea are no match for the maddened, pain-hazed juggernauts tearing through their streets. They fight well, and some of them fight gloriously. But they don't fight for long.

In time, the survivors grow wise to the futility of such tactics. The Colchian warriors fall back in more disciplined order than their panicked civilian kin, abandoning their futile attempts to end the battle by brute force. There are other ways to fight, after all.

The feeble spellcasters and acolytes of the kingdom's citizenry can hardly match Aeëtes' grasp of witchcraft, or even that of his less gifted children, but they do what they can. They whisper curses through broken lips, spitting words of power through bloodied teeth. They try to boil their assailants' blood, stoppering their courage, rewriting the cartography of their fears.

Pointless, all of it. Arrows lodge in throats, cutting off guttural chants. Enemies throw off their elemental spells, too pained and enraged to be subdued by such assaults. Blades and blows crash through shields of mystic focus, pulling back veils that occlude sight and sense. Flames of astral force burn across stolen robes and armour, ignorant of how badly these men have been burnt and maimed already. If torture like that can't break their spirit, how can this break their bodies?

The last of the sorcerous novices dies, her neck broken by a vengeful strike from Peleus. With the majority of Aea's human occupants fled well beyond their reach, they are left with only the kingdom's truest defenders to face them now.

The final attack comes without warning, because how could they have possibly expected it? Who in their right mind – hero or otherwise – would have rightfully expected the great pods and bowers hanging from the trees on every avenue to sprout their grisly fruit? Who would expect the half-rotted cadavers of dead Colchians to stir into shambling unlife, and fall upon them like a tide of long forestalled decay?

Still, the *why* of it hardly matters. The attackers, wearing and wielding whatever scraps they could find from their kills and former jailers, haven't made it this far by railing against the odds.

They have made it this far by chasing a dream across the world, and refusing to let go no matter what it costs them.

They are the last men standing of the Argonauts, and they haven't come all this way to fail now.

'Come on!' Atalanta urges them as she nocks a fresh arrow. 'Don't forget what we're here for!'

The opening moves of the battle have, for her, been a struggle of stealth and shadow play, stealing across alleys and slitting throats before her red-robed foes could rally against her comrades. But somewhere in the chaos of the mêlée she has found more arrows for her stolen bow, and that has fundamentally changed the game. It is a crude, sloppily hewn willow, no match for the work of exquisite teak craftsmanship Sybele took from her, but it is a bow all the same.

She puts shot after unerring shot through her enemies' throats, their hearts, their eye sockets. The legion of undead flesh is another matter, however. They do not fold and break like living men, but shuffle on through death wounds until destroyed wholesale. The huntress is reduced to her short blades more often than she cares for, slashing and hacking at grasping, maggot-ridden hands.

For a time, she fought together with the others, when they were clustered as a pack. The tides of the running battle have taken her on different paths, cutting foes down between shadowed alleys with Nestor and the Spartans, tailing Meleager and Laertes as they vault over walls and masonry, fighting her way across rooftops and balconies with Theseus and Telamon. But the maelstrom of oncoming foes have swept them all apart now, like minnows in a storm surge, and that slims her hopes of keeping their cohesion. They have survived this far, and slain this many foes, by capitalising on the shock of their attack. They have never stopped moving all the while, plunging themselves deeper into Aea's underbelly, like poison coursing through a bloodstream.

But now they face a foe with one goal, and one will. If they lose momentum now they will be picked off one by one.

A half-rotted hand clasps Atalanta's face from behind, shocking her from her moment. She cries out in alarm, stabbing her elbow back to throw her assailant clear. It half works, as the skeletal soldier tumbles back off the first storey ledge, pulling the huntress with it.

She crashes back down to ground level in the shadows of abandoned market stalls as Orpheus and Nestor scramble into cover behind her. Atalanta jerks up long enough to shoot another skeleton through its temples, before thudding back down as the pain of her shoulder hits home.

How different they all look to her now. Peering over the fractured counter, the huntress watches Peleus, wrapped up in torn Colchian red and bleeding from a dozen flesh wounds, barrel through a host of osseus attackers like a living battering ram, roaring all the while. Castor is at his side a moment later, fingers rammed through empty eye sockets, tearing the next dead Colchian's skull apart with raw strength alone, before snatching up its cobweb-wreathed metal shield and bludgeoning another two of its deathless cohort. But even they have dallied for too long in one place. Peleus and the Spartan slam together, back upon back, as they wheel about to present nothing but bladed vigilance to the next horrors that reach for them.

'Go!' Atalanta implores them through a hoarse throat. 'I will give you cover.'

She has another arrow in her hand before they even move. Nocking a fresh shaft is harder with a sprained shoulder, but now is no time for pain. An arrow through the femur knocks a cluster of them over, and a thrown knife shears the spine of the skeleton hanging from Castor's back.

Nestor takes this moment to scamper on after them, taking a fleshless head from fleshless shoulders with one swing of his looted axe. At the huntress' side, Orpheus is still far too petrified to even move. Like Atalanta, he has taken no armour or clothes from the slain. Unlike her, he has no real practical use in the chaos of this fight.

'It's no good,' she curses, firing over her makeshift barricade and transfixing the nearest half-decayed corpse. 'The others are taking this too far. We need to be fighting our way to the river, not scattering across this running battle and losing ourselves.'

She is running out of arrows, and knows it all too well. The dead Colchian she relieved them of was only carrying a handful. She turns back round, to see if Orpheus has any insight.

Only to find herself alone, once again, as the bard presumably scrambles towards the sound of his friends.

Not for long, however, before another Argonaut crashes down over the nearby wall to share her precarious cover with her. He wears a rusted old battle helm that looks comically large on him, clutching a stolen spear and dagger that have clearly seen better days.

'This is going well,' Meleager greets her. Another skeletal attacker clambers over the short wall after him, a process that is far from rapid with its legs both severed at the hips. The Prince of Calydon turns back, ramming his spearpoint into the bobbing skull's forehead and ending its second lease of life.

'We can't be here,' Atalanta tells him, snapping her shoulder back into place and swallowing the cry of agony that wishes to blast up through her throat. 'This isn't going to deliver us.'

'No?' Meleager asks her, abruptly springing up fast enough to lose his helmet and grabbing the huntress by the hand. Another throng of Aeëtes' reanimated dead are emerging from the walkway behind them, in large enough numbers to flush them from this latest hiding place. They have dithered here too long. It is now time to move again.

'Medea is making a move for the Fleece,' she says, as Meleager leads her beneath another marble colonnade. With luck, they can steal across the roofs again, hopefully beyond the reach of their shambling pursuers. 'And Jason will be with her. I don't know how they'll do it, or even where they're truly going. But our salvation lies that way, not drowning in this bloodbath.'

They stumble into the empty antechamber, pausing only to hack down a trio of half-comatose undead who flounder mindlessly in their way. They then freeze, at Atalanta's behest, halfway up the cold marble steps to the topmost floor.

'Do you trust me, Meleager?' the huntress asks without warning. There is no preamble this time, no dance between stinger and stung. They are both too far down this path for that, and the quest doesn't come into it.

'I do,' the prince replies.

'Then you must trust me now.' She steps past him, back down the stairs, bow drawn. Only for Meleager's hand to find her shoulder once again, and clasp it with a firmness borne of need.

'Mel. Please.' She is barely whispering, though the Calydonian hears her just fine over the outside clamour. 'This is hunter and hunted. This is a game I can play. I can pick up their trail, Mel. I know I can.'

'Then take me with you.' Meleager can scarcely stop himself speaking the words. He regrets none of them.

'I need you here.' The huntress stands closer to him, making no move to dislodge his hand. 'Lead the others to the river. Make them come to their senses. Somewhere in the city are Colchians who still draw breath. Someone will know where Medea would have gone. Get the truth from them and make the Argonauts heed it. If they can't recover their heads, it's over for all of us.'

She reaches to her bruised hip, unsheathing one of her few remaining blades and pressing it into the prince's hand. She has nothing else of value to give him, no other way of throwing open her heart.

'What was it you said, in the Hellespont?' Meleager's hand curls around hers, the blade clasped tight between them. 'About me needing a chance to prove something?'

Atalanta hauls him close by his stolen robes, fingers hooked in its tears. Their kiss is the driest, sweatiest, and most tender moment of her life. And maybe, just maybe, of his.

'Not to me.'

XLII
THE FURY AND FAVOUR OF GODS

Walk for long enough, and all the earth beneath your feet feels the same.

He has barely heeded where his steps are taking him. The Phasis is long behind him, that much he knows. He no longer hears its silken sibilance, no longer feels the coolness of nearby water. The steppes around him are dry as bone, kissed to death by the rays of Colchis' sun. Somewhere far behind him, Admetus is driving Medea's abandoned boat toward the innermost heart of Aea. Maybe he will make it in time. Maybe he won't. Herakles cannot think about that now. He has a higher reckoning to answer to.

It doesn't matter where he goes, if he even keeps walking or not. He will find it, or it will find him.

When the shadow finally darkens the sky above him, he is almost relieved. Not even this kingdom's sickening sunlight can outshine it, a void the colour of utter absence. Not even black, but the emptiness of something never meant for mortal eyes to see.

How long has it sought the scent of his soul, hunting for him in his years of self-inflicted exile? How long has it waited for him to step aboard Jason's accursed boat?

The Allslayer loosens his grip on the club's head, tightening it again only after the handle has sunk into his hand. He braces his legs, his whole body, in a fighting stance as he raises the weapon once again. By doing this thing, he has stepped off the path of Fate at last. Or has finally locked it around his feet for good.

He does not know which, and for the first time in his gods-touched life, he does not care.

The shadow takes corporeal form before him, humanoid but far from human. A shroud of shadowed night haloes its shifting form like an aura. Like a mirage of sepulchral flames, another trick of the desert light. Two hands of fleshless, spindly bone reach upward, removing the piece of pewter armour from its crown, and raking back the pall of blindness from Herakles' eyes.

The Allslayer recognises that sheenless armour, as well as this umbral figure itself, from his last trip to the World Beneath in search of Cerberus. But he has never seen them together like this, before.

'The Helm of Hades,' he observes. 'So that is why I couldn't see you this time.'

His awe is genuine enough. A relic of an age before an age, that helm was forged by the first of the Cyclopes for Hades' own head, granting the gift of invisibility whenever he wore it. Hades put that gift to devastating use when the gods cast down their Titan forebears, as did his two brothers with their own Cyclopes-smithed relics: the searing, coruscating thunderbolts wielded by Zeus, and the trident of the seas gifted to Poseidon.

And here the Helm is, borne by Hades' most prized servant. The Lord of the Dead would have never granted such a boon willingly.

'You aren't here at your master's whim, are you?' Herakles challenges the shade that stands across the desert from him. 'He did not send you to this place. You have followed me here on your own behalf, to settle this debt of ours.'

Nothing. No mortal sound, at least. The Allslayer starts a little at the sight of his own breath, an all too visible wisp that billows from his mouth. The faintest of cracklings whispers its way across the lionskin. Hoarfrost, coalescing into being. Unlike last time in the burial grove, there is no grass or greenery underfoot to wither and die before his eyes, but he takes eerie note of how the Lion's tawny fur seems to lose a little lustre.

I am Death. The silently roaring tornado of shadow draws closer, somehow without blowing any sand from its path.

'I know.'

I have been your boon companion all your days. You have meted me out to men and babes and monsters. But when Fate came full circle, you threw me back from my rightful prize.

Herakles does not step back. He *won't* step back. He squeezes his club's hilt hard enough to throttle a giant.

'You should not be here,' he spits through gritted teeth.

Neither should you.

'My Fate...' he breathes, another cold and condensed puff of air. 'My Fate was written for me. It was not to fall on Colchian earth at your hand.'

The Iolchan maiden's Fate was to die, in her husband's place. Yet still she lives.

Death's airless aura has risen to blot out the sun. This close, Herakles can feel the breath being sucked from his lungs. None of this is new to him. He knows these signs; from the previous times he's crossed paths with this shade.

'She does, aye.' He forces his voice to sound nonchalant, forces his legs not to turn to water beneath him. 'And that is by my doing, son of Nyx. You should heed that lesson well.'

By your doing, you incurred this debt. Death's shape is now disturbingly human, its sightless shadows a dark and ragged burial cloak, its form a set of stained alabaster bones. *And by my doing, I shall settle it.*

The shape in its skeletal hands keeps shifting, defying whatever form the Allslayer tries to focus on. A sword, for cleaving hair from the recently departed. A scythe, for reaping men and barley when the time for reaping comes. A deceptively welcoming open hand, ready to lead the slain to a place of shadowed sanctity.

No more dreams, Child of Thunder. No more running from your Fate. With oblivion at my hand, you will finally have the solace you cra—

An arrow spears Death's chest like a thunderbolt. Rib bones fly from their shattered cage, already turning to inky smoke. Voiceless words halt in a breathless, lungless throat.

Herakles lowers his colossal bow, this weapon that has slain beasts and innocence alike. The hydra's blood burns and hisses in the breezeless desert air.

'I am done,' he spits. 'I am done with the fury and favour of gods. Whatever freedom this world has left, I will take with my own hands.'

He tosses the bow aside, snatching up his famous club once more. An Allslayer, facing an enemy that cannot be slain. The very unlife he has wielded so well, the very void that has followed him, snapping at his heels, all his years.

Death raises its hallowed blade, its surface reflecting no light. The shadows spread. Warmth dies. The stars go out.

'What… what is happening?' Jason asks. It is the first time he has spoken in hours, for fear of disturbing his companion, but the darkening sky above their heads is enough to unravel his patience.

Medea's shimmering eyes open at last, briefly pausing in her hypnotic litanies. The deftly hidden flicker of unease across her face hits the son of Aeson like a war hammer.

'It is not your doing, no?' Jason points a finger upward. 'This darkness. The sky here has not been this dark since our arrival. What is this, witch?' he demands, his fury dancing dangerous close to panic. 'What trickery is now afoot?'

A wave of calm radiates from Medea's swirling fingers, even as she takes up her meditative enchantments once more. Just listening to her voice, without grasping her language, is enthralling enough. An entrancing fall of aural honey, it is already melting the shepherd boy's defences, seeping into his pores and thoughts.

'Oh, my Achaean friend,' the sorceress soothes him. 'Now's not the time to play the proud champion. Show me a hero, after all...'

'And I will write you a tragedy,' Atalanta finishes, derision thick on her tongue. The huntress pulls herself up over the topmost mountain crag, dusty feet striking the ground, shortbow already up and ready to fire.

'Ah...' Medea turns her treacle gaze upon the new arrival. 'So King Iasus' little orphaness knows something of our folklore. How very quaint.'

'This was not the deal, witch.' Atalanta practically spits the word. 'You helped me free our friends, only to leave them to their Fate. You led Herakles and Admetus on a merry dance and have abandoned them also. One more word from your lips, enchanted or otherwise, and you'll get a throat full of iron. My captain has had his fill of womanly wiles for one voyage, thank you.'

The Arcadian's aim doesn't falter, but her eyes flick to Jason.

'My friend, *please*. She has *proven* she can't be trusted. Whatever you hoped to achieve by aligning with this...' Her arrowpoint falters. '...with *her*... come with me, Jason. We can't trust her. Come with me and be rid of her.'

The son of Aeson says nothing. He looks at Atalanta and scarcely sees her.

'Why are you here?' he finally murmurs, almost by rote.

Atalanta forces herself not to crumble. She senses the smile bloom across Medea's golden face, but she doesn't look at it. She *won't* look at it.

'Jason, enough!' she shouts, fighting down the broiling wilderness urge to put an arrow through the witch's heart. 'The Argonauts are loose in Aea with nothing and no-one to help them! We must find them! Find them and fight our way out of this place together!'

The shepherd boy stays mute once more. Medea leans in, whispering in his ear as her breath caresses his face.

'What have you done to him?' Atalanta hisses. Oh, how she aches to kill this Colchian bitch. To cut out her forked tongue for all to see.

'Let them be,' Jason answers her at last. 'Let them die. They are not my kin. They would do the same to me. Medea and I are taking the Fleece. The others' Fates are their own.'

Atalanta's jaw falls open. Of all the thawing bonds that have snuck up on her these last months, and all the fraying ones that have undone themselves at last, this one breaking she could never have seen coming.

But then, the Huntress of Artemis has always been alone. Fellowship always seems to disappoint her in the end.

'All these months, I have defended you...' Her aim now falls upon Jason. 'You aren't fit to lead this quest, shepherd boy. You never were.'

She fires. The arrow strikes Jason in the neck.

Only… it does not.

The arrow wavers, shaking in the air, a finger's width from its rightful target. Medea's hissed, fevered curses are building to a crescendo. Her billowing eyes never leave Atalanta's face. They never need to.

The arrow turns, almost unwillingly, in place. And shoots across the air with renewed power.

Flesh punctures. Iron strikes bone.

Atalanta crashes into the dirt, crying out in unfeigned pain. Her dusty clothes are splashed with scarlet, soaking deeper into the fabric with each moment. Her own arrow is buried halfway into her side.

'You think too small, Arcadian.' Medea moves to stand over her fallen form, calm if not magnanimous in victory. 'Jason and I have grown beyond your petty quest. I'll thank Hecate that none of you sorry Achaeans will be taking the Fleece with you. You would only have squandered its potential.'

The huntress cannot reply, cannot even speak. If she opens her bloodstained mouth, enough pain and anguish for ten thousand lifetimes will pour from it.

The last thing she sees before her sight fades is Jason, taking Medea's place to stand above her body. He looks… furious. Or anguished. Through her darkening eyes, it is hard to say which. His lips move, but if the words even matter anymore, Atalanta does not hear them.

She will never find out what he meant to say, for they will never again meet in this life.

XLIII
FALLEN STARS

Somehow, in the ebb and flow of their battle, they have fallen down the mountain.

To a mortal man, this alone would have been a death fit for the sagas, but neither of these combatants are mortal men. Not truly.

Herakles roars out his pain and anger, the sound as leonine as the pelt wrapped around his body. Clasped in the Allslayer's iron embrace, Death has no such indulgence. Its skulled face gazes impassively, inches from its foe, its halo of shrieking night shifting in and out of focus.

Each time they crash down onto the sloping summits, they spiral out into the chasmic air once more, a pair of falling comets locked in a lovers' embrace. Herakles' bones break with each meteoric crash, and so do Death's. Blood cascades from one of them. From the other, only shadow.

The Allslayer kicks back with all his might, powering bare feet into his dark assailant while holding its fleshless arms fast. The sickening, crunching tear sounds like the world's fabric being unseamed. It jars his senses, shaking his sanity. But it works.

Death's osseus frame comes apart, ripped by too much force to keep integrity. The billowing blindness of its cloak spills out like ink devouring parchment, grave-cold where it licks Herakles' skin. Its articulated finger joints still dig into his shoulders, pale arm bones still somehow joined. But then they are gone, dissolving into the air like funereal ash.

And then he strikes the earth.

The impact reverberates like the War God's spear. Miles across the desert, bands of itinerant Colchian nomads hear the distant thunderstrike in their sleep, awaking to the belief that their gods demand new servitude. Shockwaves trickle down through the World Beneath, lying as far below the earth as the earth does the sky, to the gloomy depths of Tartarus. Things that should never have been born open stinging eyes, remembering how wind and daylight feel upon skin. Untold leagues above, at the great banqueting hall on Olympus' topmost spire, the ambrosia in Ganymede's pouring flute ripples.

The Allslayer rises to his more than mortal stature. Blood and sand streak him like a child's painting, like the paintings his boys used to love. The lionskin still hangs about his shoulders, tattered and shredded. His beard is a blood slicked, half burnt ruin, that only heightens the feral fire in his eyes.

He stretches out one arm, opening his hand, and the spinning club falls into his grip once more. He is alone, but he does not believe for one second that the fight is over. Their last encounter in Pherae was a contest, a tournament of wills, bound by rules. This battle, tonight, is no such contest. No weapon, no ploy, is beyond them. It will end when one of them is unmade, or when neither can afford to fight any longer.

The sound of tectonic agony steals his focus. The mountain is not strong enough to take so mighty an impact. Cracks, fissures, worm their way up toward its peak like lightning streaks. They grow louder, more pained, more desperate.

'Child of Thunder, indeed.' Herakles wills himself one more moment of witness, as the mountain's timeless corpse keeps on fracturing.

And then he starts to run.

Chunks of broken rock rain down in his wake, like the heavens' most heinous and stony outpourings. He hurls himself forward, dodging the most perilous and deafening rockfalls.

With a crash even louder than his own fall to earth, the mountain collapses in on itself.

Where once shadows darkened his world, now that role is played by dust. He has seen it happen on battlefields uncounted. Buildings falling into rubble, throwing up clouds of grit that darken the sky, settling over eyes and faces like suffocating blankets. Here, the dirt of the mountain hits him like a tidal wave. His eyes burn in protest, his stomach retching. He is falling, rolling, blown over like a doll by the mountain's last breath.

Death comes for him again.

A cloud of ashen grey reaches for his throat, dust coalescing into skeletal claws. Once more the Allslayer is lifted off the ground as his assailant takes ephemeral form beneath him. The cloying air thickens and darkens, and before long Death's shadow-robed bones are back before him.

You should submit.

Herakles drools defiance through a clasped throat. The club swings out blindly beneath him, where Death stands, but passes only through gritty air.

There is nothing in your life worth struggling for.

Its pale, time-charred knucklebones clench tighter, biting deeper into the meat of Herakles' neck. Not even muscle as thick as oak, flesh born from the stock of

Olympians, can resist the oncoming creep of Death. Time comes for us all soon enough.

But not here. Not today.

The Allslayer's head jerks forward, as far as Death's vicelike grip will let him. His teeth sink into shadow-robe and fleshless forearm. It feels like biting into the rock of Olympus itself. Memories and flavours score themselves across Herakles' mind, sinking into his soul.

The black flowers that grow along the Styx's banks, their roots radiating unlife through the barren soil.

The shining, miasmic vitae that leaked from Pholus' death wound, mingling with the odour of Hydra blood.

The chewed fragments of goats and farmers' lads, crudely strewn across the Nemean cave floor.

Divine bone and demigod teeth break like pottery. Death's arm shatters like porcelain for the second time, and its mortal opponent falls from its grasp.

A shoulder barge from below knocks it off its feet. It flies across the gorge, ready to crash back down upon the rocks... and dissolves once more into the mountain dust.

When it lands upon Herakles' shoulders from behind, still falling along the very same trajectory, the Allslayer is scarcely even surprised. A blade of jagged, shifting shadow flies toward his throat. His gnarled hands clutch Death's, keeping the fell blade just at bay.

The Fates will be kinder to you, if you submit. That icy, sepulchral voice caresses his skull from the inside. *Submit, son of Zeus. Memory will be kinder to you this way.*

They are falling together once again, rolling perilously down through the mountain's broken body. The Allslayer's club is gone from his aching hands. His bow is nowhere to be seen.

'No gift from your pantheon is ever kind,' he spits. They crash down upon the gorge's floor, and he wonders how many of his bones he has just fractured. 'And memory is a battle I've lost already, shade. What is the point of *kleos*, if nothing else remains? Look at me. Look at the men who walk in my shadow, crying out my name in awe. Two thousand years from now, what will they remember? My name. My kills. My Labours. None of the rest. None of what truly matters.'

He forces himself to his bloody feet, ignoring how his shattered joints cry out in pain. Above him, Death rights itself with no such struggle, coalescing this time from the arid silt that shrouds the mountain's feet.

A man lives for as long as others remember him.

The midnight wind sculpts its shadowed rags into being, billowing and breathing out behind it. Its skeletal outline is still visible beneath the 'robes' of flowing sand.

By which reckoning, Child of Thunder, you are already dead.

This time, Herakles does not even wait. He hurls his broken body into Death's oncoming storm. Fists strike swirling sand, abrading themselves raw. Bones break beneath the onslaught. Some turn to ash, others to molten agony.

'If I am dead,' the Allslayer howls through misshaped teeth, '*then why can't you claim me?*'

XLIV
GUARDIAN OF THE GROVE

It is a miracle any of them are standing to reach their journey's end.

The flight from Aea's streets was long, and not without sacrifice. Meleager's mad gambit was right, as it happened. Once he convinced Theseus and Telamon, in their rage, not to murder him, they managed to mob one of the last gangs of boatmen scrambling to flee down the Phasis. Eight looted, bloodstained swords at the merchant captain's throat made the decision very simple, and before long the last of the Argonauts are sailing ever closer to their destiny.

Clambering up to the foot of Medea's dream tower, the Prince of Calydon scarcely recognises any of them as the men he met in Iolchus. Sanguineous filth and sweaty grime carpet their ragged, stolen clothes, ice-blue eyes somehow the only human part of their faces.

Nestor is missing one of his hands, left behind in a forgotten market square, while a deep laceration across Telamon's back will be the death of him if he can't find a way to staunch the bleeding. Orpheus cannot walk unaided, still carried beneath one shoulder by Meleager himself, while Laertes and Theseus have cuts and burns that no lifetime of healing will ever wipe away.

But it is not the physical damage that worries Meleager.

They are coming to the end now, in all the ways that matter. Not one of these haggard, bloodied survivors threw in their lot with Jason from a desire to truly help him. Once the Fleece is within their grasp, things will play out very differently.

For Laertes, Nestor, Meleager and Orpheus — *the weak ones*, as the son of Aeson himself once derivatively claimed — the contest is already, blessedly, over. Whatever desires they ever had to claim this fell thing are rid from them, burnt out upon the floor of Colchian torture chambers. They have no means of contending with their stronger comrades, and no wish to even countenance it.

But for the others... for Theseus, the Spartan twins, and the princes of Phthia, a reckoning is coming, one way or the other. A reckoning and a fall.

Meleager pulls himself up over the final parapet of rocks, thankful at last for some level ground to stand on. And then he sees her, sprawled across the dirt nearby. Her chest rises and falls, but nothing else about her moves.

'Atalanta!' he cries, swooping down to her side and getting a closer look at her wound. An arrow, one of her own, lodged in her hip and lodged there deep.

Behind him, he hears the other Argonauts haul themselves up onto the plateau. Laertes carries Orpheus' lithe form over his back, while Peleus leads the rest of them over not long after.

They will be concerned for the huntress' safety, of that Meleager has little doubt. But they will not stop for her. Not with their prize so tantalisingly close.

'Mel...' she suddenly gasps, her eyes flickering uncertainly open. 'I... I'll live. I can't f... fight. But I'll live.' Her shoulders clench as she tries to rise upright, a rather futile ambition.

'Well, I'm not taking that chance.' The Calydonian bends over to give her wound a better look, only for Atalanta to shake his attention off.

'They were *here*, Mel!' she hisses the words as loudly as her frantic, shallowing breaths will allow. 'Jason and Medea... they were here. The witch... her rite...'

'This is the place!' shouts Castor as the others fan out behind Meleager. 'This path, in the tower's great shadow, leading down to that grove of golden leaves. This is where that sorcerous bitch keeps the Fleece. This is where she'll have come!'

The Prince of Calydon is about to rise up and join them, only for Atalanta's eager hand to clasp his forearm. Bloody stain notwithstanding, it is not an unpleasant feeling. Circumstances be damned.

'She knew... she knew we were coming.' The huntress seems afraid, and she is only ever afraid while bearing calamitous news. 'They were conducting a ritual, she and Jason. She sought to... awaken... the Fleece's guardian.'

Meleager's eyes narrow, and he opens his mouth to speak. Only a panicked scream behind him gets there first.

Later, he will recall the memory that could have saved them. That could have seen this terrible threat coming before too late.

Later, later, later.

It was one of the Allslayer's old stories, funnily enough. A story Hylas told them in hesitant tones, as a clutch of them had a beachside campfire on the shores of distant Lemnos. How Herakles had raided the Glade of Hesperide, on the world's westmost edge, and stolen golden apples that were sacred to Atlas himself.

Such fruits had not lacked guardians, however. Beyond the nymphs of the dawn with their windchime voices, dancing in the fractal sunbeams, the innermost grove harboured Ladon, an immense beast from the age before Olympus. A reptilian beast with wyvern wings and molten breath, earlier races of men would have called Ladon a dragon. A clutch of Herakles' tainted arrows had ended this primordial legend, killing the great beast in its sleep before it could rise to the intrusion.

How obvious it would all seem to Meleager, in the cold light of hindsight. How obvious that the witches of Colchis could summon a similarly terrible enemy, in defence of their blessed Fleece. How obvious that out here, at the opposite end of the world, another divine garden holding another golden relic would be protected by another such creature of myth.

There is balance in all things, after all.

It swoops down upon them from on high, on wings of fiery, wrathful abandon. Nestor is first to see it, simply because he is standing in the right place, at the right time. He is also the first to throw himself from its path, and for that he survives the next few moments.

Not all of the Argonauts are quite so lucky.

It lands feet first, hard enough to shake the very world to its foundations. A vision of nightmare-red scales, overlapping in a rippling wave like shields in a warriors' phalanx. Eyes the colour of summer meltwater, pricked with infinitesimal dark pupils, roll as far forward as their sockets will allow. Snakelike nostrils snort geyser-breath as they sense fresh meat.

Its tail — its lightning fast, crimson armoured tail — flicks out with a sickening crunch. Polydeuces of Sparta, caught by its bulbous, chitinous tip, sails across the clifftop, striking the rocky edges hard enough to turn his skull into a crimson stain.

By the time the others have even seen this happen, the dragon has opened its mighty maw. Roaring flames sear across their vision, the fire hot enough, visceral enough, to boil what little air remains in their lungs. When the screaming flames have ceased, all that remain of Orpheus of Pieria, and Laertes of Ithaca, are a pile of charred and blackened bones, fused together by a raging gout of dragonfire.

'*Scatter!*' Telamon screams.

As Castor's heartbeat fades from his ears, he takes a moment to consider the way he ought to die.

None of them can face this thing. Perhaps not even Herakles, if he is even still alive. They have come all this way from home, suffering Jason for all this time at sea, only to fail at this very last step.

But *Castor* has failed more than any of them. He has failed his beloved brother by not protecting him when it truly mattered. He has failed Tyndareus, and the rest of his beloved sisters, by not bringing his twin home with them. And he has failed all of Sparta, by letting one of her precious heirs perish in pain.

With a deafening whipcrack of foul-smelling wings, the leviathan takes flight once again. To chase down its fleeing prey, no doubt.

Castor is no coward like Jason, nor an ambitionless pup like Meleager. He remembers the pact of his youth, the one he swore with Polydeuces the night they donned their first breastplates. *Your sword, and my shield, wherever we go. There is no me without you, nor you without me.*

The words of fawning children when the world had all seemed that much simpler. And yet sometimes words like that are all you have left.

A colossal shadow flashes over him, followed by another howl of draconic rage. Somewhere behind him, a voice that sounds like Peleus cries out. In fear or in agony, Castor cannot tell which.

He has little doubt he will be joining Polydeuces in the Underworld shortly. He cannot swear to have ruled their kingdom justly, nor can he swear to have brought the power of the Fleece back to Sparta.

But those are not the only oaths they swore.

In the corner of Castor's eyeline, a hulking, haggard figure takes cover behind an old rockfall.

Theseus. Slayer of Minotaurs. King of Athens. Thief of princesses.

Castor's hand tightens around the hilt of his stolen sword. In Iolchus, Herakles begged them both for clemency. But Herakles is no longer here.

If Castor is Fated to join the World Beneath, he can perform this last duty to his family first.

As the shadow swoops over them once again, Castor howls a battle cry that puts the dragon to shame. And then he barrels into Theseus, sword raised high to spill blood.

Meleager has no time for any of that. Not now.

Slayers and champions can try to kill the dragon. Heroes and kings are welcome to fight over the Fleece. Meleager knows that he is none of those things, nor does he have the potential to be any of them.

None of that matters. This does.

In his arms, Atalanta whimpers absently without opening her eyes. She lives for now, despite her last assurances, and Meleager has no intentions of leaving her among such company any longer.

The world comes to a fiery end around him as he carries her clear. Dragonfire blasts whole tracts of earth into blackened glass, searing the plateau with every pyre. Rocks and men crash to the ground, thrown clear by the beating of mighty wings or the rending of ebon talons. The song of blades striking dragonhide, echoing off segmented scales like the cracking of temple bells, is enough to make his ears bleed. That, and the anguished shouts of men too proud to cry in pain.

But Atalanta still lives, and he has to get her out of here. All the way down the cliffside, all the way to the gods-damned Phasis if need be. Somewhere he can tend her wounds. Somewhere she'll be safe.

Here, at the foot of Medea's dream tower, ends a pointless quest performed for ignoble ends. And here stands one truly shining example of human heroism, performed not by a demigod champion, nor a mighty king, but by the youngest, least tempered among them. The unscarred one. The naïve one. The one too afraid to even turn back.

Far away in their distant cavern, the Fates share an ironic chuckle as they work.

XLV
THE GOLDEN FLEECE

The club strikes home, and this time it lodges deep. Sordid shadows curdle around the buried head, like pus or vitae from a blade wound in a living being.

The Allslayer wrenches the weapon back with all his might, and the wound tears open like a rend in reality itself. A screaming, ravenous void, hungry for his life and hopes and longing. It pulls at him, but this is not the first time Hades' denizens have tried to drag him under.

'Go back to your own realm!' he bellows.

He kicks it, harder than he has ever kicked anything. The blow feels like it will splinter every bone in his leg, but it achieves the desired effect. Death is hurled across the parched ground, crashing back in a heap of flickering darkness.

When it rights itself once more, the broken, splayed bones of its ribcage are plain to see. And that is not all.

Something shimmers and writhes within that dark, bloodless torso. Several somethings. They grow in potency until they can be caged no more, breaking free and soaring across the canyon like uncaged ephemera.

Which is precisely what they are. As they fall upon Herakles like storm winds, their forms have become unmistakeably human. Argus, or a numinous wraith resembling him, shrieks after him in a language the old shipwright never spoke in life. Tiphys is next, the ethereal outline somehow conveying his youth and otherworldliness at once. Idmon's ghostly avatar is as sallow and spent as the seer ever was, even as Herakles clubs him into aetheric smoke.

And then come others, dead for far longer but casting far greater shadows. Amphitryon, ravaged by the wasting sickness that plucked him from this life, reaching for to his adopted son with imploring hands. Theiodamas, the bellicose father of Hylas, his spine still crooked from where the Allslayer broke him over his knee. He dispatches the first risen shade with anguish, the second with unbound vitriol.

And then more. So many more. Linus, raging at his imperfect lyre-playing as if no years have passed. Megara, curls of luminous hair still falling about her perfect face. Pholus the centaur, still pleading to know how he came to be among such wraiths. His friends. His victims. *His sons*, those perfect little boys.

A lifetime of regrets, mistakes, and trophies. Kills made in anger, kills in cold blood. The ghosts of Herakles' past halo him in a hurricane of anguish. At the storm's dark eye, the man who slew them all howls his sorrow and loss to the heavens.

But fight them he must, and fight them he does.

Many of the spectres are not even human beings. Death's broken corpse vomits forth the Birds of Stymphalus, their spectral selves still shattered by the wounds that ended their lives. The Hydra of Lerna follows, most of its many heads already severed and burnt into oblivion. Even the Nemean Lion cannot resist, its flayed, skinless ghost roaring after the man who wears its hide. Its translucent form is as impervious to blades in death as it ever was in life, and the Allslayer despatches it in much the same way as last time, hammer blow after hammer blow reshaping its form out of being.

As the Lion's corposant shape fades into the night, Herakles' red-veined eyes pick out one final spirit rising from Death's wounds. Even as it takes bipedal shape, he tightens his haft on the club.

There is only one more personal demon left to face. One last truth that he pretends he is ready for.

The face that coalesces into being is young, without scars. It is full of doubt, just as it was on that dark day in Lerna's toxic swamps. But doubt was far from all it held, and he'd been brave enough to push through those fears, even at the darkest pits of the world.

Look how that worked out.

'Iolaus,' the Allslayer whispers, making an evocation of his nephew's name. 'My boy.'

The spectre reaches for Herakles' throat, falling upon him like a banshee of folklore. Eyes that once held such mischief burn with a malice that scars the sight.

You left me in that place you said you'd always come for me but my body turned to peat and rot you turned your back on me for fame and songs while my memory turned to foetid mulch and—

Herakles holds the screaming phantom by the neck, almost lovingly, as its spectral claws scrabble for his broken face. He looks at the feral wraith one last time, trying so hard to see any scrap of Iolaus still in there. Anything at all.

'My Iolaus...' he murmurs in the half-light. 'Forgive me, boy.'

And as gently as he can, the Allslayer lays his nephew's ghost to rest.

The resultant silence screams as loudly as the wraiths did. As Herakles steps closer to Death's sprawling, reforming skeleton, he doesn't even tense his muscles. No more spectral memories and nightmares assail him, because there is nothing they can do. They cannot hurt him anymore.

'It seems,' he growls through swelling lips and shattered teeth, 'that you and I are at an impasse.'

The club is back in his hand, although he cannot remember snatching it back up.

'My fists can't break your body,' he admits, 'and your ghosts can't break my spirit.'

Now it is his turn to loom over his opponent, whose bones are still reforming in inky shadows even as Herakles' own dark outline falls over them.

'So which of us will it be?' the Allslayer asks, raising the club high. 'Which of us will give up first?'

The wooden head falls, and hammers the blade rising to meet it.

The wind carries with it a dragon's distant roars, and Jason of Pelion tries not to pay them any attention. The prospect of what that beast is doing to his former comrades, however, is less easy to ignore. Even for a man willing to abandon them.

'Focus!' Medea's silken voice chides him, sensing his lapse all too easily.

The shepherd boy does not respond, his head craning back the way they came.

'Jason.' The sorceress pulls him close by the folds of his chiton, snapping his focus back to her. 'We are past the point of turning back. We made our choice, and both of our lives as we knew them are over. We must adhere to that choice now. Come on. We are nearly there.'

Which isn't a lie. Through the grove of golden, petrified trees they have walked through, a clearing is drawing close upon them. And when they enter it...

'It cannot be,' the son of Aeson speaks aloud. Before them stands a crescent of timeworn stone pillars, circling the inner altar in imperfect, concentric rings. Upon that altar lies the artefact that has haunted Jason's dreams his whole life, before Pelias, Hera or even Chiron could give them any meaning.

But it is so much more than an artefact. Why else would it be treasured so?

'You see?' Medea's satisfaction takes no prisoners. 'The Golden Fleece is not what my father guards. It is not what your uncle craves. Its power is.'

And the truth of that is plain for them to see. An aura of golden, iridescent flame shines out from the Fleece's brittle outline, hanging as it is from a fallen wooden branch, like a tunic left to dry in summer sun.

'What power?' Jason asks.

'The power of the gods themselves.' Medea's smile shows no signs of fading, nor does the auric majesty of the Fleece. 'A god, or demigod, would be destroyed by its potency. But a man of mortal stock, with common blood flowing through his veins, is inert enough to bear it aloft.'

The shepherd boy cannot wait any longer. He strides forward into the clearing, reaching out with fevered hands—

And recoils with a gasp of agony, swatting away the flames that lick at his sleeves.

'Now, now,' Medea chides him. 'Such power is nothing without control, my friend. Binding, Jason. It must be *bound*. You are welcome to try and take it without me, if you wish. But you won't be able to harness its power, or even survive it. Not without my help.'

Jason looks over his shoulder back at her. Neither surprise nor vindication mars his features. He had suspected this, in part at least. For a few moments, he truly felt he'd done it. Cleaved every obstacle from his path: every petty ruler, every troublesome Argonaut, every stupid, spiteful, twist of the Fates. He truly thought he'd done it. Reached the destiny the gods ordained for him at last.

What is Fate, anyway? A cosmic jest at their expense. A jest played on gods, and mortals, alike.

'This is your price for helping me.' The son of Aeson turns back to the shimmering altar. 'You wish to leave Colchis with me. As... as what? My ward?'

'Oh no, my dear Jason.' Medea's smile spreads like a trap swinging shut. 'As your queen. Your royal line will need a royal mother, will they not? And you know full well who sired my father. I think my pedigree speaks for itself.'

Jason says nothing. What little self-awareness remaining in his soul – whatever isn't blinded by the godly artefact before his eyes – realises just what he has walked into.

Chiron. Pelias. The Argonauts. Now this serpentine temptress, with sins brewing in her alluring eyes. He has simply handed over the reins of his soul to yet another stranger.

Will it always be this way? Will he ever be Jason, King of Thessaly? Jason, his own man? Jason, the boy worthy of standing with heroes? Will any of that ever be remembered? Or is he doomed to be no more than the choices he makes, the devils he strikes deals with?

Another blast of bestial hunger carries across the woods. The dragon, in its element. And the Argonauts, struggling to stay alive.

The shepherd boy – for that is who he has always been – sighs, knowing he has no other choice left to him.

'It will be as you say, sorceress.' Jason takes a step towards Medea, stretching out his hands for her ritual daggers. 'Show me the rite.'

XLVI
THE GODS' LAST SON

They are broken, in ways neither one of them could ever have foreseen. Their gifts and might are spent, mortal and undying both, and neither combatant has much to show for it. Weapons fall from hands that cannot grasp them. Blood patters from wounds that have little left to leak. Unlife billows into the air like a desert haze.

'What were you trying to damn well prove?' Herakles drawls, lurching up for another graceless blow. 'That you and I are beholden to the same forces?'

Another strike, from Death's degrading fist, that barely connects. Enough to send the Allslayer reeling, regardless.

'That I'm as much their thrall as you are?'

He surges forward like a collapsing tree, grabbing Death with bleeding hands and hurling it back into a shard of mountain. Its body crumbles and breaks, the shadows coiling around more sluggishly than ever before.

'That the gods can take whatever they want from me?'

Flesh and bone meet as one, two clenched fists crashing together, and both combatants are blasted apart.

'Well, you were wrong!'

The club is gone. The bow is gone. But its unspent arrows are spread across the basin floor, deadly only to foes with breath and heartbeat.

'I am *done* with obligation!'

The Allslayer rams an arrow, reverse grip, into the brow of Death's pale skull.

'I am *done* mourning a past I cannot change!'

Another arrow, smashing through its unspoiled teeth.

'I am *done* being a weapon of Fate, to be tossed and turned like a tidal wreck! I am *done* living with Zeus' hopes and fears hanging over me!'

He swoops Death's flailing form into his arms, the way he did with Megara the day Tiresias wed them. And then he breaks Death's spine across his knee, the way he did to that wretch Theiodamas. Shattered vertebrae cascade in all directions, the smallest of them already dissolving into black blindness once more.

'*No more*, servant of Hades! Take this message to the Styx's shores! Take this to your undying kin!'

He slams Death's pitiful remains into the earth, crumbling more bones, scattering more shadows.

'I, Herakles of Tiryns, born of Olympian Zeus, son of Amphitryon and Alcmena, bow to no one! Not the gods who gave me life! Not the mortals who give me kinship!'

Beneath him, Death tries, in vain, to crawl free of what is coming. But this is futile, as Death surely knows. Nothing can escape its Fated time.

'From now on,' the Allslayer declares, 'I live for me, and me alone!'

His foot slams into the ground, shattering Death's skull into a million pieces. The scream of suppressed blackness mingles with his cry of triumph.

He cannot recall how long he waits there afterwards. Contrary to his more inevitable fears, no thunderbolt burns him to ashes from on high. No earthquake shatters the ground around him, swallowing him down to a fiery death.

He has rejected the Fate he was born for, and the gods have done nothing about it.

No divine retribution. No punishment from the sky.

Nothing.

'You hear me?' Herakles finally snarls up to the heavens. 'Keep your miserable Fate. Keep your war to end all wars. Keep your vows of glory everlasting. Whatever Fate I choose for myself, whatever life I now decide to lead... it is mine. No one else's.'

XLVII
THE HUNT'S END

When she opens her eyes, she isn't sure which sounds she is imagining. The gentle tinkling of the Phasis, or the distant howls of some great beast.

'Where are we?' Atalanta croaks. It is all she can do to even lift her head.

'Truth be told, I've no idea.' Meleager's arm is a soothing presence around her body. Her eyes brush the young prince's face, and she understands that right here, right now, no harm will befall her.

'But we're away from it all, and that's what matters. I've made as best a running repair as I can to your wound, but you're still weak. I'll get us out of here, Huntress. I'll find a way.'

That opens Atalanta's eyes for good, as the adrenal memory of the last few hours trickles back to her.

She starts upright, the beginning of a foolish journey to trying to stand once more.

'They'll be upon the Fleece by now!' she gasps. 'I have to get back there.'

But she is already collapsing before the sentence is even spoken. Fiery pain flares up her left side, where the arrow no longer protrudes, and not even her legendary will can force it down.

'You're too weak!' Meleager protests. For all he knows.

'I *have* to!' the huntress cries, trying in vain to rise again. 'Jason is there, with Medea! The Argonauts are dying! Now's our chance, Mel! I... I have to get it! Before they do!'

The Calydonian wraps his arm around her struggling form.

'Atalanta,' he says. 'Just stop.'

She turns back on him in a frenzy, and the serenity in his eyes dowses her resolve. He has moved on, she sees at once. Of course he has. This naïve, pompous prince has done what none of the men up there can do. He has let the idea of the Fleece go.

'I don't want to be remembered with them.' Meleager's boyish gaze flashes up the distant cliff. 'Nor as the person I was before we came here. Do you, Atalanta? Do you truly?'

She strains one last time, begging the last of her failing strength to break the prince's grip.

'I am... the Huntress... of Arcadia,' she gasps with shortened breaths. 'I am Artemis'... foremost... ward.'

'What do you want?' Meleager asks her, refusing to break contact with her eyes.

'She taught us... to win...' Atalanta murmurs. 'If I don't win, if – if I can't claim it... *then I'm nothing.*'

Meleager won't let her go, though what he is doing isn't clear. Is he restraining her, or cradling her?

'Atalanta...' he murmurs. 'What do *you* want?'

And for once, the huntress finally acquiesces. When was the last time any soul asked her that question? Since Pagasa? Since leaving her patroness' enchanted glades?

Whoever she has found company with since then – whether they respect or revile her, whether they see her as ally or annoyance – when has any mortal ever cared about what she truly wanted? When have any of them seen past the mantle of huntress, to the woman forced to wear it?

'I want...' Atalanta wilts in the prince's arms, as a tear streaks down her left cheek. She has never before allowed a human being to take care of her, and she never will again.

'I want to go home,' she confesses, as she melts into Meleager's shoulder. 'But I don't know where that is.'

XLVIII
DELIVERANCE

Polydeuces' eyes flick open, as if waking from a restful bout of sleep.

'Wh…' Laertes chokes, rolling onto his back not far off. His gaze drifts down his body, seeing flesh uncharred, skin not blackened by dragonfire.

Far above them, the winged menace is still flying across the sky, but it seems agitated now. Disturbed, even. As if it senses something more troublesome than a gang of tedious mortals.

'It would seem,' a familiarly melodic voice drifts over to them, 'that Death has not come to claim us after all.'

The Bard of Pieria smiles a knowing smile. He has met the son of Nyx before, after all. He doesn't know what could possibly drive such an emissary back. But he can guess.

Around them, the other Argonauts are finally scurrying from hiding, not quite believing that their draconic oppressor has let them go. Castor and Theseus are nowhere to be seen, nor are Meleager and Atalanta, but Nestor and the Phthians pull the others to their feet with unfeigned relief.

And then the dragon roars once more, but this time not with rage.

The Argonauts crane their heads to look up at it, but such an act is hardly necessary. The fell beast alights – if that is truly even the right word – upon the earth beside the dream tower, wings snapping back against its scaled torso, immense horned head dipped in...

In supplication.

And that is when they see it.

A corona of golden light spills across the clifftop, like the coming of dusk after an evening of cloudless sun. It finally recedes from their eyes, leaving an outline of two figures standing together. A man, and a woman, neither of them old.

And in their hands, the Golden Fleece. But it is just a fleece. Nothing more.

'Jason?' Laertes risks asking. 'Medea? You... survived?'

They have, and have done so much more from that. The auric light now emanates from Jason, a halo of godly power that shines like the heat of a thousand sun flares.

And in that tortuous moment, the warriors of the *Argo* know that they have lost. They cannot match this power, not now he has bound it to his will. And that isn't even reckoning with Medea's magicks. None of them, alone or in concert, are any match for the shepherd boy and the sorceress together.

'*Argonauts!*' Jason calls to them. 'The prize is finally mine. Your oaths have been fulfilled. But our Colchian foes snap at our heels, and time is short. This winged beast is slaved to my lady's will. We will ride it down the Phasis, and make for the open sea. And to that end, I would have you swear a second oath to me. We still have much to do.'

Silent disbelief answers, disbelief at the change the Fleece has wrought in him. *Jason* as they know him is gone. His obsession with Hera's promises – Hera, who only ever saw him as a pawn in her own game – has led him to this point. He has gained everything he wanted, and lost the part of him that was worthy of having it.

'Well?' There is more than mortal mettle in his voice, now. 'Aeëtes will be coming for us! Do I have your oaths? Or not?'

At his side, Medea smiles a knowing, blissful smile. That smile will haunt each Argonaut to their dying day.

ACT IV

WHAT THE
THUNDER SAID

'Know thyself.'

– Inscribed upon Apollo's Temple at Delphi

XLIX
COMPOSED, I KNOW NOT WHERE

I think this will be my last letter, Iolaus.

Whether any of these scrawled confessions have somehow reached you where you are, I cannot guess. Writing to you these last months has healed something in me. But I think it is time to let you go, the way I have managed to relinquish my grip on so much else.

In life, you were the most loyal of my blood, the one survivor of my madness who refused to desert me. In death, you have still been my confessor, my conscience, the one man I could trust with my doubts and secrets. More than any other soul, dead or alive, god or mortal, you have been my family.

But I have changed. I have risen past my pains and regrets, or have started to at least. I have broken through the walls of my own making.

I might drop dead before I finish scrawling this sentence... but I do not think I need you anymore. And it isn't fair to keep on troubling your fallen shade, dear nephew. You have guarded my back, been the voice that kept me straight, in death as well as life. It is time to let you go, for your sake as well as mine.

Still, you deserve to know what happened, so let me be the one to tell you.

Jason triumphed, against all odds. He secured his prize, though the debt he paid to do so was a weighty one. A debt, I fear, that will fatten and fester, only repaid on the direst of future days.

Medea's presence is the starkest reminder of that. Right now, the Colchian witch prowls our decks, speaking to none of us, and yet assailing us with the searing force of her presence with each step. She spends her seaborne days below decks, talking with Jason in hushed, fevered tones. None of us hear what they speak of, and none of us have even seen Jason since reclaiming the Argo. *What snatches of his voice drift up to us — whimpering, fervent, pleading — do little for our doubts.*

Still, even sailing aboard the Argo *once again is a welcome nostalgia. The Argonauts' dragonborne flight across Colchis was a perilous one, and all of them were glad to be greeted with mine and Admetus' stolen boat coming the other way to seek them out. The two of us appreciated the extra pairs of hands on the oars, and with Medea's draconic steed left to drive off Aeëtes' outriders, we made swift enough progress away from Aea.*

And from there, in the yawning mouth of the Phasis, the Argo *was waiting for us. She had broken free from her backwater cove, somehow slaying her Colchian guards with mighty swings of her oars. When we came upon her, she was thrashing around in the open bay like some wild oceanic leviathan. But she calmed the moment we came back aboard. Or perhaps, more accurately, when Jason came back aboard. And our sailing has been smooth, ever since.*

We are not free of danger, yet. Aeëtes' fleets will come for us, no doubt, and we've ways to go, even if the seas still favour us. In truth, I don't even know where in the Unquiet Sea we are, right now. But we have room for cautious hope. The Argo *sails promisingly well, with little need for rowing, and Medea, in Tiphys' and Argus' absence, has had little difficulty in bonding with the vessel's heart.*

We are not a full company, though. We are down a helmsman, a seer, and a shipwright. And, of course, a slave. Meleager and Atalanta, too, seemed to disappear during the chaos of our escape, though none of our ragged cohort saw them fall or flee.

But I cannot bring myself to worry, not truly. The Huntress of Arcadia is resourceful, and the Prince of Calydon is not the fool he pretends to be either. I do not think their story ends here, in the Colchian wastes. Somewhere, beneath the chaos of our own retreat, they will have made their flight.

Few of the others have tried to talk to me since our reunion aboard Medea's skiff. Their surprise at seeing me was robbed, mainly by the prospect of a swift escape, and for that, at least, I am grateful. The façade has cracked asunder, the flawed and heroic idea of me in their heads shattered by my actions. Something has broken that will never be the same again, a rupture that won't ever fully heal. But perhaps, Iolaus, that is no bad thing. They can peer through the rubble of a simple lie, and witness for themselves a complicated truth.

Apart from Theseus. The King of Athens harangued me with a fanciful tale of his mercy in extremis. Of how he struck Castor unconscious in a rage, but didn't follow through with the killing blow, and how that made him a better man than any of us. A man deserving of every scrap of kleos he'd ever earnt.

Oh, Theseus. My Athenian boy. The child who wanted to help me kill my monsters. What have I made of him?

But we have a long sail ahead of us, and I am done ruminating on the past. Theseus' path, from now on, is his own. He will rise, or fall, on the choices he makes. As will we all. The other Argonauts swore to follow Jason back to Iolchus, an oath they see no choice but to keep.

What will happen at that point, I cannot guess. With that second oath discharged, it will no longer be any of our concerns what Jason does with his newly seized power. Or just who will reign from Thessaly's throne. Or how Medea, and her duplicitous, hastily forged agenda will come into it.

In truth, I suspect not even Jason can see that far ahead. I doubt he fully realises what he is bringing home with him, or how far into the future those consequences will echo.

I don't know why I worry. Thessaly's regnal woes are not my dilemma to solve.

As for whatever lies in my own future... that, dear nephew, I cannot tell you. Perhaps I can expect a visit from the Erinyes, *those starving Furies, who will hound me past the edges of my mind in punishment for* hubris, *and for daring to rise above my allotted path. Perhaps tomorrow I will awake to the sky splitting in two, and gods battling monsters in a struggle for all creation.*

Or maybe I will live quietly, content in solitude, cherishing the dream of a normal death like a candle flame.

What I do know is this.

The world will go on either way, the doings of gods and men unfolding whether I choose to interfere or watch. There will always be another quest, another grudge that needs settling. There will always be another Boar, another Lion, another Bull. And there will always be heroes to oppose them.

But that day in Colchis, dear Iolaus, I did something the gods could never have foreseen. I broke their hold over me.

And my life, from this day forth, is my own. No darkened dreams laced with guilt. No prophecies etched in blood. Mine, and mine alone. I do not know what tomorrow holds. It is a new, and welcome, feeling.

Thank you, my boy, for helping me realise that. And now, Iolaus, son of Iphicles... I let you go.

L
OLYMPUS

Far above the mortal world, the impact of Herakles' choice hammers home.

The King of Olympus draws in an unimpressed breath. Thunder crackles across dark skies. He lets out that languid breath, and lightning streaks the night.

What have you done, Hera?

The Queen of Olympus swallows her anger at her husband's tone. Across the Achaean kingdoms, thousands of labouring mothers cry out in their birth pains. Thousands more unborn babes cough out their only breaths, entering the cold dark world as stillbirths.

I wielded the son of Aeson against Alcmena's bastard, Zeus. I sought to blot out the most sordid of your many mistakes.

The King of Olympus turns to face his wife, golden eyes flashing with damning knowledge. His fist strikes the ebon table between them, and earthquakes ripple across the lands of Hellas.

No, Hera. You have done something far worse.

EPILOGUE
SHADOW OF THE PROW

You are on the move once more, the ocean parting beneath your battered, unbroken hull. You feel malevolence following in your wake, and the uncertainty rising in your future.

But the Many are finally back within your decks, as is the One whose touch you have missed.

And right here, right now, you feel alive.

The shadow of your prow falls across new waters, and you feel alive.

The Saga will continue in Ajax

AUTHOR'S NOTE

Well. Here we are then.

If you've made it this far, then I suppose a thank you is in order. Thank you for taking the time to make it to the other cover. I hope you've enjoyed this story as much as I did writing it.

As any novelist will attest about their work, *Herakles* was far from a breeze to write; the first draft alone took me around ten months, on and off. Almost every weekend and evening after work saw me holed up in my bedroom, the office out of hours, or any library around Oxford with unenforced entry policies.

It wasn't easy, certainly. But I'd be lying if I said it hadn't been the most enjoyable thing I've ever written by a long stretch. After one 500-page foray into Ancient Rome, I'd always known I'd enter the well-trodden world of Greek mythology retellings at some point, and having this idea on the backburner for so long gave me just the rocket I needed into the genre.

At this point, I'm naturally looking to the future, and where the Saga will take me next. In the name of courting literary agents, I deliberately framed this novel to set up the start of a trilogy, while also functioning just fine as a standalone. A full series is an awful lot for a publisher to gamble on, after all. Especially from a debut author.

I still have plenty of notes for how the next two books would have unfolded; from the Calydonian Boar Hunt, and a heartbreaking reunion with several Argonauts, to the Battle of the Giants that Herakles was always headed for, to the tragic story of Nessus and Deianira, and the Allslayer's agonised final hours before Poeas (or is it Philoctetes?) finally puts him out of his misery. The very last scene would have him wake up on Olympus, at long last, as the god he was always Fated to become. How triumphant, or horrific, that final moment is would have been left for the reader to decide.

But I've had doubts since then, and even assuming my publishing journey goes smoothly, I'm not sure the rest of that trilogy would have lived up to its beginning. As I'll mention later, the Allslayer's emotional journey – this part of it, at least – comes to what I hope is a satisfactory end in *Herakles*, and the last thing I'd want to do is overstay my welcome, or undo the work of a previous novel purely to spin out two more. I don't want to be *The Mandalorian*. Sometimes it's better to leave them wanting more.

The way I'm envisaging the Saga right now is with two more self-contained (and dare I say, publisher-friendly) instalments. They won't be picking up the immediate story of *Herakles* – that journey is over – but chronologically, they'll follow in vague progression. At the moment, Ajax is shaking me by the shoulder. Beyond that, I can just about hear Orestes calling out in the distance. They'll each work perfectly well when read separately, but thematic overlap will be there for people who look for it.

Telamon is the best example of this. What he goes through in *Herakles* will certainly affect how he raises Ajax and Teucer, and Telamon's fracturing relationship with Peleus will cast a deep shadow over Ajax's bond with Achilles, decades later. And as we know, many other

Argonauts have sons who meet at Troy. Laertes is already the father of Odysseus in this novel, Oileus and Poeas surface briefly in the early chapters, and an older Nestor will also answer the call as king, rather than prince, of Pylos.

But for now, at least, the first part of the Saga is over.

THE LURE OF THE ARGONAUTS

I've always had a fascination with this myth, ever since my Latin teacher showed us the (rather age-inappropriate) 2000 TV miniseries, as well as reading us snippets from Roger Lancelyn Green's *Tales of the Greek Heroes* and *The Tale of Troy*. His efforts are wholly to blame for the book you hold in your hands.

The tale of the *Argo* is the archetypal 'heroic quest' story in western literature, and at first glance, it surprised me how rarely it comes up as a retelling. Until Mark Knowles began his sublime *Blades of Bronze* trilogy in 2021, I couldn't find a story or novel in recent memory that tackled it. It has a deep cast of characters, a well-established plot, and consequences in every passage ripe for exploring.

Until you look closer. Like many Greek myths, Jason's quest generally strings together a bunch of plot and character beats that are essentially non sequitur, for the sake of an appealing story. If anything, it's harder to fill in the gaps in between with something creatively appealing. Let alone extrapolate character growth that speaks to a modern audience.

And the mythology in some instances is scarcely even chronological. It is generally accepted that the *Argo*'s voyage takes place a generation before the Trojan War. But the three main chroniclers of the *Argonautica* — Apollonius of

Rhodes, Valerius Flaccus, and whoever the hell wrote the Orphic version – don't agree on much else. Different versions place different people on the ship. In Apollonius' version, Theseus has already wound up in Tartarus by this point, and misses all the fun. In some versions, he's along for the ride – before or after his attempted kidnap of Helen, it isn't always clear – and in others, his chronology becomes snarled up with Medea's, as the Colchian witch's seduction of King Aegeus cannot predate her meeting the Argonauts.

Some sources quibble over the names of minor crewmates, while occasionally even the presence of major characters – like Atalanta – is totally omitted in others. And that is before we even begin to consider the return journey, which I glossed over quite deliberately. Every route chronicled is completely different; many of them, as pointed out by Mr Knowles, are straight up impossible.

This comes down to the main issue with telling a story like this: in what is, essentially, mythology's equivalent of *The Avengers*, crafting a story with a score of different characters, each of whom is at a certain point on their own distinct yet chronologically incompatible journeys, is impossible to do. Not without taking your own stance. There is no one definitive tale of the Argonauts, or any Greek myth, in ancient sources or modern fiction.

RETOLD, REIMAGINED, OR RECLAIMED?

This brings me on, quite neatly, to the next point I wanted to make. Over the course of this novel, I exercised a degree of creativity. I changed events, some slightly, others colossally. I placed characters in different places, either where ancient material drew a blank, or in direct contradiction of it. Not because I didn't respect the older stories, but because I wanted to make a new one.

I had the Argonauts number sixteen people, instead of the fifty or so that other sources agree on. I built an *Argo* from oracular, semi-sentient Dodonian oak, rather than have one beam of it at the prow that speaks whenever the plot demands it. I had Medea summon a dragon to fly her Achaean friends away from danger, rather than have them sail their ship all the way into and out of the lion's den. I had Herakles slaughter the Earthborn with his arrows, as he does in the *Argonautica*, but framed it to be an emotional flashpoint in his arc of self-destruction, rather than an epic triumph. That scene's resemblance to the Argonauts' battle with Poseidon in the 2000 miniseries is also a feature, rather than a bug.

These changes don't convey a judgement on the original stories, and it doesn't make me a better or worse writer than someone who cleaves to the source(s) more zealously. The line between retelling, reimagining, or reclaiming an ancient story for a modern audience is a blurry one, as many Goodreads battlefields attest, and every reader in this genre doubtless has their own opinion on where it falls.

And of course, for writers seeking to 'reclaim' a story on queer or feminist grounds, the line is even blurrier. Again, that isn't a judgement; at the time of writing this note, I've yet to read Phoenicia Rogerson's *Herc*, though I have no doubt it will be fantastic, and will accomplish all it sets out to do. I didn't set out to write a reclamation in that way, but 'queer' and 'feminist' are building blocks of believable fiction, not extras you can choose to sprinkle on or ignore, and so they are present in *Herakles* if not always centre stage. The story of the *Argo*, while featuring several famous women, is predominantly male, and while wordcount stopped all of them from getting airtime (sorry, Hypsipyle…) I worked hard to ensure Atalanta, Medea and even Sybele would have the same care and nuance as their male counterparts.

Where I could, I tried to put my changes in context. I liked the idea of only a handful of Jason's peers choosing to join his quest, for less noble reasons than the official line. I liked the symmetry of two magical golden gardens at opposite ends of world, each one guarded by a draconic monster of myth. And I liked the prospect of Medea using a flying dragon to escape a sticky family situation, a trick she'll go on to repeat in her titular tragedy.

I had my own ideas about characters too, and naturally this is where things get even more subjective. I knew, even before reading his brilliant books, that my Jason was never going to be Mark Knowles' Jason. I knew that my Meleager and Atalanta wouldn't be Jennifer Saint's Meleager and Atalanta. And, of course, I had my own ideas about Herakles.

THE MIGHTIEST OF MORTALS WALKS INTO A BAR…

There is no getting around it. Herakles looms over all other characters in Greek mythology, both in-universe and out of it. No other hero has deeds as mighty – or as many – to their name. No other mortal (except, perhaps, for Achilles… a question for Reddit, I think) can match him. He is the subject of more myths and episodes than any other character in the 'canon'.

So naturally, trying to compress them all down into a timeline is a fool's crusade. Today we have a vaguely, generally accepted chronology, but it is by no means ironclad.

He is born. He kills two snakes as an infant. He marries. He kills his wife and sons in a fit of divine madness. He completes the Twelve Labours. He is forced by Queen Omphale to wear women's clothes and spin wool for twelve months. He spends fifty nights in a royal palace and beds one of its fifty princesses each night. He helps the gods of Olympus slaughter the race of giants. He wages war on Troy – before waging war on Troy was cool – and wipes out its royal family. He sets himself on fire, after a love potion goes horrendously wrong, and dies, only to be reborn as a god.

And somewhere between all that, he joins a band of heroes to sail the *Argo* to Colchis, only to get abandoned by them at Pegae in a row about his missing servant.

I knew I wanted Herakles for my main character almost as soon as I knew I wanted to write about the Argonauts. That he was one is almost universally agreed by every source, though Apollonius has him join up between his Fourth and Fifth Labours, whilst other writers place his involvement long after the Twelfth. That he stays behind at Pegae, after his slave and lover Hylas is abducted by a water sprite, is also generally accepted, though other revisionists like Lancelyn Green have him rejoin the quest later. In both cases, I opted for the latter, as it gave me more freedom and suited the themes I wanted to crack open.

The direction I wanted to take Herakles in came about from several factors. As explained above, I wanted to take the tangled, nebulous chronology of the Allslayer's life and set it into a kind of emotional context. Herakles has the deepest, most well-versed path of any of these characters. It is only natural that it should weigh on him. How would it feel if a goddess drove you to murder your wife and children? What would it feel like, for your debilitating Labours to make you the most famous man in all Greece, but do nothing to salve your spiritual wound?

The second factor was a far more prosaic question, one that I posed myself when I was framing the outline of the story. I had this titan (small 't') of a character, the Superman of his day, among a crew of men he could punch holes through, ready to face a sea of dangers he could effectively solo without much effort. How then does the story have any jeopardy? How do you begin to hurt a character like that?

The answer is blindingly simple. Emotionally, of course.

I NEED A HERO!

And like that, I had my protagonist and my premise. It didn't take much wiggle room to make it fit; Herakles already had some precedent for making his own way to Colchis, after all. The way I got him there made sense to me contextually. Admetus would never forget the debt he owed Heracles for Alcestis, and in some sources, both he and Iolaus are even Argonauts.

While Herakles is generally held to have no especial impact on Jason's stay in Colchis, I rationalised that by giving the Allslayer his own (largely) self-contained story in Act III; while Jason and Medea faff about escaping her father's clutches, Herakles has demons of his own to face. His final arc in this novel, to me, is his *Obi-Wan Kenobi* spinoff. I didn't want to break the 'canon' of the Argonauts' story, or undermine it with some new and pointless additions. I simply wanted to fill in a gap, in terms of plot and character growth.

The Herakles who completes the Twelve Labours won't be the same man who faces down the giants, or dies so horrifically on that funeral pyre. This is simply my attempt to show how that change happens, or at least how it begins to happen. *A New Hope* will still take place, but it has some extra context now.

Admittedly, I had to sacrifice a few things along the way to make it all work, most obviously the erasure of his and Hylas' romantic relationship. That wasn't a decision I took lightly — Apollonius isn't even subtle about their love, and gay erasure should be as unwelcome in ancient scholarship as anywhere else — but for me, this version of Herakles needed to feel truly alone, in himself as well as in the world. Having a partner to love and confide in would only have jeopardised that.

Nevertheless, I took pains to make their bond as loving, if unromantic, as possible, and to show the seismic change that Hylas' loss wreaks on Herakles in Act III. Early drafts of this novel actually narrated the whole thing from Hylas' first-person perspective, before I realised that not only would this be a shameless Madeline Miller pastiche, but would effectively end the story at Pegae.

Because Herakles was always going to be the focus. Not Jason, not the Argonauts, not even the Fleece. That is why great tracts of the quest are skipped over in his 'letters', why the camera follows him instead of the *Argo* after Pegae, and why the title is his name, instead of *Shadow of the Prow*, as I originally intended.

This depth and introspection is why I wanted fifteen Argonauts, rather than fifty. The myth of the *Argo* features almost every 'canon' hero you can name, but for many of them, it is merely a box tick. A brief stopgap in their personal legends. Which wasn't, remotely, the approach I wanted to take.

I wanted the quest to be a defining moment for each of them, perhaps even *the* defining moment. The moment Theseus finally owns his shitty behaviour. The moment Meleager and Telamon wake up to the reality of heroism. The moment Nestor learns to fight with words, rather than fists. The moment Atalanta realises she can't go on living the way she has, as Artemis desires.

And above all that, it's the moment Herakles puts his life in context. The moment he chooses how he'll live out the time remaining to him.

On that pseudo-philosophical note, I will leave you. Congratulations, if you made it this far. A Thirteenth Labour, if ever there was.

I promise, *Ajax*'s note will be shorter.

Vijay Hare
July 2023

ACKNOWLEDGEMENTS

Here we go again.

As always, I must trace the root of my gratitude to my folks, for furnishing me with hearth and home, and enabling my self-inflicted authorial isolation. For better or worse, this all began with you.

Continuing the familial theme, Nisha Hare and Michael Orrell deserve a special mention for distracting the clan with wedding planning. Writing is so much easier when you're not your parents' main concern, for once.

Once more, several of my friends have had the pleasure of being unwilling test subjects for early drafts; Enrico Manfredi-Haylock, Kester Bond, and the Ashokides all made the encouraging noises I feed on, as usual. Alice Clarke also gave me the courage to bin that first godawful prologue, and for that you all have my thanks.

This time round I owe some mention to places, as well as people, as Covid's passing saw a lot more writing done beyond my walls. Rewley House, on St John's Street, and the barren expanses of Oxford Brookes have all helped this novel on its way.

As usual, I've a hefty debt of gratitude to my friends on the production side of things – the editorial wisdom of John Rickards, who plucked about half a million excess commas from the original draft, and another stunner of a cover from Book Beaver – for making these 400ish pages of nonsense look and feel palatable.

Since writing my last novel, I've been fortunate enough to step into the online Classics and Classical retelling communities. Thanks must go to Erica Stevenson for indulging my ramblings on her YouTube channel, and for not giving me *too* much grief about Hypsipyle (wait till you see what I've got planned for Diomedes…); to Mark Knowles, for paving the *Argo*'s way and sharing timely publishing advice; to Rosie Hewlett, for her wisdom on breaking into the Big Leagues™, and above all to Lorna Lee, for being the first person to follow the Allslayer's journey in its entirety.

My love for the *Argo*'s voyage goes back far further, however, and is owed to many more people. Professor Michael Scott's timely recommendation of a sourcebook helped me a great deal, but I'd be hard-pressed not to spare some thanks for the late, great, Roger Lancelyn Green, whose writing has altered my life so much already. As well as the teacher who made us listen to it. You know who you are, damn it.

And lastly, as always, I owe mention to the eclectic denizens of my writing playlist. To the Mysterines, Idlewild, Ghost, Holly Humberstone, Sufjan Stevens, Mumford & Sons, Hozier, and Lord Huron, go my undying respect and thanks.

About The Author

Vijay Hare comes from Oxford, and read Classics under Michael Scott at the University of Warwick.

Some misguided early career steps, a bout of appallingly poor health, and the coronavirus pandemic all left him trapped at home for almost two years, where he begun novel writing as a way to weaponize the ominous-looking gap in his CV.

Outside of work, he enjoys starring in amateur dramatics, long solitary walks, and the occasional Kopparberg.

Visit www.vijayharewriter.com to find out more about his upcoming projects.

If you enjoyed this novel, then please consider leaving a review on Amazon and/or Goodreads.

Printed in Great Britain
by Amazon

37659566R00273